THE EMPIRE

Michael Ball OBE is a singer, actor, presenter and now author. He's been a star of musical theatre for over three decades, winning the Laurence Olivier Award for Best Actor in a Musical twice; he's also won two BRIT Awards and been nominated for a Grammy. Michael regularly sells out both his solo tours and his Ball & Boe shows with Alfie Boe and has multiple platinum albums. *The Empire* is his first novel.

www.michaelball.co.uk

🐦 @mrmichaelball

📷 @mrmichaelball

f www.facebook.com/MichaelBallOfficial

MICHAEL
BALL
THE EMPIRE

ZAFFRE

First published in the UK in 2022 by
ZAFFRE
An imprint of Bonnier Books UK
4th Floor, Victoria House, Bloomsbury Square, London, England, WC1B 4DA
Owned by Bonnier Books
Sveavägen 56, Stockholm, Sweden

A CIP catalogue record for this book is
available from the British Library.

Hardback ISBN: 978-1-80418-054-9
Trade Paperback ISBN: 978-1-80418-055-6

Also available as an ebook and in audiobook

3 5 7 9 10 8 6 4 2

Typeset by Envy Design Ltd
Printed and bound in Great Britain by Clays Ltd, Elcograf S.p.A.

Zaffre is an imprint of Bonnier Books UK
www.bonnierbooks.co.uk

THE EMPIRE

THE LASSITERS, LASSITER ENTERPRISES & LASSITER COURT

Barnabas Lassiter, Sir, *deceased* .... b.1845 d. 1922, aged 77

Emilia Lassiter .... first wife to *Barnabas Lassiter,*
b. 1846 d. 1889

Lillian Lassiter, *formerly* Lil Lyons .... second wife to *Barnabas Lassiter*

Albert Lassiter, *deceased* .... *Barnabas Lassiter*'s son by his first wife,
Emilia, b. 1872 d. 1907

Constance Lassiter .... wife to *Albert Lassiter*

Edmund Lassiter, Major Sir .... eldest son to *Constance* and
Albert Lassiter

Tom Lassiter .... second son to *Constance* and *Albert Lassiter*

Agnes de Montfort .... sister of Sir Barnabas's first wife, *Emilia,*
great-aunt of *Edmund* and *Tom*

Tobias Seymour .... former board member, Lassiter Enterprises

David Tompkins .... former board member, Lassiter Enterprises

Richard Moyle .... new board member, Lassiter Enterprises

Anderson Hargreaves .... accountant, Lassiter Enterprises

Naomi Hargreaves .... wife to *Anderson Hargreaves*

Sir Jonathan Foss .... donor to the Veterans' Fund

Fenton Hewitt .... butler at Lassiter Court

Williams .... footman

Gladys .... lady's maid

Miss Fortescue .... secretary to *Lillian Lassiter*

Mrs Booth .... housekeeper to *Constance Lassiter*

Susan .... maid

THE EMPIRE

Alexander Mangrave .... manager of The Empire

Cecilia Mangrave .... wife to *Alexander Mangrave*, sister of *Peter Finch*

Grace Hawkins .... assistant to *Alexander Mangrave*

Jack Treadwell .... doorman, former captain

Ollie .... a grey and white long-haired terrier

Flo Briggs .... cleaner

Jessie Keane .... cleaner

George .... carpenter

Little Sam .... carpenter and set designer

Bobby .... scenery shop worker, stands in as doorman

Frederick Poole .... Front of House

Marcus .... boy to *Frederick Poole*

Mrs Gardener .... head of costume

Milly .... assistant dresser

Herb, *deceased* .... former doorman

Clifford .... master of light

Ruben .... master of light

Barry .... printer

Charlie Moon .... former manager of The Empire

Alma Moon .... wife to *Charlie Moon*, 'chairman' of musical revue

Danny Moon .... son of *Charlie* and *Alma Moon*,
badly injured during the Great War

THE TALENT

Stella Stanmore .... starlet

Billy Barlow, *aka* Bill .... lauded music hall performer

Lancelot Drake .... film star

Evangelista D'Angelo .... Broadway star, born Evie Wilkins

Geraldine Grey .... Broadway star

Mr Marvel .... magician

Worton Webster .... theatrical agent

Ivor French .... actor-manager of the French Company Players
Sylvia French .... wife to *Ivor French*
Mr Fields .... comic actor with the French Company Players

Usher Barton .... director of *Riviera Nights*
Ruby Rowntree .... composer, accompanist and signing coach
Mabel Mills .... bandleader
Josie .... chorus girl
Miss Perkins .... aspiring chorus girl

OTHERS

Fred Treadwell, *deceased* .... father to *Jack Treadwell*
Bessie Treadwell, *deceased* .... mother to *Jack Treadwell*
Hilda and Walter Beattie .... friends and neighbours of the
Treadwell family

Joseph P. Allerdyce .... rival impresario who owns seven assorted
venues of entertainment in Highbridge and
eight more across the North-West
Arthur Allerdyce .... son of *Joseph P. Allerdyce*
Francis Allerdyce .... son of *Joseph P. Allerdyce*
Aaron Cooper .... manager of the Palace of Varieties

Edison Potter .... editor of the *Highbridge Illustrated News*
(weekly) and the *Highbridge Gazette* (daily)
Miss Lee .... secretary to *Edison Porter*
Wilbur Bowman .... reporter
Roy .... business editor

Ray Kelly .... crime boss
Sharps .... employee of *Ray Kelly*
Hanson MacDonald .... lawyer for *Ray Kelly*

To Cathy . . .
. . . for keeping the engine running!! Xx

OVERTURE & BEGINNERS

At five minutes past midnight in the smoke-stained offices of the *Highbridge Gazette*, Edison Potter heard a clattering of footsteps up the staircase from the print room. Checking the time, he turned the dials on the brass perpetual calendar on his desk so that it read *Wednesday 22 March 1922*. His section editors had heard the footsteps, too. As the office boy handed Edison the mock-up of the first edition, warm and inky from the press, they shuffled into his glassed-off office and stood in a hushed arc around his desk, hardly daring to breathe.

Edison turned his attention to the paper, chewing on his unlit cigar with the steady deliberation of a watchful bull. He looked at the first page: advertisements and announcements; the prices of corn and cotton. No repetitions, and the layout clear enough. He turned the page and reached the meat of it.

City Mourns Sir Barnabas Lassiter, Baronet. Funeral of Highbridge Industrialist Takes Place at Cathedral. Crowds

Line City Streets, Packed service a celebration of remarkable life of city benefactor.

Edison sniffed.

He continued to turn the pages with a slowness that made the men around him break out in a sweat. Tributes to Sir Barnabas, some in verse; a couple of letters praising the dead man's charitable works, then on to other news. A murder trial, pleasingly squalid. Foreign Affairs and the Court Circular. The Sporting World. A nature piece. Theatre News.

Good, Edison thought.

He gave no comment but an occasional grunt. The only other sound was the barely audible hum of the electric lights, and, at the other end of the newsroom, the distant chatter of the telegraph machine.

He made the final turn and studied the advert which filled the back page. THE QUEEN OF PARIS, it blared, above a sketch of a young woman in an old-fashioned ballgown.

Miss Stella Stanmore stars in a magnificent revival of Sir Barnabas Lassiter's favourite musical entertainment. A tribute to the beloved owner of The Empire. Two weeks only from 15th April, commencing with a Gala Evening Performance. All proceeds to the Lassiter Veterans' Fund.

Edison raised his eyebrows.

'Bold choice of entertainment, given Lady Lassiter's former career,' he observed.

The men around him, eager as whippets, remained motionless and silent. This was the crucial moment.

'Print it.'

The office boy raced out of the room, and the section editors relaxed, secure in their employment for another day. They lit cigarettes and slapped one another on the back. Edison leant back in his chair, finally ignited his cigar and looked up at the ceiling. His editors were still fumbling for ashtrays and matches when they felt the vibration of the presses starting up, thrumming up through the building.

'A bold choice,' Edison repeated.

As the longcase clock in the hall of Lassiter Court chimed one, Fenton Hewitt, butler and valet to the late Sir Barnabas, pushed open the door to the library.

'Many apologies, Lady Lassiter,' he said, with a start on seeing Lillian Lassiter at her husband's desk in the centre of the long, shadowy room. 'I believed you had retired.'

Lady Lassiter glanced up and smiled at him. She had an old-fashioned kerosene lamp on the table alongside a pile of manila folders in front of her. She held a silver fountain pen in her pale, gloveless hand, and at her elbow stood a cut glass tumbler with an inch of whisky in it. She was still in the neat black outfit she had worn to the funeral, not a hair out of place, and, in this light, she could have passed for thirty.

'I shall retire in a little while. I sent Gladys to bed an hour ago – the poor child was fit to drop. Don't wait up, Hewitt, I'll see to the lights.'

'It has been another long day, madam,' Hewitt said, hoping to persuade her to retire at once.

'It has, but I think if I fail to read everything I sign the moment poor Barney is in his grave, he will come back and haunt me.'

'Indeed, madam, I think he might,' Hewitt agreed.

'Please do thank the staff for me, Hewitt. It all went off rather well today, I think. Don't you?'

They both glanced up at the portrait of her late husband, which hung above the fireplace. Sir Barnabas had been a broad man, with strong shoulders and a wide girth, and a thick brown beard and moustache that gave him the look of Edward VII when he took the throne. Here, he had been depicted in his ceremonial robes to commemorate the day he was given the freedom of the city of Highbridge. As well as his physical likeness, however, in all that pomp and presence, the portraitist had also managed to catch some of the baronet's humour – the glint of mischief in his eye. Hewitt was glad his master had found a wife who could appreciate that side of him. He could think of a dozen times when he had found the Lassiters – the Prince of Industry and the Showgirl he had chosen as his second wife, a woman who had worked in one of his own factories in her youth – giggling like schoolchildren over some nonsense they had read in the paper.

'Very well, madam. Is there anything I can fetch for you?'

'No, thank you. But send Miss Fortescue straight up to me when she gets here in the morning.' She paused. 'Hewitt, I may as well tell you now, I have decided to take a trip as soon as the gala reception at The Empire is over.'

Everyone in the servants' hall agreed that Lady Lassiter had nursed her husband admirably through his long last illness, showing a wifely devotion no one would have expected when he brought her home from Paris. She was younger than his own son, after all. Yes, their devotion had been mutual and touching to see. She'd brought him a great deal of happiness, and he'd bought her a theatre.

'I am glad to hear you will be taking a little time to recuperate, madam. And may I ask where you might be travelling?'

'New York, I think.'

'How stimulating. And will you be taking Gladys and Miss Fortescue with you?'

She smiled. 'I shall indeed. They have looked after me too well these last twenty years, Hewitt. I can't be expected to learn how to dress myself again, or make my own telephone calls.'

He bowed slightly. 'Very good, madam. I shall say goodnight.'

'Goodnight, Hewitt.'

He shut the door softly behind him and Lillian returned to the papers in front of her. Half an hour later she signed her name at the place indicated, then capped her pen and pushed the folder aside.

Enough paperwork for now.

Leaning back in her husband's chair, she pulled out a letter from under the files. It was written on rose-pink paper in a looping, uneven and very familiar hand. Lillian lifted her glass of whisky and reread it as she sipped.

Darling, darling Lil! I was so sorry to hear the news about your Barney. You must be in pieces. My love, I am just starting rehearsals for a new Broadway show. It'll be an absolute smash and I have oodles of room in the apartment. Do come over! I can introduce you to absolutely everyone who is anyone in New York and oh, it is such a town! The music, the lights – and the Yanks are all utter sweeties. They also absolutely love a title – even if Barney was just a baronet, not a duke or anything. Please do come! Stay for a month or two. You can get a bit of recuperation after these last hard weeks. I will look after you and we shall have a blast. It will be just like old times, only with much nicer digs! Do you remember those rooms in Place Pigalle? And that funny painter who was such a tyrant when we posed? Come at once! All my love, always, always, always, Evie.

Evangelista D'Angelo, born Evie Wilkins – and a lot longer ago than she led other people to believe – was one of very few people who could call Lady Lassiter 'Lil' now. Lillian folded the letter. She did remember the digs – a squalid little room where she had been hiding from her own terrible heartbreak until Evie arrived like a whirlwind. She had a wicked sense of humour and a sharp tongue, and had blazed like a comet through Paris, dragging Lillian with her into the city of light, till in the maelstrom of parties and people, cheap red wine one night and champagne the next, Lillian had begun to recover a little. Then she had met Sir Barnabas.

The 'funny painter' was Edgar Degas – typical of Evie to have forgotten that – and Lillian still had the portrait he had done of her and Evie preparing to go on stage hanging in her bedroom. Perhaps being with Evie would help her heart heal. A couple more weeks of papers, tributes and dealing with Barney's family, then a night at The Empire, waving from the royal box like the Queen of Sheba, and she could run away for a while. She pictured the train to Liverpool and a first-class cabin on the White Star liner to New York.

She raised her glass to the portrait.

'I wish you were coming, Barney, but I promise, I'll try and have enough fun for both of us.'

*

Constable Peters was cold, and Sergeant Chapman was moving too slowly to get the blood pumping through his young and eager veins. They made the turn from Singer Street into the broad thoroughfare of St Mary's Parade, which was quiet in these early hours of the morning. That is, until a door swung open in front of them, and two young men in dishevelled evening dress and a couple of women spilled out of the Royal Café's stained-glass doors with a sudden explosion of light and noise. The women both held open bottles of champagne. The taller of the men spent some time struggling to connect his cigarette with the flame of his lighter, till one of the girls laughingly assisted him, then the entire party clambered into a cream Crossley Bugatti which was parked a few yards along the road.

'They shouldn't be driving, should they, Sergeant?' Peters asked, hoping his shift might be about to get more interesting.

'Probably not,' his older, wiser companion replied, coming to a discreet halt in the shadows. 'But best not interfere. Those are the Lassiter boys.'

'What?' Peters was shocked. 'But they only buried their grandfather this morning! Well, yesterday morning.'

Sergeant Chapman sighed a sigh which sounded like it had been brewing for years.

'True, Peters. The older one, who's now perpetrating terrible crimes on that gearbox, is Major Sir Edmund Lassiter, now the second baronet and chairman of Lassiter Enterprises.'

The car bunny-hopped forward, stalled, then started again with an angry roar.

'He served, did he?' said Peters, with the careful curiosity of a man who had been just too young to do so himself.

'Some say he did.'

Only four weeks into the job, Peters had already learnt not to press his superior. He watched as the car screeched around the corner at the bottom of the parade at speed, and out of sight.

Ray Kelly sat at the scrubbed kitchen table, reading the second volume of H.G. Wells's *The Outline of History* by the light of a hurricane lamp. It was, he thought, reasonably well argued. When someone tapped at the door, he removed his wire-rimmed reading glasses and closed the book.

'Come!'

The latch on the cottage door lifted and his man Sharps entered, bringing a cold blast of air with him. He examined his knuckles, and fetched a handkerchief out of his pocket to wipe them.

'Partridge has seen his error and sends his apologies, Mr Kelly,' Sharps said. 'He'll make it right.'

Kelly nodded. 'As he should. We'll do no more business with him. Give him a week to repay what he owes, and Turton can take over the betting on his patch. We want Partridge out of Highbridge by the end of the month.'

'He'll have healed enough to carry his suitcase by then, Mr Kelly.'

'Good. And I'd like our theatrical friend to come and see us. The accounts need to be tallied.'

'Yes, Mr Kelly.'

Sharps nodded and withdrew, letting the latch fall very carefully. Ray Kelly returned to Mr Wells, and made a small neat note in the margin.

Five hours later and sixty miles away, the bus from Leeds rattled to a stop in the village of Winchurch. No one got on, but one passenger got out. He was a tall, good-looking young man with a cheap suitcase but a decent coat and an open, friendly expression. His grey, soft-brimmed hat protected him from the Yorkshire mizzle.

He was met at the stop by a much older man, a foot shorter than him, dressed in labouring clothes, with a collie at his heels.

'Jack Treadwell!' the older man declared, stepping forward to shake his hand. 'I'd have known you anywhere – though looks like you've got some polish on you now, eh?'

'Still just me, Mr Beattie,' Jack replied with a smile, bending to ruffle the dog's ears. The strong Yorkshire accent he'd left home with had softened. 'How are you and Mrs Beattie? It's awfully decent of you to come and meet me like this.'

'Ah, we're Walter and Hilda to you now, Jack.'

The dog barked and wagged her tail furiously, pushing her nose into Jack's hand again. Jack smiled down at her.

'You remember me, do you, Molly? After all this time? I suppose we've both changed a bit.'

'Way you spoiled her when she was a puppy?' Walter chuckled. 'I saw you smuggling her scraps. She'll not forget that.'

A change came over Jack's face and Walter followed his gaze. He was looking at the new war memorial set up on the village green. Walter gave his young friend a moment to contemplate it before he asked, 'What do you think?'

Jack nodded. 'It's very fine. A fine tribute.'

'Aye, it'll do. Too many names on it, though,' Walter agreed, before brightening his tone. 'Now, won't you come to the cottage for a brew?'

Jack shook his head, like a dog shaking off raindrops.

'I'd like to look in on Mam and Dad first, Mr— Walter, if that's all right with you. Then I can enjoy tea and a catch-up with you and Hilda. I wrote for a room to the Bay Horse.'

'Mr Shipley said as you had, and we cancelled it. You'll be staying with us, lad.'

'Thank you,' Jack said with a smile.

'There's a cake been made.' Walter nodded towards the churchyard. 'Well, then.'

Jack took his hat off and ran his hand through his wavy chestnut hair.

He'd been a boy when he went off to war, but he was fully grown now, Walter thought, watching him. Still lanky, but a bit of an air to him now. Bessie and Fred would have been proud of the lad.

'They got the good news before they passed, you know, your mam and dad,' Walter told him.

Jack was still looking up the path towards the graveyard, like he was stuck somehow.

'They heard you were missing in action just before they got sick,' Walter went on. 'And those were hard days when they thought they'd lost you. Then the telegram arrived saying you were a prisoner of war. Meant the world to them, knowing you were alive.'

Jack sighed. He felt tears prick his eyes and blinked them away. 'I'm glad of that, Walter.'

Walter sniffed. 'Hilda has a few things for you, from your mam and dad's place. We've kept them nice and safe in the attic. I fetched them down when we got your note. Come on, then.'

He turned resolutely towards the little church, which stood slightly up the hill. The daffodils planted among the graves and around the lychgate were coming out, their bright yellow trumpets heralding the spring sunshine to come after the mist and mizzle of dawn.

Jack picked up his suitcase and followed him, the collie weaving excitedly around their ankles.

'So, you were driving in France, Jack?' Walter asked as they walked across the green. 'Hilda liked the postcards. Drove her mad she never had an address to write back to.'

'I'll apologise. I was moving around a lot. And then I did shop work in Paris for a while,' Jack replied. 'I was selling some matron a very expensive hat, when I heard a fellow challenging his bill in broad Yorkshire, and I found I was missing home.'

Walter smiled. 'Took you long enough. You know what you're planning to do now you're back in England?'

'I've no idea,' Jack replied frankly. 'I have to settle to something, though. Do you and Hilda have any suggestions?'

The old man smiled crookedly. 'Happen we might. You ever heard of a theatre over in Highbridge called The Empire?'

Joseph P. Allerdyce was a stickler for a schedule, starting with his breakfast in the dining room of his Highbridge town house, punctually at eight in the morning, dressed and ready for the business of the day. It was one of his rules, and he had a lot of them.

He took tea every morning, brewed very strong – with kippers on Tuesdays, Thursdays and Saturdays, and scrambled eggs and sausages every other day of the week. As he ate, he read – the *Highbridge Daily Echo* first, followed by the *Highbridge Gazette* and then *The Times*. At nine o'clock he stepped out of the front door as his chauffeur-driven Rolls-Royce drew up, with one of the weekly newspapers under his arm, and half an hour later, he was at his desk in his office, barking orders to his secretary. Today, he had her summon the managers of the Palace of Varieties, the Playhouse, two music halls and three moving picture houses he owned in Highbridge. Once they were gathered, he threw down his copy of the *Highbridge Gazette* on the conference table in front of them. It spun along the polished wood, so they all had the chance to see the huge advertisement for *The Queen of Paris* on the back page, and the date of The Empire's gala performance.

'We go dark, gentlemen,' he said as it came to rest in front of the manager of the Regal. 'Saturday matinees as usual, but on the night of the gala, we go dark. Mark of respect for Sir Barnabas.'

He turned his back on them for a moment, hands clasped behind him, and raised himself up on his toes. Then, he turned back slowly. They braced themselves.

'But, from the Monday morning I want you to smash 'em! On Monday the seventeenth of April, you'll make your moves, and by the time Miss Stella Stanmore finishes that fortnight's run, I want The Empire to discover they're outbid on every quality act, every decent company on tour, and undercut on ticket prices from the gods to the royal box. No one who plays The Empire'll be allowed in any of my theatres in Hartshire, Lancashire or Yorkshire for a year.' His voice dropped into a low growl. 'That new manager's a disgrace to the city and that theatre. If the Lassiters want to play patrons of the arts, let 'em sponsor concerts at the assembly rooms. I want 'em out of the theatre business in Highbridge. Understood?'

The managers nodded.

'Is that quite sporting?' the manager of the Playhouse dared to ask.

Allerdyce stared at him until the man's thin, chinless face went pink.

'Sporting? This isn't tennis! We're not on the playing fields of Eton, where the gentry just swap around their prizes and tell each other what peaches they are. This is *business*.' He grunted. 'Sir Barney would've understood that. He made his money from hard graft. His progeny don't command the same respect. The second the Lassiters find it too hot for them, I'll buy The Empire – and at a fair price. But make no mistake, I want that theatre, and I want them out of show business.'

'We make eighty pounds profit a week, Joe,' Aaron Cooper, the manager of the Palace of Varieties said. 'Ninety if we get a top-class act in. If we're going to overpay and undercut, we'll run at a loss.'

'I'm willing to do it,' Joe continued. 'It won't take long. And you only made seventy-six pounds, six shillings and five pence profit last week, Cooper. Now, make your plans, then come and make your case to me here.' He stabbed at the table with a fleshy forefinger. 'Come in person. Any morning between ten and eleven, and God help you if you don't show your face and a bit of initiative before this month is out.'

He dismissed them with a wave of the hand and returned to his private office. His telephone was already ringing.

Miss Grace Hawkins stepped off the number 7 tram and paused on the pavement, just so she could see her workplace revealed in all its glory on the other side of the road. Whatever sort of day she had had yesterday, and whatever might face her today, this moment of looking up at the theatre always put a bit of steel in her spine and a bounce in her step.

The Empire stood right in the heart of the city, a hundred feet from the pavement to the tip of the stone torch held by Melpomene, the Muse of Drama, on the roof. The theatre *was* the heart of the city, facing the town hall across St Mary's Parade and the old market square. Her walls were all rust-orange brick with white limestone trim and terracotta ornament, with towers on the corners, double-height and single-height windows, ordered and arched together to give a stunning impression. It was a joyous, glamorous, welcoming building that made everything around it look staid by comparison. No wonder Sir Barnabas had got the idea of buying it as a compliment to his new wife all those years ago.

Grand.

It was just *grand*, and Grace got to work there every day.

Straightening her coat, Grace extracted a great bundle of keys from her handbag and skipped through the trams, carts and cars to reach the safety of The Empire, before going round to the side door and letting herself in. Two short flights up, a right and a left, and she was opening the door to the manager's suite of offices with another heavy key. The stale smell of cigar smoke didn't bother her much anymore. But still, she yanked up the sash window behind her desk and smiled as the clatter of a busy Highbridge morning tumbled into the room. Without even sitting down, she picked up the telephone receiver on her desk and dialled. It was answered immediately.

'Good morning, Front of House speaking,' said a nasal male voice from the other end of the line.

'Good morning, Mr Poole,' Grace said cheerfully. 'This is Grace Hawkins. The manager's office is open, and I am switching on the lights.'

'Very good, Miss Hawkins,' came the response. 'I'll have the post sent up straight away. And a cup of coffee, perhaps?'

They had the same exchange each morning, and Grace enjoyed their formal little performance.

'That'd be most welcome, Mr Poole. Thank you.'

'Of course, Miss Hawkins,' Poole replied, and cut the connection.

Grace placed her notebook on the table, alongside her fountain pen and two freshly sharpened pencils. After removing the cover from her typewriter, she crossed to a wooden cupboard beside the door to the manager's private office, opened it to reveal a panel of neatly labelled switches, and flicked one on.

Outside, one or two passers-by paused and looked up as the electric bulbs spelling out THE EMPIRE in letters six feet high burned into life.

ACT I

CHAPTER ONE

'*Who* the bloody hell do you think you are? And *what* the bloody hell are you doing here?'

Jack Treadwell dragged his eyes away from the stage and blinked at the red-faced, pencil-necked man leaning over him. It wasn't an unreasonable question, but it was posed in a rather unreasonable manner.

'You're not Tom Lassiter!' the man continued, his voice trembling with outrage. 'He and his guests have just come in.'

When Jack had arrived at The Empire theatre, full of pluck and hope, the young lad hanging around the foyer had taken one look at him, ushered him to this seat, and scarpered before Jack could introduce himself or state his business. Then the action on stage – a stunning young woman leading a large chorus dressed like angels – had induced Jack to sit down, be quiet and enjoy himself.

'My name's Jack Treadwell,' Jack said, taking the easier question first. 'Never pretended I was a Tom Lassiter. That lad showed me in.' Now the harder bit. 'I came to ask about a job.'

This seemed to enrage the man even more.

'You've no bona fides! You're not even on the guest list for this dress rehearsal!'

'Oh, that's what this is!' Jack said with a grin. 'I wondered why there was no one here.'

Not quite no one. Jack had noticed a large table at the back of the stalls with a couple of grim-faced fellows sitting at it, whispering to each other urgently and passing notes.

'The boy's new! He was thinking you were a gentleman!' Pencil-neck hissed, his outrage disturbing his grammar.

Jack shrugged apologetically. His mam had always told him 'gentleman is as gentleman does', though he'd heard some other opinions at school, and in the army. The thought of her, the thought that she would never again repeat that old saying, made a familiar dull pain spread through him. It had been three years now, but the loss of his parents still stung. He had been away for so long before their deaths that he almost felt he'd lost them twice.

'You're here after the job? Well, round the back with you! Stage door. You'll want Grace.'

Jack stood up awkwardly, unfolding his long legs from under the seat, and glanced around. A group of young people were settling into their seats in the middle of the stalls and making quite a fuss about it. A champagne cork popped, and Jack saw the two men sitting at the back exchange a glance. If the performers on stage noticed, they didn't show it.

Standing up, Jack had the satisfaction of towering over the outraged usher. The man's righteous anger seemed to drain out of him when he found himself looking up, rather than down.

'Round the back you say, Mister . . . ?'

'Poole. Frederick Poole.' Poole's lip twitched, and Jack was quite sure he was fighting the impulse to call him 'sir'.

'I was hoping to speak to Lady Lassiter. I understand she owns the theatre.'

Poole's eyes flashed. 'Jointly with Major *Sir* Edmund Lassiter, but they don't work here day to day, young man! Sir Edmund is now chairman of Lassiter Enterprises.'

'But they do own the place, don't they?'

Jack looked around him.

The theatre was spectacular, all soaring columns, Muses in classical drapery holding torches around the boxes, and a vast dome far, far above them. He wondered if he should mention he had served with Edmund Lassiter in the war, and decided against it. The less said about that, the better, in Jack's opinion.

How unfair a man like Edmund could end up owning a share in a place like this!

Poole's face contorted as if he was trying to discourage a troublesome fly from sauntering about his face without using his hands.

'Ownership of the building and producing company is split between the late Sir Barnabas's wife, Lady Lassiter, and his heir, Sir Edmund.' He sniffed. 'Not that it's any of your business as far as I can tell, but the day-to-day running of the theatre falls to our manager, Mr Mangrave.'

Jack couldn't help taking a certain mischievous pleasure in seeing how many questions he could ask before Poole actually exploded. He was already an exciting shade of purple.

'And the two fellows sitting at the back, giving evil looks to the youngsters with the champagne?'

Poole's voice sounded like the squeal of an enthusiastically boiling kettle.

'The director and choreographer of the current production.

And they're not just *any* youngsters. Tom Lassiter down there is Sir Edmund's younger brother.'

No need to give the fellow apoplexy. He's just trying to do his job, after all.

Jack smiled at him.

'Sorry for the misunderstanding, Mr Poole. Absolutely cracking theatre you have here.'

Apparently these were the magic words. Poole's attitude softened dramatically and he blinked rapidly. 'The Empire's a jewel, Mr Treadwell. A corker, a paradigm, a diamond of the first water! There's not a finer theatre north of London, and I don't care who hears me say it.'

'Quite right. Must be a marvellous place to work.'

Jack looked around again. The auditorium was massive. The stalls were a field of ploughed velvet, the armrests and backs ornamented with golden scrolls. Above his head, the grand and dress circles formed an elegant horseshoe, with boxes at either end, almost over the stage, topped with plaster foliage and draped with heavy curtains; then above those, the gallery.

The theatre. What a thing to be a part of!

He'd been a bit thrown when Walter and Hilda suggested it – he'd only been to the theatre once a year for the pantomime when he was a kid – but over the last couple of weeks, chatting things over with his former neighbours and staring up at the ceiling of their second bedroom, the idea had grown on him. Now it throbbed, a single, strong, commanding beat of his heart.

'A jewel indeed, Mr Poole. Round the back, you say?'

'Yes, stage door, if you please. Off you trot!'

Jack brushed down the front of his coat, picked up his case and his hat, and, with a nod and a smile to a now more subdued Frederick Poole, made his first exit.

Poole watched him go, then retreated to the foyer where he took the opportunity to give the new lad, Marcus, a clip round the ear.

'He's here for the stage doorman's job, you little tyke.'

Marcus rubbed his ear. 'Looks a bit grand for a doorman, don't he?'

'Takes all sorts,' Poole replied. 'And a doorman with a little presence is no bad thing. It puts off the riff-raff.'

It took Jack a while to find the stage door. The architecture of the theatre didn't seem to make any sense. That stage, that auditorium, had been vast, glorious; it should have been set in formal gardens, like a country house. But, once Jack had walked down the side of the building, and into a back lane, he found he had to turn past a cheap-looking restaurant into a large and evil-smelling yard with a pair of black wooden barn doors taking up half of a dirty brick wall. Next to the barn doors was a human-sized entrance in need of a sand and a varnish, held ajar with half a brick. He must have made a mistake. But no, it had a sign above it: STAGE DOOR.

He pulled the door open and, sweating slightly under his collar, slipped inside. He found himself in a sort of lobby, with pigeonholes and a chalkboard on one wall, and a counter on the other with a door behind it. Directly opposite him, a short, wide flight of stairs led to a landing and another double door. This one had THEATRE STAFF ONLY painted across it.

The paint on the walls was scuffed and grimy, and the air smelt of strong pipe tobacco, blended with the cabbage and suet smells from the restaurant out the back. Dust motes floated in the silent air.

He should have written to make enquiries about a job here,

instead of just turning up. Hilda had said as much, but once the
idea had taken hold, he'd wanted to get here as quickly as he could.
Plunge into the thing.

A snuffling noise behind the counter startled Jack. He leant
over carefully, half-convinced he was going to come eye to eye
with a rat, but instead met the gaze of a grey and white long-haired
terrier with very expressive eyebrows.

'Good morning,' Jack said.

The dog did not reply directly, but trotted round the edge of
the counter and sniffed Jack's ankles, brief and businesslike, then
sat on his haunches and stared up at him.

'Your master here at all, boy? Or mistress?'

No answer.

Well, no point chatting with the dog. Best foot forward.

Jack tucked his cardboard suitcase behind the counter and laid
his coat and hat on top of it, then smoothed down his suit. The
dog watched but made no protest.

'I'll just . . .' Jack pointed vaguely towards the internal doors.
'Any advice?'

The dog looked at him, sneezed, then trotted round the counter
again, pulled Jack's coat off the suitcase onto the dusty floor, then
curled up on it with a satisfied huff.

The double doors opened on to another sort of lobby with a much
lower ceiling, but this one had narrower corridors leading off it.
Jack could hear music and singing from the stage now. A rack
of costumes – white ballgowns – came barrelling down at him
from the left, with the grim determination of a bus packed with
debutantes. He stepped back smartly as it rattled by him, then,
apparently of its own volition, made a ninety-degree turn and
rattled off down another corridor. It was being pushed by a small

barrel-shaped woman with bright red hair, a tape measure round her neck and a pencil behind her ear.

'Excuse me . . .' Jack said, but she didn't seem to hear him, and before he had a chance to try again, she had disappeared. A boy of no more than ten jogged past with a bundle of music in his arms. Again, Jack's greeting was ignored.

He decided to follow the sound of the music. Low-wattage electric lights were wired along the ceiling, and the dark grey walls were lined with mirrors and odd narrow shelves filled with the strangest things – a dozen identical bonnets, a tea service, a powdered wig. Where space allowed, advertising posters had been pasted up, then left to fray. The smell of tobacco and cabbage was replaced by a blast of talcum powder, mothballs and damp paper. A human waft of sweat, machine oil and sawdust. Jack liked it, and he felt his face twitch into a smile. Through half-open doors either side of him he saw more mirrors, set on dressing tables and surrounded with light bulbs. The walls around them were heavy with all manner of fabrics, the tabletops scattered with face paints and telegrams. He caught sight of a young woman in one room leaning forward, her mouth slightly open, making dark marks in the corners of her eyes. Jack smiled hopefully at her reflection. Without looking away from the mirror, she reached out a long stockinged leg and kicked the door closed.

The sounds from the stage were getting louder. Jack headed towards them with renewed determination. Another door stood at the end of the corridor – he pushed this one open, too, and came to a halt as his eyes adjusted to the sudden darkness. He was in the wings, almost on the stage he had been watching from the auditorium mere minutes ago. The walls were painted black and ropes ran up into a vast, deep darkness above him. Metal staircases zigzagged upwards against the walls, occasionally joined to narrow gantries. A number of men in shirtsleeves stood about, as oblivious to Jack's presence as everyone else had been.

He could see right out on to the stage from here. The stunning woman was still performing, surrounded by whirling confections of other girls, singing to a fellow whose jacket looked a bit tight. Jack took another step forward, eyes wide, entranced, as she lifted her arms and sang a note so long and pure it felt like it was melting his bones. A phrase on a violin seemed to curl round the note like ivy round a slender trunk. Then, her face full of joy, she ran off the stage and towards him.

The look of joy disappeared at once. She grabbed a cigarette from an inlaid box on a shelf just behind Jack and lit it, then started pulling at a tie on the side of her dress. It had a sort of cape of feathers attached, which seemed to be getting in the way.

'Oh, bloody hell!' she cried, exhaling a plume of smoke. She thrust the lit cigarette at Jack, and he took it automatically. 'Thank you, darling.'

The tie yielded, and the whole confection slithered off her shoulders, revealing a long ivory satin slip. She stepped out of the frock, reclaimed the cigarette, and, in the same movement, hoicked the great feathery gown into Jack's arms.

'If that bloody fiddler wants to be the star of the show, he can get his arse up here and wear the dress, too. Where's Milly?' she added, looking at Jack directly for the first time.

Jack gaped like a goldfish. She had already turned away, dragging furiously at her cigarette and tapping the toe of her high-heeled shoe. The chorus line started pouring off the stage and, seeing Jack with the frock, each girl unhooked her own feathered cape and chucked it into his arms as they passed. Soon the pile of pink and white feathers was almost up to his chin.

On stage the man, the last person out there, stepped forward and began to address the audience. At once, all the men in shirtsleeves who had been standing round like statues became animated. A gauzy curtain swung shut behind the actor. Ropes were unwound, and huge panels, the size of the side of a double-decker bus, began whistling up into the air, as others descended out of the vastness above, hurtling down, then slowing suddenly to touch the floor with the delicacy of a mother kissing her infant's forehead. Two men picked up the table which Jack had been half-leaning against and propelled it out onto the stage, while another picked up a pair of dining chairs and followed them. Another fellow seized a pair of what looked like bronze candelabras and swung them onto the table as soon as it was set down, all done in silence and in a murky gloom.

'There you are!' A young woman in a smart-looking wool skirt and jacket, her brown hair in a neat bun and a clipboard held up to her chest, appeared from somewhere in the maelstrom of moving furniture and men. Her voice was a sort of shouted whisper. 'Stella! You'll miss your cue!'

'Grace! Where's Milly?' the singer who had dropped her dress on Jack demanded. 'I can hardly go out there in my slip!'

'She's waiting for you stage *right*, Stella!'

'Oh, Hell! I'm such a goose!'

She took one final drag from her cigarette and crushed it out in an onyx ashtray which was sitting on the shelf next to the cigarette box, then flashed a smile at Jack that had the force of a mortar shell.

'Bye, darling!'

As she ran off, Jack stood blinking after her. The men in their shirtsleeves seemed oblivious to this angel passing between them.

'Who on earth are you?' said the woman with the clipboard.

'I'm Jack . . .' he said, trying to stop the pile of treacherous silks and feathers slithering out of his arms. 'I was told to come and see you about a job. You are Grace, aren't you? Mr Poole said I should speak to you.'

'Yes, I'm Grace Hawkins. You're the new doorman? Did Mr Mangrave hire you?' Grace said, with a frown.

'I . . . That is—'

'Why on earth did he tell you to turn up in the middle of a dress rehearsal?'

Before Jack had the chance to explain, one of the shirt-sleeved men whistled. Grace glanced up, then took hold of Jack's arm and pulled him three feet to the right. A heartbeat later, a sandbag tied to a rope the thickness of Jack's wrist descended with uncomfortable speed from the darkness above him and settled in the place where he had just been standing.

'Not that we really need a doorman, as we have Ollie,' Grace continued. 'Come to think of it, how did you get past Ollie?'

Jack's head spun.

'Is Ollie the dog?' he asked. 'He sniffed my ankles and now he's asleep on my coat.'

'He let you pass?' She looked impressed. 'Perhaps you'll do, then. He barks like all-get-out at anyone he doesn't like, and he has *such* a nose for the over-enthusiastic admirers. Doesn't matter if they come dressed as doctors or tradesmen, he knows every one of them for a rat and won't let them pass.'

Jack was about to reply, but Grace held up her hand. The stage curtains had disappeared and Stella was sweeping on from the other side of the stage in a huge scarlet satin ballgown, arm in arm with that fellow again. From this angle, his skin seemed a little orange.

They exchanged a few lines, then the orchestra started up. Behind the actors a man was painting some scenery, seemingly unconcerned. Stella glanced offstage towards Jack and Grace and rolled her eyes. Grace gave a little hopeless shrug and hissed between her teeth.

'Oh, he trod all over her line again! Thank goodness Stella's such a pro.'

'Are you an actress, Miss Hawkins?'

She looked at him properly then.

'Good Lord, no! I'd rather set my hair on fire than go out there. And call me Grace. I'm Mr Mangrave's assistant, though I came up working for Charlie Moon, the old manager.' She said that last bit in a defensive sort of way; Jack filed the observation away for future consideration. 'Did Mangrave tell you about your wages and hours?'

'No, he didn't. Look, I've never met him. I just turned up here. But I don't mind what the wages and hours are. I'm awfully eager to get into the theatre business and delighted to take any job you have.'

As he said it, Jack realised this was true. The last ten minutes had been the most exciting and stimulating of his adult life. True, the war had had its excitements – and its horrors – and he had come close to a sticky end under a sandbag a few seconds ago, but this was *fun*. One could not say that about life in the trenches.

'You don't have any experience in the theatre?' Grace said, looking at him doubtfully. 'Stage doorman tends to be a job men take towards the end of their careers, not the beginning.'

'I've always tended to do things the wrong way round,' Jack replied cheerfully. 'I'm in search of a new profession and some friends suggested the theatre – here, specifically. I think my mam knew Lady Lassiter from when they were both factory girls in Highbridge. Thought that might get my foot in the door. But I like it much better that the door was being held open by half a brick and this doorman job was behind it. It's a stroke of luck, and I believe in following those up.'

'Wasn't a stroke of luck for old Herb,' Grace said dryly.

'Herb was the previous doorman?'

She nodded.

'He hasn't moved on to a better position?'

'His new position is six feet under. He had a heart attack.'

As she spoke, she was looking past him at what was happening on stage with fierce interest, occasionally making notes on her clipboard. Her frown created a charming little crease between her eyebrows.

'Look, Miss Hawkins, it took me a long time to come home after the war. I was at a bit of a low ebb, wondering if I'd ever find a career to suit me. Then it turns out my mam has left me a scrapbook full to bursting with clippings about this place. And my neighbour says that on her deathbed, Mam said when I came home, I should go to see Lady Lassiter. So I thought, well, why not? Seems it was my mam's last wish I should give it a try. Now here I am asking for a job, and you have one! I'm a hard worker and I'll do whatever you need me to, so please, give me a chance to do it.'

As he lifted his chin defiantly, a draught from the wings stirred an ostrich feather under his nose, and he sneezed. Grace's rather serious expression shifted, and her lip started trembling. She was trying not to laugh.

Jack twisted his head, but the damned feather seemed to follow him.

'And the dog liked me!'

'Yes. That is a point in your favour,' Grace conceded. 'But then you did let him sleep on your coat. So, love or work? The reason you were at a low ebb, I mean.'

She sounds amused. Good.

'Work. A foul little tyrant named Garnier, head buyer for La Samaritaine department store in Paris. Apparently, he didn't like my sense of humour. Or my face. An hour after he told me so, I heard someone speaking with a Yorkshire accent and I thought, "Right. Time to go home."'

'Seems severe of Mr Garnier. It's not a terrible face.'

He smiled, and she coloured slightly and looked away.

'I'm sorry, Jack. I have a hundred other things to do and eighteen places I should be right now. Honestly, I'm not sure you're right for this job. There are department stores in Highbridge – excellent ones. If you've experience and some Paris sparkle to you, go and work there. You'll earn twice the money in half the time. Mr Mangrave hasn't hired you, and I haven't seen any of the Lassiters for a week.'

'I didn't like shop work. I want to work here. And I think there might be a Lassiter out front,' Jack added helpfully.

'Oh, yes – Tom, probably. He's the younger brother. Is there a woman with him?'

Jack nodded, avoiding the feathers this time.

'Three, actually.'

'Makes sense. And probably not the sort of women he'd dare bring to the gala night with Sir Edmund and their mother in attendance.' She gave Jack a long, assessing look, then sighed. 'Bobby from the scenery shop has agreed to be on stage door this evening. If you really want to be the new doorman, you can start tomorrow.'

'Thank you!' Jack beamed. 'You won't regret it. Didn't you have a moment when you knew this – the theatre – was the only thing you wanted to do? Well, I'm having it now.'

She smiled again and it made her eyes shine.

'I did. Fine. You're hired.'

Grace pulled a pencil from her clipboard and wrote for a minute, then tore off the page and held it out to him. Jack shrugged apologetically, unable to take it without dropping the ostrich capes, so she tucked it swiftly into his jacket pocket.

'Show that to whoever's in the box office, and they'll find you a decent seat. There's a party afterwards in the grand circle bar. A great deal of champagne and frayed nerves, so that will be fun. All the Lassiters and Mr Mangrave will be there. Black tie, please. And take those costumes downstairs to Mrs Gardener before she has a heart attack.'

Jack felt a shiver of elation, like a shock of electricity from head to toe. It left him numb and completely happy.

Probably not the moment to mention I don't own black tie.

Grace turned on her heel and started to walk away. As she reached the wings, she looked back over her shoulder.

'Welcome to The Empire, Jack.'

CHAPTER TWO

If anything, Jack's day had just got better after that, and busier, but at half past seven precisely he took his seat in the grand circle in a happy daze. He told the man sitting next to him, whose beard reached down to his third waistcoat button, he had met the star of the show that afternoon and she was an absolute gem. The man asked if he had served in the Great War, and Jack fixed a polite smile on his face and gave the old walrus the outline. It went down well. Turned out the older gentleman had fought in the Boer War, and they chatted amiably about matters military until the Lassiter family arrived. Tom he recognised from that afternoon, and Edmund was with him. He looked very sleek. The last one into the box, the walrus said warmly in a slightly hushed voice, was Lillian, Lady Lassiter. The crowd applauded her to her seat, and she smiled gently and waved.

To think she once worked in a factory. You'd never know it now.

The band launched into the National Anthem and after it was done, everyone settled back into their seats as the overture began.

Jack felt a strange surge of pride in his chest as the curtain came up, as if he'd already played some crucial part in proceedings. He had to fight the urge to tell his new friend that he'd watched the show from the wings this afternoon, and listened to the director's notes and the little changes he had made to the second number, how he had held Miss Stella's cigarette for a moment, and delivered the silk capes from the third number down to Mrs Gardener, the red-headed head of wardrobe. He wanted to tell him how he'd spent twenty minutes in a maze of corridors that smelt of Lime's detergent, all lined with props and costumes, trying to find the wig lady – with whom Mrs Gardener seemed to be engaged in some subtle war, the tactics of which were far too dark and devious for Jack to understand. He wanted to explain that the moderately respectable ensemble he was wearing had been worn by a magician called Mr Marvel, who had left it behind when escaping through the wings from his burly creditors, who, Mrs Gardener assured him, the audience had believed were part of the show. Mr Marvel's disappearing act had proved more effective than any of his usual tricks, and his creditors had to make do with his rabbit, an alarmed canary called Theophilus and a round of applause.

Jack had the eagerness of the convert to share his knowledge. Surely his new friend and the other swells sitting around him, tapping their feet to the first big number, had no idea of how much they could *not* see: the men with the ropes; the musicians Jack had placed bets for at the bookies; the scene painters who had clambered on ladders to touch up the stained glass of Notre Dame, reproduced on pine and canvas, while Stella was delivering her very moving final speech at the dress rehearsal just a few hours ago.

It had been the best day of Jack's life. He risked another glance at the Lassiters' box. Lillian was looking at the stage, but something about the careful neutrality of the smile on her face told Jack that she knew she was being watched herself. Strange – everyone else seemed so caught up in the show, even the other members of the Lassiter family. Except Jack, too excited to concentrate, and Lillian, too aware of her own audience to relax.

As the final curtain came down, the applause lifted the roof. A little girl in a white dress presented Stella with a bouquet of roses, then a man in uniform appeared and made a speech about how all the proceeds of tonight's performance were going to the Lassiter Veterans' Fund. Something about teaching crafts to the fellows who couldn't return to their old jobs, and decent housing for their families. Jack stared at his hands and waited for it to be over. He was glad those poor devils were getting some help. He wondered how many of them had been like him, so eager to sign up, clambering on to a train grateful he'd get a chance to fight before it was all over. Then two years in the trenches, Ypres, and waking up with a bullet hole through his shoulder and a prisoner of the Hun. And there had been others far worse off.

'Coming for a drink then, young man?'

The speeches had all ended with him not even noticing. He took a breath that went down to his boots and looked up at his walrus chum.

'An excellent idea! Did you enjoy the show?'

He had, and told Jack so with great enthusiasm as they were ushered out of the auditorium.

Someone very kindly offered Jack champagne, which he very gratefully took as he began to look around the room for any of his new acquaintances. He spotted Grace – or rather, he saw her reflection first in one of the huge mirrors which lined the dress circle bar, and caught her eye for long enough to sketch a tiny wave. She looked very busy, so Jack thought it best not to bother

her. Two glasses of champagne later, Stella swept in on the arm of her director and she blew him a kiss which was like another glass of champagne all in itself.

'I know you, don't I?'

Jack looked round.

Edmund Lassiter.

He had a bit more of a chin than his younger brother, but his sandy hair was already receding and his cheeks had a slightly sallow tinge.

'You do, Sir Edmund. Treadwell – Jack Treadwell. We served together in France. I was second in command of B Company. I've just taken a job at The Empire. I'm the new stage doorman.' Jack kept his voice level and friendly.

'Oh, yes – Treadwell.' Edmund's face broke into a broad smile and he slapped Jack on the back. 'Good man.'

He kept his hand round Jack's shoulder and Jack fought the impulse to shake him off.

Thank God I didn't actually have to ask this man for a job. I wouldn't have been able to stick it.

'I say, Mangrave?'

A slightly older man who had been bending over Stella's hand looked up. Edmund beckoned him over, gesturing with his champagne glass.

'Mangrave, this is your new stage doorman. Joe Treadwell.'

'Jack,' Jack corrected him. 'Jack Treadwell.'

'Is he?' Mangrave said, with minimal interest. He wore small round glasses, which he took off and polished with a tartan handkerchief. 'Well, I don't suppose we'll see you round this side of the house much, Treadwell. As manager, my duties tend to keep me here. If you need anything, see Grace.'

'Treadwell and I served together, Alexander,' Edmund said.

'Really? How fascinating,' Mangrave replied, with no interest whatsoever. 'A full house tonight, Edmund. And I'm pleased to say the rest of the week is booked solid. Now, are we going to stay here for the newspaper notices or shall we go to the club?'

Edmund finally dropped his arm from Jack's shoulder, and shook his head.

'Too many of my tribe around for me to make a discreet exit, Alexander. I'd better stay and see Mother home.'

'You must look after your mother, of course,' Mangrave said.

A perfectly innocuous statement, but Jack couldn't help noticing he managed to say it with a sneer. But then Mangrave's attention was attracted elsewhere.

'What is *he* doing here?' he said, his voice dripping with disdain.

Jack followed the direction of his gaze and saw a large man climbing the stairs. He had an astonishing girth and a wing of black hair swept back from his red face. As he reached the top of the stairs, conversation in the bar seemed to falter for a second, then resumed at a slightly higher volume. Lillian emerged from the centre of a knot of people, reached the top of the stairs and offered the newcomer her hand.

'Mr Allerdyce! How good of you to come!'

He smiled at her, an easy open grin, and he bent over her hand with surprising grace.

'Lady Lassiter! Never let it be said that Joseph P. Allerdyce couldn't put professional rivalry aside to support a noble cause.'

Lillian took his arm. 'So generous of you to darken your theatres tonight. Barnabas would have been touched. And you must stay with us till the notices come in. We have a boy waiting to bring them along the moment they come off the press.'

'The notices are good. I've a boy who reads them while they're setting the type and telephones my office from the print room.'

'Remarkable,' Jack heard Lillian murmur, though he suspected she said it through clenched teeth.

Joseph P. Allerdyce had enjoyed the show. Stella Stanmore had agreed to take part as a compliment to Lillian and Sir Barnabas, and her talent meant they had attracted a decent director. Still, what he had enjoyed most was sitting in the centre of the grand circle and planning all the changes he'd make when he owned The Empire himself. First, he'd put in his people from the Palace of Varieties, shift over the whole company, and turn that rather cramped and old-fashioned theatre into a moving picture house. A nice one. In five years – ten at the most, he reckoned – the Hollywood Johnnies would've got the hang of talking pictures, and he was going to be ahead of the game. He had, in his darker moments, thought of changing this venue into a cinema, but no, given its place in the heart of Highbridge, a theatre it would remain. He smiled to himself. It had been pique anyway, that plan. Joe had been negotiating carefully for months with the previous owners to buy The Empire for the best possible price, then Sir Barnabas had swept in and paid over the odds for the place as a tribute to his new wife. It had been a galling experience.

Once the curtain calls were done he took his time, checking for dust on the gilding and calculating the numbers of seats on each level, made a couple of calls from the telephone booth in the foyer, then walked upstairs with a feeling of warm satisfaction. Telling the lovely Lillian about her notices made it warmer still. His hostess had just turned away to summon him a flute of champagne, and he was considering the costs of extending the bar another foot or two in each direction, when a woman who, for all her pearls and satin, smelt of hay, handed him her fur coat.

'And what,' he asked her, 'am I supposed to do with this?'

'Put it in a cloakroom, my good man,' the hay-smelling lady responded. 'That is your job, is it not?'

'Madam, I am Joseph P. Allerdyce. I own seven assorted venues of entertainment in this city and eight more across the North-West.'

She frowned at him. 'Then why are you working as a footman?'

'I'm not! I'm a guest here!'

For a moment they stared blankly at each other, then down at the offending coat in his arms.

'I was too warm,' the woman said. 'There are far too many people in here.'

Joe wondered if that was supposed to be some sort of apology.

'I hope you didn't pay more than ten pounds for this coat,' he said. 'Can't be more than a year old and the stitching on the lining's coming away.'

'I paid twelve!' She bent to peer myopically at the place he indicted. 'You are quite right. How awfully shoddy.' She paused, as if deciding to start the conversation over again. 'Very pleased to meet you, Mr Allerdyce. My name is Agnes de Montfort.'

The light dawned on Joe.

'Well, of course you are – the sister of Sir Barnabas's first wife! I won ten guineas on your filly Princess Polly last year.'

Agnes beamed, and Joe took in the woman standing in front of him. She was on the gentry side of Highbridge society, while Joe made his friends among the businessmen, so their social circles rarely intersected. Her features were strongly marked, and her hair, though streaked with grey, was thick and glossy still, like the pelt of one of her horses.

'Do you like horses, Mr Allerdyce?'

'Can't stand 'em,' he replied, dumping the fur coat on a chair behind him and dusting his palms together. 'But I take a flutter once a year, and I liked the name. Only time I've been near a horse in person, it tried to bite me.'

The smile faded. 'They are very good judges of character.' She looked him up and down. 'Perhaps that horse was simply afraid you might try and ride him.'

Joe Allerdyce laughed. He didn't do it often and it surprised him, coming out in a sharp sort of bark, like an old dog suddenly woken by a knock at the door. A waiter appeared with a tray, finally, and without thinking too much about it, he picked up two glasses and handed one to Agnes. She took it.

'Agnes, whatever are you saying to Mr Allerdyce?'

Another woman had come to stand beside them – but this one was wearing a considerable amount of face powder and an outfit similar to Lady Lassiter's, creating an unfortunate comparison. It was amazing how some people could do everything right and still look a bit off. Perhaps it was the fact this woman had an oddly long neck, and a smallish head with dark beady eyes, while Lillian was, whatever her faults, a natural beauty. At least Agnes de Montfort made no bones about her looks and clothes. She wore her expensive, ugly dress with an obvious and unconcealed air of reluctance, which Joe thought refreshingly honest. Joe recognised the new arrival, of course: Constance, widow of Albert, Barnabas's deceased son, and mother of Sir Edmund Lassiter.

'Dear Agnes spends so much of her time with her horses and fallen women, we never know what she is going to say when we bring her into polite society.'

'You did not bring me, Constance,' Agnes said. 'Lillian invited me and I drove myself.'

'Miss de Montfort and I were having a good chat about horseflesh and the sad decline in the standards of modern tailoring, Mrs Lassiter,' Joe said.

'Hmm,' Constance said, then addressed herself to her aunt-in-law. 'Edmund would have been only too happy to drive you, Agnes. You should have rung us upon the telephone.'

'Why in God's name would I want him to do that?' Agnes replied, looking genuinely surprised. 'Edmund's an awful driver.'

Women's rights, Constance mouthed at Joe.

He noticed a blush creep up Agnes's throat.

'My last chauffeur was a lass,' Joe replied cheerfully, thickening his accent and watching Constance's nose crinkle, as if his voice smelt off. 'And she was a damned fine driver. First class. I was sorry to lose her.'

'She married, did she?' Constance asked with artificial sweetness.

'She won an engineering apprenticeship at Rolls-Royce, as a matter of fact, Mrs Lassiter,' he replied, then added in a conversational tone to Agnes, 'I paid her fee and now I get a very tidy discount on the new models.'

'You have the 1922?' Agnes said with sudden animation. 'I should love to take a look.'

'I'll bring it over and you can have a drive as well, if you'd like. Just don't threaten me with any horses.'

'I could borrow the farm shire horse – that might carry you.'

Constance looked piqued at the direction their conversation was taking; then their attention was caught by a high female voice, crying out in alarm.

'Oh, Lady Lassiter!'

Joe turned, and saw that Lillian was sitting on one of the low chairs that lined the room, her head bowed, while an elderly female fanned her in what looked like a very irritating manner. A dropped glass lay at her feet.

'Always drama with Lillian,' Constance said.

Joe caught the look of surprise – then disdain – Agnes directed at her nephew's wife, before he firmly made his way through the crowd and persuaded the woman with the fan to back away and take her fan and smelling salts with her. He picked up the empty flute before it was smashed – *no need to waste good glass* – and asked Lillian if she needed a doctor.

'No, no, I'm quite well, Mr Allerdyce,' she said in a low voice. 'Why on earth did that woman shriek like that? Only it's terribly warm and this place is so full of memories. Then . . . Well, I thought I saw . . . Oh, it's nothing.'

'I hope for your sake it was the theatre ghost.' Joe offered her his arm. She rested her light weight on it as she stood. 'Doesn't the one here only turn up to alarm everyone when he approves of the show?'

'Yes – a playwright or some such. We haven't seen much of him lately, but if he'd turn up for anyone, it would be for Stella.'

Lillian still seemed distracted, looking through the crowd as if searching for someone. Agnes arrived with a glass of water and thrust it at her.

'Drink this. I bet you haven't eaten all day, Lillian,' she said, noticing the other woman's hand was shaking as she took the glass. 'Who are you looking for? Edmund and your manager are making fools of themselves over your star, but she is fending them off admirably, if that's what worrying you, and your leading man is getting lachrymose in the corner with the lord mayor. If he drinks any more, I dare say he shall trip over his chain.' She put her hand out to take the glass back. 'Oh, and your notices have arrived.'

Lillian dragged her eyes from the crowd. 'Good, yes. How exciting.'

'Much too exciting for me,' Agnes said. 'I'm off. Enjoy yourself in New York, Lillian.'

'Can I get your coat for you, Miss de Montfort?' Joe asked.

She laughed, a musical sort of chuckle. 'I can manage, Mr Allerdyce.'

'Thank you, yes. Goodbye, Agnes,' Lillian replied, but Allerdyce couldn't help noticing she was still looking round the crowd as if searching for her ghost.

Jack was chatting in an animated fashion to two of the band members and trying – not too obviously – to search the crowd for Grace. He wanted to thank her again for the job, and also he liked looking at her. He'd decided now was not the moment to introduce himself to Lady Lassiter, though he had caught another glimpse of her through the crowd. He wasn't sure that, surrounded by all these sleek-looking society types, wandering up and saying, 'My mam, Bessie Treadwell, worked with you at the Lassiter textile works' would go down very well. Nothing wrong with the work, of course, but officer training had taught him the upper classes had some odd ideas about their working brothers and sisters. Most of them were astonished to find he knew which way up to hold a book.

'Jack! Darling! There you are! I'm ready to go now.'

He turned to discover the star of the show, Stella Stanmore herself, reaching for him through the throng.

He accepted a lipstick kiss on the cheek and noticed over her shoulder Edmund Lassiter and Alexander Mangrave looking daggers at him.

'Save me,' Stella whispered to him. 'They are trying to drag me off to their ghastly club to watch them play cards. Sounds like Hell. I said I was going to the Metropole with you. There's a new jazz band playing, and we might catch the midnight show if we hurry.'

The looks the owner and manager were casting at him didn't look very promising for Jack's career, but he was nothing if not gallant.

'Marvellous!'

He offered Stella his arm, then wondered for a wild moment if they might invite Grace, too. But it seemed advisable on balance to get away from Mangrave's and Edmund's demon stares as fast as possible.

'Who is that very large man with the slicked-back hair?' he asked Stella as they made their way to the lobby.

'That's Joe Allerdyce. Biggest man in theatre north of Watford, in all senses. He owns dozens and dozens of theatres. Why do you ask?'

'He was looking at Mr Mangrave just now as if he was a particularly off bottle of milk.'

She snorted. 'Oh hell, it's raining! The Metropole is only a step, but my hair gets awfully frizzy if it gets wet.'

'Mr Poole, may I?' Jack said, reaching for a large red umbrella in the stand by the door.

Poole, who was chastising Marcus and wishing good evening to a number of departing patrons at the same time, nodded his assent. Jack pushed open the door, opened the umbrella with a flourish and beckoned Stella out to join him under it.

Not bad, he thought as she took his arm again. A job, a star on his arm, and the prospect of a glass of champagne and some decent music to finish off the evening. And he would see Grace again tomorrow. It was a shame he had no idea where he would sleep, but that, at this moment, hardly seemed like a problem at all.

CHAPTER THREE

Lady Lassiter left for New York the day after the gala. Ten days later, the souvenir issue of the *Highbridge Illustrated News* commemorating the life of Sir Barnabas was nearing the top of the pile of fish wrappings at the shop behind The Empire, and the glowing notices which had been cut out and stuck around the dressing room mirrors were beginning to curl in the heat of the electric bulbs. But the houses were still full, and Stella's co-star remembered his lines most nights.

And Grace Hawkins was in a pickle – and as vinegary a pickle as she had encountered so far working at The Empire. Something was going on. The touring company who were supposed to come in a fortnight for a short repertory season of Shakespeare had cancelled.

She had told Mangrave this disastrous news, and he had shrugged and told her to call up the variety agents and book in whatever second-string revue shows were still available. She had spent the rest of that day, and this morning, trying to do just that, but every halfway decent act was booked – allegedly – and the agents she spoke to didn't seem to want to blow the dust off their books to look for anyone else. This was far worse than acts being booked up, and her suspicions grew ever stronger. She opened the paper and looked again at an advert she had noticed that morning. Yes, Joe Allerdyce had cut his ticket prices in most of his venues, and his upcoming attractions list looked like he had hired half of the West End and was bringing them all to Highbridge simultaneously. She felt sick.

After some frantic thought, she remembered one more agent – a greasy and unreasonable man whom she was sure had bribed Mangrave to put on a company he represented for a humiliating week last year. She asked Mangrave to call him, but he said he didn't have time, gave her the agent's number out of his pocket book with a sigh, then left for his club. Grace sat there staring as the door closed behind him. She must have failed to make the situation clear. If they didn't get something in place today, The Empire would go dark, and when would they open again? Mangrave said they could get the local schools and amateur dramatics societies in.

In The Empire? No.

She had to get something – anything – but they had to be professionals, at least. She rang the number.

'Horse and Hounds,' a gravelly female voice announced.

'Oh, I'm sorry, I'm looking for Mr Worton Webster, the theatrical agent.'

The line crackled as the person who had answered turned away from the instrument.

'Warty! For you!'

A minute passed, then a voice crumpled by cigarettes and bile spoke.

'Webster here.'

'Mr Webster, this is Grace Hawkins from The Empire in Highbridge. We've had a late cancellation and I was wondering if you might have a production for us. Get in from May the first, opening on the fifth. Four weeks guaranteed.'

He laughed, and it was not in any way pleasant.

'Having trouble getting a show in, are you? Not surprised.'

Her throat went a little dry. 'Well, do you have anything?'

The agent was, she remembered quite clearly now, a woman-hating, slimy, vicious fraud.

'Shoe's on the other foot now, isn't it, missy? Yes, I have something. A *Macbeth*. Small company of seasoned professionals, currently resting. But it will cost you.'

It would have to be *Macbeth*, Grace thought. Mrs Gardener would be burning sage in the corridors for a month.

'They've added songs to it,' the voice added, in curdled amusement.

Macbeth as a musical? It was a terrible idea – no wonder no one else would put it on. But it was either this or school plays.

'How much?'

The voice became darker and more hateful still.

'I'm not negotiating with Mangrave's fucking typist. Get him to call me back here – himself, mind – three o'clock this afternoon, and tell him to have his chequebook ready. I'm his last hope, and if he doesn't know that yet, he's an even worse manager than I think he is.'

The connection was cut. Grace put her receiver back in the cradle, her heart thumping. Webster didn't scare her, and if he thought foul language would shake her, he'd have to think again, but the odious little man was right: they needed him, and Mangrave was gone for the day. She leant forward slightly over her desk, her fingers to her forehead.

Then, with a lurch, she remembered she had yet to cancel the order for the now-defunct posters advertising the Shakespeare season. If they went ahead, that would be ten pounds wasted, and the printer didn't have a phone. She grabbed her handbag and dashed off.

The idea occurred to her when she was coming back from the printer. It was a ridiculous idea, but it was the only one she had. The new doorman, Jack Treadwell, with his Paris polish, would make the call, pretending to be Mangrave. There was no alternative. Poole sounded all wrong and would get flustered; Stella's co-star might have the voice, but unfortunately he also had the brains of a chicken. The lads backstage were all Highbridge to the bone and voice box, but Jack Treadwell . . . his voice wasn't far off, and he seemed to have some sense about him. She could coach him through it.

Rather than using her usual entrance to the management offices, she went straight round the back of the theatre, and through the yard to stage door. She was already starting to speak as she pushed it open, then the words dried in her mouth.

She had heard that Jack had been making some improvements to his place of work, but this was the first opportunity she'd had to see them for herself. She was astonished. The lobby smelt of fresh paint, and the scuffed magnolia had been replaced with a subtle pale green. The desk and pigeonholes glowed with fresh polish. The blackboard had been replaced, and was neatly marked with the availability of the rehearsal rooms and this evening's performance times. Under the pigeonholes was a dog basket, or at least a basket which was now being used by a dog. Ollie was curled in it on a clean tartan blanket. He got up when he saw her, gentleman that he was, wagged his stumpy tail and barked once, then settled again. Grace was still too amazed to do anything more than blink. A large vase of flowers – pinks and baby's breath – sat on the counter. At the sound of Ollie's bark, the door to the tiny back office behind it opened and Jack emerged, in a clean shirt, dark tie and Herb's old jacket, now altered to fit him. He had a copy of *The Stage* under his arm. He looked very well; the jacket looked like a high fashion accessory of a man around town rather than a uniform, and it made his shoulders look broader than she had remembered.

'Grace! A good afternoon to you.'

'What?' she managed to say.

'I said good afternoon.'

'I know – I mean, what has happened here? How did you . . . ?'

Jack grinned. 'Elbow grease, mostly. Mrs Gardener altered the coat for me in exchange for a bit of work on the cupboard door that was sticking in her workroom and a new rail put up in the chorus dressing room. The old one was coming loose and dumping everything in a heap once a week. Meant a lot of extra ironing.'

He pointed out his various improvements, from the ceiling to floor, rattling off the names of the backstage company like they were lifelong friends, and with half a dozen references to local businesses who had been having a clear-out of useful odds and ends.

'Flo and Jessie came in on their afternoon off to give me a hand, too.'

Flo and Jessie?

Grace realised with amazement that Jack was referring to Mrs Briggs and Mrs Keane – two no-nonsense cleaners who had worked here since the year dot, and whom Grace treated with careful respect. They had certainly never invited her to call them by their first names.

Jack produced a tin featuring the Relief of Mafeking from under the counter.

'Flo baked me biscuits. She's an artist. Would you like one?'

Grace was staggered. She might even have actually staggered, had Jack not put down his copy of *The Stage* and produced a stool from behind the counter, setting it down for her in front of the counter. She vaguely recognised it from a scene in a nightclub from *All Aboard*, a rather poor drama set on a cruise ship they had produced in 1917, the year she had started working here. Jack had a matching stool on the other side of the counter. The look of concern hadn't left his face.

'I haven't spent a penny of The Empire's money. I even bought the new blanket for Ollie myself, but I had to do that to get my coat back. He'd grown attached and I didn't want us to fall out over it.'

'How do you get everyone to do things for you?' she said at last.

Jack had sprung up again and was now busying himself heating a little camping kettle on a spirit stove. It sat on a shelf under his window, which allowed him a view of the dank yard outside.

'Oh, well, it's normally just a case of finding a way to be useful. Then other people are helpful back.'

That had not always been Grace's experience, especially working with Alexander Mangrave.

'And where did you learn to do all of this? Are you a carpenter?'

He laughed. 'Lord, no! I leave all that up to masters like George and Little Sam in the chop shop. Honestly, the way they can conjure a staircase a dozen girls can run up and down twenty times a night in a couple of hours. I'm ever so grateful you took a chance on me, Grace. I've been learning so much. Ruben took me round the lighting galleries last week. Did you know Ruben's mother was born in Goa? She popped in yesterday with these spicy pastries. I've never tasted the like.'

'So how did you . . . ?'

He shrugged. 'Jack of all trades!' His face became graver. 'We had to build our own shelters in the prisoner of war camp. Picked up a lot then.'

He handed her a cup of coffee and looked as though he wanted to change the subject. She sipped, still struggling to take it all in.

He's been here ten days. Where on earth did he find the time?

A sudden suspicion crossed Grace's mind, and she stood up from her stool and leant over the counter top. Jack tried to tuck the rolled-up canvas camp bed further out of sight, but was unsuccessful.

'You're living here!' she said.

Jack grimaced. 'Yes, I am. Sorry. I hadn't the time to look for digs, and I saw this in Bertram's Goods on sale, so I thought a day or two wouldn't cause any harm.'

She stared up at him, a severe frown on her face, then caught sight of the clock on the wall behind him.

'Blast! We've no time to argue about it now. Do you still have the brick for the door?'

'I've kept it as a memento.'

'Good. Well, deploy it. Ollie will have to hold the fort for an hour or so. I need you to pretend to be Mr Mangrave and negotiate with a crook for me.'

'What? When?'

'In twelve minutes. Come on, I'll explain on the way.'

When they arrived, Jack looked around the office, then turned back to Grace and smiled.

'This is nice!'

'You've never been in here as yet, I suppose?'

'No. I do have a walk round every evening to check everything's in order, but I wouldn't dream of snooping about in management's offices after hours. Anyway, they're locked.'

Grace laughed in spite of herself. 'So you are our nightwatchman as well?'

'My way of making up for sleeping downstairs.'

'You have made yourself very comfortable, haven't you?' she said dryly.

He felt briefly crestfallen.

'You don't mind too much, do you, Grace?'

She frowned for a second, then shook her head. 'I suppose not, if you are our nightwatchman, too. But the only person officially allowed to stay here is Lady Lassiter. She has a flat over the auditorium.'

'But isn't her house nearby?'

Grace glanced at the clock and got ready to place her call.

'It's about quarter of an hour's drive, but I think she and Sir Barnabas liked staying here if they'd seen a show. She hasn't used it for years. Now, are you ready?'

Jack took off his coat and rolled up his shirtsleeves.

'Not in the slightest. I understand I have to pretend to be Mangrave and book this musical *Macbeth*?'

'That's it,' she said. 'Mangrave seems to think we can just have the local schools put on talent contests, but that would be utterly humiliating.' Then she spoke into the receiver. 'Horse and Hounds? Yes, is Mr Webster there? Thank you!'

'What's the problem? Why can't you get a show in?'

'I think Joe Allerdyce is trying to force us out of business,' she said, with one hand over the receiver and looking a little sick. 'Lady Lassiter is out of town and Mangrave doesn't seem to care what's on stage, as long as we keep the doors open!'

Worton Webster was making her wait.

'I even tried to call Edmund Lassiter yesterday, but his secretary just told me all matters related to the theatre are to be dealt with by Mangrave. The Empire will go dark, and all of us here will have our reputations ruined. By the time Lady Lassiter gets home, it'll all be over.' She held up her hand. 'Yes – Mr Webster? I have Mr Mangrave for you.'

She beckoned Jack around to her side of the desk and tilted the receiver so they could both hear.

Jack thought of that bored drawl he had heard Mangrave use when speaking to Edmund at the party.

'Webster? Mangrave here. A musical *Macbeth*, is it? Is that all you've got?'

Grace gave him an enthusiastic thumbs-up as Webster's throaty voice crackled on the other end of the line.

'It's all you're getting, Mangrave. Hundred pound a week, fifty pound booking fee and fifteen per cent of the box office. Six weeks.'

The sudden success went immediately to Jack's head.

'Well, that sounds . . .' he began cheerfully, then noticed Grace was frantically shaking her head. He cleared his throat. 'Well, that sounds like the sort of deal you *would* ask for, Webster.'

Grace thrust the receiver into his hands and started writing frantically on the notepad on her desk. Jack tried to peer over her shoulder. Her perfume had a lemony hint to it.

'You won't get any better terms from me,' Webster growled.

'There are other agents,' Jack drawled back.

'Not for you. Joe Allerdyce's theatres have put the word out. Anyone who plays in his venues can't play The Empire for a year. It's called a non-compete.'

Grace suddenly shot upright and the back of her head caught

Jack's chin. He stumbled slightly, grabbed the telephone to stop it falling on the floor and knocked the table lamp off the desk in the process.

'What was that?' Webster said sharply.

Jack put his hand to his jaw as Grace mimed an apology, her hands pressed together.

I'm fine, he mouthed.

'Pigeon!' he said into the phone.

'What?'

'Err . . . a pigeon flew into the window!'

Grace mouthed a *sorry* at him, and looked very sorry indeed. He struggled to focus on the man on the other end of the phone.

'Listen, Webster, I don't give a damn about Allerdyce or his non-compete. He can go whistle.'

Grace grabbed hold of her pad and thrust it at him. Jack read, squinting a little at her handwriting.

'Booking fee of fifteen pounds, seventy-five a week for the company. And five per cent of box office after costs.'

'Pay me what I want or you'll have to shut the theatre.' Webster's voice had gone oily again.

Jack looked at Grace and she shook her head, stabbing at the page again.

Jack took a deep breath. 'Then we'll go dark and your musical *Macbeth* can find another theatre. How's your bar bill at the pub, Webster? That landlady happy for you to turn down a nice booking fee, is she?'

Silence; the connection crackled. Jack reached for another pencil from the desk, but the fallen lamp had sent them everywhere. Grace passed him hers. Their fingers touched as they both listened to the silence at the other end of the line.

Booking fee twenty? Jack wrote.

Grace bit her lip, then nodded. Jack dropped the pencil, straightened his back, then he gave a short sharp sigh.

'Very well. Twenty pounds for the booking fee, take it or leave it.'

'I'll take it.'

'Wonderful!' Jack exclaimed in his normal voice, then when he saw Grace's appalled face, coughed and repeated it in Mangrave's bored drawl. Grace clapped her hand over her mouth to stop a laugh. 'We'll send the paperwork today, Webster,' he added. 'A pleasure, as always.'

'Good day,' Webster said with a snap in his voice, and the connection was cut.

'How was that?' Jack asked, slowly hanging up the receiver and dropping into a chair.

Grace leant against the desk. 'Oh, Jack, that was smashing! How is your poor chin?'

He rubbed it. 'I'll live.'

She reached down and put her hand on his face, examining the red spot where the back of her head had made contact. Her fingers were cool.

'Oh dear, you might have a bruise. A pigeon! Honestly, Jack, where on earth did you spring from?'

Her touch could remedy all ills; he was sure of it.

'Winchurch. Little village about ten miles from Leeds.'

'But how did you end up here? You just walk in off the street, and next thing I know you've cast a spell over everyone from Ollie to Mrs Gardener, and now Worton Webster!'

'Are you under my spell?' he said, lifting his gaze.

Their eyes met for an interesting second, then she blushed and stood up, going to sit on the chair on the other side of the desk.

Lord, why did I say that?

He pushed his hair back. Regrouped.

'I told you.' He deployed the boyish grin. 'My mam sent me.'

'Yes, she gave you some cuttings and told you to go and see Lady Lassiter when you came home. Why *did* your mother say that?'

'Well, I think they knew each other before Lady Lassiter went on the stage. Mam worked in Lassiter's textile printing works. Lady Lassiter did too, didn't she?'

'That's right,' Grace said. 'Sir Barnabas was a great innovator and engineer. He started the printing works, then bought the North End factory, which makes cutlery, and the Mitchell Works, which does fancy goods.' She counted them off on her fingers. 'Got them all using electricity before anyone else in the county, and made an absolute mint. Then he goes off to Paris and sees Lillian, asks her out for supper, and they find out she used to work in his first factory.'

'Sir Barnabas didn't mind?'

'He wasn't grand at all, you know.' A fond smile touched her features. 'He would have thought it was an absolute hoot. They fell in love spending nights on the Champs-Élysées together, chatting about their home town. It's terribly romantic, really.' Then she straightened up again. 'But why did your mother think you'd want to go work in the theatre?'

'I have no idea!' Jack said with a shrug. But he was so grateful she had. Coming to the theatre, starting a career she'd picked out for him – it was almost like she wasn't gone at all. His heart ached with missing her and Dad. 'I'm beginning to think she was a genius,' he went on, forcing himself to brighten. 'I love it here. Mam always said she knew me better than I knew myself. Seems she was right.'

CHAPTER FOUR

Three weeks later, Jack found himself in close proximity to the star, producer, director and arranger of the musical *Macbeth*, Ivor French, in his stage door lobby. And Ivor French, actor-manager of the French Company Players, was not happy.

'It is a witch-hunt!' he shouted, pounding the counter with his fist and making Jack's latest bunch of flowers quiver slightly under the force of his indignation. 'A travesty! These critics are weak, soulless, ink-bloodied little men. Without vision, without poetry!'

Jack nodded in what he hoped was a sympathetic manner. The notice in the *Highbridge Gazette* of the Players' production of *Macbeth* had been about as cruel a thing as he had ever read in print. It was also painfully accurate.

'I am an *artiste*!' Ivor continued at full volume, and he beat his fist on the counter again for entirely unnecessary emphasis. 'I lead a company of *artistes* in the best actor-manager traditions of the theatre. My wife and brother-in-law are artists – Mr Fields is a genius the like of whom has not been seen in this country since the time of William Kempe, the great Shakespearean clown, who once danced from London to Norwich!'

Jack sincerely wished that Ivor French and his entire company would head off to Norwich, too. No such luck. Ivor's eyes glistened with a manic intensity and he leant over the counter, fixing Jack with his basilisk stare.

'Shakespeare,' he hissed, 'would have adored me.'

With that, he flung his scarf over his shoulder and strode up the steps and through the THEATRE STAFF ONLY doors.

'Has he gone?' a quiet female voice asked from under the counter.

'He has,' Jack confirmed.

Grace stood up from where she had been crouching next to Jack's carefully furled camp bed.

'I was sure he was going to see you,' he added as she smoothed her skirt. 'What on earth would you have said?'

'That I was looking for a hairpin or something.' She slumped onto the counter and groaned. 'This is too terrible.'

'I bet you wish you hadn't asked me to impersonate Mangrave now.'

She groaned again.

Seasoned stagehands had looked on in pity at the sets and flats Ivor French's company had brought in with them, then watched the rehearsals with horror. The stage manager Ivor had brought with him was a drunk – not offensive, but continually mildly sozzled – and operated the show in a free and easy spirit of improvisation. The band had discovered that the parts given them for the musical numbers were faded and torn, then soon found this was a perfect match for the voices of the principals.

God alone knew when last this abomination had been staged. Ivor, playing Macbeth, and his wife, were both in their sixties, and the music was definitely pre-war – *Pre-Boer war*, the clarinettist had remarked with a sneer in his voice. The witches were juveniles – new hires Ivor must have grabbed off the streets: a pert and talentless trio of young ladies, only one of whom had bothered to learn her lines. The tallest of them, though English by birth, improvised around the Shakespearean verse with an American twang. They could hold a tune, but very little else. The dress rehearsal had left the employees of the theatre slack-jawed with horror. Ivor, however, had told his company it was superb, and so profound were the man's delusions, he seemed to believe it.

It was a shame that Ivor couldn't put the passion he showed when discussing the notice into his performance in 'the Scottish Play', as Jack was being trained to call it. He had slipped twice so far and been forced to turn circles in the yard, spitting over his shoulder, under the baleful supervision of Mrs Gardener, head of wardrobe. She had told him a variety of exciting horror stories – actors accidentally hung on fly ropes, chunks of the ceiling falling down on the audience, and one unconfirmed report of spontaneous human combustion – to illustrate why the actual name of the play must never, ever be said aloud within the theatre.

It was a disaster. Flo and Jessie told Jack that bookings had been slow anyway, given the extravagant entertainments that were on offer elsewhere in town, and since the notice had appeared this morning, the box office was getting a stream of cancellations. Frederick Poole was planning on papering the house, giving away tickets just so there was some sort of audience in the building.

Grace groaned again.

Jack's lip twitched.

'Still, I wouldn't have missed "The Weird Sister Waltz".'

'Stop it, Jack. It's not funny.' She was trying to look severe, but Jack wasn't convinced.

'You didn't think the fight where it looked like Mac— him, and Macduff were both going to die of old age before they traded blows was funny?'

She looked him straight in the eye.

'It was the worst five minutes of my life, other than the five minutes before it, and the five minutes directly after. What have we done, Jack?'

Ollie must have sensed something was up. He got out of his basket and headbutted Grace's calves until she scratched his ears.

Jack had no idea what to say, so he said nothing.

'I tried to resign this morning,' Grace said, as Ollie made it clear the scratching should continue. 'I was expecting Mr Mangrave to come in raging about the notice, but the fact he didn't seem to care was even worse.'

'But, Grace, you can't leave! This place relies on you.' He hesitated. 'You'd have left without telling me?'

'No! I would have come down and cried all over you and Ollie within five minutes.' She smiled crookedly. 'I've got used to coming down here and complaining about Mangrave and Joe Allerdyce to you every day.'

'Ollie and I are always very pleased when you do.'

'Anyway, I haven't resigned. Mangrave told me to wait five minutes, and when he came out of his office again, he gave me this.'

She took an envelope out of her handbag and handed it to Jack. He read the single page inside.

Miss Grace Hawkins has my full permission to act as an agent for The Empire in all matters financial and artistic.

Jack frowned. 'That's good, isn't it? I mean, you can get round him now.'

She took the letter back and put it back in her handbag.

'I don't know. I just don't understand why he doesn't *care*. I was told he's run theatres before, but he just seemed to spring from nowhere. I wish Edmund hadn't hired him. He's either at his club or locked in the inner office with the account books.'

'But with that letter, we can fight on, can't we? Bugger Allerdyce and his plotting.'

'I want to, Jack! But what can I do if the only thing we can get on stage is' – she gestured towards the door Ivor French had gone through – '*that!*'

'What – "the worst production of *Macbeth* ever to have been staged outside a borstal"?' Jack snorted, quoting from the notice.

'Oh, you said it again, Jack! Get out and spin three times.'

He protested very mildly, but she shoved him out of the door. Ollie barked excitedly.

'It's a complete farce!' she said, and leant against the wall while he spun round in the yard and spat over his shoulder.

'Thing is, some of the tunes aren't half bad, even if they are old-fashioned,' he said between enthusiastic spins. 'It's just such a horrible, horrible idea to start off with.'

'Keep spinning. It was all that stamping during the sound and fury speech which got me.' She began to laugh again, in spite of herself.

He spun again. 'Not the Yankee witch saying "Who's got the frogs' bits, then?" as her opening line?'

Grace gasped. 'Oh, stop it, Jack, my sides are hurting.'

He stopped, and if a sudden beam of sunshine didn't shine through the clouds like a spotlight on his unturned face, it should have done. He could almost hear an angelic choir.

'That's it!'

'What is it, Jack?'

'You said it yourself. It's a farce! What did the notice say? "A night in the theatre unlike any other"?'

'What? But it's not meant to be funny!'

'But it *is*, Grace! We sell it as a comedy! What about the bit when the end of Macduff's sword fell off and he had to pretend to knock Ivor down with the hilt?'

'Jack, that's—'

'Bloody hysterical. Grace, we sell it as a comedy.'

'It . . . It might work,' she said very slowly. 'Do you really think . . . ?'

'Come on! Let's see if Ivor will play it for laughs in the matinee. Honestly, Grace, what have we got to lose? And you're allowed to do *anything!*'

'That doesn't mean I should!'

'You were ready to resign anyway! Please, let's just give it a try.'

She pushed herself away from the wall. 'This is mad.'

'So is the play!' he said. 'Think! How can we sell the idea of playing it as a comedy to Ivor?'

She bit her lip then looked up, her eyes dancing.

'"O heaven, the vanity of wretched fools!" I might have an idea.'

Grace and Jack tumbled into the number one dressing room, flushed with enthusiasm, and found Ivor French at his dressing table. He wore a slightly ragged scarlet dressing gown over his breeches, had his eyes closed and his fingertips tented together. He was humming as they opened the door, then opened his mouth to give a long, sonorous *maaa*. He sounded like some sort of demonic sheep.

'Mr French?' Grace said.

The eyes remained closed, and the long single *maa* became a series of staccato blasts.

Grace tried again. 'If you have a moment, Mr French, we—'

'*Ma!*' French enunciated with remarkable energy. Then slowly and wearily, he opened his eyes. 'I have finished. What do you want, Miss Hawkins, Mr Treadwell? As you can see, I am preparing for my performance.'

His performance that afternoon would be to a dozen street urchins, bribed into the theatre with boiled sweets.

'We just wanted to say, Mr French,' Jack said, 'how terrible it is that your bold interpretation of the play has been so misunderstood by the critics.'

Ivor eyed him suspiciously.

'Terrible,' Grace said. 'And I was just saying to Jack, how I wondered if, given the lack of sophistication in this city, you might need to broaden it up, just a little. So that the audience understand what it is they are seeing.'

He sniffed. 'Broaden it?'

'Yes, Mr French!' Grace went on. 'I think that perhaps the Highbridge crowd, in their ignorance, don't understand the revolutionary—'

'And incredibly modern,' Jack interjected.

'Exactly – incredibly modern concept of turning the Scottish Play into a hysterical satire of the theatrical arts.'

A long pause. Ivor narrowed his eyes.

'Satire?'

'So wickedly funny!' Jack said. 'An absolutely joyous theatrical experience. The wit!'

Ivor was staring at them now. 'The Scottish Play is a study in ambition, young man – how it can turn a hero into a murderous tyrant, and finally drive him into madness.'

'And yet – so much fun!' Jack's voice cracked a little under the strain.

'Like the moment . . . just one example,' Grace rushed in, 'where you actually say out loud "lunge, lunge, parry, shield" while fighting Macduff. So . . . So . . . innovative. You are reinventing the whole concept of performance in front of us.'

'With tunes!' Jack added.

Ivor's face gave away nothing.

Jack tried to force the squeak out of his voice, lowering it in a desperate attempt to regain some gravitas.

'Only a man like you – a visionary, Mr French – could stage such a remarkable, playful, bold reframing of a Shakespearean tragedy as a perfectly performed satire . . . with cracking tunes. Wouldn't you agree, Grace?'

'A thousand times "yes",' Grace replied.

Ivor stood up suddenly, flicking the tassels of his dressing gown behind him as he strode past them into the corridor.

'Have we made it worse?' Jack hissed.

'Impossible,' Grace replied.

'Company!' Ivor called, then when nothing and no one stirred, he did it again. '*Company!*'

Lady Macbeth, unwigged, but with her whiteface and bald cap on, stuck her head out of the number two dressing room. Macduff, Banquo and the porter stuck their heads round the door of dressing room three; the witches from dressing room four.

Ivor cleared his throat.

'It has been suggested to me by these young people,' he began in the same slightly warbling voice he used on the stage, ' that for the audiences of Highbridge to understand what we are doing here artistically, we might *broaden* the comedic aspects of the play.'

'Not a comedy,' said Macduff flatly. 'It's a tragedy.'

'With dance routines!' Grace squeaked, then turned away.

'Which is exactly what makes our approach,' Ivor continued, as if she had not spoken, 'of playing it as a comic musical revue so remarkable.'

He looked at each of them in turn; it was, Jack had to admit, a mesmerising performance. Far more mesmerising than anything Ivor ever managed on stage.

'So make it *funny*?' the porter said in a wondering tone.

'Though, of course,' Jack interposed, while the cast looked at one another from their doorways, like rabbits sticking their heads out of a warren to test the weather, 'it's the conviction with which you play the roles that makes it really work.'

'Exactly,' Grace jumped in. 'Mrs French – Sylvia, if I may . . . ?' The bald-capped Lady Macbeth nodded her permission. 'Your mad song, "Blood, Blood, Blood", wouldn't work if you just played it for laughs. No, of course, it's the way you keep singing the words with more and more conviction each time which makes it . . . unforgettable.'

Jack choked, but managed to turn it into an earnest grunt of agreement.

'What?' Macduff said, scratching his unshaven chin. 'So we should just keep doing what we are doing, then?'

'What about the witches?' Ivor said, frowning at Grace.

Grace looked thoughtful for a second. 'They shouldn't change a thing. I think the one with the American accent should play up the gum-chewing, though.'

'Such a clever way of emphasising the American takeover of our culture,' Jack said.

'The matinee is in an hour,' Grace said warmly. 'Perhaps, just see how it plays there?'

'I shall speak to the rest of the company,' Ivor said as the other players in the corridor shrugged or nodded.

Grace thanked them and dragged Jack away, through the double doors and all the way into the yard, before the laughter overtook them completely.

'What now?' Grace said, wiping her eyes.

'We need new posters, another advert. If it works today, we'll have to paper the town tomorrow.'

She shook her head. 'Jack, stop. If it does work this afternoon, or looks like it might work, we need to close for a couple of days.'

He was baffled.

'Don't worry, Treadwell. It's still an absolutely insane idea. But if it looks like it might fly, we'll need to restage the whole thing. Comedy is hard! They need to get the pacing right. I'll cut some of the speeches, and ideally we want a couple of new tunes. Do you believe in God?'

The conversation seemed to have run away from him.

'I served in the trenches, so I'm not sure I believe in Him, but we are definitely on conversational terms.'

'Then start praying.'

He closed his eyes. 'Grace, listen. Do you hear that?'

'What – the sound of Shakespeare spinning in his grave?'

He shook his head and listened again. Someone was playing a piano somewhere in the theatre. It was a version of "The Weird Sister Waltz", but it had some sort of strange syncopated pop to it, which transformed it from dirge to something light and unusual.

'Where is that coming from?'

Grace shook her head in amazement.

'Heaven, possibly. Or practice room seven.'

Without thinking, Jack grabbed her hand and she threw him

a glance. Then they were off again, racing up the narrow, scuffed staircases until they bundled into a small room near the top of the building. A middle-aged woman was sitting at a piano, idly strumming the keys. Her long hair was piled insecurely on top of her head with an enormous number of hairpins, none of which seemed happy in their work.

'Miss Rowntree?' Grace gasped, slightly out of breath.

'Just call me Ruby, dear.'

'Jack, this is Ruby Rowntree. She coaches singers and plays for us in rehearsals sometimes. Ruby, this is Jack Treadwell.'

'Delighted. You're the one Flo's been baking for, aren't you?'

'That's right. I'm sorry we haven't met before.'

Jack took in the little room. It was very cosy, and littered with manuscript papers and pencils. There was even a knitted comforter over an armchair in the corner.

'I come in through the front, dear. What can I do for you?'

'Was it you playing a version of "The Weird Sister Waltz" just now?'

She laughed, a gentle little trill. 'Yes, I saw the show last night. Absolutely awful, but a couple of nice melodies.'

'We're thinking of redoing it as a comedy,' Grace said, her tone suggesting she did not quite believe the words which were coming out of her mouth. 'We'd need to do something to their tunes, just like you did with the waltz. And perhaps write a couple more.'

'An excellent idea,' Ruby said. 'Though you mustn't touch "Blood, Blood, Blood". Making that funny is all about the orchestration. A little oboe on the offbeats.'

'Exactly!' Jack was not completely sure he understood what she meant, but it sounded right. 'Could you help?'

'Turn that abomination into a comedy?' Ruby said. 'How long would we have?'

'If we go dark for three days,' Grace said, 'would you be able to do . . . say, two new songs, and re-orchestrate the rest?'

'You'll need three new songs. And yes, I can, as long as you deal with the words, dear. I know you're good at the words. I'll need to cancel a few piano lessons.'

'We'll pay you, of course,' Grace said.

'In that case,' Ruby said, suddenly beaming, 'I'll cancel all of them.'

'You're really that fast?' Grace asked.

'I am. I can just reach up and grab good tunes out of the air. It used to annoy my teachers at the conservatoire no end. That, and my being a girl.' She smiled sideways at them.

'Are we doing this, Grace?' Jack felt a bubble of excitement rising in his chest. 'You have the note of authority, after all.'

'Even if it doesn't work, at least we're going down fighting! Oh, I hate the idea of Joe Allerdyce just stomping all over us!'

'We'll show him what we're made of!' he said and saluted, which made her smile again.

'It'll be expensive to close the theatre, but we have to.'

Jack thought for a moment.

'Listen . . . This might sound peculiar, but I have an idea about the money – Palgrave's Soap. Ring them up! We'll print up bills with "Out, damned spot" and "Should've used Palgrave's" over a picture of Mrs French doing her bit, washing the blood off her hands.'

Grace smothered a laugh. 'Do you know, that might work. How do we explain going dark for three days?'

'Mr Poole can put up a poster – due to circumstances beyond our control . . .'

Grace waved her hands; inspiration had struck.

'No – due to *mysterious* circumstances beyond our control,

Macbeth will close tonight. Grand reopening of *Macbeth*, with exclamation marks, on Friday!'

'Perfect!'

Grace flung her arms around him, and their eyes met for a long moment, then she pulled away.

'I'll ring the soap people and then I'll have time for a word with the band and stage crew before the matinee. They'll get it. You go and see Mr Poole and explain what's going on. Ruby, I'll be back as soon as I can to work on the text, and we can rehearse with the French Company Players from tomorrow.'

And she was gone again. The woman could disappear on you like she had trapdoors in every corner of the building.

Frederick Poole had run the front of house at The Empire for fifteen years. It was a career he was proud of; it had been, as he remarked to his wife, a calling. Sarah Bernhardt had, on her last appearance here, greeted him by name. He had once ushered King George into his seat in what was now the royal box. He had been on hand during triumphs and tragedies, hits, flops, failures and successes. And some oddities. He had once, for example, dealt with a performing seal who suffered an attack of nerves and had tried to exit the theatre through the lobby. The night *Macbeth!!* reopened after its disastrous first night, and three days of frantic restaging, however, was even stranger. And he didn't see a second of the actual performance.

He often watched the show from the back of the stalls; it was one of the pleasures of his position that he had his own neat fold-down seat just inside the lobby doors. He didn't need to occupy it, however, to know how a performance was going. The mood of the audience altered the quality of the air. Even when he was outside, carefully neatening the piles of tickets, coloured according to the days of the week, and smoothing out the banknotes in the till, or piling up the coins paid for the gallery seats at the side door, you could feel it – the collective pleasure, enjoyment, excitement, or even boredom.

On the first night, the knowledge that the performance was a disaster had seeped into his kingdom like a bad smell. Even before the interval, people were leaving.

'I am ever so sorry I made you sit through that,' he heard an elderly patron whisper to his wife as they hurried out into the rain.

More left at the interval. The final curtain was greeted with a half-hearted smattering of applause, and then the audience fled. Poole had taken his usual position by the door, wishing his patrons a good evening. Most had dashed past him into the night with their heads down. The few who did meet his eye did so with a look of rage – the expressions of men and women who had been cheated out of a shilling or two and an entire evening from the span of their short, precious lives.

When a show was a success, patrons took the programmes with them. That night, the programmes were balled up and thrown into the waste paper baskets. One had even been thrown at him.

Poole did not need to read the notices.

Then, during the matinee, Jack Treadwell had ambushed him as he took his tea. He was telling Jack that his and Miss Hawkins' 'plan' was ridiculous, and they'd be better off cancelling the run entirely and save on heat and light, at least, when the first ripples of boyish laughter had become audible from the auditorium.

So he had allowed himself, eventually, to be persuaded into the sign about 'mysterious circumstances', the auditorium going dark for three days, and the show had been retitled, through a manic wielding of paintbrushes and fountain pens, *Macbeth!!* on each printed programme, ticket and poster. At the end of the first day of restaging, Jack and Grace had remembered they'd need an audience for their reopening – one that would know to laugh, and talk about the show. Poole made some suggestions which were received in a flattering and enthusiastic manner, including bribing a few members of the theatre staff to walk around the lobby in civilian clothing, talking about what a hoot the show was as the audience arrived. Jack Treadwell was proving to be an interesting sort of doorman, and Miss Hawkins had a fresh spring in her step.

And so it began.

On the evening of the reopening, a good-sized crowd, curious and bemused, made their way into the theatre just before seven o'clock. They had shut the balcony, and Poole had sent the boys from the carpentry shop to give tickets to the sales girls in the department stores, the doormen at the better hotels, and waiters at the gentlemen's clubs. They all came decently dressed and nicely behaved – if a little nervous. Poole closed the doors on them as the overture began, then retreated to the box office and waited.

Three minutes in, there was a laugh so loud it startled him into knocking over the balcony tickets for the Saturday matinee. He lifted his nose and sniffed. Another laugh; this one started small, then grew like a gathering sea. Then applause and cheers. The air changed. A thousand people in a single space who are having a very, very good time does something to the atmosphere. It tastes different. It conducts pleasure and compounds it.

Poole looked at the doors and made a curious high humphing noise in the back of his throat. He could almost see it. Ten minutes . . . twenty . . . and it could not be mistaken. Joy – sheer ridiculous joy – was streaming like flood waters from the auditorium, and was now spreading through the corridors, empty bars and lobbies of The Empire, pouring down the stairs into the foyer like a waterfall. It would spill out into the streets, and when the audience left, the news would sprinkle the city like a fine rain until everyone within five miles would wake up knowing that they just had to get tickets for this show. The shop girls would tell their customers, the waiters their guests. The air of Highbridge would thicken with the news.

Remarkable.

Poole fetched an envelope and put a selection of the tickets for the best seats in the house into it. He knew personally some of those regular patrons who had left looking so beaten down and betrayed only a few days ago. Tomorrow, he would have Marcus and his friends act as messenger boys, sending those carefully selected individuals personal notes inviting them back to witness a miracle, a resurrection, a theatrical event like no other. He started humming to himself as he selected some seats from the stalls. Everyone who worked in the theatre – from Mrs Briggs, to Little Sam, to Barry, who always did their printing and charged a little under market price – would be desperate for tickets. In such moments, Poole played Highbridge and its society like a concert pianist.

'A hit,' he said to himself, as he sealed the envelopes and placed them in a locked drawer under the tills. He slipped the key back into his waistcoat. 'It's a bloody hit.'

CHAPTER FIVE

That Sunday, Grace took Jack on an outing. Jack looked at the passing streets with interest. He hadn't been more than a quarter of a mile from the theatre since he had arrived, and was intrigued by these affluent suburbs. They got off the bus outside a grocer's and post office, serving streets of semi-detached villas built just before the war. Opposite them stood the gates to a bowls and tennis club. Grace led him up a wide avenue, lined with comfortable detached houses in orange brick, which glowed where the afternoon sun reached them through the foliage of lime and plane trees. She turned through a metal gate, and up a path of black and white tile, then knocked at the door. The knocker was modelled on the masks of tragedy and comedy.

'Grace! How are you, my sweet?'

The woman who opened the door was in late middle age, with handsome features and a smile which made her eyes glint.

'Oh, I'm managing, Alma. Just. This is Jack. He's the new doorman at The Empire.'

Alma gave him a long look up and down.

'You make a bit of a change from Herb! You'll be looking for Charlie, Grace?'

'Yes. Did he read the *Gazette* last week?'

Alma laughed. 'Of course he did, treasure. And yesterday! We've been agog. You've done something remarkable. I'll bring tea.'

She ushered them through the house, and Jack noticed it was decorated with a mix of mirrors, fresh flowers and old playbills. A door from a comfortable-looking sitting room at the rear of the building opened out on to a terrace, and a long garden beyond.

'Go on,' Alma said. 'He'll be delighted to see you – it'll give him a chance to stop weeding the shrubbery.'

Grace headed down the flagged path, Jack at her heels.

'I like her.'

'She was a great turn in her day. A male impersonator – like Vesta Tilley, although Alma was better, I think. Charlie was always hard as nails as a manager, but he melted when he met her.'

For Jack, the days of the restaging and rebirth of *Macbeth!!* had passed in a sort of frantic blissful haze. It was one thing to make stage door look nice, and bury himself in finding out everything he could about the business of theatre by reading Herb's archive of copies of *The Stage*, but actually taking a hand in things had been exhilarating. Once the company had arrived, Jack latched the door and put Ollie in command then hurried to join them in rehearsal. Ivor and his company, buoyed by the titters of a few schoolboys, had proved enthusiastic collaborators. Ivor directed, though he consulted with Grace between each of his commands to his players. Ruby had delighted the band with her reworking of the old songs and the new numbers she and Grace had composed together. And Grace – marvellous, brilliant Grace – had, in the midst of all this, brandished her letter of authority at the printer's and at the makers of Palgrave's Soap, and five hundred new programmes with SHOULD HAVE USED PALGRAVE'S printed on them would be delivered in time for next week's performances. The box office was besieged all day on Saturday, and Frederick Poole was in his element, handing out tickets like they were royal favours.

Warton Webster had called yesterday, and reminded Grace that The Empire's contract was for six weeks only. After that, the newly stupendously successful Ivor French would be taking his production elsewhere. That meant Grace was faced with the same problem as last time: no agent would place their acts at The Empire, and none of the touring companies would come in. No matter the coup they had pulled off with *Macbeth!!* – Allerdyce owned most of the best theatres in the North-West as well as many smaller venues. At least the agents sounded slightly sorry about turning her down now, but they were still turning her down. They needed another success to show that The Empire could stand up against the might of Allerdyce – that the triumph of *Macbeth!!* was a sign of renewed spirit, not an accident – or they'd all go down with the ship.

So, despite their triumph, they had come to the old theatre manager for advice and inspiration. Charlie Moon, a small man nearly as spherical as his namesake, emerged from the shrubbery and beamed at them. Grace made the introductions, and when she told Charlie it had been Jack's idea to make *Macbeth* into a comedy, he had his hand shaken again, but even harder this time.

Alma came out with the tea, and after Grace had explained about Allerdyce and their present worries, Alma asked Grace some questions about her family. Soon they were chatting about people Jack had never heard of, in a flurry of names and professions. Charlie noticed Jack's confusion.

'Grace is my god-daughter,' he said. 'I've been friends with her parents for forty years.'

'That's not why you hired me as your assistant, though, was it, Charlie?' Grace asked defensively.

'Of course it was!'

'Oh, Charlie!'

'But I kept you on because you were bloody good at the job.' He looked at Jack. 'So are you two stepping out?'

Grace blushed and they both stuttered their denials.

'What are you doing here if you're just the doorman, then?'

'I told you – it was his idea, Charlie. To re-advertise the show as a comedy. And Mangrave's no help, so I've ended up talking everything through with Jack.'

'More your assistant than a doorman, I'd say,' Alma said, smiling over the rim of her teacup.

'Grace has taught me an awful lot,' Jack said promptly. 'I'm delighted to be her assistant.'

Charlie gave Jack a long assessing look while sucking on his pipe. Alma pushed a plate of fruit cake at him.

'Glad to hear it,' she said. 'So what brought you to The Empire in the first place?'

Jack drew a deep breath and told them about spending time driving in France.

'Who did you drive?'

He frowned. 'Mostly wealthy couples wanting to see where their sons had fought. Then, later, people who didn't trust their chauffeurs on French roads. It meant I got to see a lot of the country.'

'So how did you end up in the shop?' Grace asked.

He laughed. 'I fancied a change and one of my clients recommended me. It was fun for a while.'

'Until Mr Garnier took against your sense of humour,' Grace said, her eyes dancing.

'And my face,' Jack added with mock seriousness.

Then he explained about his return to Winchurch, the scrapbook of clippings Bessie had left behind, and her message to go and see Lady Lassiter.

'So what do you want to be, Jack, when Grace has no more use for you?' Alma asked. 'A director, an actor?'

'Theatre manager,' he said promptly. 'I didn't know what one of those was a few weeks ago, but it's the job for me. But a real theatre manager – like Grace is, and how you were, Mr Moon. In the thick of it.'

'Is it now?' Charlie said, still scowling over his pipe. 'The hours are terrible, you know, if you do the job properly.'

'I shouldn't mind that. Grace will tell you I have been firmly and irredeemably bitten by the theatre bug. Can't think how I believed any other job would do for me.'

'It's true, we can hardly get him to leave the building,' Grace said dryly.

'Why did you leave, Mr Moon?' Jack asked.

He half-smiled. 'I got old. Nothing more complicated than that. I recommended a few people when I said I was retiring, but Edmund turned up with Mangrave and Lady L. . . . Well, she agreed.'

'When was that?' Jack asked.

Charlie sniffed. 'Eighteen months ago – about that, wasn't it, Grace? Lady Lassiter was a powerhouse during the first part of the war. We raised a lot of money at the theatre, then I think it overwhelmed her – the state the boys were in when they came back. For the last year of the war she kept pretty much to herself at Lassiter Court, looking after the wounded who were sent there.

Then Sir Barnabas had his first stroke. Mangrave seemed an odd fish, but it wasn't my place to argue.'

'At least Mangrave has had the sense to put Grace in charge now,' Jack said.

Grace produced the letter with a certain amount of pride.

'Yes,' she said, 'Mangrave's just locked up with his account books or at the club now.'

While Alma and Charlie bent over the letter, Jack heard the sound of the French window opening. A man of about his own age, in rough trousers and shirtsleeves, leaning heavily on a walking stick, emerged from the house and lifted his free hand in greeting.

Jack set down his teacup and jumped to his feet.

'Danny! Danny Moon! As I live and breathe!'

Danny began to walk down the path towards him, Alma looking pleased and confused. Charlie leant towards Grace.

'He never comes down when we have company. Did Jack say that he served?'

'Yes.' Grace realised she had never asked Jack much about what he had done in the war. He'd just mentioned the prisoner of war camp. 'But I didn't realise he'd served with men from Highbridge! How is Danny, Charlie?'

'He's much the same. But he's here, my love. And we're grateful for that every day.'

The two former soldiers had met on the path and were shaking hands. The unscarred part of Danny's face was pink, and he was smiling.

'Good to see you, C-captain.'

'I'm just Jack now, Danny,' Jack said cheerfully. 'I had no idea I was calling on you today. I should have worked it out! How are you keeping, old man?'

'T-today is a good day,' Danny said quietly. 'Mum, Dad, this is Captain Treadwell. I . . . told you about him.'

Alma gasped and Charlie's jaw dropped.

'Doorman Jack is Captain Treadwell?' he said. 'Blow me down!'

'What's happening?' Grace asked, looking between the various shocked and beaming faces.

'Captain Treadwell was Danny's company commander – he saved Danny's life,' Alma said, her eyes filling with tears. She jumped up and hugged Jack so hard she almost knocked him over onto the lawn. 'We never thought we'd have a chance to thank you.'

'No thanks needed,' Jack said as he recovered his balance. 'And I was second-in-command actually, and not for long. Anyway, we saved each other's lives often enough over there. I'm glad to see you made it back, Danny. You must have got the shock of your life when you looked out of the window and saw me having tea with your folks!'

Danny only nodded.

'Will you have tea with us, Danny?' his mother asked.

He flinched, and it seemed to Grace he must have run through his stock of words for the day. She had seen him half a dozen times at most since he had come home, and normally wearing a painted mask which covered much of the scarred right side of his face. He wasn't wearing it today.

'Now I know you're here, I hope you'll let me come and call again, Danny. So we can have a proper chat.'

'I'd . . . like that,' Danny said, whispering now.

'Leg giving you gyp? Shall I walk you back in?'

Jack was answered with a look of mute gratitude. The two men turned back up the path, Alma and Charlie gaping after them.

'I can't even believe it!' Alma said. 'Captain Treadwell, and you giving him the third degree, Charlie!' She turned around. 'He's a hero in this household, Grace. I'm very glad to see him looking so well.'

Grace was sure she meant it but felt the pain under the words, too, as the door closed behind her son.

Before she could enquire further, Charlie cleared his throat.

'Are you still writing, Grace? You haven't sent me anything to read in an age. Can't have you slacking off.'

Grace felt an uncomfortable turn in her stomach. 'I haven't been, honestly, Charlie. I did some bits for *Macbeth!!*, but I've been terribly busy.'

She was saved from having to explain any more by Jack coming back from the house. He was smiling broadly.

'What a treat to see Danny.' He glanced round. 'Do I have something on my face?'

Grace blinked at him, sounding suddenly indignant. 'You don't even come from Highbridge! How did you end up serving together? Did you serve with Edmund Lassiter, too?'

Jack sat back down and sipped his tea for a moment before replying.

'Same battalion, different company. I was promoted from the ranks and so they shipped me away from my own regiment. By Ypres, we were all just members of the Hartshire Rifles. Men from all across the region.'

'I see, but . . . Jack, you're a terribly confusing person! Did you even tell me you were an officer?'

'Does it matter?' he asked with a crooked smile. 'I'm still just the son of a mechanic who managed to survive. I wasn't an officer for long. It mostly meant I got a better deal than most of the men when I was a prisoner of war.'

'No,' she replied quietly. 'It doesn't really matter.'

'It shows your senior officers saw you had leadership qualities, Jack,' Alma said. 'Seems to me they were right.'

Jack looked uncomfortable. He didn't like talking about the war or his role in it. Grace might not have known his rank, but she had worked that out by now.

'Perhaps they just saw you have a tendency to charge into impossible situations,' Grace said, with a slightly arch tone.

Jack laughed and flashed her a grateful smile.

'Grace, I just had a thought looking at the old posters in Mr and Mrs Moon's hall,' he said. 'What about an old-time music hall show? We go and find the old acts that aren't on agents' books anymore and bring them to The Empire. Allerdyce couldn't stop us doing that.'

'No, he couldn't!' Grace said, sitting up straight. 'It's a good idea. What do you think, Charlie?'

'Allerdyce has his theatres full of great turns,' Charlie replied. 'Who would come and see a bunch of old has-beens?'

Grace shook her head. 'Nostalgia? It could be a sort of revue version of the old days!'

'Nostalgia sells,' Alma said, proffering the pot. Jack nodded his thanks as she poured him more tea.

'We could have a chairman,' Grace went on. 'Sort of string it together with a bit of a story, even.' She could almost see it already. 'All clean stuff, old songs and daft speciality acts. And Alma! You could be chairman!'

Alma paused in her pouring. 'Go back on stage?'

Charlie looked at his wife. 'You've still got plenty of fans in Highbridge, Alma. And I'll bet ten shillings you still fit into your white tie and tails. Fancy taking another spin for these young people?'

'Charlie, you can un-retire for a bit, help us put it together,' Grace added.

Charlie frowned. 'I don't know about that.'

'No, my darling,' Alma said, smiling sweetly and topping up his cup. 'If you're going to volunteer me for this, I'll volunteer you.'

'I can't argue with that, I suppose,' Charlie said slowly. 'It'll be quite a job to find the acts, though, and I'm too old and comfortable in my home to dash about the place looking for them.'

There was a pause.

'Why's everyone looking at me?' Jack asked eventually. 'Oh – you mean I'll have to go looking for them?'

'I have to stay at the theatre, Jack,' Grace said. 'And Mangrave's not going to help.'

Charlie started refilling his pipe. 'Jack, you'll need a new job title. You're not just a doorman any more.'

'What about company manager for now?' Grace suggested. 'I can appoint you right this minute. We can go over the engagement contracts for the turns on Monday morning.'

'And I'll be off Monday afternoon!' Jack said. 'I can take all my old copies of *The Stage*, and there's a stack of postcards of old turns, too, I've inherited from Herb! Should be lots of leads there.'

Charlie lit a match and puffed till he had the tobacco glowing as he wanted. 'Go to the pubs near the theatres, Jack, and ask about the old-timers there. You'll probably meet half a dozen acts at the bar.'

'I shall!'

Alma tilted her head to one side. 'You won't mind, will you, Jack? Heading off again just as you've settled after all this time?'

'It'll be an adventure, Mrs Moon,' he replied stoutly. 'As long as The Empire doesn't forget about me while I'm gone.'

He looked straight at her while he spoke, but Grace felt herself colour slightly as Alma glanced at her.

'I'm sure there's no danger of that,' Alma said. 'Is there, Grace?'

'Of course not. Ollie, in particular, has the most splendid memory for faces.'

Jack grinned at that.

'All right then,' Charlie said with a sigh. 'Let's talk this through.'

On Monday morning, Grace was at her desk at the usual time, sorting through the contracts for the acts Jack might possibly engage on the road, and puzzling over the rough budget for the production they had worked out yesterday afternoon in Alma and Charlie's garden. They had also come up with an ideal running order – the mix of speciality acts, singers and comedians who would make up the quintessential old-time music hall revue. Mangrave appeared, nodded curtly when she told him about their new idea, then left, taking a bundle of papers with him and saying he intended to work at the club. Grace watched him go. Her distaste for the man had grown, and she was aware of something else whenever he was in the room – an unpleasant creeping sensation under her skin, as if an alarm was going off somewhere deep inside her. Grace knew he was married, but his wife never came to anything at The Empire. She shook her head and hoped he stayed in the club as long as possible. She had better things to think about than him.

Jack appeared just after eleven, leaving Ollie in charge at stage door, to go through their plans with her, and they spent the next hour happily going through them again. She watched him as he reread the model contract, his brow deeply furrowed in concentration and spinning a pencil round in his fingers. He was certainly handsome, but unlike most of the actors who arrived at The Empire, all chiselled jaws and soulful gaze, he didn't seem aware of it. He must have met all sorts of beautiful girls in Paris, yet he never mentioned any.

He looked up. 'What?'

Grace found it necessary to rearrange her pencils briefly. 'Nothing. I was just thinking how you've a knack for picking up all sorts of complicated things rather quickly, Jack. Charlie had to explain those contracts to me a dozen times before I understood them!'

He scratched his nose, as if uncomfortable with the compliment. 'That's the army for you. When I was promoted from the ranks, we had about two months to learn all sorts of things, from which fork to use for what in the officers' mess, to orienteering and the general military codes. These contracts are almost understandable in contrast to them, I assure you. And besides, you're an awfully good teacher.'

His eyes did crinkle in a very winning way when he smiled.

'Miss Hawkins!'

Grace straightened up sharply as Frederick Poole burst in through the door. Jack jumped to his feet and dropped to the floor in pursuit of his pencil.

'What is it, Mr Poole?'

'There's a man from Palgrave's Soap downstairs! He wants to give away free samples after the show tonight!'

'Oh, yes,' Grace said, standing up. 'I'm so sorry, Mr Poole, I did mean to discuss that with you. That was my suggestion. They have offered us quite a handsome sum of money to do it, and they'll print the wrappings with Mrs French's picture and "appearing at The Empire".'

'That sounds like a marvellous idea!' Jack said, clambering to his feet again and brandishing his pencil. 'I wish I'd thought of it.'

'Oh, Mr Treadwell, I didn't see you there, rolling around on the carpet.'

Jack pointed at the pencil by way of explanation.

'Yes, well, that's as may be,' Poole said, returning his attention to Grace, 'but there's a flow to the lobby, a system! I don't want a bloody great soap stand in the way!'

Grace nodded very seriously. 'Naturally, Mr Poole. Very true. Why don't we go downstairs and discuss it? I'm sure with your advice we'll be able to find a way to make it work.'

'I can't have my flow disturbed.'

'Of course not, Mr Poole.'

She took him by the elbow and began to steer him towards the door.

'Grace?'

'Yes, Jack?'

'I suppose I'll be off this afternoon to start recruiting these new acts.'

She nodded. 'Do you have everything you need?'

'Yes, but . . .' He seemed to be on the point of saying something more to her, then grinned again. 'I'll return with the best acts Joe Allerdyce can't buy!'

'*What?*' Poole squeaked. 'What's happening?' So the rumours are true! I knew it! That Joe Allerdyce! He'll do for us in the end. We'll be joining the bloody unemployment lines, and he'll turn The Empire into a picture house just to spite us! And who's to be stage doorman while Mr Treadwell is gone?'

It took five minutes to calm Poole sufficiently and explain the idea of the old-time music hall revue to him, and another ten for Jack to assure him that Little Sam, who – though very sweet-natured – was built like a steam engine, had agreed to stand in for Jack on stage door. Poole eventually conceded that *if* Jack managed to get some decent turns, Joe Allerdyce might be prevented from bankrupting them for another few weeks, but he needed a cup of tea before he was ready to do battle with the soap man again.

By the time Grace had finished the discussions of flow in the lobby, Jack had left. To Grace, The Empire seemed suddenly very empty without him.

CHAPTER SIX

The business editor knocked at the door of Edison Potter's office at the *Highbridge Gazette* and the *Highbridge Illustrated News*.

'Come in.'

Edison was not at his desk. He stood at the window, which looked out across the city centre. Not much of a view by some standards. He could just see a couple of trees in the municipal park, but then he didn't care much for trees, and he liked looking at the buildings, and the people coming and going on the streets below. It reminded him he was at the centre of things.

He always took his lunch at a pie and mash shop two streets from the office. He had a table near the counter, and he would read one of his competitor's papers while he smashed his potato into the gravy and listened to what people were saying. For the last week they'd been talking about *Macbeth!!* at The Empire, quoting lines, then collapsing into gales of laughter, which would, Edison thought, have come as a bit of a surprise to William Shakespeare.

'Edison.' His business editor sidled his way into the office with a slender young man in tow. 'This is Wilbur Bowman. He's come to me with a story and I want to run it by you.'

Edison abandoned the window and returned to his desk as the two men settled themselves in front of him.

'Spit it out then, Mr Bowman,' he said.

'People are talking about Lassiter Enterprises, Mr Potter,' the young man began.

'Of course they are, son – biggest employer in Highbridge.'

'There are rumours . . .'

Edison sighed as he looked at his section head.

'Roy, do we print rumours?'

'We don't.'

'Do we print "what people are saying"?'

'No, Edison.'

'No, we don't.' He turned his stony gaze on the young reporter. 'Because we are a newspaper. We print news. Now do you, Mr Wilbur Bowman, have any of that?'

'No . . .'

Edison drew breath, like a dragon readying himself to deal with an ill-prepared adventurer after the gold of his reputation, but the young man hurried on.

'However, I *do* have ears in my head and a brain between them. Sir Edmund Lassiter is no businessman. He's vain and he's weak and he needs keeping an eye on.'

The lad had fire of his own in his belly, it seemed.

'And that's your job, is it? Keeping an eye on him?'

'Should be the job of his board of directors. Only there have been some changes there.'

'Carry on,' Edison said, settling himself more comfortably into his chair.

'The board consists of his mother, his brother Tom, and his step-grandmother, Lady Lassiter, who hasn't been to a meeting since Sir Barnabas's first stroke and is now in New York. In fact, I can't find any record of the board meeting in the last eighteen months. Three months ago Sir Edmund removed Tobias Seymour and David Tompkins from the board, and has made one appointment: Richard Moyle.'

Edison frowned. He knew Seymour and Tompkins – good men who had come up under Sir Barnabas. Bit long in the tooth, though, and every new chairman of the board had to stamp his authority on the place.

'Who's Richard Moyle?'

'Not sure, Mr Potter. But I did some digging, and a Private Richard Moyle served as Major Lassiter's batman during the war. He now lives in Sheffield. Owns a pub.'

There was a pause.

'Could be a sharp business mind,' Edison said, but he thought it unlikely. 'What do you propose, Mr Bowman?'

Bowman looked sideways at his section chief, who spoke up.

'Wilbur wants to do some digging, Edison. Get beyond the rumours to see if there is trouble at Lassiter Enterprises. I said we'd have to talk to you.'

'There's something else,' Wilbur said. 'The manager at The Empire. Edmund Lassiter hired him. The *rumour*' – he leant on the word a little, the cheeky bugger – 'is that he does no work, doesn't even like the theatre – but I've been told he meets with Ray Kelly sometimes.'

Ray Kelly, Edison thought.

Whenever something was wrong in Highbridge – illegal gambling, black market food which poisoned a bunch of poor families, or dark spasms of violence on the backstreets – if you went up the chain far enough you found Ray Kelly. And when you did, most people stopped asking questions and went home sharpish. Mostly he kept to his cottage in the dale, but he had his finger on the pulse of this city just as much as Edison did.

Edison got up from his chair again and went to stare out of the window. He could smell the story, like rain on the pavements after a hot day. There, but indescribable somehow. Think about it too long and it was gone again. Could Lassiter Enterprises be in trouble? The connection with Ray Kelly was thin – and libellous. But if it was true, it would be one hell of a story.

'An interview,' he pronounced at last, turning back into the room. 'It's an important story for the city. We want to hear about Sir Edmund's vision for the future. Sell it to him as an opportunity for the people to get to know him. Not for the paper – for the *Highbridge Illustrated News*. With a photograph. Then he'll imagine it on the tea tables of all the high and mighty in the city. Take your time over it – and that should give you an excuse to ask a few questions.'

Wilbur Bowman nodded. 'I might need to grease a few palms, Mr Potter.'

'We'll cover you. You'll need to talk to some of the top businessmen in town, too.' He reached into his pocket and pulled a few notes from his wallet. 'Buy yourself a decent suit.'

CHAPTER SEVEN

The road, Jack was discovering all over again, was a lonely place. Straight after the war, he'd embraced that loneliness like a long-lost friend. After being locked up with his fellow prisoners for so long, he had been desperate for a bit of peace, time to mourn his parents and let himself heal. But he'd found The Empire since then, and it was a wrench to leave it.

'Jack, I have to go,' Grace said in his ear, her voice distorted by the telephone line. 'Mr Poole wants something. Chin up!'

'I'll ring again tomorrow.'

He was about to try and finish with something witty and charming, but she only said 'Yes, do! Goodnight!' and cut the connection.

Jack replaced the receiver and allowed himself, forehead against the glass of the booth, a moment of despair. Grace was always encouraging and enthusiastic about his finds, and he had found some good acts, he reminded himself. A juggler called Horatio

Jones who looked about ninety, but who had entranced Jack by juggling his wife's tea set in his little parlour while she squeaked with laughter. He'd also found a comedian and a speciality dance act – an athletic bunch, who had been training their children as performers and marking time doing circus gigs along the coast until music hall called them home. The ventriloquist wasn't bad either, and there was a conjuror who had turned being a bad magician into twenty minutes of comic delight. Jack had a sentimental singer for the early part of the show, and a unicyclist to keep things lively going into the second act, but he needed something spectacular to finish with – and so far he had nothing. It was a big cast, more expensive than *Macbeth!!* had been by a mile, and if he didn't find something to make Highbridge really excited, and pack the theatre, they'd be running at a loss and doing Joe Allerdyce's work for him.

He stepped out on to the street and looked about him. He'd come here to talk to a female impersonator who had been quite the draw in her day, but she now ran a boarding house stuffed with cats and teddy bears and travelling salesmen and who had no intention of leaving any of them. He'd go and try his luck in Newcastle. The next train was in an hour.

Opposite the station, the steamy windows of a fried fish and chip shop caught his eye. The door swung open, and a pair of working men in flat caps, their faces flush and smiling, called their farewells to the people still inside. Jack smelled vinegar and batter, and his stomach grumbled. He checked his pockets – he had enough change for a plate and a tea. The world always looked better after a decent meal. He picked up his case and crossed the street.

The café was small – a dozen bolted-down tables and the kitchen at the back. Though it was busy, he was able to take the table just vacated and settled himself down. Pulling out another old copy of *The Stage* from his pocket, he began to study it.

A man emerged from behind the counter, carrying fully laden plates in his hands and up his arms.

'Haddock and chips, and the love of your favourite fryer for fourpence,' he declared. 'Who's up?'

Two respectably dressed young men sharing a table with a couple of women raised their hands. The man swung between the crowded tables towards them, making a show of just missing the heads of their fellow diners with the dishes, fainting a drop, pivoting on the balls of his feet, then delivering the plates onto the table. The whole room enjoyed the show, and Jack looked around him. It was the same feeling you had in the theatre on a good night – a sense of communal pleasure.

Jack stared at the man. He was in his late forties, maybe, with a full head of hair and a solid frame, although he moved very lightly around the tables. There was a small scar over his right eyebrow. Jack ordered a fish supper and tea from a cheerful waitress, and recognition stirred somewhere deep in the back of his mind. He stared at the tabletop, trying to lay hands on the thought.

He put his case on the chair next to him and opened it, then rifled through the old copies of *The Stage* that had been his guides and maps across the country, and the collection of postcards and photographs from Herb's archive. He flicked through the latter – a city's worth of forgotten comedians, dancers, clowns and speciality acts. And there he was – the fryer in his striped apron, though in this picture he was wearing a suit, with a warm smile for the camera, and was a lot younger. But it was him all right. Jack flipped the card: BILLY BARLOW. He'd read that name, too! He went back to the copies of *The Stage*. They had spilled some ink on this man in the nineties. A young man of exceptional talent – Prince of the Music Halls. Then he had disappeared. 'Sudden illness', a diary entry bemoaning his absence in the halls said. He didn't look ill now.

'Here you go, mate.'

Jack looked up at the man as he set down Jack's fish supper in front of him, his face flushed with the heat of the kitchen.

'You're Billy Barlow, Prince of the Music Halls,' Jack said to him.

The man frowned. 'No idea what you're talking about – my name's Henry.'

'Oi, Bill!' a voice called from the kitchen. 'We need more flour!'

The man who claimed to be Henry grinned at Jack. 'Coming, Giorgio!'

Jack reached for the salt.

Fine. I like a challenge.

William Barlow was happy to lock up for Giorgio after the fish shop closed. He lived in a tiny flat above the place – one of the perks of being Giorgio's best fryer, along with all the chips he could eat – so cleaning and locking up was part of his routine. The safe, comfortable routine he was planning to follow until he popped his clogs.

He'd spent half his night hiding out the back from the persistent young man who'd called him 'Prince of the Music Halls', then waved that old postcard in his face.

God, I haven't thought about those days in years.

The lad had insisted on introducing himself – Jack Treadwell – and started on at him about making a triumphant return to the stage. No thanks. Never. They'd had to be quite firm about showing the man out.

Bill began to mop the floor tiles and in the warm, foggy quiet the old tunes started going round his head. He started to hum along, then step round his mop and bucket like it was a stage partner as he began to sing out loud. Giorgio, Gilda and Fred had all headed home, after all, so there was no one to hear him. He'd always done his act with an outsized walking stick, breaking up his songs with a half-casual soft-shoe shuffle. It had given him the chance to work in some fancy bits – those moments when it looked like you were going to topple over, then swung your weight back and landed with a spin on your heels. The words came to his lips, and the moves took over his bones, like slipping on an old jacket from the back of the wardrobe and discovering it still fits. He swung the chairs up onto the tables in rhythm with his internal orchestra, the tune singing out of his blood now, as he rested his weight on the mop for one line, then swung it over his head like a baton on his next. The song bounded out of him, echoing across the tiles, bouncing across the mirrors as he tested his slides and slips. He drove the mop into the bucket and swung it around in a circle. It gave a satisfying percussive clang as he let the last long note of the tune snap off in the air, and went straight into a low bow to the steam-fogged windows. Then he lifted his head.

Jack bloody Treadwell.

He was standing outside, his face pressed to the glass and shining with delight. Bill frowned darkly, letting the mop rest against the table, and walked towards him. Jack obviously thought he was going to open the door – he started speaking. Bill didn't hear a word of it. He got to the window and slammed the shutters closed.

But Jack was there when Bill opened them again in the morning. He ate fish for breakfast and lunch, then waited outside till the

last of the rush had left, and Bill had run out of excuses to avoid
talking to him. Jack sat down very meekly with a cup of tea while
Bill wiped down the tables, and made his case.

'No,' Bill said when he was done.

'Why not?'

'Because I don't want to,' he told him. 'I can't do it, and I won't
do it. Go home, Jack.'

'I can't – not without you.'

It sounded so like a line from a cheap romantic novel that Bill
laughed at him. Then felt sorry – Jack was obviously sincere.

'Look, Jack, when I say I can't, I mean it. The idea of going on
stage makes me feel like I'm about to have a heart attack. I'm sorry
you've got your hopes up, but I'm not going anywhere. I've got a
job I like, and a room, and there were a lot of years when I never
thought I'd even have that again.'

'Mr Barlow,' Jack said, 'please, we need you. The place I work,
The Empire in Highbridge – do you know it?'

He pulled a promotional card out of his pocket. It showed
Lillian and Sir Barnabas, smiling delightedly in front of the
illuminated building.

Bill's energetic wiping at the tables slowed slightly.

'Yup. I played there once, many years ago. Good theatre.'

'It is . . . or rather, it was. When Lady Lassiter had a hand in
the running of it, it was one of the best. Variety, revues, plays. She
was on the stage herself before she married, you know, and she was
brilliant, by all accounts. But she's in America right now, and Joe
Allerdyce is trying to force us out of business.'

'Allerdyce?' Bill replied slowly, rubbing at a grease stain. 'He
runs good theatres.'

'Doesn't mean he has the right to run all of them. And The
Empire could be great again. I'm amazed by how brilliant the

people are.' Jack paused for a second, thinking of Grace, then rattled on. 'If we can hold out a while longer, Allerdyce will have to back off eventually. And we'll have shown what we're made of.'

Jack told him about the cancelled shows, about the agents refusing to work with them, and did an impersonation of Worton Webster. As he started telling him about *Macbeth!!*, Bill finally paused and sat down. The description of the show started him laughing, so Jack hammed it up, and by the time he was describing the songs on the first night, Bill was laughing so hard tears were running down his face.

'So we told everyone it was a comedy! We've sold out the entire run.'

'Good for you, Jack,' Bill said. 'Looks like you gave Allerdyce what for. But why do you need me?'

'Ivor French is taking his show to Glasgow, Edinburgh, Birmingham and Newcastle. We need another show, and no one will book with us. So we're doing an old-style music hall revival – bit like a revue with a chairman. Alma Moon is going to come out of retirement to do that, but we need a singer. A headliner. That's you.'

'Everyone's forgotten me.'

'We'll remind them! Watching you through the window last night, I saw the best turn I've ever seen. Trust me! By the time you're on stage, we'll make sure everyone remembers how much they've missed you!'

Bill sighed. 'You know what stage fright feels like, Jack?'

'Yes! I had to go on once in *Macbeth!!*. Didn't have a clue what I was doing. I only had one line and I made a mess of that. Hated every second.'

Bill was shaking his head. 'That's not stage fright, that's just nerves. Everyone has nerves. Stage fright is something else.'

And Bill was there again. He'd been doing the same act all season – twenty minutes exactly, four songs and a bit of chat with the audience in between – and he'd been doing it twice a night across music halls in the Midlands, the North-West and Yorkshire and bringing the house down, having a ball. Then one night, ten minutes in, a voice in his head had spoken to him.

What are you doing here? it said. *Who are you trying to fool? You don't even know what the next line is.*

And the voice was right – he didn't know, couldn't remember it for the life of him. Somehow it came out anyway, but his body was moving like a puppet and someone else was holding the strings.

Just stop now, the voice said. *You'll never even make it to the end of this song anyway.*

His breathing had started to get shallow, and he could feel the sweat breaking out under his collar, soaking the back of his shirt under his checked jacket. He breathed faster, gasping down the air between his lines. A blackness started to close down the edge of his vision, leaving him trapped by the spotlight in a tiny sliver of Hell.

Then he was in the dressing room, taking off his make-up. Someone slapped him on the back, told him what a great show it was. Back on stage and it happened again. Earlier this time, almost as soon as he got on, and this time someone had cut the strings. The words went. He tottered around the stage as the band vamped. Turned to the audience, where he thought the audience was. He couldn't see them anymore, just felt the light on his face. He told them he'd come over all queer. Told them he thought he'd had a bad oyster. And he ran. Fleeting images of the shocked faces backstage, the chairman stubbing out his cigar and cursing, then heading out to talk nonsense till they could get the next act prepped behind the heavy curtain.

He walked straight out of stage door and straight back to his digs without breaking his stride. The blackness, the thudding heart, never went away. He was done. He packed his case and left. Disappeared. Didn't even leave a note for his girl – one of the chorus dancers who followed the same circuit he did. She'd be better off without him, he was certain. In Birmingham he found a pub and drank until his ready money ran out. Then he pawned his gear and drank through that, too, with nothing but the voice for company. He drank right through the reign of Edward VII, and a good way into George V's, taking whatever casual labouring jobs were available until he had enough cash to get drunk again. Then war broke out and he took a look at himself. He joined up, but he was already too old to fight, so they taught him to cook. He worked behind the front line in hospitals and field kitchens, and found when he wasn't drinking he could still project some of that old good humour, make people smile, drive away their ghosts for a second. He finished the war sober and knowing how to serve up hundreds of meals at a time. Two days after he left the army, he saw the HELP WANTED sign in the window of this fish shop and walked in. Within an hour he was wearing that striped apron and he hadn't left since. He reckoned he was a lucky man.

'Bill.' Jack was talking to him again. 'You were great. You still are. And I need you to be the star. You'll be in the headlines! The man who walked away when the world was at his feet! A living legend!'

'I'll sink it,' Bill replied.

'Give it one more try, Bill. Otherwise you'll never know, will you?'

Bill ran his hand over his face. He knew that if he did send Jack away now he'd spend months wondering if he'd done the right thing. Perhaps, he thought, he should take the chance and visit The Empire just for old time's sake.

'Come to Highbridge. If you dry on stage, well, you can come back here and carry on working in the kitchen and mopping floors and know you were right.'

Bill studied Jack. The lad had a quality which he had seen in some of the really good officers he'd known in the war. You couldn't help it, you wanted to please him.

'You're in trouble if you need a washed-up old has-been like me, matey.'

'You're not a has-been, Bill. You didn't go off your game and lose your audience. You left them begging for more. And I'm betting they'll want you back.'

Blast it.

Something in the lad's face got to him. Bill stood up, went to the back of the restaurant and called over the counter.

'Giorgio! If I bugger off for a few weeks, then come back with my tail between my legs begging for my job again, will you give it to me?'

Giorgio came out from the kitchen, wiping his hands on his apron.

'Where you going?'

'I used to sing a bit. This idiot . . .' He jerked a thumb over his shoulder at Jack. 'He wants me back on stage.'

'I knew it!' Giorgio said, beaming suddenly. 'I knew you were a singer. I have heard you when you are washing up. I think to myself, that man can sing, why is he frying my fish? I told my wife: Bill has secrets.' He clapped Bill hard on the shoulder. 'Yes, go, and may all the saints go with you. If you decide you want to fry fish again, I'll take you back.'

THE EMPIRE

PRESENTS

THE OLD-TIME MUSIC HALL REVUE

FEATURING

THE TRIUMPHANT RETURN OF

BILLY BARLOW

PRINCE OF THE MUSIC HALLS

A CAVALCADE OF SPECTACULAR DELIGHTS!

MAGICIANS, ACROBATS, SINGERS AND COMEDIANS!

STALLS: 2/-
CIRCLE: 1/6 PIT: 1/-
UPPER CIRCLE: 9d

A FEAST OF ENTERTAINMENT
LIKE NO OTHER
NIGHTLY SHOWS AT 7.00

Printed on 127 High Street

CHAPTER EIGHT

Against all the odds, preparations for the music hall revue were under way. Grace had got decent parts made up for the band and the backstage crew had outdone themselves, creating unique sets for each of the acts. Alma and Grace worked together on the patter between the turns, playing up the nostalgia, peppering the chat with local gossip.

Bill arrived for his rehearsals punctually. The plan was he'd start mopping the floors of a recreated fish shop in his striped apron, then halfway through the act, he'd knock the head off the mop and it would become his cane. He'd snap his fingers and his trademark bowler hat would be thrown on stage. The whole fish shop would collapse and transform into a street, complete with lamp post and bench and paper flowers. Bill was affable with the crew and the band, half-singing through his songs, and walking through his steps. Mrs Gardener made him up a new checked suit and found a bowler which fitted him. Mangrave remained in his offices, grunting whenever Grace tried to tell him the latest news, but immune to the excitement everyone else felt building in the air.

And Jack threw himself into selling the show to Highbridge: the best of variety with stunning new arrangements and choreography, all topped off by the return of the lost Prince of the Music Halls, Billy Barlow. He gave newspaper men tours backstage, and put up photographs of the rehearsals outside the theatre. He had the acts out in the street in full costume, handing out coloured postcards with the dates of the performances and prices on the back. Bill said he'd rather not do that, so Jack told every gossipmonger in the city the management of The Empire would not let Billy Barlow sing in public until the first night, and anticipation for his return increased. Frederick Poole reported that bookings were brisk, and a general feeling of excitement rippled through the company.

The dress rehearsal on the afternoon of the opening day had the usual glitches and hitches. A rabbit bit its way out of its cage and relieved itself on the first singer's second gown, and the magician's trick table needed oiling. Then Bill came on, and walked his set again, caught the hat, gave the follow spot operators their cues, tested that the fake lamp post could hold his weight if he wanted to lean on it or kick his heels against it. Then he left – to rest, he said – before the opening night.

'Is he all right?' Grace asked Jack when she found him an hour later, brushing Ollie and fixing a bow to his collar for the occasion. 'It seems . . . like he's got smaller somehow since the day he arrived.'

'I know,' Jack replied. 'Is he saving it for the performance? That's not unusual, is it?'

Grace looked slightly confused. 'Well, no, especially since he's a solo act, but it doesn't feel right, does it?'

'Miss Hawkins!' Poole burst in through the doors, holding

them open at the head of the short flight of stairs. It was quite an entrance. 'I've just been told the most marvellous news! I'm all of a flutter!'

'Do tell us, Mr Poole!' Jack said, smiling up at him.

'Stella Stanmore's dresser was just in. Miss Stanmore's in town for a week before her next engagement in Manchester, and is coming this evening.'

'That's lovely,' Grace replied warmly, though Jack could tell from her voice she didn't think their old friend popping in for the evening should cause this much excitement.

Poole trotted down the stairs to join them, and Jack noticed he had a newspaper in his hands.

'No, no! The dresser bought a ticket for Miss Stanmore's guest, too! You'll never guess who it is . . . Go on – guess! No, I'll tell you. It's Lancelot Drake! *The* Lancelot Drake!'

Jack jumped off his stool in excitement. Lancelot Drake drew crowds just walking down the street. He had gone from child star to romantic lead on the stage, mixing light entertainment with serious dramatic roles, then shot to another level of stardom playing in a series of films about the French Revolution opposite Madge Stuart and Mabel Poulton.

'Look!'

Poole thrust the afternoon edition of the *Highbridge Gazette* into Grace's hands and tapped the central column with one well-buffed fingernail.

'"Mr Lancelot Drake was spotted arriving in Highbridge today, our sources say",' Grace read out loud. '"And our correspondent managed to snatch a conversation with him before he was swept away by his friend and occasional theatrical co-star Miss Stella Stanmore. This remarkable young man tells us his glittering career was inspired by an evening watching Billy Barlow as a little boy, and he has travelled up from London purely to see the Prince of Music Halls perform again. "I wouldn't miss it for the world," he said. "Stella telephoned to tell me he was on the bill and I headed straight for the railway station."' Grace looked up at Jack. 'This is fantastic! We'll be booked solid all month with publicity like this!'

'Miss Stanmore's dresser brought the article in case I thought she was telling taradiddles!' Poole exclaimed. 'Naturally, I've put them in the front row, stage right. Now I'd better tell my people front of house, and he ought to be protected from autograph hunters, I think. Perhaps a roped area on the pavement for non-ticket holders would be just the thing? Oh, his performance in *The French Gentleman* had me in tears. I saw it three times.'

'An excellent idea, Mr Poole,' Jack replied, and Poole zoomed out of stage door. Then Jack cast an anxious look at Grace.

'Grace, when I met Bill, I did push him a bit. To perform, I mean.'

Grace looked at him narrowly. 'How much?'

'I laid it on pretty thick. If he doesn't turn up tonight, what do we do?'

Grace looked at her watch. 'Judging by your performance in *Macbeth!!*, I don't think there's much point in sending you on.' She studied the article again. 'Jack, why did you push Bill so much in the press if you were worried about him? If he doesn't go on now, the whole audience will want their money back! And all the other acts are great. Oh, Jack, you should have told me.'

Jack shook his head. 'I know. I didn't want to worry you, but that's stupid, isn't it?'

'Very,' she said, looking severe, then put her hand on his sleeve. 'But we'd never have got all these bookings otherwise. Theatre is ... well, it's like jumping off a cliff sometimes. An act of faith.'

'You're awfully kind to me, Grace.'

'Very important to treat one's assistant properly,' she said with an awkward smile, and took her hand away.

'He'll be here,' Jack said, though the words stuck in his throat.

'I'll have a chat to Alma and Charlie, see if we can come up with a plan B – but I really hope he comes!'

She threw him a worried look and headed backstage again.

Jack told himself Bill would turn up at least once a minute for the rest of the afternoon, as the other acts began to arrive, start their warm-ups and get into costume. He was telling himself Bill would turn up as Grace strode out of stage door and found him standing about in the yard, tapping his foot, half an hour before the curtain was due to go up.

Bill didn't turn up.

'Jack, I've been on the phone to Bill's landlady.' She took a sharp breath. 'He's packed his case and just left. And . . . he asked about the best bus for the railway station.'

The crowds thronged the pavement outside The Empire as the last of the early summer sun faded from the sky. Lancelot Drake arrived with Stella Stanmore – flash bulbs popped, and they spent a quarter of an hour signing autographs for the besotted crowds before making their way in and being led by a fluttering Frederick Poole to their front row seats.

That was where, ten minutes before curtain, Jack found them.

'Jack, darling!' Stella greeted him. 'How is Ollie?'

'He's in disgrace – he ate Little Sam's sausage roll and has been looking pleased with himself ever since.'

Stella snorted with laughter and introduced him to Lancelot Drake.

'Mr Drake?' Jack said.

Lancelot looked at him. The man was so handsome, with cheekbones you could use as steak knives and ice-blue eyes that it took a moment for Jack to regain use of his voice. He felt like a donkey trying to chat with a Grand National winner.

'What you said to the newspaper about Billy Barlow inspiring you . . . was that true?'

'Absolutely,' Lancelot replied, a slight frown on his perfect forehead. 'What's up and how can I help?'

'He's a no-show. We called his boarding house and we think he's heading for the station. Any chance you might try and talk him into coming back?'

Drake looked surprised, then nodded. 'Damn straight, I will. I travelled three hundred miles for this performance. Let's take Stella's car.' He stood and bent over Stella's hand as he took the keys. 'Enjoy the show, sweets.'

Lancelot drove as if the demons of Hell were on his back. Jack held on tight as he told him about the stage fright, and how Bill had seemed during rehearsals.

'Got it,' Lancelot said, as they came to a halt with a squeal of brakes outside the station. He leapt out of the car and they raced into the main building, through the light crowds, with Jack following and feeling more like a donkey than ever.

They hesitated, but then Jack spotted a lonely figure on platform four and pointed like a trained gun dog.

'There he is!'

Lancelot ran ahead while Jack fumbled with the coppers in his pockets to pay for platform tickets, then looked at his watch. A quarter past seven. Alma, in white tie and tails, would be introducing the second magician.

What have I done?

All that money and effort on the basis of watching a man sing to himself as he wiped down the floor.

Jack emptied his pockets and ended up handing over a mix of coins and a spare button to the guard, who stared at the contents of his palm with disapproval, but allowed him to dash up the platform after Lancelot.

He had come to a stop a yard away from Bill.

'Billy Barlow?' Lancelot said.

Bill stared out across the empty tracks in front of him, fixing his gaze on the air and refusing to look round.

'Our Bill? Prince of the Music Halls?'

'Never heard of him,' Bill said bitterly.

He looked haggard, like a man torn from a ghost story or a wood engraving in a penny dreadful.

'He was the best,' Lancelot said. 'First time I went to a theatre, I saw him perform, and I knew then all I wanted to do was be on the stage. I owe him everything.'

Bill looked round with a frown and Jack saw recognition dawn.

'You . . . ? What are you doing here?'

'Good question.' Lancelot took a cigarette case out of the pocket of his dinner jacket and offered it to Bill. He refused. Lancelot took a cigarette himself and lit it while Jack fought the urge to look at his watch again. 'I'm supposed to be sitting in my front row seat at The Empire, happy as a coot and ready to watch my hero sing. So what am I doing here, Bill?'

'I can't,' Bill said, shaking his head hard. 'I can't do it, mate. I'm sorry for those kids – Grace and Jack – but I can't do it. Every time I've been to the theatre it's got worse. Last night I almost took a drink – first time I've been tempted since war broke out. This evening I made it off the tram, saw my name on the posters and all but passed out. I'll never manage it. I don't know the songs or the steps. It's just mush in my brain.'

'Well, I know how you feel,' Lancelot said, blowing out a long stream of smoke.

Bill laughed harshly. 'You? You've got no idea, lad. Second you walk out on a stage, people fall in love with you. You haven't put a foot wrong, and then it turns out you look like a bloody hero waggling a sword about in the flicks, too. You've got no idea.'

'Last time I saw you walk out on stage, they fell in love with you, too.' He tapped the ash off his cigarette. 'As it happens, the first time the terrors got me I was twelve years old.'

On the other side of the station, one of the local trains from the coast drew up in a cloud of steam. Little embers flitted through the smoke, and the doors began to clatter and bang as people clambered down, gathering their kids and packages and heading out of the station.

'I got on stage and thought I was going blind,' Lancelot continued. 'Had my mum take me to a specialist in London.'

Bill looked at him again. 'When you were twelve? Why did you go back?'

'I've got a little brother. Smart as paint and studying to be a lawyer now. My wages were paying the school fees. And my mum, she'd had a hard time of it with my dad and was just beginning to enjoy herself. I went back on for them. Nearly killed me.'

Bill hunched his shoulders. 'Well, good for you. But I can't and I won't. I didn't ask for it. They made me.' He raised his voice a bit. 'I can feel you skulking about there, Treadwell. You wouldn't bloody well take "no" for an answer, and now here you are.'

'Sorry, Bill.' Jack looked at his watch again. Half past. And he was sorry. He hadn't meant to make anyone miserable.

'Do it for me, Bill,' Lancelot said, so quietly Jack could hardly hear him.

'What?'

'Do the act for me. I'll be sitting right at the front, stage right. Just do it for me.'

'No.'

'Bill, I'm not taking "no" for an answer either. This is a command performance. I want to see your act again.'

Bill looked at him, a terrible mixture of hope and despair chasing around his face.

'How did you beat it? The fear?'

'I remembered that the audience was my friend, not my enemy. Oh . . . and when things started to go dark, I flicked my thumb with my index finger. Like this.' He demonstrated – a tiny gesture. 'It seemed to stop the terrors getting so loud and I was myself again. For a while, at least.'

'You call it the terrors?'

'Worst bloody feeling I've ever had in my life. Come on, my car's waiting.'

Lancelot picked up Bill's suitcase and started walking away. Bill followed him.

Jack looked at his watch again. If they went now, they could make it.

Grace was waiting at stage door, looking pale as a ghost in the pool of light which spilled out from Jack's little kingdom.

Bill got out of the car, slowly. Lancelot followed and led him backstage to the number one dressing room. From the auditorium they heard applause and laughter as the act before Bill – a comedian – started her opening, trading wisecracks with Alma.

'Just for me, Bill,' Lancelot said. 'Remember.'

He nodded to Grace and Jack and headed off to retake his seat in the auditorium, waving away Jack's thanks.

Bill started putting on his make-up, his movements mechanical, and when he reached for his costume, Grace pulled Jack out of the room and shut the door.

'Can he do it, Jack? He looks like he's drugged, or sleepwalking!'

'I don't know. He's here – that's a start. Are you going to watch from the front?'

'Yes. Will you stay here?'

A gale of laughter rose from the auditorium, and waves of warm applause and cheers. The comedian was going down a storm.

Jack took Grace's hand and squeezed it.

'Like jumping off a cliff, you say?'

'Yes. Certainly what it feels like now!'

She squeezed back, then released his hand and hurried off into the wings, leaving Jack to stare at the closed door to Bill's dressing room. More applause, then cheers.

God, she's coming off already!

Time had started to distort for Jack, as if he was drunk. The orchestra began to vamp Bill's intro music, and Alma launched into her last bit of patter before introducing him.

Then Stella Stanmore appeared. She must have come round the back of the stage. Her long red evening gown made her look like a bird of paradise, a messenger from the gods. At the same time, Bill opened the door from his dressing room, his frying apron over his trademark suit. Both men stared at Stella.

'Darlings! I know it's an absolute cheek to ask, but may I walk Mr Barlow out on stage for his triumphant return? My mother used to sing your songs to me, Bill, and if there's a night she'll bother looking down from Heaven, it will be tonight.'

She gave her mortar-shell smile. Lancelot must have sent her, the genius. Bill offered her his arm; she took it and led him through the doors to the wings without another word. Jack followed. There was a rushing sound in his ears and he couldn't feel his feet or his hands.

The orchestra were still vamping and the curtains had opened on Bill's set – the fish shop, with Bill's mop and bucket waiting for him.

Stella swept straight on, carrying Bill with her, and smiled at the orchestra leader.

'Ladies and gentlemen!' she announced, throwing her arms wide. 'It gives me all the pleasure in the world to present to you that lost legend, master of varieties! The Prince of the Music Halls has come back to us a king! Mr Billy Barlow.'

She bowed and the audience erupted into fresh applause, Alma joining in from the side, before discreetly backing off into the wings. More cheers, as Stella swept a grand bow to Bill and exited stage right. The orchestra continued, waiting for Bill to begin, and he faced the crowd.

He looked blank, whiter than any stage make-up could render a human being. From where he stood in the wings, Jack could see the sweat dampening his collar, running down the back of his neck. His fingers moved over the end of his mop. A flick. Another. Then he glanced down at the front row, where Stella was settling into her seat again, next to Lancelot.

Lancelot gave the slightest, almost infinitesimal, nod. Bill put out one hand towards him and began to sing.

Alchemy. Jack had heard about that at one of the impromptu lectures in the POW camp. Base metal transformed by ritual and fire and human longing into precious metal. And from the wings of The Empire that evening, Jack watched it happen. Two numbers . . . three . . . Bill, with his mop and striped apron, turned the stage, the orchestra, the audience, the air, into gold.

When he caught his bowler hat, tossed in from the wings, and the stage transformed around him, the audience went wild. Shrugging on his jacket and dropping his apron into the orchestra pit, he was every inch a king. Between numbers he talked to the audience, and something about the way he turned his head or widened his eyes made them incapable with laughter. He broke the order of the set, talking nonsense with the orchestra leader as the musicians rearranged their parts, to sing a sentimental tune about being with friends again. The audience were weeping; you could hear sniffing and nose-blowing from the stalls to the gods.

While they were recovering themselves, Bill told them he'd been so nervous that Lancelot Drake had had to come and fetch him from the station. Lancelot got an ovation of his own. He asked Stella from the stage if she knew 'My Old Dutch', and got her up to sing it with him. He danced round her, while she shimmied and spun and made it look as if they'd both been performing together for years.

Jack leant against the wall, then he felt a hand on his shoulder. One of the stagehands had fetched him a stool.

'Sit down before you fall down, fella,' he said.

Jack did, resting his head against the wall, mouth gaping.

Bill applauded Stella off the stage, then waved at the audience and exited stage left. He shook his head as he noticed Jack, but that dead look behind his eyes had gone. Instead, there was a sort of concentrated energy coming off him – not joy exactly, but the sense of force and power you might feel watching a lion shaking its mane after a hunt. He went back out again, and again, and again. Three encores. Then Alma led on the whole company for half a dozen curtain calls, and the crowd didn't stop stomping and cheering for more until the house lights went up.

CHAPTER NINE

J oe Allerdyce sat to the right of his hostess in her shabby but comfortable dining room. She was cooking an omelette for him at the table, with the efficient competency he had come to associate with everything Agnes de Montfort did – other than dress herself.

His visit to show her the Rolls-Royce had been a success. She had enjoyed the car, and he had enjoyed her enjoyment of the car. He had invited her for lunch in town, and she had asked him to lunch here at Manor Farm, the rambling stately farmhouse bought wholly, he was sure, because the stabling was excellent. A bargain was struck, and she agreed to accompany him to one of his shows, and he was quite sure she had enjoyed herself. This morning he had been induced to visit the stables. No one had tried to bite him, and after a certain amount of reluctance he had been persuaded to pat one of the threatening-looking beasts on the nose. It had responded with a friendly snort which rather reminded him of Agnes when she was in a good mood.

'Tell me,' Joe said, stabbing a forkful of omelette, 'did you read the article about Edmund?'

'Yes,' Agnes said.

'A change in direction for Lassiter Enterprises.'

'Yes.'

'And that's all you have to say about it?'

'Yes.'

Joe set down his fork. 'Now then, let's be clear. We're friends, right, Agnes?'

She nodded without looking at him.

'Then let's be frank! I asked what you thought of the article and what you think of your nephew.'

Agnes put down her own fork. 'No, you didn't, Joe. You asked me if I had read it. And I have, and I thought his own mother could not have done a better job of making him sound like a decent human being.'

Joe picked up his fork again and took his last mouthful, slightly ashamed of his own temper. The omelette was excellent.

'Why in God's name would you want my opinion, anyway?' Agnes said, patting her mouth with her napkin.

'Because I value it.' He realised he meant it quite sincerely. 'Look, Agnes, I think you should read over that article again. There's not a line in it that's outright rude, but if you read between the lines, there's plenty of hints. Little hints. Like his bold decision to clear out his grandfather's pals and put his old batman on the board. Bold can be good, but it's also what we say when someone's done something bloody stupid.'

She sighed.

'I get the feeling you don't like him much, Agnes? Am I right?'

'I have enough family loyalty to feel a little bad about saying so, but yes, you are.'

'Can I ask why?'

She sighed. 'When Edmund was a little boy, he and Tom were

playing football by the greenhouse in Lassiter Court, and I saw him quite deliberately kick the ball at the gardener's old dog. And I saw the grin he gave when the poor old thing yelped and stumbled off.'

'What did you do?'

'Twisted his ear and told him exactly what I thought of him. He said the dog had been growling at Tom. Utter nonsense. Then, of course, Constance swept in, told me to get my hands off her child, and smothered her brave boy with kisses. Honestly, that woman! To think I smashed some perfectly good shop windows to get women like her the vote.' She paused and refilled her glass and his with a very good German white wine. She had bought up the entire stock from the local Highbridge wine merchant the month before war broke out. 'I had some shares in Lassiter Enterprises. I sold them off quietly as soon as Edmund became chair while Barnabas was ill.'

'Because Edmund kicked a ball at a dog when he was a little boy?'

She checked his expression for any suggestion of mockery, and found none. 'Yes. Largely. My sister Emilia chose her husband well – Barnabas was a good man. He always refused to have any worker under fourteen in his factories, while most of the mill owners were using eight-year-olds to keep the looms running, and he reduced the working day long before the government took an interest in such things. His people rewarded him with loyal service. But Edmund does not look to me like a man who would inspire loyalty.'

Joe considered this quietly; something about the way Agnes was holding her wineglass, studying the colour of the liquid, suggested there was more.

'Have you ever spoken to any of the men who served with him, Joe?'

'I must've done. Not about him, though.'

'Lillian's fund has sent a few veterans up here to work in the stables. Good men. If Edmund's name comes up, they all say something complimentary about him.'

'But . . . ?'

She looked at him, lips pursed. 'But they don't look you in the eye when they say it.'

'Ah.'

'Exactly. Have you finished? Fill up your glass and we can sit on the terrace while you have one of your horrible cigars.' Then she paused. 'Joe, are you asking me about Edmund because you want to buy The Empire? God knows that I don't hear much from the city up here, but even I know your theatres are at some sort of war with them.'

He filled his glass and followed her out to the terrace, which had the same faded elegance as the dining room. Weeds grew between the flagstones, and the grass on the lawn was long and studded with wild flowers.

'No,' Joe said eventually. 'I trust my own judgement in those matters, but I don't think much of Edmund either. Nothing to do with dogs, but he's out too much on the town and goes too wild when he is. He's careless. And I don't like the company he keeps. I'm happy you don't depend on the family fortune, Agnes. Whatever happens to The Empire, I don't hold out much hope for Lassiter Enterprises with him at the helm.'

'You think he'll sell his interest in The Empire?'

'I do. But I'll be wanting Lady Lassiter's shares, too, or no sale.'

Agnes settled in one of the wrought-iron chairs. There was a heavy glass ashtray on the table, Joe noticed, which had not been there the first time he came for lunch. He took it as a compliment, and it pleased him.

'Have you heard,' he said, once his cigar was lit, 'how my battle with The Empire's going?'

The corner of her mouth twitched. 'According to my second stable boy, you are getting what I believe is referred to as "a right kicking".'

He laughed, startling a wood pigeon out of the eaves. 'He's not wrong.' He studied the end of his cigar. 'Mangrave's handed over half his authority to his assistant, that lass Grace Hawkins. She's roped in the new doorman as *her* assistant, and he's bloody charming everyone's socks off, and blow me if it doesn't seem to be working. That *Macbeth!!* will be talked about for years. They made Ivor bloody French a star, and now I'm fighting to pay him a hundred and twenty quid a week for a run in my house in Birmingham. Then they dig up Billy Barlow! Billy Barlow! I thought he was dead, but he turns up like Jesus bloody Christ, and now they're turning punters away at matinees and I'm just picking up the crowds that can't get in, even though my acts are established favourites and I'm charging twenty per cent less than them on every ticket.'

'How very aggravating for you, Joe.'

'It bloody well is, so stop your smirking, woman. Let me tell you, I didn't bargain on those two. The Empire is their cause and they're sticking with it.'

The smirk turned into a smile and she patted his hand. 'Are you going to give up?'

'No. Just because it's working doesn't mean it's *right*. Mangrave's a poison. I see him at the club from time to time. He knows nothing about the theatre, and it's an affront that the Lassiters put him in charge. No one knows where he sprang from, and he never invites people to his house. I don't like it. I could make The Empire what it should be. And I want it.'

'I know. Still, I do like young people with a cause.'

'I've heard rumours you were one yourself back in the day. Tell me, is it true you were a communist?'

'I was. I even married one. Turns out he had a rather limited revolution in mind. I was still expected to cook and clean and leave all the thinking to him and his friends.'

'Bet that went down like a ton of bricks.'

'Quite right. Mother and Father had disowned me, so I left him and lived with Emilia and Barney. I started using my maiden name again. Barney said he owed me for making him look like a good son-in-law by comparison.'

'What happened to your husband?'

'The marriage was annulled. Mother and Father put me back in the will, and I went from outcast to respectable eccentric spinster. And I place a considerable value now on my independence.'

'I can see that.'

'So what if Lillian doesn't sell?'

'She's been out of the game for years, and even before the war she leant on old Charlie Moon. He was a decent manager – I didn't mind going toe to toe with him – but Mangrave? That's another thing altogether, I don't mind telling you. Two jammy kids aren't going to drag her back into all that again. Especially when I'm making life hard and offering good money.'

'I don't know,' Agnes said. 'Lillian is an unusual woman.'

'Tell me, do you like her?'

Agnes snorted. 'I've certainly never seen her mistreat an animal! I thought of her as rather unserious when she turned up as Barney's new wife, but she showed some grit in the war and when Barney was ill. So I'd say she is . . .'

'What?'

'Unpredictable, Joe. I have no idea what she'll do when she hears about all this.'

CHAPTER TEN

Constance Lassiter lived with her two sons in the same city square as Joe Allerdyce, though on the other side. The private garden at the centre of the square, with its mature lime trees and its border of glossy evergreens, meant they rarely saw each other.

The *Highbridge Illustrated News*, with its article about her oldest son, was folded neatly on the side table set in the window, next to a cut glass vase filled with roses. They had been arranged too tightly, and she found the smell suddenly oppressive. She tried to open the sash window but it stuck, and as she banged it with her palm, she stumbled against the table. The vase tottered and fell.

She twisted and caught it. A few water drops landed on the pale carpet, but the vase was safe.

She set it down on the embroidered table-runner – her own work – and found her hand was shaking slightly. She couldn't think why. The interview had been read by her friends as a laudatory piece extolling the forward-thinking dynamism of her son. But it had left a nasty taste in her mouth.

The summer season was upon them, and her project now was to find Edmund a wife. She had her eye on a couple of young women. Edmund would need someone with a little backbone, she knew that, and someone whose own reputation was unsullied. No need for a title, but a girl from a family of independent means with connections to a title would be perfect. Lillian's stain still needed to be wiped off the Lassiter name. Ridiculous that a woman like her, who had started her working life on the factory floor, should be Lady Lassiter. The music hall stars of Constance's youth had at least had the grace to remember where they came from, but Lillian had acted as if she had the right to be a leader of Highbridge society when she returned from Paris on Barnabas's arm, and Highbridge had let her.

Their compliance with her sham of being a lady still burnt Constance. It had been her role after the death of Sir Barnabas's first wife – *hers*. She was married to the eldest son; she was the daughter of a gentleman. Her father had shot with earls and dukes. Edward VII had once pinched her cheek. But Lillian had arrived; Constance's briefly ascendant social star was eclipsed, and she had been forced to cede precedence to a showgirl. Albert hadn't supported her at all and seemed quite content to welcome Lillian into the family. There had been a softness to him Constance had grown to dislike, and now she saw it reborn in Tom. Neither of them had Barnabas's drive, or her sense of what was proper and fitting. Then her husband, Albert, had died – a heart attack before he was thirty-five – and she had decided to pour all her energy into her eldest son. It started as a necessity, and as he grew up, he had became the fixed passion of her life.

But why was she nervous now? Edmund had dined at home only once this week, and seemed disinclined to tell her with whom he was breaking bread. When he came home at lunch, he refused to talk business, even though she was on the board. He only lectured Tom about sport, or leadership, leaning heavily on his army experience, and gave occasional grunts as he consumed her carefully planned meals. Albert had always talked to her about his work. They had sat up over the books together, discussed his colleagues, the workers, Sir Barnabas. And when Edmund had come home after the war, he had at least listened to her advice. Now he did not even pretend to do so.

Then David Tompkins, Edmund's godfather and former member of the board, had come to see her. He had been warm, charming as always, but when he asked about Edmund his voice had taken on a certain level of uncertainty. Was Edmund sharing his strategic plans with her? Tompkins understood he was old and stuck in his ways, but he was not convinced that Edmund's latest investments had been wise, and he was concerned he was taking a far more aggressive attitude towards the management and the workers than was necessary. Ambitious targets for production and cost-cutting were excellent, but they had to be practical, Tompkins had said gently. Simply shouting that a thing must be done could not alter the physical laws of the universe.

The maid came in to lay out tea, and Constance realised she had been standing by the window for a long time.

She was pouring a second cup, still brooding, when she heard the car outside and looked out of the window in surprise. Major Sir Edmund Lassiter walked up the front steps, and within moments he was in the room with her. The clouds disappeared. She really was terribly glad to see him. She rang for another cup, and cake.

'What brings you home at this hour, Edmund?' she said. 'It is most pleasant to have your company.'

'Oh – yes!' He crossed and uncrossed his legs, and leant sideways on the chair. 'Office was driving me potty. Thought about going out for a drive, clear my head. Then I thought as it was near tea, I'd drop by.'

'Will you be joining me for dinner?'

'What? Yes . . . I don't know. Might go to the club.'

His tea and cake remained untouched in front of him.

'Edmund, dear, I'm sure it is only an oversight, but the dividend from your father's shares is normally paid into my account on the tenth of each month. That was last week, and it has not appeared as yet.'

'You've still enough money for roses and fruitcake, though, haven't you?' His tone was unpleasant.

'I do. I merely wished to draw the matter to your attention, my dear. If it is only me, that is one thing, but if the other shareholders are not receiving their payments, that might create a bad impression. All eyes are on you now, Edmund.'

'Don't you think I know that?' He got to his feet very quickly and turned his back on her. 'The damned reporter who wrote that thing in the *Illustrated News*. Such an insidious air about him! And he went round talking to everyone in town about me.'

'I'm sure it is very hard, dear,' Constance murmured. 'Such a great deal of responsibility. I am planning an entertaining summer for you! Once you are married, Lillian will move out of Lassiter Court, and you will have a real home of your own and a wife to comfort you on difficult days like these.'

'I wonder where she'll go.' Edmund looked at her, showing his teeth. 'Probably move into that dashed horrible flat above the theatre! I can't believe Grandpa used to stay with her there. Done up like a bordello, I'd bet you a thousand on it.'

'No doubt it reminded them of where they met,' Constance suggested.

Edmund laughed. 'Yes, by Jove, it probably did.' He bent over and kissed his mother on the forehead. 'You're a good old stick.'

She dared to say more. 'Do remember, Edmund, I'm always here if you want to discuss anything.' His face crumpled with disapproval and she held up her hand. 'No, not that I have any intention of giving you advice, I'm sure you have quite enough people trying to do that. I mean that sometimes it can be helpful to talk things through, in an informal fashion. Simply to organise one's own thinking – sort out any knotty problems.'

He bent over the empty fireplace, his foot on the brass fireguard and his arm on the mantelpiece. 'Yes. Yes, that's true.'

'Though your father used to say I had an awfully devious mind! I think he meant it as a compliment.'

Edmund was silent for what seemed a very long time.

'I'm sure you have been doing the right thing, Edmund,' Constance said, making her way carefully through this dark and thorny thicket, 'and the best thing for Lassiter Enterprises. Sometimes, though, there are circumstances outside our control, a little bad luck. It can usually be managed . . .'

Now he stared at her again, and the haunted look behind his eyes – one she had only ever seen on charitable visits to hospitals and workhouses – scared her. She smiled, confident, compassionate.

'Can it?' he said. 'Can anything be managed?'

'Yes, Edmund. Would you like to chat?'

The moment evaporated. 'No. There is nothing to be concerned about. The proceeds from the North End factory will start showing up soon. Another slight inconvenience, that's all. I'll go back to the office and speak to the accountant, Hargreaves. There is no need to worry, Mama.'

But she did worry. She paid a return call to David Tompkins and called in on Naomi, the wife of Anderson Hargreaves. She opened the safe her husband had installed in the cellar, and took a chilling inventory of its contents on the maids' afternoon off. She sat up late in the library with her old diaries, which contained a careful record of all Edmund's achievements, his boasts about his plans for the company and how he meant to put them into action. She read in her own handwriting his complaints that his grandfather and the board were holding him back. Then the entries began to clot with references to Barnabas's health, and Edmund became silent on the page.

Two weeks passed, then three. Constance put off arranging tennis parties, and one of the young women she had thought of as a possible daughter-in-law announced her engagement. She sat up late more and more. Then one night as Friday slipped into Saturday morning, she heard Edmund opening the door, and his step hesitating outside the library door. A knock.

'Come in!'

His sandy hair was dishevelled and his tie undone. She thought he looked like a hero from the moving pictures. She smiled in welcome, not daring to say anything.

'Mama? I don't suppose you have time for that chat, do you?'

'Of course I do.'

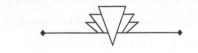

CHAPTER ELEVEN

'Waiter, we'll need another bottle of champagne.'

'Sure thing, Miss Evangelista!'

The really rather glorious boy who had been serving them flashed Lillian a smile as bright as the Broadway lights themselves and weaved his way off among the tightly packed tables of one of the best illegal nightclubs in New York.

'I thought we were supposed to ask for tea?' Lillian said, and Evie dragged her attention away from the boy's lithe retreat.

'What? Oh, prohibition is such nonsense! The chief of police is in here twice a week. You know, I once went to a little bar in Greenwich and the prohibition enforcement officers turned up. Honestly, I was worried that they might throw me out of the country, and they did look terribly fierce.'

'What happened, darling?'

'It turned out that they weren't happy with the pay-off the barman had offered! They ended up passing round a hat. I put in a dollar.' She sighed, her chin in her hand. 'Perhaps it would have been better if I had been thrown out. As opposed to staying here, to be heaped with infamy.'

Evie's new show on Broadway had not been a success.

'Honestly, Evie, if I see that theatre manager I shall spit in his eye. What a way to find out! You were such a trouper to finish the week in such style.'

It was true – the manager of Evie's theatre had been brutal. Ten days ago Evie had arrived at five o'clock to prepare for the Monday evening performance and found MUST END SATURDAY banners plastered all over her posters.

'I was, wasn't I?'

'And the cast and crew loved the Tiffany money clips!'

'I refuse to have anyone think I'm mean. Now do give me a cigarette so I can look suitably tragic for five minutes. Then I shall cheer up again. What do you think about getting a house in the Hamptons for the rest of the summer? It's beautiful. We can play tennis and make bathtub gin and just have party after party.'

Evie really is remarkably resilient, Lillian thought as she offered her friend a cigarette. And Lillian was enjoying her stay in New York very much. She had listened with interest to the jazz which had drifted across the Atlantic, but, of course, she had gone out very little in these last years. In New York, jazz seemed to shiver up from the pavements – or sidewalks, as they called them here. It was like the taste of salty air. With its informality and urgency, it sounded like liberty – the pleasure of free movement caught by piano and trumpet.

Shame Evie's show hadn't had some of that spirit in it. The fact the show was closing should not have come as a bolt from the blue, Lillian thought as she took another cigarette from her bejewelled purse. When she had arrived in New York, two months ago, the writing was already faintly visible on the wall. Evie came home from rehearsals each day complaining bitterly about the director, the choreographer and the musical director in rotation, and insisted on drowning her sorrows in half a dozen illegal nightclubs, all filled to the brim with aspiring actresses twenty years younger than both of them.

Lillian could sleep in each morning between peach-coloured satin sheets, before taking long, pleasant walks around Central Park and doing a little shopping. Then Evie would return with a new chapter for her Book of Grievances. Unsurprisingly, her director began to complain about her timekeeping, and her costume designer made catty remarks about a slight thickening of her waist.

Evie had been disastrously miscast, at her own insistence. She was still a very beautiful woman, with a fine voice and a wonderful stage presence, but to put a woman of her age in the ingénue role then surround her with a leggy chorus of twenty-year-olds was to invite ridicule. But Evie had fought hard for the role, charming elderly investors and calling in favours with a commitment which would have made the most corrupt politicians of Tammany Hall blush. She'd described her victorious campaign and invited Lillian to share in her glee, but Lillian had felt nervous for her friend even then.

'They just needed to keep their nerve!' Evie said, snapping her lighter shut and sighing with relief as the waiter returned with the champagne to fill her glass. 'We played to full houses . . . well, full-ish, for the last few days.'

'Darling Evie, you've been absolutely wonderful,' Lillian said, being supportive, but keeping her comments vague.

She had tried to help during previews, mentioning to the choreographer that he had it in his gift to showcase Evie's talents rather than mercilessly underlining her deficiencies, and trying to persuade the set and costume designers that if they both kept to the same colours, no one would be able to see anything anyway.

The musical director had quit before the first preview – not just the show, but the theatre world entirely – and the director had left for Brazil after the opening night.

Lillian wouldn't have chosen to start this week, with the show closed, by going to see *The Fabulous Follies* at the Winter Garden Theatre. It was the absolute hit of the season, but Evie had insisted.

'Oh no!' Evie said, spotting something.

Lillian looked over her shoulder.

Perfect.

Geraldine Grey, star of that very hit, was bearing down on them, with a man on her arm and diamonds in her hair and everyone turning their heads to watch her pass.

'Evangelista! How too wonderful of you to come and support us this evening! You should have come backstage afterwards, but it is always such a scrum.' Evie stood and the two women air-kissed. 'And after you've had such a rough go of it, too,' Geraldine continued with a pout. 'I do appreciate it. I said to Ivor – Ivor Novello – Evie is a legend in the theatre, even if the public don't know her that well. And is that the role for a legend? Couldn't they have written in a mother or a maiden aunt for her? A character part?'

Oh, Geraldine, Lillian thought as she raised her glass, *what have you done? The fairy glow of a hit show will not defend you from Evie if she decides to get her claws out.*

Evie stiffened dangerously. 'No need to worry about me, darling,' she said with a purr. 'Sometimes audiences and critics take a while to recognise what the next big thing is going to be, and prefer watching the same old thing done in the same old way. But how sensible of you to stick with what you can manage!'

Geraldine's smile remained precisely in place, but Lillian noticed a glitter of nerves in the woman's eye, a quick sideways glance at the young man in white tie standing beside her. Evie smiled, too, but hers was more genuine now.

If an anaconda could smile, Lillian thought, biting her lip to stop herself laughing, *it would have just that expression on its face*.

'But I must ask, Geraldine,' Evie said, bending slightly towards her with confidential concern, 'were you nervous this evening, darling? That closing number of the second act is a little high for you, isn't it?'

'No, not nervous at all! It's been such a smash.'

'Ah yes. Nice songs, even if they do sound rather familiar, but straining your voice like that for weeks could cause permanent damage. Where is your chest voice?' Both women glanced down – Geraldine was a little flat-chested. 'I mean, doing everything from the throat like that can just about carry over the stalls, but it gets a bit . . . shrieky.'

'I-I think . . .' Geraldine stammered. 'I think our table is ready.'

'Have a lovely evening,' Evie said warmly. 'And try a little honey and lemon before bed.'

Geraldine walked off very quickly, and when the gentleman tried to put a hand on the back of her glittering gown, she shook him off.

Evie caught Lillian's eye as she sat down and drank off her champagne, then giggled.

'She deserved it, Lil.'

'Oh, she did! It's all I can do not to break out in applause.'

Evie put down her glass and took Lillian's hands. 'Look, it's been an absolute hell the last couple of months. I have no idea how I would have managed without you, and if that stupid director had listened to you during previews, we probably wouldn't have closed. Have you thought about going back on stage?'

'Good God, no!' Lillian said with a laugh. 'I'd be treated as an absolute freak.'

'Directing, then?'

Lillian had not given much thought to her future. Her recent losses had staggered her, and throughout Barney's illness her approach had been to take life one day at a time. In New York, Evie's dramas on and off the stage had kept her mind off her grief.

'Tomorrow and tomorrow and tomorrow,' she murmured.

Evie ignored her, her usual reaction to anyone who quoted Shakespeare. 'Come on – you own a theatre!'

'I part-own it. Edmund inherited Barney's shares, and I am supposed to go back and play Lady Lassiter until Edmund gets married and I can be a dowager.'

She made a grim dowager face that made Evie choke on her fresh glass of champagne. Then she bounced to her feet and started waving. A gang of Evie's friends were just funnelling in from the dark and secret little lobby, and the band struck up a new tune.

The following morning, the two ladies were drifting into the salon of Evie's rather luxurious apartment and considering how to fill their day when the newspapers arrived.

'Evie!' Lillian said as she moved the *New York Times* to one side, 'what on earth is the *Highbridge Gazette* doing here?'

'I ordered it for you, darling. I get the London papers as a matter of course, all a couple of weeks late, naturally, but one should try and keep up. Then I asked the man at the docks if he got the *Highbridge Gazette* and he said yes. Then when you arrived you were talking about how glorious it was to leave all that behind – the civic leadership and the hoo-ha over Barney's death – so I've been hiding them. Forgot this morning!'

'You can be very thoughtful, Evie,' Lillian said warmly.

'Yes, I can, but only briefly. It gives me a terrible headache if I try and keep it up too long.'

The two women poured coffee and selected reading materials. Lillian found herself turning to the theatre news almost at once. ANOTHER STUNNING SUCCESS FOR THE EMPIRE, the headline ran.

Lancelot Drake and Stella Stanmore had front row seats last night for a triumphant revue of music hall, chaired by local favourite Alma Moon and featuring the triumphant return of songster Billy Barlow. Your correspondent caught up with the manager's spokesman, Mr Jack Treadwell, and the show's artistic director, Miss Grace Hawkins, shortly after the triumphant opening night.

'Of course, we always knew it would be a fabulous show,' said Mr Treadwell, 'but having Lancelot and Stella with us to cheer Bill on was the icing on the cake. We're negotiating with them both to star in a new musical revue towards the end of the year, and of course Bill will be part of that, too. Miss Hawkins will write it.'

Lillian felt her heart pounding and heard a rushing in her ears. She could not breathe. She blinked and read the paragraph again, then once more.

'Darling, are you all right?' It sounded as if Evie's voice was coming from a long way off. 'You've gone a very worrying colour.'

'Evie, we must go home immediately.' Lillian thrust the paper at her friend.

Evie read, then shrieked, her coffee slopping into the saucer.

'Oh, my goodness!' She reached for the telephone. 'There is a sailing tomorrow afternoon. I shall book the tickets. You ring the bell for the maid – we must start packing at once.'

ACT II

CHAPTER TWELVE

Grace sat alone in the centre of the stalls, a notebook on her knee, staring at the empty stage. Anyone looking at her face would conclude she loathed with a passion the poor stagehand stuck with sweeping it today.

'There you are!' Grace heard the lobby doors close as Jack strode in and sank down in the seat next to her. 'I've been searching for you all over, Grace. Funny how sometimes the middle of the auditorium is the best place to hide.'

He clambered into the row of seats in front and twisted round to look at her with his usual grin. She stared daggers at him.

'I'm not hiding.'

She was absolutely hiding.

'Fair enough. Are you still cross, though?'

'I'm absolutely livid.'

He craned his neck, trying to get a look at her notebook. 'Any ideas at all for the musical?'

She snatched the notebook back against her chest. 'No! None! Go away!'

He didn't – only scratched behind his ear and stared into the air above her head.

'I heard Ruby singing through an absolutely lovely ballad upstairs yesterday. She said it was your lyric, and she played me a cracking little flirty duet, too.'

Grace groaned. 'I wrote those ages ago – they'll do absolutely fine for Stella and Lance, but I don't have a setting or a plot or anything for them to say yet. They're all expecting to start rehearsals in a month! This is all your fault! Honestly, Jack, how could you? Announcing a brand new musical to the *Gazette* and saying I'm going to write it, just like that, without talking to any of us!'

'It's not entirely my fault,' he said, making his eyes wide. 'I was provoked. And possibly a little overexcited.'

'It's *entirely* your fault.'

'And Stella and Lance and Bill are all up for it!' He rested his chin on the back of the seat. 'I managed to calm down their agents eventually. Though I had to spend a fortune on flowers for Stella's. She's a force of nature. "So unprofessional, Mr Treadwell,"' he added in a high fluting tone, very like the grande dame of the theatre who was shepherding Stella's career.

Grace refused to be amused.

'Well, it was!' she glowered. 'What about me?!'

'Do you want flowers?'

'No, I don't!'

'Well, then,' Jack replied, as if that solved the entire problem.

'Jack, I've never written a full musical! The fact Ruby has turned out to be a one-woman Tin Pan Alley was pure luck, and I can't think straight because all I want to do is throttle you. Honestly, I can't sleep or eat, I'm so cross.'

'I did think you were looking a bit peaky,' he said in a concerned tone. 'Come out with me this evening. I'll buy you dinner. Food always make everyone feel better.'

'Why did they ask you to comment, rather than me, anyway?'

'I've been bothering them to get stories in the newspaper about the music hall revue, so they know me.'

She sighed lustily. 'I suppose so, but there's absolutely no chance of me forgiving you until I get at least one idea.'

'You do want to write, don't you?' he asked, a little tentatively. 'Alma and Charlie mentioned it a few times. They said they hoped doing Mangrave's job for him wouldn't divert you.'

'I do. I just don't like being bounced into things.'

He looked contrite, and she wondered what going out to dinner with him might be like. He managed to make Mr Marvel's old suit look rather good, and there was this closeness between them at times which felt . . . felt like something . . .

She shook herself, reminding herself she was still angry with him and anyway, he charmed everyone, not just her. She decided to change the subject.

'How is Danny getting on?'

'Getting more confident every day. He'll make a very good doorman whenever you need me to be your assistant.'

'Miss Hawkins! You out there?' Grace had been so focused on Jack that she hadn't noticed Mrs Gardener bustling out onto the stage. 'Ah, I see you! I can't be having it! They're disarranging things!'

Grace plastered a tight professional smile on her face. She got up so smartly that the seat banged in a startling fashion, making Jack jump, and walked towards the stage.

'What's happening, Mrs Gardener?'

'They simply can't block the corridors with boxes and tea chests!

And I caught one of 'em actually *moving* Jemima's costume for the quick change! If I hadn't have seen that she'd be trying to do the ribbon dance, ribbon-less!'

The threat to the ribbon act aside, Grace was perplexed.

'Who is moving things, Mrs Gardener?'

'The man in the suit with the neck. He's clearing out the everything-else rooms next to the rehearsal studio.'

Jack wandered down the aisle to join Grace, hands in his pockets. 'Thank goodness you spotted it, Mrs G! But rest assured, the varmints will be dealt with *tout de suite*!'

Mrs Gardener beamed, and visibly relaxed. 'Oh, Jack! How wonderful. If you'd be so kind, I'd appreciate it terribly.'

He saluted her and she giggled. Everyone had feelings for Jack, it seemed.

'Thank you, dear!'

Then she walked back into the wings, still smiling.

Jack caught Grace's look.

'What?'

'Is there anyone you don't flirt with?'

He shrugged. 'It's the theatre – as far as I can tell, *not* flirting is seen as downright rude.'

He isn't entirely wrong about that, though, Grace thought.

'Let's just go and see what's going on, shall we, Jack?'

The Empire was utterly disorientating once you left the gilt and velvet of the public areas. Grace went through one of the side doors from the stalls and headed up flight after flight of stairs, while Jack followed and tried not to pay too much attention to how appealing her figure was in motion. They passed the chorus dressing rooms, and the domain of wigs, a couple of costume storage rooms, and the large workroom where Mrs Gardener's assistants sewed up tears and steamed out creases, then up again to the rehearsal room corridor. It held one large studio, big enough for the chorus, an overspill, and the everything-else rooms.

'What *is* in the everything-else rooms?' Jack asked as they approached them.

'They aren't large enough for wardrobe or wigs,' Grace said. 'So they've become a sort of storage place for old papers and posters – things which don't have an official place.'

'Bit of lost property, too,' Jack added.

They came to a halt to watch a liveried footman walk past them carrying a crate overflowing with scarves, opera glasses and a perfectly decent, if somewhat ragged, top hat. Grace turned into the room the footman had just exited, with Jack at her heels, and found a man in a high collar and black suit directing operations.

Grace cleared her throat and he turned towards them with a pleasant smile on his pale face.

'Are you Miss Hawkins and Mr Treadwell?' he asked, his voice so deeply sonorous Jack felt it vibrate through the floorboards.

They nodded.

'Excellent. Two maids from Lassiter Court will be coming this afternoon to wash down the walls and windows, but I wonder if we might borrow one of your carpenters to rehang this connecting door before the gentlemen from Bertram's come in to install the carpets and furniture tomorrow morning. Miss Fortescue will be in the outer office here—'

Grace found her voice. 'Who are you, exactly?'

He inclined his head, gracefully accepting the interruption. 'I am Mr Hewitt, butler to Lady Lassiter at Lassiter Court. Now, the footmen encountered a rather angry lady downstairs, I understand, who protested at the placing of some of these items in a largely empty room near to the stage. Could you explain the situation to her, Miss Hawkins?'

Grace was not sure that she could. 'That is the green room, and it is to be kept clear for the performers. You are aware, I hope, Mr Hewitt, that this is not Lassiter Court?'

'I am,' he replied, with only the slightest wobble of the jowls. 'If it were, I'd have a better notion of where to store the . . .' He waved his hands at the papers being piled into tea chests. 'The ephemera.'

'What is happening, Mr Hewitt?' Jack said. 'You've just turned up and started rearranging things, and I know we might look a little chaotic at The Empire, but it's carefully arranged chaos.' A thought struck him. 'How did you get past Ollie at stage door?'

'We came in through the front, Mr Treadwell.'

'Dashed sneaky,' Jack muttered.

'Mr Hewitt,' Grace said, 'let's start at the beginning. Why are you clearing these rooms?'

'Lady Lassiter is coming home,' Hewitt replied with obvious satisfaction. 'She has her flat above the auditorium, naturally, should she wish to spend the night in town, but she also requires a place to do business in the building. She has chosen these rooms. My understanding is she intends to involve herself in your exciting new production. And Miss Fortescue is her private secretary.'

'Oh,' Grace said, hugging her empty notebook more tightly to her chest.

'That's dashed good news!' Jack said, his moment of bad humour forgotten. 'We can find room for this stuff in the carpenters' shop for a day or two, don't you think, Grace? Until you know what sets you want them to build for the musical, anyway. I think Little Sam would like that topper, and some of those old posters might be framed and hung around the place. When's Lady Lassiter due back?'

'Thursday,' Hewitt replied. 'I understand she intends to take up residence in these offices on Monday.' He hesitated, then continued in a more confidential tone. 'I feel it is appropriate to tell you that her friend, Miss Evangelista D'Angelo, is accompanying her, and we have been asked to prepare rooms for her at the Court, suitable for an extended stay.'

'How pleasant,' Jack said.

Hewitt leant forward. 'An *extended* stay, Miss Hawkins, her Broadway musical having just closed. If I am to believe what is printed in the local newspapers, you are writing this new musical. Is that correct?'

'I'm trying to.'

'If I may make so bold to drop a hint, then, I suspect Miss D'Angelo will be most interested in the available roles.'

'Oh,' Grace said. 'Oh, I see.'

'Indeed, Miss Hawkins. I had the pleasure of meeting Miss D'Angelo when she stayed with us before the war.' He leant forward a little further and added in a warm, avuncular tone, 'Best of luck, my dear.'

A bark, short and authoritative, came from the corridor outside, followed by a muffled shout and a crash. They hustled out to find one of the footmen sitting on the floor and rubbing his shin, a spilled tea chest of good luck telegrams and postcards and letters fluttering around him, while Ollie stood at the top of the stairs, his head down and his tail pointing out behind him, growling.

'Did the animal bite you, Williams?' Hewitt asked.

'No, Mr Hewitt,' Williams said. 'Just scared the living daylights out of me.'

'This is what comes from wandering in through the front door,' Jack said. 'Ollie catches you on his rounds.' He put his hand out to the dog, who trotted towards him and offered his ears to be scratched. 'It's all right, lad. I know they're not theatre, but they're friendly.'

'We do try,' Hewitt said, helping Williams to his feet.

Grace set down her notebook, and they began to gather up the fallen papers. As Jack bundled a pile of them back into the tea chest, one slithered free and spun like a sycamore seed before coming to a rest at Grace's feet. She picked it up and stared, Jack looked over her shoulder.

The postcard advertised the Grand Hôtel on Promenade des Anglais, Nice, on the south coast of France. It was a long, white, classical building, its name in huge red letters across the frontage, against a deep blue sky. The promenade was fringed with palm trees and promenading along it were fashionably dressed couples. In the far corner was the lighter blue of the sea, a flat golden corner of sand, and a young woman in a red swimsuit and large sunglasses.

'Grace?' Jack said, and Ollie barked.

'I think,' Grace said slowly, 'that I might have an idea.' She looked up, bright and excited. 'Jack, can you deal with this? I've got to go and speak to Ruby!'

'Of course.' Jack felt a pang of jealously that Grace wanted to speak to Ruby, rather than him. He told himself not to be foolish. 'We'll manage, won't we, gentlemen?'

Hewitt's eyes travelled across Jack, Ollie and his hobbled footman.

'Probably.'

Grace discovered Ruby Rowntree in her room. The floor was, as usual, evenly scattered with hairpins, and the dressing table piled with manuscript paper. Recently a corkboard had been hung over the piano. It was supposed, eventually, to have a plan of the musical pinned to it. At the moment it held two cards, marked with Miss Rowntree's neat script, one saying STELLA SOLO, and the other LANCE AND STELLA FLIRT SONG.

'All right, Grace?' Ruby asked from her seat at the piano.

Grace beamed at her, then pinned the postcard she had found on the corkboard.

'What about this? A big hotel on the south coast of France. Lance's character could own it, and perhaps Stella could be the in-house singer with the band?'

Ruby clapped her hands. 'Oh, yes! Sun and glamorous strangers – perfect. We could have the in-house band on stage! I wonder if I could persuade Mabel Mills and her jazz band to join us? What a coup it would be to have them in it. If the curtain falls before ten, they could still do their late show at the Metropole – and that's a perfect role for Stella. What about Bill?'

Grace stopped beaming and sat down heavily in the armchair, pulling the comforter around her.

'I don't know! I only had this idea a minute ago.'

'He could work at the hotel, too. What if Lance was an officer and Bill was an older NCO who saved his life? Or perhaps he used to own the hotel and lost it to Lance at the tables?'

Grace screwed up her nose. 'That might make Lance a bit evil. Good Lord, it's all so complicated. My head feels like it's full of butterflies.'

'Better than having a head full of moths.'

Grace smiled ruefully. 'Lady Lassiter's coming back, and they're making the everything-else rooms into an office for her and her secretary.'

A tune began to emerge under Ruby's right hand. A few notes

at first, like a song in the distance, then coming closer, resolving into a thread of melody. It sounded, somehow, French.

'But that's excellent news, Grace – d'you ever see Lady Lassiter on stage? No, of course, you are much too young, and she didn't have any big roles until she was in Paris. Sir Barnabas's gain was the audience's loss.'

Grace was staring at Ruby's hands, amazed at watching the tune appear. It was like watching a potter at a wheel.

'We could have a big welcome number, couldn't we?' Grace said. 'The guests arriving at the hotel – that could be our opener.'

'Perfect. This is an excellent idea, Grace. Some glamour and sunshine. Just what we all need.'

'It's *half* an excellent idea. Did you see Lady Lassiter perform in Paris?'

'I did.' Ruby pulled a fat and well-used notebook off the top of the piano and began to scribble, occasionally letting her hands drift to the keys to remind herself of some corner of a melody. 'That's where the conservatoire was, where I studied. Though, if I'm honest, I learnt a lot more in the cafés and bars. That's where I met Mabel Mills first.'

'Having her would be a coup. And as she plays in clubs mostly, Allerdyce's ban on us shouldn't put her off. Lady Lassiter is bringing Evangelista D'Angelo with her, too.'

'Well, I never! She has presence, that one. She's what my Parisian friends used to call "hot stuff".'

'I don't know what to write for her!'

Ruby's hands strayed around the piano again. 'Don't worry, dear. It will come. Glamour – that's what we want. And make it funny. But sad, too, of course! With the sort of ending that people feel down into their boots. And real, so it speaks to people's hearts. But light.'

'Is that all?'

'A rags-to-riches story is always good. And, of course, lots and lots of romance.'

Grace groaned.

'We have almost a whole month before rehearsals start, dear. You'll do fine.'

'It's taken me a fortnight to find this postcard.' Grace's voice was slightly hysterical.

'Now, Grace, we did *Macbeth!!* in three days.'

'Shakespeare had already written that one!'

'You did the new songs.'

Grace was about to protest again when the door banged open and Jack tumbled in at his usual high velocity.

'Jack!' Ruby said. 'Grace has done it. A romance on the Riviera! All set round a big hotel.'

'Magnificent!' Jack said. 'I knew you'd think of something, Grace – you shouldn't worry so much.'

'Jack, you absolute—'

'I've been invited to Lassiter Court for dinner Saturday evening. Stella and Lance have been summoned, too. Whatshisface with the neck didn't mention Bill, though, now I come to think of it. Ruby, will you come?'

'Goodness, no!' Ruby said, with such shivering conviction that one of her hairpins fell out. 'And Bill will be performing.'

'Whatshisface with the neck is called Mr Hewitt,' Grace said. 'Am I invited? Oh, Lord – what about Mangrave?'

'I've no idea. Anyway, what on earth do I wear? Mr Marvel's dinner jacket is wearing out and I keep finding birdseed in the pockets. I shall throw myself on the mercies of Mrs Gardener. We're sold out again this evening, by the way.'

'I know,' Grace said quietly as the door closed behind him.

'Is he always like that?' Ruby asked.

'It varies,' Grace replied.

The door banged open again.

'Have you got a dress?'

'What, Jack?' Grace said. 'Yes, of course I have a dress.'

'Good. I told Hewitt you're coming, too, but Mangrave will have to be here as it's a Saturday night. So that's all arranged.'

And he was gone again.

The two women sat in silence for a moment.

'You know,' Ruby said at last, 'he moves so quickly sometimes, I swear I heard a sort of swooshing noise then as he left.'

Grace gulped with laughter. Then it faded.

'Are you angry Jack had to inform them you were invited, Grace?'

'A little,' she admitted. 'I mean, when Lady Lassiter last really came to the theatre I was terribly young. But I have been working very hard for The Empire.'

'I hope you'll make that clear to Lady Lassiter when she gets here. Right then, my dear. Let's give these characters some names, shall we?'

CHAPTER THIRTEEN

At the *Highbridge Gazette* and *Illustrated News* offices, Edison Potter received the news of Lady Lassiter's return to the city with Evangelista D'Angelo from his secretary.

'Photographer to meet the train,' he told her. 'Send a telegram to Liverpool for Miss Fortescue to warn them. Give them a chance to straighten their hats.'

She flipped a page in her notebook. 'And we've had a tip that The Empire is clearing out office space for her.'

He grunted. 'Send someone round for a quote from Mangrave, or that Treadwell fellow. It'll be the usual guff, but it's something to go with the photograph.' He picked up his jacket from the back of his chair and shrugged it on. 'Carry on, Miss Lee.'

As she returned to her desk, Edison walked out into his newsroom, and wandered over to the desk of Wilbur Bowman.

'Come on, lad. Breath of fresh air will do you no harm.'

Since he had started investigating Lassiter Enterprises, Wilbur had spent more time in the office than anyone other than Edison himself. For a moment it looked as if he was going to demur, but Edison raised an eyebrow and Wilbur got up swiftly from his desk and grabbed his own jacket.

Edison led him down the stairs, through the lobby where the local citizenry queued to place their classified adverts. The more prosperous ones were looking for domestic staff; the more ragged were offering whatever they had left for sale. A silent five-minute walk along the busy pavements brought them to the municipal gardens behind the town hall. Office workers ate their sandwiches, sitting on the wrought-iron benches, and nannies who worked in the larger town houses walked in pairs, occasionally watching their charges poke model boats around on the pond.

Edison's quick marching pace slackened to a stroll.

'So, Mr Bowman, what have you got?'

'The interview shook a few things loose, Mr Potter, especially on the Lassiter Enterprises side of things. I need to get the full story, but it seems Sir Edmund has invested in some dubious new innovations.'

'Sir Barnabas's motto in business was "diversify and innovate", you know. He used to say that all the time.'

Wilbur nodded. 'He knew what he was doing. He was an engineer, and a sharp businessman, from all I hear. Sir Edmund seems to write a cheque for any charlatan who comes in promising him the moon, then takes it out on his staff when the "innovations" don't work.'

'Can you prove that?' Edison asked, lighting a cigar.

'Converting the cutlery factory back from manufacturing ammunition is well behind schedule, sir. And he boasted last year about a new firing regime for the fancy goods works. Nothing's been heard of that since. The manager just shrugged when I asked him about it. The textile printing works had to shut down half its production last month because a new synthetic dye he invested in started clogging the presses.'

'Call me Edison but is that real incompetence or a run of bad luck?'

Wilbur pursed his lips. 'I've been trying to find out about those two. Where these inventors are now, and why no other manufacturer invested.'

Edison grunted. 'Remember, this is about our town, our jobs. You've got to show cause and effect.' He stabbed the unoffending air with his cigar. 'Sir Edmund's impulsive investments mean you can't put food on your family's table.'

'Yes, Edison.'

'What about that other thing? Have you heard that Lady Lil is coming back and means to get involved with the theatre again?'

'Yes, I've got friendly with Danny, the new doorman. Nice bloke. He knows nothing useful about Mangrave, but it was me who passed on that bit about Lady Lassiter. Wonder what Joe Allerdyce will make of it?'

'Let the theatre chappies worry about that. That's their beat. Have you got anything on that connection between Mangrave and Ray Kelly?'

Wilbur was quiet for a few minutes, and Edison let the man think as they continued their walk. He stared about at the town's elite, the young gents in their sailor suits and married ladies gossiping among the shrubberies.

'It's not much more than a rumour, Edison,' Wilbur said at last, and Edison laughed.

'I'll listen.'

He saw an unoccupied bench off the gravel walkway and headed towards it, Wilbur following him.

'Get out your notebook and walk me through it,' Edison said as he took his seat.

'My notebook? It's on my desk.'

Edison sighed. 'Always carry your notebook, lad. Every hour of the day. And when you go to sleep, you keep it under your pillow. Tell me what you remember.'

Wilbur swallowed. 'Well . . . I've made some friends who work at his club, and it's not just the company's money Sir Edmund likes to gamble with. He spends hours at the vingt-et-un tables most nights, and loses. Sometimes he settles the debts in cash, sometimes he just chalks them up to his account. Now, his account there is paid off regularly, but not by him. Someone turns up with a banker's draft and my source says they are brought in by Hanson MacDonald. He's a lawyer.'

'I know him. Acts like butter wouldn't melt, but represents any Kelly gang members who can't bribe or intimidate their way out of a court date. That's good work, son, and another vague connection with Kelly, but nothing illegal.'

'Yes, but why is a lawyer connected with Ray Kelly paying off Sir Edmund's gaming debts?'

'I'd like to know that myself.'

'I tried looking at it from the other end, and I've been doing some digging on Mangrave. When he was appointed at The Empire, Mangrave told a reporter he'd managed theatres in Scotland and Newcastle. Well, I've spoken to dozens of theatres and playhouses, Inverness to Hull. None of them have ever heard of him. But MacDonald used to practise that side of the country, so I went through the court records, going back a couple of years from when Mangrave turned up here.'

Edison was beginning to see why Wilbur's desk looked like it did.

'You ever sleep, son?'

'Sometimes. I did find an Alexander Mangrave who was tried for fraud in Newcastle in 1919. He was a clerk, and running a smart scheme to skim a lot of money out of his employer – and guess who his solicitor was?'

'Hanson MacDonald?'

'Spot on. I talked to the *Northern Echo* court reporter—'

'And he remembered it?'

'*She*, actually, Mr Edison, but yes. Said this Mangrave looked like a gentleman, but was a proper piece of work. Married a girl with a bit of money right after the war. Her family turned up in court, though the wife didn't – they suspected he mistreated her. Anyway, he was found not guilty. The star witness got beaten up in a street robbery and wouldn't say anything when they forced him on to the stand.'

'I'll be damned.' Edison had been listening so intently his cigar had gone out. 'His wife never comes out into society. Everyone's assumed she was ill or one of those nervous types, but perhaps there's more to it than that. Did you get the names of the wife and her family?'

'I did. The wife's name is Cecilia. And I have an address in Newcastle for her brother.'

'Go and see him. Soon as you like. As for Lassiter's follies, you'd better check those out, too, I suppose. And keep your damned notebook with you.'

The news that Lillian was coming home had reached Manor Farm, Agnes's home, in the form of a telegram from Lillian's secretary. Agnes had received it while watching her horses and read it with mild interest, being more occupied at that moment with the performance of a filly she was planning to sell. That sale completed, however, she thought of it again while tending to her roses.

'Lillian is having a welcome home dinner on Saturday night,' she said, deploying her secateurs among the straggling bushes. 'Would you like to come, Joe?'

Joe Allerdyce was holding the wicker trug of faded rose heads. As well as his usual dark suit, he wore a rather battered straw hat to keep the sun off his forehead. Agnes had insisted.

'I saw she was coming back. What's her cellar like?'

'Moderate. Occasionally good. Those two young things from the theatre will be there. Edmund, Tom – and their mother, too, of course. And someone called Angelica de whatever. Though I don't believe she came by that "de" in any legitimate fashion.'

'But your "de", Miss de Montfort, is solid gold, I suppose?'

'Twenty-four carat. Papa had heaps of vellum to prove it. I think it's all still in a chest in the cowshed if you wish to examine it.' She snipped another faded bloom and tossed it into the trug.

'I'll take your word for it. The lady you mean is Miss Evangelista D'Angelo. She was in some good shows before and during the war. Has a certain something to her, and that's my expert opinion. Did her bit entertaining the troops, too.'

'I'm sure she did.'

He laughed. '"Smile for your Boys" was "her" song. You heard it everywhere. I have it on good authority they paid fifty pounds to put her picture on the cover of the piano version.'

'Oh?' She snipped away. 'I'm sure she donated it to the war effort.'

'How're you enjoying the gramophone I sent you, by the way?'

Agnes thrust another handful of dry thorns in his direction. 'Very kind of you, Joe. Though I haven't really had much chance to listen to it as yet.'

'Really? Funny that, because you've been humming Ivor Novello tunes for the last fifteen minutes.'

'Don't you have work to do, Joe?'

Joe accepted this prickly response with equanimity. It was true; he was spending more time out of the office and away from his theatres than he had in many years. But he was enjoying himself.

'I *am* working.'

'You're holding my trug.'

'And thinking. I can do both at the same time.'

'A man of many talents.'

'I am. I'm considering my considerable good fortune. While The Empire spends all their capital on their new show, I'm filling my theatres with quality touring companies. A few straight plays for the Highbridge intellectual elite at the Playhouse, singers at the Palace of Varieties . . . I'm printing money.'

'Do we have an intellectual elite in this city?'

'Well, there's a few of 'em. And then there's the discussion groups from the working men's clubs. They stay to argue and drink my beer for hours after.'

'You are fomenting revolution. How very exciting. I notice your ticket prices have gone up again.'

'I thought you never paid any attention to that sort of thing?'

She snipped some more. 'The advertisement was next to the racing results.'

He chuckled. The swifts danced through the air above them, making their long, high calls.

'Joe, this new musical – it seems quite a gamble. They are rather expensive to produce, aren't they?'

He made a vague *hmm* noise in the back of his throat.

'I saw you talking to him, that Jack Treadwell, you know, at the reception celebrating the return of Billy Barlow, about five minutes before he started talking to the news reporter.'

'Let me tell you, a new musical is a . . . bold endeavour. I *might* have mentioned, as it happens, that a theatre like The Empire needs a couple of ambitious productions to hang on to its status of a really first-class house.'

'Joe, you are a psychologist.'

'I'd only ever let you say that, my dear.' She blushed slightly, which pleased him. 'Look, I'll make you a deal. I promise to come to Lassiter Court if you agree to wear one of your new ensembles.'

'I shall certainly do that. I think Constance might actually explode. Who knew if one had enough champagne and a friend, shopping could actually be quite amusing?'

Her secateurs moved towards another bloom. It was past its youth, its petals fully open, but lushly thick. Joe put his hand over Agnes's.

'No, don't touch that one, Agnes. It's at the height of its beauty now. A queen among these young bloods.'

She smiled at him. 'Very well, if it gives you pleasure.'

'It really does.' He gently squeezed her fingers. 'Now let's go and have a drink.'

CHAPTER FOURTEEN

Jack was trying not to stare at Grace too much as they waited
for their lift outside The Empire on Saturday evening, but he
was finding it difficult. She was probably thinking about the
play, and her small, fine-featured face was even more serious than
usual. Jack wished very much he could – that he had the right to
– reach out across the five inches of evening air between them and
take her hand. But he couldn't. He had loved every minute of the
day he had arrived at The Empire, but he did wish, very much, he
could restart his relationship with Grace Hawkins. He had fallen
into his usual way of being with people – all boyish enthusiasm
and high spirits, trying to tease a smile out of her – but he was
worried now that in the process he'd become a bit of a clown. And
now he was her assistant, which was fun and challenging and he
was learning a lot, but it made him feel as if he might seem childish
in her eyes. His doing things like committing them to a musical
because Joe Allerdyce had provoked him probably hadn't helped.

'Here they are!' Grace said, her eyes brightening.

Lancelot Drake was driving Stella's sports car again, and despite their doubts, he persuaded Grace and Jack there was plenty of room in the back for them. To their surprise, he drew up at seven o'clock, precisely on time.

'I told Stella we had to leave at six,' he said by way of explanation.

He drove just as he moved, with a great deal of elegance and little visible effort. Stella twisted round, enthusiastically kneeling up on the front seat to tell Grace and Jack how much her agent hated them both, and how fantastic she thought the idea of the South of France was.

'I love it! I shall spend the rest of the month sunbathing and call it preparation.'

'But are you sure you and Lance are doing the right thing, Stella?'

Grace was painfully aware Stella had given up a lucrative concert tour in France to take this job, and Lance had irritated his new Hollywood producers by telling them he wouldn't be available until after Christmas.

'Ha!' Stella said, lighting a cigarette and watching the breeze whip the smoke away into the summer evening. 'My agent has been looking at me severely over her reading glasses for months and telling me it's impossible to get me anything south of Bradford other than second-girl roles. That's why I was doing the tour, darling. "There are just so many girls, Stella," she says. "Roles such as you deserve are rare as hen's teeth." As if it's someone else's job to go and find them! The woman's stopped hustling. But starring in a new musical at The Empire! That'll make people pay attention. I mean, of course I loved doing the revival of *The Queen of Paris*, but it's all a bit slow and tragic. Sort of opera for people who don't really like opera, but feel they should.'

She put her hand to her snow-white throat and stared up into the evening sky, just as she had in the last scene of the revival. The ghost of tragedy passed over them briefly. Then Stella snapped her fingers and it fled.

'Being in something really fun and witty and bang-bang-bang – with Lancelot Drake, too – will do my career a world of good. Honestly, Grace, I love both you and Jack from the bottom of my heart, but I'm not doing this to be nice.'

'Have you told them?' Grace asked Jack.

'Told us what?' Stella threw her cigarette out of the car.

Jack shook his head.

'Evangelista D'Angelo is staying at Lassiter Court,' Grace said.

'Run out of New York by the critics, so I hear,' Stella said gleefully. 'She can play my mother! Or, even better, my grandmother. Write her a tune about how utterly ghastly it is to be over forty!'

'That will obviously go down well,' Lance said.

'Have you told them *our* news, Lance?'

'What news?' Jack asked.

'I picked up a rumour in London the other night,' Lance said, changing gear. 'Seems that Usher Barton might be available to be your director and choreographer if you move quickly.'

'What an awful name,' Stella observed. 'Sounds like a sheep eating blancmange.'

'Usher Barton! That's splendid,' Grace squeaked in excitement. 'He produced and directed *Summer Girl* and *Sundays at the Ritz*! He's a smashing choreographer, too. Do you really think we could get him, Lance?'

'For you, dear girl, I shall do my best to persuade him.'

'Didn't one of his actresses try and kill herself halfway through rehearsals?' Jack said cautiously.

His reading of *The Stage*, cover to cover, was a matter of religious

observance these days, and he had almost worked his way through
the old doorman's archive.

'That was Susie – she never eats anything not in pill form.'
Stella lit another cigarette. 'A pal of mine was her dance partner a
year or two ago, and he said she rattled every time he lifted her.'

'Just a thought,' Lance said. 'I have his address if you want to
write. And I'll call on him when I'm back in town, if you like.
See what he thinks of the Riviera idea.'

'Lord, how wonderful,' Grace said. 'Jack, we must have him.
I've never written a musical before and nor has Ruby. A really
experienced West End director could make all the difference.
Though it will add to the costs.'

Lance turned the car off the road and the wheels crunched on
the gravel as they passed through the gates of Lassiter Court.

'Chuck away that ciggie, Stella, my sweet child,' Lance said.
'We approach the house of the great and good.'

'Blimey, what a pile!' Stella said cheerfully as the long, low,
Neo-Gothic frontage of Lassiter Court came into view.

She flicked the cigarette out onto the lawn for the roaming deer
to find.

Lance drew up on the circular drive at the front of the edifice,
and tossed his keys to a young man in uniform who materialised
nearby. The front door was opened and, after a certain amount of
fuss and laughter getting Jack and Grace out of the car, Fenton
Hewitt bowed them into the hall.

'Ah, the young people!' he said in a rather lowering fashion. 'If
you would follow me into the library, Miss D'Angelo and Lady
Lassiter will be joining us shortly.'

In the library, which didn't have many books in it, Hewitt offered
them cocktails, so they were all clutching Old Fashioneds when

Evie made her entrance. After the briefest of introductions, she descended on Grace like a sparrowhawk on a vole.

'Miss Hawkins! I am absolutely too thrilled to meet you!'

Grace only just managed to stop herself curtseying. Evie was dressed like a queen: her evening gown of crushed velvet was a deep green, the same colour as her eyes, and she wore the most astonishing rope of emeralds around her neck, matched by cuffs on her wrists.

'So delightful to hear about the Riviera idea – Julia, tragic and beautiful singer at the Hotel Riviera. An absolutely splendid role. I shall be delighted to play her.'

Grace was startled. Perhaps she shouldn't have been. Lillian's fantastically organised-looking secretary had been at The Empire on Friday, so no wonder word of the idea had made it back to Lassiter Court.

Stella smiled daggers. 'Julia is my role, Evangelista.'

Evie looked at her sideways. 'Really? I thought you were going to play a maid or something.'

Lance swiftly put a restraining hand on Stella's arm. 'Darling Evangelista, poor Grace has only just begun. Stella will, of course, play Julia – the role was created for her – but I know our brilliant author will create something really remarkable for you! Something that will take advantage of your full dramatic range—'

'And extensive experience,' Stella muttered, but Lance spoke over her.

'. . . A real show-stopper of a role – not just another singer.'

'Is that right, Grace?' Evie asked, her eyebrows raised.

'I . . . That is . . . Oh, look, here's Lady Lassiter.'

Their hostess had just entered the room, as quiet as her friend was loud. She stood just inside the door, looking very pale and staring across at them all, more like a debutante at her first party than the hostess. She had an almost ethereal glow about her. Grace, her theatrical mind prompting ungenerous thoughts, wondered if she knew that the lighting was particularly good at that spot. But no – when Lady Lassiter moved, the glow came with her. Grace stepped forward to greet her.

'Grace, how lovely to see you again. Did I hear that you have persuaded Charlie Moon out of retirement? How is he? How are Alma and Danny?'

Her hand was cool and her voice more breathy than usual. Grace noticed she was still wearing black – widow's weeds – but she made it look gloriously chic, and her evening shawl was a loose, thin chiffon thing the colour of lavender.

'I did, Lady Lassiter! Charlie was an enormous help with the music hall revue, and Alma has been a smash as the chairman. Danny is doing rather better. He's taken over as stage doorman now Jack is company manager for the musical.'

'Has he? I'm ever pleased to hear it, especially— Thank you, Hewitt. I hope you like Old Fashioneds, everyone. Prohibition has made decent champagne difficult to get hold of in New York in all but the most splendid places, so we've fallen into the habit of cocktails.' She turned her gaze back to Grace. 'And do call me Lillian, dear. Especially as I'll be at the theatre much more.' She seemed distracted, her eyes continually straying around the room. 'One moment . . . You said Danny Moon is the new doorman? He must really be doing better than when I left for New York.'

'He is.' Grace smiled. 'I think Charlie and Alma would work for free for The Empire for the rest of their lives now.'

Lillian nodded.

'He's really enjoying the work. His speech is getting better, too.'

Lillian looked round at the faces of her young guests again. 'What a remarkable, wonderful thing.'

Grace sipped her cocktail. It gave her a jolt of pleasure whenever she thought of Danny. He had been like an older brother to her when she was young; he had come back from the war a different man, but now she saw glimpses of that boy again.

'It is, but I can't take credit. Jack served with him, saved Danny's life according to the Moon family, and I think Danny gets a lot of confidence from knowing Jack is about. Goodness, I haven't even introduced you! Jack, this is Lady Lassiter. Lillian, this is Jack Treadwell.'

She offered Jack her hand wordlessly, and he bowed over it in a courtly fashion.

'Lady Lassiter!' he said cheerfully. 'I've been so looking forward to meeting you!'

'Lillian – please. Have you?'

'I have! I think you knew my mother, Bessie Treadwell. She told me to look you up when I came home.'

Lillian did not reply at once, but stared at him – looking for some clue in his face, perhaps.

'I think it might have been from before you even went on the stage,' Jack went on helpfully. 'My mother was a supervisor at the textile printing works.'

She blinked rapidly. 'Yes, my apologies, I do remember. Right here in Highbridge. How is Bessie? And her husband, Fred?'

Jack's bright manner seemed to slip. 'I'm very sorry to say I am now an orphan.' His voice shook a little. 'They died in the flu epidemic.'

'I see,' Lillian said faintly. 'I . . . You poor boy. They were very good people.'

'The absolute best,' Jack said simply.

'You know Stella, of course,' Grace said, 'and this is Lancelot Drake.'

Lillian turned towards him. 'Mr Drake, what a pleasure to welcome you here.'

'Who on earth is driving that enormous Rolls-Royce?' Evie said, and beckoned them all towards the window.

It was a magnificent machine. The chauffeur stepped out and opened the back door.

'Good gracious!' Evie went on. 'Lillian, someone has taken that almost sister-in-law of yours shopping. What was her name?'

'That's Agnes de Montfort,' Grace said, peering into the driveway.

Agnes certainly looked different. She was wearing purple, a long dress with a cloak, feathers in her hair, and a very modern gold necklace highlighting her considerable décolletage.

'Lord, how splendid she looks!' Grace said.

'Who is that large gentleman with her?' Lance asked.

'Oh, goodie! It's Joe Allerdyce!' Stella said. 'He's a bear, my sweet, and just too cross with me for playing The Empire. A straight arrow, though.'

'I know the name. He leaves my agent in tears,' Lance murmured. 'I went round his picture palaces doing appearances where my films were playing, and I'm not sure we didn't end up paying him.'

'He's been trying to drive us out of business,' Jack said darkly. 'It's only with the most incredible luck that he hasn't managed it, either. Well,' he said with a grin at Grace, 'luck and Grace!'

She caught his eye and held his gaze softly in a way that made his heart tighten.

'You've helped, too, Jack. We'd never have done it without you.'

'Yes.' Evie was still staring out of the window. 'Lillian said something about him coming. Oh! Urgh! Edmund, Tom and his mother. I quite like Tom, but the other two are an absolute waste of food.'

'Evie.' Lillian had not come to the window but remained by the empty fireplace. 'Be good.'

'I shall be *relatively* good, Lil,' she replied.

As the cocktails were being consumed, Evie offered to sing to them. To Jack's surprise, Tom Lassiter volunteered to accompany her on the piano. He did a good job, and Jack told him so.

'Yes,' Edmund said airily. 'Tom had a chance to continue his piano lessons while we were at war.'

'Spent his time much better than us, then,' Jack said. 'Have you settled on a career yet, Tom?'

The young man deflated. 'Once this summer is over, I'm to work with Hargreaves, the accountant. So says Mother, at any rate. So I'm trying to get as much fun in as possible before then.'

Constance overheard them. 'You don't have the presence for a really distinguished legal career, Tom. Learning to manage money will see you in good stead.'

'You play well,' Jack said. 'You can come and help us out at the theatre if you are at a loose end.'

Constance pursed her lips, and Agnes made the mistake of smiling into her cocktail.

'Agnes, I have to ask you – what on earth are you wearing?'

'A dress, Constance. Joe helped me pick it out.'

'I have to say, I think it's absolutely terrific,' Jack said sincerely.

'And I like your necklace,' Stella added. 'It's too marvellous! Mr Allerdyce, did you begin your career in the costume department?'

Joe gave her an old-fashioned look over the last remains of his drink.

'I did not. But my mother worked there. That's how I got my

start in the business. And Agnes is giving me too much credit. I just told her to enjoy herself. Everybody's got to wear clothes, so why not enjoy buying them?'

'I spent some time in the ladies' fashion department in La Samaritaine in Paris,' Jack said to Agnes, 'and I think that's awfully sound advice.'

'Which is why I took it, young man,' Agnes replied.

Hewitt returned to announce dinner, and the guests were welcomed into the dining room. The same style of elegant luxury pertained here as in the rest of the house, very art nouveau – light polished woods and organic shapes. The pictures on the walls were modern, too, and as far as Grace could judge, good.

'You worked in Paris, Jack?' Lillian asked, as the soup was served. She was seated at the head of the table between Jack and Lance. 'Evie and I lived there for some years.'

'I adore Paris!' Stella exclaimed. 'Those magnificent clubs. Lance, darling, didn't you tour there in the spring for one of your pictures?'

For a while they swapped stories of evenings spent in the nightclubs of France's capital, but when the conversation turned to the music, Grace joined in too. She, Agnes and Lillian discussed the new American styles, and the relative merits of Novello and Gershwin.

'. . . now I have my offices in the theatre again,' Lillian concluded.

The soup had been removed and the fish disposed of by this point, and Joe caught the end of this remark as he was working his way through the meat of a guinea fowl. He was inclined to pick up the awkward bird and gnaw at it, rather than try and keep it pinned on his gravy-slathered plate.

'So the *Gazette* got it right?' he asked. 'You're going to involve yourself in The Empire again, are you, Lady Lassiter?'

The general conversation quietened.

'I am,' Lillian said, elegantly dismembering her fowl. 'Surely you don't object to a little healthy competition, Mr Allerdyce?'

He sawed bad-temperedly at his own bird. 'I don't. These young people have been giving me a right runaround, and all credit to 'em. The managers at all my places have had to up their game. But I don't like dabblers.'

'Dabblers? You think I *dabble* in theatre?' Lillian said, putting down her fork.

'I do.'

'Before my husband was ill—' Lillian began, but Joe interrupted.

'You dabbled more! You know it's true, Lillian. You had a fine manager, and yes, between lunch and dinner, or shopping and shooting parties, you liked to talk to him about possible plays. You gave him little bits of advice when you wandered in to the theatre during rehearsals, and you pointed at colour samples when someone showed you a few, but the last night's work you did in the theatre – the last real night's work – was your last performance in Paris, and you know it. Since then, you've just been a rich woman with an expensive toy.'

'Mr Allerdyce!' Evie said reprovingly.

Grace glanced at Agnes. She was sipping her wine and watching. Then she beckoned Hewitt to her and whispered something to him.

'And what is that to you, Joe?' Lillian asked.

'It bloody well irks me!' he replied. 'Let's be clear, The Empire is a first-class theatre. I wanted it, and your husband snatched it out of my hands so he could give it to you as a plaything! But theatre's too serious a thing to be mucked around with because you're bored. I want it, and you should sell it to me because you know I've got moral rights to it. I'm sixty-two, and I started working in the music halls at twelve and I've worked at it every bloody day since. Every day!'

Grace found herself looking at Joe more closely. He had been such a monster to her in the last few weeks, but now he looked like a man who genuinely loved the theatre – she thought of the appointment of Mr Mangrave – and a man who had a point.

'It's almost,' Constance said, with a sneer in her voice, 'as if life wasn't fair, isn't it?'

The sneer was enough to set Joe off. He threw down his napkin. 'If you had any loyalty to the place, the sort of loyalty and love a theatre like that deserves, you would never have let Mangrave go in. If it wasn't for that lass there' – he jutted his chin at Grace – 'the whole place would've fallen apart before Barnabas died.'

'Mr Allerdyce,' Jack said gently, 'you are Lady Lassiter's guest.'

'If my plain-speaking troubles her, I don't mind leaving.' He stood up.

'Do sit down, Joe!' Lillian said. 'Please.'

Joe was ashamed at his own temper already.

Damn that bloody guinea fowl.

However, he was on his feet now.

'You aren't wrong,' Lillian went on. 'I leant on Charlie and enjoyed having the fun without the worry.' It was enough, and Joe sat down again. 'But I intend to really do the work this time.'

'Are we staying or going, Joe?' Agnes said. 'Only, I've just asked Hewitt to write me out the name of this excellent red from the wine book, and he said it might take a minute.'

Joe hesitated for a fraction of a second. 'Staying.'

'I was busy being Lady Lassiter before, you know,' Lillian continued. 'It was quite a demanding role.'

Joe reclaimed his napkin. 'You are still Lady Lassiter.'

Lillian raised her glass to him. 'I shall only be doing the

occasional performance as Lady Lassiter from now on. Constance has been doing a fine job of running the charities and opening fêtes while I've been away.'

'Like your understudy?' Stella asked with a crisp smile.

Constance glared at her, her small black eyes like beads.

'Indeed.' Lillian waved to the maid to start clearing the plates. 'And I dare say Edmund will marry soon, and his wife can take all that on. I shall be working at the theatre.'

'As what?' Jack blurted out. 'I mean, it sounds wonderful, doesn't it, Grace? But we have a manager – Mr Mangrave.'

'I'll produce your new show,' Lillian said smoothly. Glances of surprise flew around the table between the theatrical contingent like a storm of paper planes. 'I shall also be interested in seeing Mr Mangrave at work.'

'Blink and you'll miss it,' Joe said.

'He manages all the money,' Grace chimed in, annoyed at finding herself defending Mangrave. 'It's true he doesn't seem interested in the artistic side of things, but all our wages are paid on the dot.'

'I appointed Alexander!' Edmund said. 'I had every right to do so. I am the co-owner of the theatre and the production company now I've inherited Grandpa's shares. You agreed to it, Lillian.'

She simply shrugged.

'So be it.' Joe watched the mangled remnants of his fowl being removed, wondering if his housekeeper would be awake to rustle him up some decent sandwiches when he got home. 'When you get bored, Lady Lassiter, I'll take The Empire off your hands – and for a decent price.' He glanced sideways at Edmund. 'But if I buy it, I want it *all*. How does it break down?'

Grace looked around the table. Jack and Agnes looked curious, Stella and Lance uninterested, and Constance mildly outraged.

Tom was tapping out some tune on the tablecloth, and Edmund was finishing his wine and holding up his glass.

'Grandpa gave Lillian fifty-one per cent of the shares as a marriage gift,' Tom chimed in, 'and Ed inherited his forty-nine per cent stake.' He caught a look from his mother. 'What? It's not a secret, is it?'

'There is a vulgarity in discussing such matters at dinner,' Constance told him.

'And what will happen to us if you buy The Empire?' Jack asked.

Joe shrugged. 'You'll land on your feet. Like cats.'

'Nothing will happen to you, Jack,' Lillian said. 'I'll never sell.'

What about me? Grace thought.

She almost said it, then held her tongue. There were enough raw feelings around the table already. Edmund drained his glass and held it up again. Grace wondered why on earth he'd come. Tom was surprisingly nice, but Edmund seemed boorish. He had taken no part in the conversation other than to support his right to appoint Mangrave. It was obvious he didn't care what anyone around the table thought of him. For a moment, Grace almost envied that.

'It's all going to be a marvellous adventure!' Evie declared. 'I have had some thoughts as to a director.'

'We have one!' Stella said brightly. 'Fellow with a name like blancmange.'

'We are hoping Usher Barton might be available to helm the production,' Lance said. Joe's eyebrow twitched, which Grace thought was probably a good sign. 'If he meets with the approval of our producer, of course.'

'I'm sure he'll do very nicely,' Lillian replied, and raised her glass to him.

*

Three hours later, Evie and Lillian were alone and sipping brandies in her dressing room, their finery discarded, or at least replaced with more comfortable boudoir splendour.

'How are you, Lil?'

Lillian stared at the liquid in her glass.

'I am most terribly, terribly happy to be here. It feels miraculous. Though it is sad, too.' Her eyes strayed to the wedding portrait by her mirror. Barney looked so proud of her – his fresh young bride, on the steps of the British Consulate in Paris.

'But mostly happy?'

'Mostly ecstatic, darling. They are fine young people, aren't they?'

Evie huffed. 'That Stella girl thinks very highly of herself – strange, given her unfortunate wrists – but I thought the rest of them utterly charming.' She drank down the rest of her brandy in a gulp and reached along her chaise longue for the decanter. 'Darling, why is your stepdaughter-in-law or whatever she is . . .'

'You mean Constance?'

'Yes, the one that looks like a goose, not the one who is emulating the Empress of all Russias. Why was she wearing fake diamonds? Do you want more of this lovely brandy?'

'No, darling, I'm awash. Constance wasn't wearing fakes – that necklace was one Barney bought for his first wife. She passed it on to Constance.'

'That was a cruel thing to do to a woman with her neck.'

'Evie, really!'

'Don't "Evie, really" me, my love. You know exactly what I mean. Is she a blue blood?'

'She is a cousin of the Earl of March. I'm surprised she hasn't mentioned that to you yet. She acts like they are close friends, but I doubt he could pick her out from a chorus line. Why?'

Evie stretched luxuriously, the pink satin sleeves of her dressing gown falling back to show her thin white arms.

'I was thinking it must be awful to have all that breeding, but not be able to carry off the family jewels, while a couple of commoners like us manage it perfectly.' She twisted her wrist so the emerald bracelet she wore caught the light. 'Anyway, she was wearing fakes.'

Lillian turned away from the mirror and frowned. 'Are you sure?'

'Quite sure. You'd have noticed, too, if you hadn't been distracted. I'd bet the contents of my nicely filled security box in Coutts on it.'

Lillian tried to remember. 'When she wore them on Victory Day, they were quite genuine. I remember I thought it rather inappropriate for the occasion. Perhaps the real ones are being cleaned.' Lillian began rubbing cold cream into her cheeks, and its delicate rose scent drifted across the room. 'I can imagine her having fakes made so she could still blind the populace while the originals were at the jewellers.'

'Are you sure she hasn't sold the originals and spent the money at the racetrack?'

Lillian laughed. 'If she bet on Agnes's horses, she'd have done very well. No, Evie – there are absolutely piles of cash lying about. Barney saw to that.'

Evie finished her drink and set the glass down. 'I shall bear those words in mind when I am discussing my wardrobe for the musical.'

She rose and came to stand behind Lillian, her hands on her friend's shoulders, and kissed her hair. 'I am happy for you, Lil.'

Lillian took her hand and kissed it. 'Your wardrobe budget is limitless, Evie.'

CHAPTER FIFTEEN

Since Edmund had confided in his mother about the extent of the unfortunate challenges he was facing at Lassiter Enterprises, the relationship between them had shifted. Constance had a steel to her that Edmund had never noticed before. He had been raised by a succession of nannies, then there was school and the war, so throughout his youth his mother had simply been another female presence in the house, like the maids or the housekeeper. He'd assumed – if he thought about her at all – she spent her time doing good works and gossiping. The discovery that she thought – and had been thinking for some years – about Lassiter Enterprises was unsettling. He discovered, too, the rusty wheels of his mind turning slowly and screechingly, that she had smoothed over many small difficulties in the past – at his boarding house, in the regiment – which he had thought had disappeared on their own. She had even taken a hand in paying off a girl he had got briefly entangled with.

Now he wanted to please her – or rather, he felt somewhere

deep in his animalistic mind that it would be better for him if he did please her.

He'd learnt that being amusingly rude about Lillian or Agnes did the trick, so he did so all the way home from Lassiter Court, only coming to a halt as the maid opened the door and Constance handed her her fur coat.

'Will you require anything else, madam?'

'Edmund and I will have a drink in the library,' Constance said. 'But we can serve ourselves. Tom is going to bed.'

'Am I? Thought Ed and I might pop to the Royal Café for a finisher.'

Constance's face was, to any casual observer, expressionless, and Edmund said nothing, but Tom got the message anyway.

'Bed it is, then. If you could bring me up a brandy, Susan.'

'Yes, Mr Lassiter.'

The girl bobbed a curtsey and retreated, while Constance led the way into the library and Tom wandered upstairs. Edmund watched him go. He had always known he was his mother's favourite, but he accepted it as his due. Tom was one of those boys whom people were vaguely fond of, but Edmund felt very few respected him. Pathetic, really, but as his mother had said, Tom was one of those people who wanted to be liked rather than feared.

Edmund went into the library and glanced round. He was fairly sure none of the books had been read since his father died, and very few of them before then. Strange how since their 'conversation' his mother had abandoned the drawing room and taken up residence here.

Constance adjusted the lamps to a low glow and sat in one of the leather armchairs by the empty fireplace. She undid her necklace and dropped it on the occasional table with a sharp sigh of disgust and a shudder, as if wearing it had sickened her.

Edmund had never thought that little fraud would be discovered, but that night when he had come in and bared his soul about the difficulties facing Lassiter Enterprises, Constance had told him she'd been to the safe and seen that some of her jewels – like this necklace – had been replaced by fakes. It had never occurred to Edmund that anyone would be able to tell the difference.

'Whisky, please, Edmund, my dear,' she said.

He poured them both drinks and took his seat opposite her. Despite her laughter in the car – Lillian's showy catering, Evie's vulgar excesses and Agnes's strange transformation had given Edmund plenty of material – she had become serious now.

'What is our topic this evening, Mama?' he asked.

'I want to discuss Mangrave and the theatre, Edmund. I could tell from your reaction to the mention of him this evening there is something going on. You said at the time of his appointment that he was an old friend of yours? We are to have no more secrets between us, remember?'

He took a swallow of his drink. 'Yes – quite. Thing is . . . I was asked to appoint him.'

She smiled at him encouragingly.

'After I got home . . . I'm not sure if you knew, but I got rather into vingt-et-un.'

'A necessary relief.'

'Exactly that, Mama!' he replied, encouraged. 'I'm afraid I went rather beyond my resources, but I was offered the opportunity to extend my line of credit if I gave Mangrave the job at The Empire. It was just after Charlie Moon started talking about retiring, and it has proved a very satisfactory arrangement,' he continued in a rush. 'But Mangrave is an excellent chap. He's very understanding about the cash flow problems one occasionally runs up against.'

'I am sure many young men,' Constance said gently, 'who suffered as you did in the war found refuge for their stresses at the table.'

'Quite so!' he said, delighted she understood. 'And the thing was, I have an excellent system, only I had the damnedest run of luck and these things can take time to even out, and—'

'You're still playing?'

'A little.'

'Is that where the money for the jewels went?'

He coughed. 'As I explained before, the investments I made on behalf of the company are taking a while to pay out. Anderson Hargreaves came to me . . . oh, six months ago, saying there was a bit of a shortfall – the wages needed to be paid. So I pawned the jewels, discreetly, in London.'

'Investing the family's private money in the business so the workers would not go hungry?'

'Exactly.' Edmund took a swift swallow of his whisky, somewhat disturbed by the dry tone in her voice. 'The banks are so slow and ask so many questions, it just seemed much more straightforward—'

'By whom?'

'What?'

'I was wondering who offered you the opportunity to extend your line of credit at the club if you hired Mangrave?' Constance's voice remained gentle.

The room was really very warm. Edmund pulled his tie loose and undid the stud at his neck. 'A rather informal arrangement, as it happened . . . I was actually at the racetrack betting against Agnes's nags when it came up. This fella and I got quite pally over a drink, and he said I should speak to his friend, and I did, and they arranged for the funds to go to the club.'

'Who, Edmund?'

He almost spilled his drink. 'The man I met was called Sharps. The arrangement was made with Hanson MacDonald. Lawyer. Works for Ray Kelly.' Then he rushed on. 'But I didn't exactly know it was Kelly's money that I was being offered – not straight away, at any rate.'

Constance looked away and drank her whisky. Edmund didn't dare to breathe. The silence became too much for him.

'What . . . ? What do you think we should do, Mama?'

'About your gambling, your involvement with a notorious gang of criminals, or the terrible state of affairs at Lassiter Enterprises?'

The edge in her voice startled and cowed him.

'All of it, I suppose.'

She sighed. 'I need to think, Edmund, my dear. Now, are you quite resolved to be guided by me?'

'Yes, Mama.'

She patted his knee and he felt a great surge of relief.

'Good. The answer lies in The Empire, of course. We shall sell it. A similar theatre in Manchester was sold for seventy thousand pounds last year.'

'Lillian doesn't look like she wants to sell,' Edmund said doubtfully. 'And then there's Mangrave. I don't suppose he or Ray Kelly would be happy if we sold. I think Mangrave uses it to move their money around or something—'

'I don't need to know. I find reasonable men can always come to a sensible arrangement. As for Lillian? Leave her to me.' Constance put down her glass. 'Now, Edmund, you should go to bed. But before you do, please leave me Mr MacDonald's address and telephone number. Just write it on the pad on my desk.'

Her desk now, is it?

The house and its contents are in my name, if I remember rightly.

Still, he glanced at her angular profile in the shadows and decided – for the time being, at least – to do as she said.

Seventy thousand pounds, eh?

Hope and disquiet roiled in his stomach with Lillian's rich catering and made him bilious. He took out his address book and did as he was told.

Constance finished her whisky, then went to a volume of Greek poetry set in the centre of the second shelf and opened it. It contained a torn postcard showing Lillian as she had been when an 'actress' in Paris. Constance had confiscated it from Edmund when he was a little boy, not long after Sir Barnabas had brought Lillian home from Paris like a souvenir. The other boys at school had teased Edmund without mercy over his grandfather's new bride. It was a terrible time for mother and son. The postcard had led to an interesting conversation with Tom's nanny – a Highbridge girl whom Constance had, for various reasons, later appointed as her housekeeper. She took it with her as she walked downstairs and knocked on her housekeeper's door.

'Mrs Booth, I'm very sorry to disturb you at this hour.'

Mrs Booth tightened the belt around her dressing gown. 'Not at all, Mrs Lassiter. What can I do for you?'

'Do you remember this?'

Constance brandished the postcard. Mrs Booth took it and snorted.

'Oh, her! Not what I'd call a lady. Yes, I remember, Mrs Lassiter.'

'You told me an interesting story. My husband was quite insistent we didn't pursue it at the time, but I wondered if you were still in touch with the friend you mentioned then?'

A malicious smile touched Mrs Booth's thin lips. 'I still know her. And she likes to reminisce, especially with a few drinks inside her.'

'I am very glad to hear it, Mrs Booth. I would be very interested in as many details as you can get from her. Take the card, if you think it would help.'

The card disappeared into Mrs Booth's pocket. 'That would be a pleasure, Mrs Lassiter.'

'Thank you so much, Mrs Booth.'

The ladies bade each other goodnight and Constance went to bed in good humour. The thing about holding a trump card was knowing exactly when to play it.

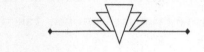

CHAPTER SIXTEEN

Lillian was leaning with her back against the office window, her arms folded.

'It sounds splendid, Grace.'

'A glamorous widow?' Evie said slowly.

It was Tuesday morning, and Lillian's second day as a producer. Grace and Jack had persuaded Miss Fortescue to let them in, to tell Lillian about Grace's thoughts about a role for Evie – and found Evie there, too. Looking at Evie's face, though, Grace felt everything was now balanced on a knife-edge, however warm Lillian's reaction.

'Very glamorous,' Jack said, leaning forward in the armchair. It was a dainty piece of furniture, and he did look a little comical squeezed into it. He also looked – thank goodness – very, very sincere. 'American, too – we thought that would be marvellous, given you've worked on Broadway – and absolutely everyone is desperate to marry her. And she's dashed good fun! Very witty.'

Evie looked at Grace, one delicately sculpted eyebrow raised.

'But she ends up with this Hector, played by Billy Barlow, not Lance's character?'

'That's right, but they have the most marvellous, scene-stealing romance.'

Grace had used the same phrase on a crackling phone line to Stella only an hour before about her romance with Lance, but there would be lots of scenes in which the stars could split the spoils between them like a quartet of bank robbers.

'Have you seen Bill perform?' Grace continued. 'He's terribly dashing. And Ruby has already started working on your first number, when Katherine arrives and all of the Riviera just falls at her feet.'

That was true, at any rate. It was a sprightly tune, called 'What's Next?', with some nice chorus work.

'Very well,' Evie said slowly. 'I suppose it *might* be interesting, but I'd really have to see some pages before I could agree. Lillian, shall we go to the music hall revue tonight? See this Billy Barlow perform?'

'I watched a little last night, Evie, and had supper with Alma and Charlie afterwards. You go tonight – see if you think you and Bill will pop.'

'Have you met Bill, Lillian?' Jack asked. 'He was awfully pleased to hear you were producing.'

Lillian started reading something on her desk. 'In passing. Now, Grace, how long until we have some pages?'

Grace took a deep breath. 'We've got some of the songs. We've got a fair bit of plot to work out yet, but I'm confident we'll be ready to start rehearsals as planned.'

'Excellent,' Lillian said. 'Though Evie will need to see the part and agree it's a suitable role. I'm glad to say Lance has succeeded in persuading Usher Barton to join us.'

Grace felt a sense of great relief and extreme pressure at the same time. She was surprised she managed to stay on her feet. Evie and Jack applauded.

'Yes,' Lillian went on. 'He'll be a great asset as long as we have a play for him to direct. Joe's shenanigans mean we'll have to hold open auditions for the chorus and other speaking roles. I'll call Edison at the *Gazette* and have the advert placed.'

'I'll organise the schedules,' Jack said, 'and talk to Little Sam and Mrs Gardener.'

'Thank you, Jack, dear. Grace, get whatever you have of the book to Usher when he arrives, including your best guess at the speaking parts.'

Lillian returned to her correspondence and Evie picked up a magazine.

Grace and Jack left them to it. In the corridor outside the rehearsal room, Jack turned to her, his face glowing.

'Are you excited?'

'I think I'm going to be sick. I have no idea what the plot is yet! I'm nowhere close to having the full book.'

'You'll get there, Grace. I have absolute faith in you.'

'Why?'

His face became briefly serious. 'Because I think you are brilliant. By the way, what is "the book"? I thought you were writing a script.'

'"The book" is the script of a musical, Jack – the libretto and spoken lines.'

He put his hand on her arm. 'See, you're the expert.'

She shook her head at him, but couldn't help smiling.

'Right, I'm going to need more pencils and a clipboard like yours.'

He swept away down the corridor, leaving Grace feeling

strangely touched and frustrated at the same time. His endless optimism was a support – of course it was – but on what was he basing his faith in her? He approached everyone and everything in this open-hearted way; she never knew if she was special or not.

Jack was up early on Sunday morning. He fed Ollie and propped open the stage door so the terrier could go through his ablutions at the same time Jack did. Within twenty minutes he was making his first cup of coffee at his spirit stove, his morning biscuit on a cracked china plate.

Something caught his eye.

There were people standing on the pavement at the bottom of the alleyway which led from the backyard of the theatre into the street behind. They looked as if they were queuing. Jack looked at his watch. It was not even eight o'clock, and the auditions were not due to begin until ten.

He walked out, Ollie at his heels. It *was* a queue – a great long snake of young people, all chattering like birds. He walked along it and found that it reached to just outside the foyer doors, under the sign announcing the open auditions for the chorus of the new musical of gigantic importance. They had thought they might get a fair few people – but a crowd like this . . . On their own or in pairs, girls were showing each other dance steps; boys were stretching in the morning air, bending from the waist as if they were made of rubber. A fellow in overalls showed off a soft-shoe shuffle to a girl in full evening dress.

Jack heard a familiar step behind him and turned to see Grace crossing the road from the tram stop.

'Good Lord!' she said as she approached. 'Are they all here for the auditions?'

'Morning! Yes, so it seems. And more coming all the time. It means we'll have our pick, doesn't it?'

A tall man in a pale grey suit, who was walking past them, paused. He leant on his cane and examined them both through small round glasses.

'It means hours will have to be spent weeding through hopeless amateurs. At least eighty per cent of these people are delusional, and another ten will be simply bad.'

'Are you here to audition?' Jack asked. 'I'm afraid the queue starts right round the other side of the theatre.'

Pale eyes blinked behind the round glasses. 'I am Usher Barton. Your director. You, I presume, are the woefully inexperienced company manager.'

'Err . . . yes.'

'I'll need coffee – and a great deal of it. May I suggest you find someone to take the names of the people auditioning? We'll see which of them can speak an audible line and sing in tune today, and I'll do dance call-backs on Tuesday morning. Are you Miss Hawkins? The debut writer? Almost a debut writer, I should say, given that the material you've sent me so far is a vague collection of half-formed thoughts.'

'I am,' Grace said in a small voice.

'The songs you sent to my hotel are adequate. When we're inside I'll give you my notes on the little you have so far in terms of a book.'

He lifted his bowler hat to them, and walked off.

'Oh dear,' Grace whispered.

'He's a charmer, isn't he?'

Jack had never seen anyone so untheatrical in the theatre before. The man was so thin as to be almost invisible from the side, bald-headed apart from a neatly razored tonsure, and dressed like an accountant. A thought struck him.

'Are you sure Lillian wrote to the right Usher Barton, Grace?'

'How many could there possibly be?'

'Thank you, Miss Perkins!' Usher called out in a bored voice. 'Next, please!'

'Found any stars yet?'

Bill Barlow sat down at the long table at the back of the auditorium next to Grace and Jack, as Miss Perkins, who had a voice like an angry Pekingese, snatched her music from the piano player and stalked off stage.

'Morning, Bill!' Jack greeted him. 'There's a few decent voices, and some half-decent actors. I keep wanting to call them all back, though, because they are trying so hard, but Grace says that wouldn't be fair on them.'

The next girl announced herself in a voice so quiet, Usher had to ask her to repeat herself.

'Bill!' Grace said. 'What are you doing here?'

He took out the latest edition of the *Highbridge Gazette*, and opened it.

'Thought I'd offer my advice. Need any help with the book? Is Lady Lassiter here?'

'She and Evie are popping in later. By the way, how did you get on with Evie?'

'She's a live wire.' He laughed. 'I think she might be warming to this idea of yours, the merry widow. And I thought, perhaps my character could be a professional dancer? Give him a bit of glamour and me the chance to show off.'

Grace considered Bill's suggestion for a moment. It wasn't a bad idea at all.

'I'll need a solo, too, though,' he went on. 'Maybe in the empty ballroom. Me dancing with the ghosts of my former paramours. First just with props, then the chorus comes in.'

'Waltz or foxtrot?' Ruby asked, settling in beside him.

He carefully picked up a fallen hairpin from his jacket and handed it back to her.

'Throw in a Charleston, Ruby, my pet – I'm game.'

'Talk like that and you'll get a rhumba, Bill.'

He laughed quietly and returned to his paper.

The auditionee was off-key.

'Thank you, next!' Usher called.

'Bill,' Grace began, 'honestly, I can't believe . . .'

Bill licked his finger and turned the page.

'Say it, Miss Hawkins.'

'I . . .'

'You'll feel better, sweetheart. Just say it.'

'Well, it's quite the change, Bill, you coming here on your day off and offering help and advice, given we couldn't get you into the theatre without an armed guard a couple of months ago.'

He didn't look up but smiled. 'Feel better for getting that out?' he asked.

'Yes, a bit.'

'And Lance wasn't armed,' Bill added.

'Only with his talent,' Ruby said. 'Which is considerable.'

Grace leant round Bill. 'Ruby, if you're here, who's playing the piano for the auditions?'

'Tom Lassiter. He's an old pupil of mine. Rather stupid, but sweet, and he can read absolutely anything. Music, anyway. Not sure he does words. I've booked him for rehearsals, too. Much easier if I can watch and take notes, rather than just play.'

They paused while their new director delivered his verdict on the next unfortunate hopeful.

Bill looked sideways. 'So that's the great Usher Barton? I've heard he is an absolute devil.'

'Don't say that,' Jack said. 'I'm dashed scared of him already.'

'I thought you were a war hero.'

Jack gave a weak shrug.

'Less chatter, people,' Usher said crisply from his seat in the stalls a row or two in front of them. 'I wouldn't want any of you to miss a second of this aural torture.'

'How many do you need, Grace?' Bill asked in a whisper.

'Ten lads, ten girls, and a couple of character parts for a start. Bill, I'm in such a mess with this plot. Do you think you might be able to help?'

'Any time, my dear,' but he was already looking over her shoulder.

Grace twisted round. Lillian and Evie had just come in through the lobby doors. She watched as Bill went to greet them. He kissed Evie on the cheek and seemed to be about to do the same to Lillian, but she took half a step back and offered him her hand instead.

'Next!' Usher shouted, and another soul shuffled out onto the stage to be judged.

CHAPTER SEVENTEEN

Ray Kelly's man, Sharps, arrived on foot and went to the tradesman's entrance to collect the car key. At the exact time arranged, Constance and Edmund left their house to find him waiting for them at the wheel of their touring car on the square. They got in, and he drove off without a word.

In ten minutes they were leaving the city of Highbridge behind them, and driving along the dale, climbing towards Atherton Tor. Constance watched the passing scenery. She had expected a house, probably in one of the poorer quarters of town – not this. It was discreet, of course. No one would be likely to see or recognise her or Edmund up here.

Sharps turned on to a narrower road; the climb steepened and he slowed. They were surrounded by moor now, purple with heather, patterned by occasional shadows from fast-moving clouds. The road dipped and Constance realised they were in a sudden shallow valley. A peat stream ran across the road at its base, and just north of the ford was a scatter of buildings, some ruined, but one or two with what looked like functional roofs. There were three motorbikes in the yard, like polished insects. One had a sidecar, and as they approached a collie tied up outside stood up and barked.

Sharps stopped the car, got out and walked to the house. Edmund scurried to get out, then hopped round the car to open the door for his mother.

They followed Sharps inside, and found themselves in a typical Hartshire country cottage: a large, stone-flagged room, deeply shadowed, with a large fireplace; a chimney you could smoke a lamb under. It was cool, even on a high summer's day like this, and sparsely furnished. On either side of the fire stood two high-backed settles. Sharps was standing, at ease, to the right of one. Sitting in it, facing them and nursing a pewter tankard, was a man in his late fifties, with hollow cheeks.

He half stood, just enough to make a sweeping gesture at the other settle.

'Mrs Lassiter, Sir Edmund, take a pew. Sharps, get them both a beer.'

'Mr Kelly, I don't think my mother—' Edmund began.

'Thank you, Mr Kelly,' Constance interrupted him. 'I should enjoy a beer.'

Ray Kelly looked at her. His eyes were a startling green, and the whites of them very clear. It made them look as if they were shining out of the shadows.

Sharps handed Constance a pewter tankard. She could feel the chill of the metal through her burgundy leather gloves. She sipped. Yeasty, but refreshing.

'MacDonald got us your message,' Kelly said. 'You asked to see us, which seems a peculiar request when we have taken some pains to keep our distance from Sir Edmund. So what needs to be said?'

'Well, the thing is, Mr Kelly,' Edmund began, crossing his legs, 'we need to make a few changes . . . The Empire, Mangrave and so on, and we thought it best to come straight to you.'

'We like the arrangement as is, Sir Edmund.'

Edmund half-laughed. 'I'm sure you do! But all good things must come to an end. It's been a useful arrangement and I'm sure you've done jolly well out of it. But The Empire must be sold, for various reasons, and I don't think Joe Allerdyce will want to keep Mangrave on. So there we are.'

Kelly said nothing for a long time, before slowly repeating his words. 'So there we are. We take it you are in a position to pay back everything you owe to us, then, Sir Edmund. What's the figure at now, Sharps?'

'A little over five thousand pounds, Mr Kelly.'

'A little over five thousand pounds, indeed. We can be generous, Sir Edmund. We'll make it a clean five thousand if you pay in cash.'

Edmund choked on his beer. 'Five thousand, is it?'

'You are welcome to see your page in our ledger, Sir Edmund. All those little advances do add up.'

Kelly held out his tankard and Sharps refilled it while Edmund blustered.

'I will, of course, repay you in the fullness of time – when The Empire is sold. Though' – Edmund's tone took on a jocular tone and he wagged a finger – 'you've done well out of having Alexander running The Empire, doing the books and so on. Perhaps you should knock off a few thousand of the debt in recognition of that. We all know what he's been up to!'

'Do we? What exactly *has* he been up to?' Kelly took his beer.

'That is . . . I mean to say—'

'And you don't own The Empire,' Kelly said. 'Only half of it.

And we know, like the whole county knows, Allerdyce wants it all, and dear old Lil has decided to get involved again. No, Sir Edmund, we'll leave things as they are. Now finish your beer.'

Constance held out her tankard. 'That is most refreshing on such a warm day. May I have some more, Mr Sharps?'

Sharps looked at his boss and received a brief nod. Silence fell while the tankard was refilled and returned to her.

'We both have a problem, Mr Kelly,' she said once she had taken a sip.

'We don't have a problem, Mrs Lassiter.'

She kept her voice very even. 'I'm rather afraid you do. If Lassiter Enterprises collapses, and it will without a large injection of capital such as the sale of The Empire would bring, a lot of people who buy your . . . wares and drink and gamble in your pubs and so on, will be out of work. That might hurt you. And Lillian, in spite of her spending habits, does not have quite the same devil-may-care attitude to finance as those young people who've recently been running the theatre. I'm sure she could tell you to the shilling what the box office should be on any given night, and the wages paid, the expenses and so on. And she has something to prove. Mr Mangrave might find it wearisome to produce all those receipts and account books on a day-to-day basis. But I have a suggestion. And please, do call me Constance. I see no need for such formality among friends.'

Kelly gave her a wintry smile. 'Friends, are we? We're listening, Constance.'

Constance wet her lips. 'Alexander Mangrave is a . . . a very talented man, one I think would be a great asset to us at Lassiter Enterprises. For example, he would make an excellent executive manager of the new North Factory and the fancy goods works. He would not have to concern himself with the everyday running, merely keep an eye on them both for us and run the books. Anderson Hargreaves only needs to see the official accounts once a quarter. The various markets the fancy goods are sold at mean we have to deal with a lot of cash business – and then stock has to be transported all over the country, of course.' She looked at him; he was listening with attention and – she hoped – interest, so far. 'Given the friendly relationship we would be building through this appointment, it would be a kind gesture if you tore out my son's page from your ledger, too.'

Kelly drank before he spoke. 'We might consider it, in the fullness of time. Not much good offering Mangrave this . . . interesting opportunity if Lassiter Enterprises is about to collapse, though.'

'It won't if we sell The Empire,' Constance replied, then held up her hand. 'I know, Lillian holds a large interest, and Allerdyce won't bite unless he can have the whole thing. But you can leave her to me.'

He held her gaze for a long moment. 'Can we now?' Then he sniffed. 'We like a woman of character, Constance, so we'll consider a new position for Mangrave if you manage to sell. Till then, we'll keep him where he is.' That wintry smile again. 'You can find your own way out.'

Constance stood up and put out her hand. She was glad to see it wasn't shaking.

Kelly stood up this time and shook it. Edmund put his hand out, too, but that Kelly ignored.

'Goodbye, Constance.'

'Goodbye, Mr Kelly,' she said carefully.

Sharps walked them out of the cottage and watched as Edmund clambered into the driving seat.

'Stay in first gear as you get up the slope, or you won't make it,' he said, taking his knife out of his pocket and cleaning his nails with it as he spoke. 'If you stall, you're on your own. No one here is going to push your sorry arse up the hill.'

Edmund flushed and opened his mouth, but Constance put a hand on his arm and squeezed, hard, while offering Sharps a gracious nod, to thank him for his kind advice.

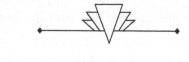

CHAPTER EIGHTEEN

The auditions had been a marathon, an endurance test for all concerned, but from the pile of crushed hopes and wrecked dreams, Usher had plucked ten young men and ten young women he deemed acceptable for the chorus, and a cluster of others for character parts.

For Grace, the days since then had grown blurred and fuzzy. Bill and Jack had kept her supplied with coffee and Flo's biscuits while she shut herself in the overspill rehearsal room and filled page after page with notes, and waste bin after waste bin with crumpled rejects. Lance took her to the Metropole to see Mabel Mills and her jazz band, and tell her stories about the South of France. It was useful, and the music was exhilarating, but she remained befuddled. Sometimes she could see it – Evie's entrance, Lance and Stella's passionate duet by moonlight – and sometimes it seemed to dissolve away again. The feeling that there was something there – something good, if she could just get a grip on the thing – itched at her and kept her working, even when she knew she should sleep or eat.

Late on Friday evening, feeling she was trying to make a patchwork quilt out of pieces which didn't fit together, she had actually shrieked at her typewriter – what had looked workable in her notebook looked ridiculous stamped out on the page. Seconds later a gentle knock at the door heralded an unusually cautious Jack. She tore the page out of the machine and threw it at him. He didn't make a joke, didn't tease her. Instead, he picked up her coat and suggested they go to the stagehands' favourite gin palace round the corner.

He sat her in the corner of the salon, got her a port and lemon, and then said nothing at all. In the strange silence, Grace began to talk about what she thought was working in the play and what wasn't, all by herself. She talked about pace, and character, and how hard writing something light could actually be. Jack got her another drink. Something about his attention, and the sensible questions he asked, made lines and ideas bubble up in her head. That sense she could trust him with all her half-sentences seemed to unknot her muscles; slowly at first, then in a rush, the pieces started to fit together. He got her another drink and she felt, even in her daze of tiredness, very alive. It was as if he was lifting her into cleaner air. Everyone in the bar was a potential character, every sight and smell suddenly inspiring, each scrap of overheard conversation a revelation. Jack let her think, then walked her to her tram stop. She went to bed and woke up two hours later with everything stitched together in her head, grabbed her book and started to write.

Grace walked into town on Saturday morning, before the first tram. While the summer dawn was still blinking its eyes open, she went in through the usual side door to The Empire so as not to disturb Jack and Ollie round the back. From there, she marched through the dark and silent auditorium and up the stairs to the overspill rehearsal room, dropped her coat and bag, got out her book, and began to type. And this time it looked right.

By nine o'clock she had the whole first act. She took it through to Miss Fortescue to cut the mimeograph stencil on her machine while Grace wrote up the entire outline, her typewriter bristling with carbon paper.

'I'm not sure,' Evie said slowly, two hours later.

Grace had handed her the outline of *Riviera Nights* and the first act only moments ago.

'Now, Evie, let Grace tell you about it properly at least.'

Lillian was sitting at one of the trestle tables in the main rehearsal room, looking as lovely as ever in the morning light. Usher was beside her, his hands folded together on top of Grace's work, his face unreadable.

'Jack, are the others coming?' Lillian asked.

No reply was necessary. Stella and Lance entered together, apparently both laughing at something Bill had just said. All three snatched up their copies of the first act, neatly lined up by Jack with their names on the first page and the date in his surprisingly neat handwriting. Ruby was sitting at the piano, reading avidly and making rapid marks on the page with a soft pencil.

'Now we are here, Grace,' Lillian said, 'would you like to tell us what you have? In general terms, at least. I heard Miss Fortescue laughing as she was preparing the copy, and anything which amuses her must be rather good. But perhaps an idea of the plot for both acts?' Usher shot her a stony look. 'If you think that would be useful, Usher.'

'I should be delighted to have the vaguest idea at the moment.' Usher enunciated his words very clearly.

Grace took a deep breath and launched in.

'Evie, your character, Katherine, as we discussed, is a terribly glamorous widow. She's been married three times and each time her husbands have been killed in tragic accidents, but they were all millionaires, so now she's one of the richest women in America. And so she's getting chased by all sorts of fortune hunters all over Europe, but she's terribly bored. Then she spots Johnny.'

'Lance's character?' Evie said. 'I bet she does.'

'That's right – she likes him, but Johnny's in love with Julia. On the other hand, his luxury hotel is in trouble and he needs a new investor. Julia realises this, so Julia tells him he should marry Katherine, not her. Bill plays Hector, Julia's father, but he doesn't know she's his daughter because he ran away to sea when she was a baby. Now he's a professional dancer at the hotel, and a sort of father figure to Johnny.'

People were beginning to look slightly confused. Grace rushed on.

'Then, Evie, you, as Katherine, are set upon by thieves after your jewellery. Hector saves you, and you have your first duet with him. You offer him a reward, but he's much too proud to take it and that intrigues you. Also, there are lots of strange men staying in the hotel and you're worried they're after your money, but actually they've been tracking down Hector, because it turns out he's heir to a kingdom.'

'Hector didn't know he was royalty?' Bill asked.

'He comes from a seafaring family, and the realm has suffered a spate of revolutionary assassinations,' Grace told him, improvising rapidly, 'so when they changed their minds and decided they wanted a king after all, they had to go out on quite a long narrow limb on the family tree. Now he's a king – or nearly – he proposes to Katherine, and she thinks that's an excellent idea, because Lance may be pretty, but she's fallen for Hector and likes the idea of being queen.'

Evie was frowning, and Grace found her heart was beginning to thud like a bass drum.

'Then one of the genealogists finds out Julia is Hector's daughter – so they have a nice reconciliation, but Johnny won't propose to her because she's now a princess, and he's just a commoner. So the genealogists get to work and discover Johnny's actually a duke, so he does propose, and the Hotel Riviera becomes the favourite haunt of all the royalty of Europe.'

'The ones with heads still on their shoulders, at any rate,' Stella murmured.

It had all sounded a lot better in Grace's head, or in the pub with Jack. There was a long moment of silence

'What do you think?' Lillian asked at last.

'Sounds perfect.' Lance jumped up from his chair and kissed Grace on the cheek. 'You're a real gem, Grace.'

'Marvellous, Grace!' Jack smiled at her.

'Talking it through with you was terribly helpful, Jack,' she said, then swallowed. 'And what do you think, Evie?'

Evie looked up and pouted for a moment. Grace couldn't breathe. Would Evie go for it? Would Lillian cancel the whole production if she didn't?

'I would make an excellent queen,' Evie said. 'I mentioned the fact to the Prince of Wales when he came to see me in *Lovely Lady*, but he didn't take the hint for some reason.'

Grace still wasn't quite sure. 'So . . . you're happy?'

Evie winked at her. 'You've given me a story to work with. I shall play Katherine.'

Grace felt a sense of relief so powerful she thought she was lifting into the air. Everyone's voices became indistinct and the edges of her vision grew pink.

'I think it'll be top-drawer,' Bill chimed in. 'Smart, and some nice set ups. Evie, stop counting your lines.'

'Sounds like *East Lynne* on the Riviera,' Usher said, leafing through the pages in front of him. 'But the first act appears competent, and the concept is sound.'

'*East Lynne?*' Lance had wandered over to the piano, and Ruby had gone an alarming shade of scarlet at his proximity.

'I know the one,' Stella said, laughing. 'Where the woman abandons her children, then comes back in disguise as the governess, then the little boy dies. "Dead! Dead! And never called me Mother!"'

'Oh, that!' Jack leant back in his chair and stuck his hands in his pockets. 'My mam had a copy. She said it was sentimental nonsense, but she read it four times. And she cried all the way through.'

'Lil— Lady Lassiter, are you all right?'

'Yes, I'm fine, Mr Barlow. Well done, Grace. I must leave you to it.'

Lillian left the room quickly.

Bill gathered up his copy of the first act.

'I better start learning my words. Ruby, can I run through my nostalgia song with you later? I've got the lyrics, but there's a corner round the key change I can't make stick.'

'Of course, Bill. You know where to find me.'

'Very well,' Usher said. 'Grace, go and write me a second act. Jack, do a breakdown of the first act and take copies of what we have so far to Mrs Gardener and Little Sam. I want the staging areas for Act One marked out on the floor before the chorus joins us on Monday morning. Stella, pick out your first ballad on a piano and learn the lyrics. Mabel Mills will be visiting us with her band on Wednesday. I want you to have all your numbers with them prepared by then, or she will make you look like an idiot in front of the company. Miss D'Angelo, I'd like to talk through the staging of your arrival song. Do you know it?'

'I have had a few thoughts about that, Usher—'

'I said, do you know it?'

Evie stared at him and blinked. 'Yes.'

'Then let's begin.'

Grace floated back to the overspill room and sat on an armchair in the far corner, just for a minute, before she started work again. When she finally woke, late in the afternoon, she found someone had laid her coat over her as she slept.

Bill Barlow did not look for a quiet place to learn his lines. He'd been overjoyed when he heard Lillian Lassiter was coming back from New York in time to see him selling out her theatre every night, but then she'd greeted him like he was no one and barely met his eye since. The anticipated pleasure of the meeting had turned sour on his lips. Lillian was friendly and warm to everybody else in the theatre, but Bill she addressed as 'Mr Barlow', and only spoke to him at all when it couldn't be avoided. He'd waited for her to come to him, not pushed himself forward, but if she was producing this show, something needed to be said, and he was going to say it before he did another minute of work on this play. Full of hurt and indignation, he went straight to Lillian's office, passing Miss Fortescue with only a shake of the head.

Lillian was reading the script at her desk, and her look, when she glanced up, was not welcoming.

'Mr Barlow,' she said, her voice glassy and cold. 'What can I do for you?'

He shut the door behind him.

'For a start, Lil, you can stop acting all high and mighty and say 'hello' like an ordinary human being! If you need to act all 'my lady' in public, fair enough, but it's just us here.' He opened his arms. 'Haven't you got a hug for your old friend?'

Lillian stood up and walked round the desk.

It's going to be all right, Bill thought. He prepared to welcome her into his arms, and that was when she slapped him with enough force to make him stumble.

'Blast it, what the hell, Lil?' He rubbed the sore spot and stared at her. Her eyes weren't cold now – they were blazing. 'I know we didn't part on the best of terms, but there's no need for that!'

'How dare you!' she said. 'How dare you amble in here, and smile at me like that and call me "Lil"? "Didn't part on the best of terms"? We didn't part on any terms at all! You just *left*.'

'Well, forgive me, my lady!' The hurt and confusion curdled into anger. 'That was almost thirty bloody years ago. Now I'm your star! I've packed your theatre for weeks on end. It's my name that's paying the wages of everyone in here at the moment.'

'How kind of you! I heard until Jack Treadwell turned over a rock and found you, you were an alcoholic fish fryer.'

Damn it, I didn't mean it like that, he thought. 'I'm not doing him and Grace and the rest out of the credit they're due. But I'm working hard now . . .'

She turned away, crossing her arms across her chest.

'Lil, we were friends. More than friends . . . When I saw your picture and they told me you were Lady Lassiter, I knew you at once. Lil Lyons! All grown up! I was looking forward to seeing you. Telling you about the hole I got into, and how I ended up back here again. And I didn't tell anyone I knew you back then. I don't know if you're ashamed of those days before you became a big star in Paris, and knowing people like me.' He paused. 'And I stopped drinking during the war, for a matter of fact. I didn't have a lot when Jack turned up, that's true, but I had a job and a place to live and friends – and I did that much on my own.'

She half-turned and he could see the girl, fresh as spring rain, lovely as meadow flowers, and with all that talent and spark, just as he remembered her. He used to watch her from the wings every night.

'I only hoped we could be friends again, Lillian. That's all I was hoping for.'

'Friends?' she said bitterly. 'Is that what we were?'

He studied her face and felt his heart ache. 'No, I'm sorry, Lil. You're right – of course you are.'

He thought of the trains they'd take between theatre towns, her small blonde head resting on his shoulder; of long games of cards in the dressing rooms; her giggle, and watching her drink her port and lemon in a saloon bar, her eyes like saucers.

'But it was a long time ago.'

'You left me, Bill. You disappeared. Do you have any idea what that was like? You walked out of the theatre and were gone. Everyone was asking me where you were. I walked the streets for hours every day for the rest of the engagement, desperately trying to find you. We thought you were dead. I went to the hospitals, in case you were lying injured somewhere.'

Bill had relived that night – the night he dried on stage and walked out – a thousand times, drunk and sober; gone over it again and again. He had never once thought, though, about what it had been like for Lillian and the others.

'I . . . I didn't think.'

'You could have waited!' She balled her hands into fists. 'They bundled me and the other girls straight out on stage the moment you walked off! Twenty minutes, Bill! If you'd waited twenty minutes for me to come off stage again and said something

– anything . . . Even if it was just goodbye . . . But you had disappeared! Not a note, not a word. I came running off to find you, to see what had happened, how I could help, and you were just gone.'

He swallowed, but his throat was dry. 'I honestly thought everyone was better off without me, Lil.'

'Ha!' A single, explosive syllable.

'I did! I swear I did. You were so lovely, so talented, and I was . . . broken. I swear I believed you'd never give me another thought. I loved you . . .'

'Love! You call *that* love?' She looked disgusted. 'I was sixteen years old. God, what a little fool I was. Honestly, when you started taking an interest in me, I thought, "Oh, lucky me, Bill is nothing like the silly boys in the chorus! He's an old hand at all this. I'll be safe with him." And then you ruined my life.'

Bill was startled. Ruined her life? He was beginning to see how bad it must have been, but surely that was going too far given everything she had now.

'Ruined your life? Come off it! Look where you are, Lil! Whatever I was wrong about, I wasn't wrong about that – you were a million times better off without me. You saying you'd rather have been saddled with a drunk in a hovel, rather than having all this?'

'I would trade it all – all of it in a heartbeat – to get back what I lost!'

'Then you'd be a fool! What did you lose? What did I take from you? I was always honourable with you.'

She laughed – a harsh, miserable sound. 'What a gentleman!' She spat out the words, then took a long shuddering breath, trying to control herself. When she started speaking again, her voice was soft. 'You broke my heart, Bill. I loved you, and when you went without a word, it was like the sky had fallen in. I had no family, no one to protect me, and I was scared and miserable and alone. And I thought your leaving was my fault. I thought I must have done something wrong for you to treat me like that.'

'No, Lil. You didn't—'

She held up her hand and continued. 'What do you think happened? Do you think another man didn't spot a defenceless girl when he saw one?'

Of course there had been a man like that, Bill thought. *Why had he never thought of that?*

'Lil . . .'

'I blamed myself for that, too, of course. I should never have let him take me out. I shouldn't have drunk champagne, but I was so miserable and alone. And I should never have let him follow me. I wanted to find the powder room, splash some water on my face. But he pulled me into one of those private dining rooms some of those places had. Locked the door. After a while I just wanted it to be over.'

He didn't want to hear it – didn't want to know.

'It was weeks and weeks before I even realised I was in trouble. I was back in Highbridge then. The other girls in the chorus told me to get rid of it, and I even went to the appointment. A miserable, cruel-faced woman in the back streets of this town! God, my heart goes cold every time I pass the end of that street. But I couldn't go through with it.'

She went to the window, though the view was nothing but one of the light wells of the theatre, and looked out.

'You had the baby?' Bill said. 'Lil, I'm so sorry. How did you manage?'

She sighed. 'I made a bargain, and another woman took my child as her own. I had two days with my baby. *Two days.*'

Bill leant on the back of the armchair, the shock of it all making him dizzy. He had left her to the wolves, and the wolves had found her.

'Bill, I would trade everything that comes with being Lady Lassiter – the money, the theatre . . . God, I loved Barney, but I would have traded my marriage, too. I'd trade them all in a heartbeat for just one day more with that baby.'

His legs couldn't hold him any more. He sat down heavily and wiped his face with the back of his hand.

'I thought you were just too grand to talk to me, Lil. I am so, so sorry. I was a fool and you suffered for it. What happened to the child? Do you know?'

She took a handkerchief from her pocket and wiped her own eyes. 'He never found out he was adopted. I promised – swore – never to try and find him. The woman who took him sent a letter once a year to the post office in London to tell me how they were doing. She raised him well.'

'I should have married you. He should've been mine.'

He put his head in his hands, as a different past unspooled behind his eyes: years of being Lillian's husband; Bill and Lil playing the circuit, good years and bad; teaching their kids the trade.

She gave another half-laugh, a low weary sigh, and he felt for the briefest, most blessed moment, the touch of her fingers on his cheek.

'You could have just left a note, Bill.'

It unmanned him, the deep sadness in her voice.

'Do you want me to leave? The show, the theatre? I'll do it in a second if you want me to. The musical will be good, and you have Lance and Stella and Evie. You'll find someone else to play Hector. I'll understand if you can't bear to look at me. If I remind you of all that.'

He heard her sit down opposite him and risked looking up; the anger seemed to have burned out of her, leaving her pale as ash.

'I don't need to see you to remember it every day, you idiot. Don't leave. Stella, Jack, Lance . . . it would break their hearts if you left. You've made a conquest of Evie, too. Stay, please. Do a good job.'

'Evie doesn't know it was me who left you high and dry?'

A gurgle of laughter. 'No, she'd have tried to throttle you when she met you if she knew. The rest of it she knows.'

'Tell her if you want. I can take it.'

'I will. But I'll tell her I got the chance to deal with you myself.'

'And the man?'

'I'm sure the name he gave me was false. I never saw him again, after that night.'

'Lillian, would you mind if I just stayed here a moment? I can't face leaving this room for a minute.'

She sighed, a long exhausted sigh. 'Yes, Bill, do stay a little.'

And they sat together in silence for a long while, as all the years and memories moved around them in the shifting shadows.

CHAPTER NINETEEN

Wilbur Bowman had had a long day, and he walked through the Barrows with his shoulders hunched as dusk gathered around him. His mother didn't like him living here, though she had been born just three streets over. She and his dad had managed to find a place with a patch of garden up the hill now, and felt that their son living here was a downward move – literally *and* figuratively. He'd explained to her for a man in his profession – a journalist who wanted to keep his eye on the banks and the big industrial players – living this close to the business centre of Highbridge was ideal. What he didn't tell her was that buying rounds in the pubs frequented by the clerks and shop girls, and the hole-in-the wall places favoured by part-time hoodlums, was also perfect for a young man who wanted to know what was going on. Some things you could only find out over an expensive lunch at the Royal Café, some things you found out treating typists to buns at the Lyons' Corner House, and some rumours circulated only in rooms with sawdust on the floor, which stank of sour beer and sweat. Here in the Barrows, he had a good room in a decent boarding house and access to it all.

He passed kids running races with sticks and hoops, and women gossiping over their sewing outside their front doors. Some of the steps were polished till they gleamed; others were neglected, like rotten teeth in an otherwise healthy mouth. He wondered about turning in to the Prince of Wales for a pint of mild, then decided against it – his feet were sore from a day pounding the streets of the city trying to work out exactly what Lassiter Enterprises, and Edmund Lassiter in particular, were up to.

The visit to Newcastle had been interesting. Peter Finch, brother to Cecilia, had plenty to say about his brother-in-law. He painted a picture of a petty tyrant who had charmed his sister, then transformed her from a pretty, carefree young girl into a cowed shadow of herself. He begged Wilbur to tell his sister she would always have a home with them. He was less clear on what Mangrave's criminal activities were, or where he had been for the year between escaping the fraud conviction in Newcastle and arriving in Highbridge.

Wilbur opened the door to his boarding house and climbed the stairs to his room. It was on the first floor: a good-sized chamber with a bit of light, a decent bed, a table and desk, and an armchair to read in by the fire.

Someone was sitting in it, reading.

'Evening, Wilbur. Shut the door behind you.'

The man sitting in the chair was in his forties, with a waistcoat over a very clean linen shirt, and his features were smooth, and strangely bland. A face you walked past and never noticed.

Wilbur hesitated. 'Mr Mangrave.'

'That's right. No need to be nervous. Your landlady is downstairs. I'm not going to cause a fuss in a respectable house like hers.'

Wilbur shut the door behind him and noticed Mangrave's hat and coat hanging on the hook. He took off his own jacket and put it on the hanger. Mangrave had lit the kerosene lamp on the side table. Once Wilbur had taken off his coat, Mangrave put the book aside. It was *The Wealth of Nations*.

'How did you get in?' Wilbur asked.

'Knocked on the door and suggested I wait for you. Do you think I fell in through the window? You've been asking a lot of questions about me, Wilbur. Telephoning people over half the country. Made me curious about you.'

Mangrave tented his fingertips together. His fingers were long and thin, and the backs of both hands were scarred with white slashes.

'How did you get those?' Wilbur asked.

He retrieved his notebook from his jacket and pulled the pencil free before he sat down at the desk. Mangrave watched him with an amused smile on his face.

'A little dog attacked me. Funny, everyone told my mother and father – get the boy a pet. Turns out my pet didn't like how I played. There, I've answered your question. Now I have one. How long you been working at the *Gazette*, Wilbur?'

'Almost two years.'

'Eager little pup, aren't you? That's what all the young men your age look like to me. Like little puppies, yapping and scurrying about. Undisciplined. No experience of the real world – the world as it really is, I mean.'

'It was the war that turned you into the man you are today, was it?' Wilbur asked.

Mangrave half-laughed. 'Indeed it was. I learnt a great deal in the war. A great deal about men – how they live and die. The sounds they make when they are full of holes, but don't quite realise they are dead. Then I came home and found the whole country is riddled with holes, too. Like the sappers had been at work on the home front, burrowing weaknesses into every institution. Collapse of society, some say – new avenues to explore, I say . . . as does my employer.'

'Ray Kelly? Hanson MacDonald?'

Mangrave spread his hands wide. 'Mr Bowman, as you know, I am employed by The Empire theatre and was appointed by Edmund Lassiter. A bold and innovative thinker if ever there was one. I can't imagine why you'd think anything else.' He examined his neatly manicured fingernails for a moment. 'I came here to explain that to you, and to have a little chat.'

'I still have some questions. Did you have a witness attacked to get off a fraud charge in Newcastle in 1919?'

The man blinked. 'What an imagination you have! I said a chat, not an interrogation. That charge was the result of a misunderstanding and I was discharged without a stain on my character. Wilbur, you are just starting out, and you seem like a bright boy, even if you do have fanciful thoughts. You've done well. Got a bit of education. A nice comfortable future in front of you.'

'Thanks very much.'

Mangrave leant forward, as sudden as a snake, and Wilbur only just managed to hide the instinctive flinch. He was staring into the face of this very respectable businessman, but he could taste steel and blood in the air.

'Watch your tone, boy.'

Then he sat back slowly. The threat disappeared and the fingers were tented again.

'Be sensible, Wilbur. I do have friends in this town, I am happy to admit as much. My friends can be your friends, too. A few juicy stories, a little gossip. The inside track – who knows? – sometimes, on some scandal among our besuited brethren at the Royal Café or the club. A tip or two for the races. But there's a trade to be made. In exchange for all that friendly gossip, I want a little discretion. Stop asking about me. Do you understand?'

'I understand.'

Mangrave fetched his hat and set it on his head.

'But that doesn't mean I'll back off,' Wilbur added in a rush. 'Where did you go when you left Newcastle?'

Mangrave opened the door.

'Yap, yap, yap,' he said quietly. 'Remember, Wilbur, puppies don't like how I play. I've asked politely. Now do as you're told.'

He started whistling between his teeth, an old music hall number, and left, closing the door behind him. A minute later Wilbur heard him bidding goodnight to the landlady at the street door, and whistling again as he ambled down the street. Wilbur listened without moving till the sound had faded entirely away, then took a deep breath. The air now, it seemed to him, smelt slightly of sulphur.

CHAPTER TWENTY

Usher slapped down his copy of the book on the table and all conversation immediately ceased. For an uncomfortable minute he stared round the room. Stella, Evie, Bill and Lance were facing him, with the other speaking parts ranged in a horseshoe around them. Beside Usher sat Grace and Ruby, notebooks at the ready. Lillian sat further left. Jack was on Usher's other side with his own copy of the book in front of him, Grace's completed first draft of the play with the songs inserted, an empty notebook, four pencils and a sinking feeling.

'Good morning,' Usher said, his voice dark and heavy. 'Welcome to the first morning of rehearsals for *Riviera Nights*.'

Evie began applauding, but no one else did and, catching the repressive look in Usher's eye, she stopped.

'The principals in this production are not without experience,' he continued, 'but the rest of you are amateurs. You barely know how to sing or act, let alone dance. The writer is an ingénue, and the book needs work, plus our composer is an unknown. The set designer was painting flats a month ago, and our producer has more experience opening fêtes than musicals.'

Jack was not convinced this was a good pep talk.

'If I am to turn you into a cohesive company of seasoned professionals within a month, and it seems I must, you will be expected to do what you are told, when you are told. You will not turn up on time for rehearsals – you will arrive early. You will not go home until I say you can, and when I do say you can, you will then decide to stay late and carry on rehearsing. For the next four weeks, I own the breath in your lungs and the blood in your veins. Usually rehearsals for a production of this sort would start at ten in the morning. I will expect you all here at 8.30. There will be dance training in the morning and singing practice after lunch each day.'

He sat down as Jack scribbled on the first page of his notebook.

'The songs the principals know, they will sing. The other numbers, Miss Rowntree will play to us herself. Begin.'

There was silence. Jack realised everyone was looking at him for some reason.

'Oh, for Heaven's sake!' Usher exclaimed. 'Mr Treadwell, as company manager, you will read in the stage directions.'

'Right! Wonderful. Sorry, everyone.' Jack cleared his throat. 'The entrance to a grand hotel on the Riviera, morning. Johnny, Hector and members of the staff prepare to greet their latest guests.'

Tom Lassiter began to play the vamp of the first song.

'Welcome to the Hotel Riviera!' Lance said, and they were off.

By the end of the first week, Jack had lost all sense of time, all sense of what the theatre was, or art, or music, and no longer possessed a clear idea which direction 'up' lay in. Usher was a tyrant – a tyrant among tyrants, the sort of tyrant who made other tyrants back away in embarrassment.

The only high point had been the appearance of Mabel Mills and her band on Wednesday afternoon. Mabel set her trumpet case on top of the piano and clicked the catches open. She and Ruby hugged and then she turned to the company.

'I hear this show needs some heat. Let me show you what we've got.'

And they did. The other rehearsal rooms emptied as everyone hurried in to listen, and as soon as they started listening they began to dance. When Mabel hit the high notes, the glass in the windows seemed to flex.

When she was done, she put the trumpet back in the case.

'That's what we call jazz – take it or leave it.'

'Oh, we'll definitely take it,' Grace said promptly. 'One hundred pounds a week. Eight shows a week and three numbers a show.'

Mabel raised an eyebrow, considering.

'You'll have two numbers with Stella as vocalist,' Grace added, 'and one just you and the band. On stage, not from the pit.'

Mabel nodded slowly. 'That is acceptable, young lady.' Then she looked over her shoulder at Stella. 'Think you can keep up, sweetie?'

'I'll keep up or die trying!'

Mabel laughed. 'That's the spirit, Miss Stanmore, that's the spirit.'

Then she nodded politely to Usher, who put his hands together and bowed towards her before she left with the rest of her band in her wake.

But that was the only high point.

Since then, Usher had made Stella cry twice – 'For Heaven's sake, Stella, I was told you used to be a competent dancer' – and even Grace – the incomparable Grace – had had to leave the rehearsal room fairly quickly on one occasion: 'Miss Hawkins, this lyric is so trite even Lance can't make me believe he has the vaguest interest in the girl, and he is, when he wants to be, a reasonable actor. Could I please have some lines with spirit in them? It's meant to be the Riviera, and you are giving me tea in Shropshire on a rainy Tuesday.'

Evie actually had sprung to Stella's and Grace's defence, agreeing with her phrasing of the final love song and standing up for Stella, making – miracle of miracles – Usher back down for once. After that, the two female stars of the show seemed to have formed a strategic alliance against their director.

The company snatched what moments away from him they could, practising their steps and lines in corridors and storage rooms. Lance seemed to have made bucking up Grace his special project, as Jack kept seeing them together, Lance staring at her, full of enthusiasm and telling her what a marvellous job she was doing, Grace recovering a little under the praise. Jack would have done that himself, of course – Grace was doing a wonderful job under awful pressure from a maniac – but he spent his whole time running messages to and from Usher and the costume and staging departments, trying to make Usher's insults sound like creative suggestions, and the tart responses like reasonable compromises. Little Sam, in spite of his prizefighter build, trembled at the sound of Usher's voice. Ruby hardly went home, rewriting and re-orchestrating every song half a dozen times, her only reward a pause in Usher's withering commentary. Even Ollie seemed disinclined to do more than sit with Danny at stage door. Only Tom appeared to be enjoying himself, playing the piano ten hours a day and loving every minute of it, in spite of the storms of tears and argument breaking like sudden squalls over his head.

Grace, who had thought once her struggle with the book was over she would be rewriting a line here or there, discovered she was expected to rework page after page until the characters began appearing in her dreams, and one by one they transformed into Usher, snarling at her like a starving wolf. She took to fleeing onto the patch of flat roof outside the rehearsal corridor window to write, even though the weather was unreliable. The overspill room was always packed with people hiding from their director and comparing their blisters. She was sitting there, shivering slightly and staring at her notebook, trying to think of 'hot' things her suddenly lifeless characters could say to one another, when the window opened. For a terrible moment she thought Usher had found her, but it was Stella.

'I knew you had a nook somewhere, Grace!' she said.

Her head disappeared, but she was back two minutes later, a fur coat over her rehearsal suit of shorts and blouse, and carrying a long scarf, which she slung around Grace's neck.

'Last thing we need is for you to get ill, my sweet.' She extracted cigarettes and lighter from her pocket. 'My feet are actually bleeding, and I found Josie, the short girl who does that bit in the "Please Be Our King" number, in full-blown hysterics in the auditorium. Mr Poole summoned me to stop her throwing herself over the edge of the gallery.'

'Is she all right?' Grace asked.

'Yes, we had a chat. Now she's having tea with Marcus and helping him and Mr Poole put the threepenny bits into piles. Apparently it's very soothing. I've never seen someone have actual hysterics before.' She blew out the smoke and put her chin in her hands. 'It's quite something.'

'He's so horrible. Why on earth did we hire him? Honestly, if it wasn't for Lance, I think I'd give up completely.'

'Darling, that is the way they work, you know. Usher tears us all to shreds and Lance builds us up again. And somehow in the middle of all that, we become good.'

Grace stared at her in surprise. 'It seems like a terrible way of doing things – why can't everyone just be nice?'

Stella laughed. 'Oh, stop it, I've seen you crackle when you need to – especially when you're giving Jack a hard time about something, I can tell there's blood in your veins, then. Nice is fine, but too much nice is *dull*. Usher is just trying to get you to spill a bit of *oomph* into the book. Think of the last time a lover made you really angry – throw-the-furniture-at-him angry.' She looked at Grace. 'You've never had a lover? Blimey, how on earth have you managed to preserve your virtue this long? I suppose Charlie Moon warned all the rakes off you when you first turned up.'

'Probably,' Grace said, feeling strangely inadequate. 'Are you and Lance . . . ?'

Stella snorted. 'No, darling. But it helps if everyone thinks we are. Lance is not that way inclined. I rather think he and Usher were lovers once, back in the dim and distant.' She realised Grace was looking perplexed. 'Didn't you know? Usher had to leave London because he was caught with the second male lead of his last show. Would have been all right, but the boy's father got all Marquess of Queensberry about it, so Usher had to hand over a great big pile of cash and then disappear up here.'

'Marquess of Queensberry?'

'Yes, the man who sued Oscar Wilde – "the love that dare not speak its name"? Usher doesn't like women *that* way, darling. Neither does Lance. Did you really not know, you goose?'

The light dawned very slowly upon Grace. 'Oh, I . . . How on earth was I supposed to know without anyone telling me?'

Stella laughed her rich, throaty laugh, which made grown men fall flat on the ground in front of her. 'I suppose I assumed that sort of gossip is just inhaled with the smell of sweat and bad coffee.' She put her arm through Grace's and shuffled up close to her. 'Now, how can I help you? How did you come up with all that fantastic lost children and missing relatives stuff?'

'Jack took me to the pub, one of the scruffy little places some of the stagehands go to. It all sort of tumbled out of me there. But maybe it was a one-off? Lance thinks I should go to America and write scenarios for the pictures. I'd rather stay here with The Empire, but honestly, perhaps I'd be better just typing again and answering telephones!'

'Nonsense,' Stella said. 'Only a real writer could manage what you have. Now I've realised how nun-like your life has been, I'm even more impressed by the power of your imagination.'

'What about you, Stella?'

Stella winked. 'I love everybody when I get the chance.'

Grace shook her head. 'But I can't put all that in the musical!'

'No, darling, that would be an absolute disaster for us all. But you do have to remember this is all about heightened emotion – everything is bigger and brighter in the theatre. Colours, fights, laughs. And look at us all! Sweating and singing and sweeping each other around. Our bodies are our tools, so we're all a little bit more . . . physical than people who spend their time in an office or a factory.'

'I told you I should work in an office.'

'And I hate to repeat myself, but that's nonsense! You ended up in the theatre, Grace. That means you're just as much an animal as the rest of us. Even if you have got that "buttoned up, but what will happen when she lets her hair down?" thing going on.'

'I don't have a "thing" going on!' Grace squeaked.

Stella ignored her. 'You just need to write more from your . . .' Stella gave her a long look, which made Grace feel a little hot. 'Heart. And stomach. The Riviera is hot – *be* hot.'

'I'm not sure I know how. I've lived in Highbridge my whole life. I don't think I'd know hot if it bit me.'

Grace stared at her notebook. She was thinking about Jack: a dozen small moments that had felt as if they were teetering on the edge of something. But he had always pulled away, gone back to his boyish, bouncing manner. Or she had – running away from the edge, frightened of what would happen if she allowed herself to tip forward.

Is that what they are talking about? That moment – and whatever comes next?

She would have to use her imagination. What would happen if they held each other's gaze a moment longer? If she stepped towards him, rather than away? She felt a little breathless.

'That's it, Grace! You, my darling, are coming back to my flat tonight. We'll order in champagne and cocktails and caviar, get stinkingly drunk, and I shall tell you five years' worth of deeply scandalous and deliciously inspiring filth.'

'That would be very helpful actually, Stella,' Grace said, and Stella started laughing again.

CHAPTER TWENTY-ONE

By the end of the second week of rehearsals, the entire company was in a state of nervous collapse. It was Bill who broke in the end. They were rehearsing the 'Please Be Our King' number – a complicated piece with full chorus weaving around one another, improvising thrones out of dining chairs and tablecloths. One of the boys stumbled into Bill and Usher laughed, harsh and derisive. Bill crossed the rehearsal room and got a hand on the director's tie, his fist pulled back ready to swing. Only Lance's catlike reflexes, sending him leaping across the space between them and catching Bill's elbow, saved Usher from being knocked out cold.

Evie shrieked and ran from the room, and Ruby leapt to her feet so quickly the latest parts for the orchestra tumbled to the floor. Usher's coffee cup, thrown from his hand as he cowered from the coming blow, landed right on top of them. Josie and Tom leapt forward with towels to save what they could, while Lance marched Bill off to the far side of the room and kept him there.

'Ten minutes' break!' Jack yelled.

He dropped his book, grabbed Grace's hand and dragged her from the room.

'Are we going to see Lillian?' Grace asked.

'We are,' Jack said. 'This has gone too far.'

Miss Fortescue took one look at their faces and let them pass into Lillian's office.

'Jack! Good morning. Hello, Grace.'

'Lillian, you have to do something about Usher,' Jack said. 'He's been making everyone absolutely miserable. Bill almost hit him! Evie's run away, and just about everyone is in tears all the time.'

'It's true, Lillian,' Grace added. 'He's driving us all mad.'

'It's not just the rehearsal room,' Jack went on. 'Mrs Gardener kept me talking till ten last night, complaining about his costume ideas, and Little Sam daren't come within twenty yards of him.'

Lillian put down the play she was reading. 'I know he's difficult, but he does get results. I saw the first act – it's looking wonderful. You can't possibly want to fire him at this point, Jack.'

'You've no idea what he's like – you haven't been in rehearsals, Lillian. You're in here or away from the theatre half the time.'

'Lance could take over!' Grace said enthusiastically. 'Everybody loves him.'

'Surely it won't come to that,' Lillian said mildly. 'Jack, my dear, you get on with everyone. Can't you just smooth a few feathers? It won't be long now. Let the chorus know how much we appreciate them, and ask Usher to tone it down a little. Grace, tell Ruby I think she's doing charming work.'

Jack and Grace looked at each other. Lillian reached for the play again.

'No,' Jack said.

'What was that, Jack?' Lillian looked back up at him with a frown.

'I said no. I am company manager. I have no authority to tell anyone anything other than when the rehearsal starts – I certainly have no authority over the director.'

'But, Jack—'

'Lady Lassiter . . .'

Grace looked sideways at him, as his face had become terribly serious as he said Lillian's name. Not amused, or rueful at all. She hardly recognised him.

'Please, I asked you to call me Lillian—'

'Lady Lassiter!' Jack said again, with real ferocity. 'You told Joe Allerdyce that you weren't going to dabble—'

'I've been here every day!'

'You said you were going to produce this show! Not just pop into rehearsals and applaud every now and then, then read plays in your comfortable office the rest of the time! Grace negotiated with Mabel Mills, not you, and we didn't even think about it, but Grace is not our producer – *you* are! She's got her hands full writing the show! If there's a problem with the director and the stars, that's your problem. Not mine, not Grace's. If you don't want to do the work, you might as well sell us out to Joe Allerdyce.'

He turned and left the room, and Grace followed.

Lillian watched the door close behind them and set down the play. She was shocked. Things had been going well – or perhaps it would be better to say that things had been going well for her. Her encounter with Bill had loosened some tight knot in her, and being here made her happy. She remembered what Joe Allerdyce had said about the last day's work she had done in the theatre being when she was on stage. She had the awful, baffling feeling he might be right.

Has being Lady Lassiter all these years made me soft, lazy? Jack Treadwell appears to think so.

She stood up and smoothed her skirt. She was not unaware of what had been going on. She heard plenty from Evie each night, and Mrs Gardener's complaints and Little Sam's requests for a budget to build more and more elaborate sets had been silting up on her desk. She opened the door.

'Miss Fortescue, could you summon the company and department heads to the rehearsal room, please?'

Miss Fortescue picked up the telephone. 'When would you like them to gather, Lady Lassiter?'

'Immediately. Let me know when they have assembled.'

She closed the door again and went to the window, looking out on to the city street far below, preparing.

Jack went straight through the doors at the end of the corridor, then paused at the staircase as Grace came running up to him.

'Jack Treadwell!'

He leant his back against the bare wall of the half landing. Somewhere further downstairs, a girl was singing the chorus of the second act nightclub song.

'What?' he said crossly.

'You always seem so . . . unserious, Jack! The jolly good fellow and friend to everyone, and then you do *that!*'

'Was that too much?' His face was still missing any sign of amusement. He looked older suddenly, the shadows emphasising the sharp angles of his face. 'I'm just so bloody tired I don't know what I'm saying half the time.'

'I don't know if it was too much or not.' Grace replied.

'Someone had to say it, I suppose. I've just never seen you like that. It was . . . well, terribly impressive.'

Jack looked away, and Grace remembered in a sudden rush what it was so easy to forget about him: that he had led men into battle; that most of the men he had joined up with had been killed. That he'd survived one great tragedy, only to lose the family he thought he was coming back to in another. It was impossible usually to see those losses in Jack, but she could now.

'Why did you spend all that time in France?'

He smiled swiftly at her, surprised at the question. 'I wanted to see what everyone had died for, I suppose. And I wasn't really fit company. It took me a while to feel something like myself again.'

She put her hand on his shoulder, the tweed of his jacket soft and well-worn under her fingers. 'I'm glad you did find your way back, you know. It's not simply an act, then? Happy Jack, friend to everyone?'

He shook his head. 'No. I can normally laugh my way out of anything. But sometimes the laughing isn't enough, not if you care about something, and you have to care about *something*.' He sighed. 'Some fellows, they've sunk under what they saw out there. And Lord knows I sometimes feel it lapping round my feet – but mostly I want to enjoy every day I'm not in Hell, for my sake and the sake of the people I left there.'

It had felt natural to leave her hand on his shoulder; now she felt his hand on her waist. She could feel the warmth of his palm through the cotton of her blouse. Now Grace understood what Stella had been talking about.

'Grace, I—'

The door to the corridor swung open and Bill peered round it.

'Message from Fortress Fortescue. Lady L. wants to see the

company and heads of department in the rehearsal room now. She's ringing round.'

'Thanks, Bill,' Grace said, then as he retreated, 'What is it, Jack?'

His hand moved very slightly on her waist. She could feel the pressure of each finger against her skin.

'Do you think, that perhaps, you and I—'

'Oh, bloody buggering Hell!' Stella was running up the stairs towards them and the voice singing in the distance stopped abruptly. 'I only just got down to Milly for my fitting and then Marcus comes dashing in and says I have to come up again! I still have pins in me. Mrs Gardener and Little Sam are on their way up, too. And wigs.'

'Stella!' Jack dropped his hand from Grace's waist. 'Things have reached crisis point. It's the fall of the house of Usher, or something.'

Stella giggled. 'I do love a good crisis. Come on then, my little cherubs.'

She had pushed open the door and was waiting for them to follow her, her weight on one hip in her shorts and high heels, her hair slightly disarranged. Jack all but sprang after her. Grace followed a little more slowly, wanting her breathing to steady a little before she faced the company.

Usher was back in his usual place at the front of the room with his book and his pencils. Evie, wearing a long kimono over her dance practice costume, had reappeared and was sitting in a chair on the other side of the space, her arms folded. Lance and Bill were at the piano with Ruby, their backs to Usher. Stella sashayed across to Evie and the women air-kissed, then put their heads together for a bout of intense whispering. Jack took his usual seat next to Usher, and Grace went over to join the group around the piano. The rest of the chorus drifted in, followed by the backstage department heads. Then they waited.

When Lillian entered, she walked into the centre of the room and put her hands on her hips.

'Good morning!'

Several voices, mostly from the chorus, mumbled a good morning back to her.

Jack had almost forgotten she used to be on stage. You couldn't help remembering it now. The woman certainly knew how to command a space.

Evie jumped out of her seat and pointed dramatically at Usher. 'Lil, I have had it with that man! For Heaven's sake, I am Evangelista D'Angelo! I have not come here to be treated like a fourth-rate chorus girl. He *berated* me yesterday, and if dear Stella hadn't stepped in, I think I should have screamed!'

Usher said nothing, only watched, one eyebrow raised and a vague smile on his grey face.

'He has to go! Lance can take over – everyone is saying so!'

'Miss D'Angelo, sit down!'

Evie stopped dead and looked long and hard at her friend. Then sat down.

'Thank you.'

Lillian turned round, catching the gaze of each of them as she did, then spoke quietly. 'Now, listen to me, all of you. Usher Barton has turned you into a company. He has done it by pushing you all to your limits, and sometimes beyond them. Good. That is his job, and that is why I hired him. I was there at the run-through of the first act yesterday, and it's superb. You all know it, and you all know it wouldn't be superb without him.' One of the chorus girls tutted. Lillian rounded on her. 'One more sound out of anyone – anyone – before I'm done, and they'll be fired. Understood?'

The girl nodded, then stared at the floor.

'Evie, if you are late for rehearsals one more time, you'll be fired, too.'

Evie started to protest, but Lillian raised her eyebrows and her friend bit her lip.

'Grace and Ruby – put some blood into that last ballad. Everyone in this theatre, from seventeen to seventy, man and woman, needs to be desperate to take one of the principals as a lover before the curtain comes down. Enough with milk-and-water missishness. Mabel Mills and her band are supposed to be set off by this show – we haven't hired them to show us up. Jack, stop trying to be everyone's friend and let people do their own jobs. Mrs Gardener, if you have a problem with Usher's requests, you can come and tell him yourself. Jack is company manager now, not your errand boy. Little Sam – grow an inch or two. From now on, you will come up here and show the models to the company like any other set designer. Chorus? You are all of you ten times the singers, dancers and actors you were when you arrived here a fortnight ago, and I expect you to be ten times better when we open. Yes, I could sack Usher and ask Lance to run the show, and I'm sure you'd all have a much nicer time, but the show won't be as good, and we want this to be brilliant. I won't settle for pleasant. I will not settle for mildly entertaining. I want a smash. Am I making myself clear?'

A certain amount of throat-clearing and murmuring indicated that yes, Lady Lassiter was making herself clear. It wasn't enough.

'I said, am I making myself clear?'

'Yes, Lady Lassiter,' came the rather shamefaced response.

'And you,' she said, turning on Usher. 'No, there will be no swimming pool number and no, there will be no mirrored dance floor. I don't know what sort of fool you think I am, but if I see one more deluded request on my desk for light airplanes landing from the flies or steam trains pulling up centre stage, I will sack you. You can create your illusions with artistry and stagecraft because that is what you are paid to do. I will not fund whatever wild experiment comes into your head. You wouldn't dare put them on the desk of one of your West End producers, so don't put them on mine. And now that you've managed to drum some discipline into this group, you will treat them and your remarkable young creative team with the respect they deserve and some basic courtesy. But I expect' – Lillian scanned the group around her again – 'them to continue giving their all. No more tale-telling and back-biting, please. I shall be moving into my flat from tomorrow until opening night. Evie, you're welcome to stay at Lassiter Court, or move into the Metropole, whichever is more convenient.' She looked at her watch. 'Thirteen days and nine hours until we open. I suggest you get on.'

Then she left without looking at any of them.

As the door shut behind her, there was a collective exhalation and a sudden burst of chatter.

'Ladies and gentlemen,' Usher said, 'Act Two openers, please. Evangelista, do you know the steps?'

'I do, Usher,' Evie said, shedding her wrap.

'Thank you so much. Remember, everyone, it's about the third beat in the bar. Keep hitting that hard and we'll get along splendidly. In your own time, Tom . . . and Jack, please could you make a note of any of the changes we need to communicate to Mrs Gardener.'

'Yes, sir,' Jack muttered, and picked up his pencil.

CHAPTER TWENTY-TWO

Tom arrived early for rehearsals the next day. He looked at his watch, then around the quiet corridor, hoping someone else might be around. Silence. He sighed, then walked to the far end, to the staircase which led to Lillian's flat. He should have known that when his mother had given her nod to his playing piano for rehearsals at The Empire, there would be a price to pay. And there had been.

Tom didn't like his home life much at the moment. Edmund and Constance were always muttering together. The other week, they had shut themselves up with the housekeeper, Mrs Booth, for half an hour, and when she had emerged, Constance and Edmund had been gleeful. Then they gave him his orders.

The door to the flat was unlocked. Lillian, he knew, would still be at Lassiter Court with Evie, just getting ready to motor into town for rehearsals. Her flunkies would come with her clothes for the next fortnight this afternoon. Danny was already at his post downstairs at stage door, of course. He had given Tom a smile and a good morning when he came in. Jack had patted him on the back as he passed, book in hand and pencil behind his ear. Even Ollie hadn't growled at him. Their welcome made him feel even more of a heel now. Why would Lillian lock the door to her flat? They were all a team, after all.

He had protested when his mother gave him his mission, told them it wasn't the done thing. He'd even told Edmund he was very surprised that he would tolerate the suggestion; what about being an officer and a gentleman? His answer had been a look of such utter contempt that some small part of Tom's soul had shrivelled in shame.

The flat was rather grand, featuring a large room, big enough for entertaining a decent crowd. There were Turkish rugs on the wood floor and low settees and armchairs in pale green leather scattered about; light poured in from the rose window that took up almost all of the south wall. It certainly didn't look like a Parisian brothel, which is what his mother had told him to expect. He wandered over to the window and looked out. It gave quite a view over the town hall. There was a short, sloping tiled roof outside, then a sudden plunge to the pavement. To the right and left, the view down the main street was blocked by the red-brick corner towers, and he could see the backs of a couple of statues.

Interesting that they carved the backs as nicely as the fronts.

Perhaps, he thought hopefully, *there will be nothing to find here at all.*

There were a few framed posters on the wall, mostly in French, and a few sketches. He found the kitchen, a bathroom, and then the bedroom. His skin crawled. He had been very fond of his grandfather, and Lillian had never done him any harm. It felt wrong to be here.

He went in. This was a much smaller room, still modern, in

pale greens and creams. The bed had a sweeping carved head, and the furniture was all done with rather sinuous lines.

Best get it over with. Where to look?

The bedside drawers were empty, as were the cupboards and chests of drawers. One more door: a private dressing room with a large vanity table. The top drawers on either side contained a smattering of cosmetics and creams, but the second drawer was packed with printed papers: old programmes from Belle Époque Paris; yellowing menus covered in signatures. And under them . . . letters.

Tom took them out and glanced through them. Mostly short notes – love or congratulations from actors and performers, some of whose names sounded familiar. A few other friendly notes from playwrights and producers written before the war, but nothing scandalous. He shut the drawer again, his fingers feeling dirty, but his heart lightened. He could report back that there was nothing at all of interest to his mother and brother here.

Then something under the dressing table caught his eye: a small, battered leather case, tucked into the shadows in the corner. He pulled it out and placed it on the bed. Once it had been designed to lock, but it was not locked now. The leather around the catches was worn smooth, as if it had been opened ten thousand times. He slid back the clasps. Two neat stacks of envelopes, tied with ribbon, the rest of the space packed with tissue paper to stop them rattling about. Tom's heart sank again.

Yes, this would be what Mama wanted.

He took one of the stacks and pulled away the ribbon. They were all addressed to Lillian Lyons, care of the Charing Cross Post Office, 'to be collected', and all in the same careful feminine hand, though the stationery and ink colours changed. Cheap paper. He glanced at the postmarks: exactly one a year – only that, as far as he could tell. The oldest was 1890-something. He took three of the envelopes at random, then retied the stacks, put the case away again and left the flat.

All day the purloined letters seemed to exude a guilty heat in his jacket pocket, increasing to a sudden burn whenever any member of the company thanked him for his playing.

'Perfect. This is absolutely wonderful – well done, Tom.'

Tom had never earned such high praise from his mother. It made him feel sick now.

'Do you want to know what's in these?' Constance asked teasingly, waving the cheap stationery at him.

'No, I don't.'

Tom left the library, and closed the door behind him.

'Goodness, what's peeved him?' Edmund said, coming across to his mother and handing her a drink.

'It doesn't matter,' Constance said, her eyes dancing. 'Edmund, do take a look! Absolute proof! Mrs Booth's friend was right. And that's not all.'

He took one of the letters from her and read. He blinked. Read it again.

'Well, I'll be absolutely blown!' The clouds parted, borne away by the fresh, cleansing breeze of this absolutely terrific news. 'This is ripping good news! Mama, you are a marvel!'

'It's the sort of brazen behaviour we should always have expected from someone of Lillian's background. Now we have this in our pocket, she will have to sign her shares over to you! We can sell the theatre, invest the capital in Lassiter Enterprises before any more awkward questions about those unfortunate investments are asked, and appoint Mr Mangrave somewhere that will be helpful to Mr Kelly and no harm to us.'

'Are you quite sure, Mama, an ongoing relationship with Ray Kelly is a good idea?' Edmund said doubtfully.

Constance shrugged. 'It would be no bad thing. If your workers ever decide to go on strike, I am sure Ray knows a few people who could dissuade them, for example.'

'You might be right there. What's up? You're frowning again.'

Constance put down the letter and stared at the short stack, idly brushing it with her fingers as if the cheap paper was actually mink. 'Only, I wonder . . . Lillian is somewhat odd – dashing off to New York and then coming back with that awful actress friend of hers. And now getting so involved with the theatre! People of her class do the strangest things, sometimes. What if she decides simply to face down the scandal? She is spending her time with theatre people now, rather than society, after all, and they will visit anyone!'

Edmund pondered the possibility. Would respectable people go to a theatre run by such a disgraced female? Probably, as long as they weren't expected to shake her hand. He shuddered, thinking of Lillian's brazenness. His grandfather had spoilt her – addled by her Parisian tricks, no doubt. The rusty wheels of his brain turned. 'But what if it's not *her* reputation she wants to protect? Mothers do anything to protect their young, don't they? You women are like tigers when the cubs are threatened.'

She smiled and nodded at him over her whisky glass. 'That is true, dear.'

'Well . . . What if – just supposing – someone had helped themselves to something from the collection at the gala meant for the Veterans' Fund? A hundred pounds, say, in fifty-pound notes?'

Constance looked shocked. 'Edmund, you didn't?'

She cares about that now? Balderdash.

'It's not my fault! I was in the lobby waiting for you to finish talking to your set. The donation box was right beside me, and I saw Jonathan Foss and David Tompkins both put in fifty-pound notes – making a great show of it. The box wasn't even locked.'

'Edmund . . . The Veterans' Fund? Let me be clear. You, Major Sir Edmund Lassiter . . . You stole from the Veterans' Fund?'

He sniffed. 'It hadn't reached the Veterans' Fund yet, so I'm not sure I did, technically, Mama. Anyway, I *am* a veteran! And Foss and Tompkins were both just showing off to each other. You know, the big, "Oh, I shall just put in this fifty-pound note. Hard to fold up, aren't they?" "Yes, I shall do the same. They should make the slit in the top wider!" Stupid old duffers. You could just lift the lid. That's what I did. Put the notes in my pocket. Just a moment of spite – I'd probably have put them back, but you arrived right at that moment.' He crossed his legs to stop his foot from jiggling, the way it did when someone was being unreasonable. 'They were both drunk! Who puts in fifty pounds? Even the lord mayor only put in a guinea, and he made a fuss about that. I bet they both woke up with sore heads, regretting it in the morning.'

She shot him a look and he fell finally silent.

But she couldn't bear to look at him for long. Not straight away.

Love, she thought, staring into the fire, *is a difficult thing*.

She loved Edmund, but her devotion had grown more complicated of late. Each failing of his that she discovered set off a hundred small memories of times she had blindly defended him in the past. Nevertheless, the more she realised how much he needed her – how much he needed her to fight for him – the stronger her devotion grew. She had sunk her whole life into him – into the idea of him. He was Sir Edmund Lassiter, war hero, benefactor, businessman. She would brook no challenge to that, and face this challenge as she had so many others and turn it to their advantage.

'They talked about it? Foss and Tompkins?' she asked at last, and Edmund nodded. 'And I think you are right. I doubt anyone else would have put in a fifty-pound note. I can check the bank receipts, but I think it is very unlikely the bank receipts will show two fifty-pound notes being paid into the Veterans' Fund accounts the next day with the rest of the donations. That proves the theft. Now, to point the finger of suspicion. The theatre is full of disreputable characters, after all, and we want it to point in a very particular direction.' She sighed, the pieces falling into place in her head to form a very pleasing picture.

'I can say I saw the chap do it,' Edmund added with enthusiasm. 'Or saw him near there. Lots of people were milling about.'

'You'd be happy to lie in court? If it comes to it?'

Edmund only shrugged, as if the answer was so obvious that it wasn't worth wasting his breath on it.

CHAPTER TWENTY-THREE

Agnes de Montfort had never had cause or inclination to consult an architect. Lassiter Court was already built when she fled her marriage to live there with Emilia and Barnabas, and her own home had developed in its own way over several centuries. She enjoyed the odd inconveniences of Manor Farm: the strange cupboard that held remnants of a blocked-off spiral staircase, now crowded with unnecessary crockery; the way the rooms fell into and out of one another in a pleasant tumble, rather than being arranged according to a grand plan. Still, when Joe invited her to come along and see the plans for a new project at the firm of Palmer, Dixon and Brown, before lunch in town, she was interested enough to accept.

The architects were based in the centre of the city. As Agnes parked her car, she noticed posters advertising The Empire's latest upcoming attraction—*Riviera Nights*, a musical comedy. She realised she was rather looking forward to seeing it. The gramophone had opened her eyes to the pleasures of revue songs, and she was coming to think that the business of the theatre and the business of horse racing had a great deal in common. You recruited, bought or bred up talent, cared for it, trained it, and then let it loose on the world or the racetrack and hoped your instincts had been correct. There was a lot of hard work and risk involved, but when a bet paid off, the satisfaction was immense. She must share that thought with Joe over lunch – it would amuse him.

The offices were full of a certain masculine energy which reminded her of Sir Barnabas and of Joe – a mix of no-nonsense practicality and focused, inspired energy. It was rather refreshing. Joe and Dixon first showed her some of the plans they had drawn up for a new picture house Joe was building in Manchester. The drawings were lovely in themselves: delicate and precise visions of bricks and mortar; supplemental pages showing the ornaments planned for the frontage.

'This will be the one your elder son is to manage?' Agnes asked.

They had spent enough time together over the summer for Agnes to have a clear idea of Joe's family. He had been widowed before the war and had two sons, both of whom had followed him into the business.

'Yes – Arthur.'

'Almost as challenging a client as you, Joe,' Dixon said, looking at the plans with satisfaction. 'Arthur has a talent for asking for the impossible in such a reasonable tone of voice, you can't help agreeing to it.'

Joe grunted, and Agnes knew that meant he was pleased with the compliment.

'And now, for my place.' Joe rubbed his large hands together.

Dixon summoned an assistant, and together they unrolled a scroll of heavy paper extracted from the shelves behind them and weighed down the corners with glass paperweights heavy enough to fell a pony.

'Your place?' Agnes said. 'You have a house. Are you building another theatre in Highbridge?'

'No. I'm getting old. I want a bit of space and more fresh air than I can get in town. Francis, my younger lad, will take over the town house and I'll move into this.'

He tapped the plan in front of him. Agnes stared at it. It seemed that Joe was not planning a semi-retirement into a pleasant cottage or something of that ilk. The structure was enormous, like a steam turbine hall, with huge glass windows and a free-standing staircase, sweeping up to a number of bedrooms and, to Agnes's eye, what looked like an unnecessary number of bathrooms.

'I had Dixon draw up the plans a couple of years ago. What do you think?'

Agnes studied the plan and artistic rendering in front of her. 'I think you must be a lot richer than I thought.'

He laughed. 'I've had some luck, and the harder I worked, the luckier I got. But what d'you think of the design?' He had a distinctly mischievous look in his eye.

'It looks ghastly – the sort of thing one of those terrible American oil barons would build for themselves. You *are* an Englishman, aren't you?'

Joe chuckled. 'Not at all your style, I see. I spend half my days in backstage offices or surrounded by the gilt and flummery of the music hall. I want light and space in my off days.'

'It will be rather hellish to heat.'

'A summer palace. Now I've been looking for somewhere to build it, and let me tell you, I think your north paddock would be just the spot.'

He certainly had the capacity to surprise her.

'Joe, have you been surveying my land under the guise of friendship?'

'You know I haven't, woman,' he replied gruffly. 'But once I saw the spot, I knew it was the place for this.'

He tapped his large finger on the paper. Dixon had folded his arms and taken a step away – a man well used to this sort of diplomacy.

'I could not,' Agnes said emphatically, 'tolerate that eyesore.'

'Ah!' Joe's pleasure only seemed to redouble under this withering assessment. 'That's just the thing. You won't be able to see it. Orientated to the west, and hidden behind the hill and that patch of woodland. You'll be able to come and go to town, to the stables and to the training grounds along the ridge, and never know it's there. You'll only be able to see it from the Westgate road, and you never go that way. But' – he lifted his forefinger – 'if you wanted to come and see if I'd frozen to death or experience modern plumbing for once in your life, I'm planning a nice little path through the woods. So it'll be a ten-minute stroll from the bottom of your garden.'

'"In Xanadu did Kubla Khan a stately pleasure-dome decree",' Agnes quoted, staring at the plans.

'Poetry now, is it?' Joe asked.

'I think that's about as much poetry as I have.'

'Will you sell me the land, Agnes?'

'I will charge you an absolute fortune for it.'

'I'd expect no less.'

She considered for exactly fifteen seconds. 'Yes, then. I'll sell.'

Bill made his way to rehearsals in a cheerful mood. The deal that Lillian had brokered – or demanded – between Usher and the company was holding. Usher's courtesy could still be acidic, and even praise from his narrow grey lips could sound like a threat of imminent dismissal, but as the company redoubled their efforts, he had taken a slight step back.

Usher was very good. Bill had never worked with a choreographer before, and it had been a challenge to understand what the man wanted at times. Bill had never learned the names of the steps he'd performed in his own act. He had watched other stage performers, then improvised. He had never learnt to read music, either, always trusting his ear rather than his eyes. The need to learn so much, so quickly, had done something to the demon voices in his head, though. They had been stunned into silence – most of the time – by the new words and music swilling constantly round his brain. And when they did return, Lance's trick – that flick of the fingers – was still working.

'Bill!'

He turned and saw Jack heading towards him, with Ollie at his heels.

'Morning, Jack.'

'I've been taking Ollie for his morning walk. There was a fierce disagreement with a Pekingese about whose turn it was to sniff a lamp post in the municipal park.'

Bill bent down and scratched the terrier's ears. 'Who won?'

'Ollie made his opinions clear. How are you feeling about the show?'

'I think you're bloody lucky to find talent like Ruby and Grace under your own roof.'

Bill noticed Jack's instinctive smile at the mention of Grace's name. Jack's and Grace's feelings for each other were a regular topic of gossip in the company. Everyone was quietly convinced they were in love, and amused that the only people who hadn't realised this fairly obvious fact were Jack and Grace themselves.

They walked together round the back of the theatre and up to the rehearsal rooms. Flo and Jessie had worked their usual early-morning miracle of making the place respectable again. The tea urn was set up, and the detritus of the previous day had been thrown away or neatly stacked to be reclaimed by its careless owners.

Lance was in the middle of the room, arguing about something with Usher.

'Look, it will just be better if Stella crosses, and I grab her wrist and swing her back towards me. Where *is* Stella?'

'With Ruby,' Tom said from the piano. 'She and the chorus girls are learning the beach number. Shall I fetch her, Lance?'

Lance shook his head. 'No, you'll do. Just watch this, Usher. Tom, start upstage and stage right, and cross in front of me, saying Stella's line.'

Tom hurried to do as he was asked. He managed a fair impression of Stella's racehorse walk, crossing in front of Lance and announcing, 'Why are you so pig-headed?' over his shoulder.

Lance caught hold of the wrist of his upstage arm and spun him round, then put his hand to young Tom's face.

'I can't stand to see you waste your talent like this,' he said tenderly. Then he relaxed. 'See, Usher?'

'Yes, yes. Run it with Stella.'

Bill watched Tom return to the piano.

'He's turned out to be quite useful, hasn't he?'

Jack was arranging his place at the long trestle table: pencils, notebook, his expanding folder of technical notes.

'Who? Tom? Yes. Grace said he'd never spent time at the theatre before, but he was one of Ruby's private piano students. He's been staying late, copying parts and all sorts of things. I don't think we're paying him, either.'

Bill watched as the blushing Tom returned his hands to the piano keys, and suspected he knew why Tom was so interested in the theatre all of a sudden.

'Lance!' he called. 'Are you free to go through the duet before the main rehearsal starts? Usher, I want to try something. What if Johnny and Hector are clearing up the ballroom? The crowd will get a kick out of me doing a version of my musical hall schtick with the chairs, and if we make it like I'm teaching the trick to Lance.'

Usher nodded. 'How are your knees holding up, Bill? Can we risk you jumping between tables?'

'On them, under them. The next number is the beach one, so I can have a breather. Give us a challenge. Something a bit more than the usual soft-shoe shuffle and a skip up and down the staircase. What do you reckon, Lance?'

'Sold! I haven't had the chance to fight anyone with a chair since my last Western.'

Bill rubbed his hands together, and the demons said not a single thing.

Wilbur waited patiently for the woman to appear. He had been waiting for days, on and off, but Cecilia Mangrave very rarely left the neat house near the middle of town in which she lived, and she never answered the door. The maid always said she was not at home. Then, finally, Wilbur got lucky. On a sunny Thursday morning, she finally appeared.

He did not want to alarm her, so he followed at a distance, and when he saw her turn in to the Lyons' Corner House, he was relieved. It would be much easier to approach her somewhere like this. She sat in the centre of the room, and something about the way the staff greeted her made Wilbur think she was a regular customer.

He approached the table.

'Mrs Mangrave? My name is Wilbur Bowman. May I sit with you for a moment?'

Cecilia's hair was oddly arranged, covering one side of her face almost completely, and she wore an old-fashioned hat which put much of the rest of it in shade. When she looked up, he realised she was older than he had expected. The lines around her eyes were deep, and her lashes so pale as to be invisible. She seemed too stunned at being addressed to respond. Wilbur took her silence as consent, and took a seat opposite her.

'I'm a reporter, and I was wondering if you could tell me about your impressions of Highbridge? You and your husband are notable people, and relatively new arrivals. Now, before you came to us, you lived in Newcastle and then . . . ?'

'Sheffield,' she whispered. 'Highbridge is nicer.'

'And what was your husband doing in Sheffield, exactly?' Wilbur kept his tone as light as possible.

Cecilia looked back down at the table, so the hat obscured her face entirely from view. 'I don't understand Alexander's business. I don't discuss it. I mustn't discuss it. It's private.'

'He was a clerk in Newcastle, I think? He's done very well to rise to his current position.'

Cecilia looked up again. This time she lifted her head higher and her hair fell back, slightly exposing a purpling bruise on the side of her face. 'Please go away.'

Wilbur was shocked. Ferreting any details of Mangrave's past from this woman didn't seem important any more. He remembered the flash of rage Mangrave had shown him in his room. What hell life would be to be trapped by such a man.

'Mrs Mangrave, I have recently been to Newcastle. I met a Peter Finch there. I think he is your brother.'

'I don't know him. Please go away.'

Wilbur had to get this out quickly. 'At once. Only Peter and his wife both told me they wished that Cecilia would visit them.'

'No. They're glad to be rid of me. Please go away,' she said again. 'This is my one escape. Alexander doesn't know. He thinks I go to the library. I do, but first I come here. You're ruining it.'

Wilbur felt a lurch of pity. 'They did ask after you, Mrs Mangrave, and spoke of you with great affection. Peter and his wife said there was a home for you with them.'

'He'll kill me if I try to run away.'

Wilbur drew in his breath sharply. 'If you need money to leave, I'll help you,' he said, not knowing if he had the means, but knowing he had to say something. 'You can ask for me at the offices of the *Highbridge Gazette* or leave me a message there at any time.' He wrote quickly on a page of his notebook, then tore it out and tucked it under her plate. 'This is my name, and Peter's current address. Peter said he knew Mr Mangrave could be a charmer. They don't blame you for being taken in.'

'Go away.' This time Cecilia spoke loudly enough to be heard at other tables.

Wilbur stood up at once and bowed formally. 'I am very sorry to have troubled you.'

He made his way out of the tea shop, feeling the suspicious stares of the other diners as he went.

He paused on the pavement outside, more shaken at seeing Cecilia Mangrave than he had been by her husband's visit to his boarding house. And what had he learned? That Mangrave had spent time in Sheffield. Perhaps Mangrave had come to the attention of the local reporters there?

CHAPTER TWENTY-FOUR

Lillian had seen very little of Mangrave since she returned to The Empire, and hadn't gone out of her way to see him. Now she had exerted her authority over the company, she realised she needed to find out what was behind Joe's dislike of Mangrave, too. It was true some of the productions he had brought in had been unimpressive, even before Allerdyce had gone to war with them, and no one in the theatre seemed to have had much to do with him. Each head of department, from Frederick Poole to Little Sam, had been simply going on as usual, collecting their wages. Lillian arranged to be informed when Mangrave was in the building, and went to see him. That led to a dull hour, listening to him recite figures from the payroll and bills for ongoing maintenance of the building, while she stared at the scars on his hands. He knew he was boring her, and seemed to take a great deal of pleasure in it.

When asked to account for the time he spent outside the building, Mangrave looked down his nose at her and talked about sourcing materials and meetings with influential business people in town. He mentioned lawyers, councillors and licences. Did she know how difficult it had been to make sure The Empire retained the right to sell alcohol? How important his lobbying had been to ensure the new number 10 tram line had a stop close to the theatre? She thanked him through gritted teeth for his efforts and asked to see the books. It took almost a week – and some fierce reminders from Miss Fortescue – before they were delivered to her office. She had not had a chance to look at them when the technical rehearsals began: long complicated days of lighting cues, scene changes, and Jack brandishing a stopwatch for the quick changes of costume.

Poor boy is looking more exhausted every day.

Released at last from those responsibilities, Lillian went through the books carefully now, noticing where the theatre had gone dark while they turned Ivor French's monstrous sow's ear into a profitable silk purse. Grace and Ruby, it seemed, had simply given French the songs they had rearranged and rewritten. She made a note on her writing pad. Then the smash of the music hall. No payment recorded for Charlie Moon, and they had got most of the acts very cheaply.

It was so long since she had been forced to think about money. Barney had always encouraged her to get the best of everything – for herself, their home and the theatre. It had taken some getting used to after growing up watching every penny, and she had kept her eye out for a bargain and made sure that when she paid for quality, quality was what she got. Still, actually seeing the tight margins The Empire was running on was a reminder of the choices which had to be made when income was not, apparently, inexhaustible. Insurance was a ghastly expense. Necessary, though. The numbers began to dance in front of her eyes.

A thought curled in her mind. It all looked reasonable, but something wasn't right.

The figures add up and make sense, so what is it?

She thought of her own chequebook, which was written in a dozen different pens and inks. These pages were all so clean. She ran her finger over the top one. So even, and the last page of the ledger as fresh as the first . . . almost as if they had all been written at the same time. She thought of the books she had spotted in Mangrave's safe, left slightly ajar during that sadistically dull conversation. They had looked like real account books – a little worn at the edges from frequent handling. Not like this.

Miss Fortescue tapped lightly at the door.

'Lady Lassiter, Sir Edmund's office just called. Would you be free to see him and his mother tomorrow morning? They are bringing Mr Hargreaves with them.'

'What on earth could they want? And on the day of the dress? Very well. Yes, I shall see them.'

Ollie jumped up in his basket and started growling. Danny Moon looked up to see Sir Edmund Lassiter, his mother, and a sheepish man in a black suit entering his lobby. Edmund stared at Danny's mask.

'Do you know who I am?' Edmund demanded.

'Y-yes,' Danny replied, looking back at him with loathing.

'Then you'll know I am part-owner of this theatre. With that authority, I am ordering you to wait outside – and take that mutt with you.'

'We'll just be a minute, son,' the sheepish fellow said. 'Just go out into the yard for a while.'

Danny put Ollie on his lead and took him outside. The little dog was still growling.

'I don't like it either, Ollie,' Danny murmured.

Edmund's face brought back bad memories. Bad sights crowded his eyes. Bad smells filled his nostrils. But that wouldn't stop him. He put his finger to his lips, and Ollie quietened. Then Danny crept quietly towards the window.

Evie read the page and snorted with laughter, while Grace perched awkwardly on the dilapidated armchair which took up one corner of the dressing room, afraid that if she relaxed, the ancient piece of furniture would envelop her and she'd never be able to stand again. Evie had only moved into the number one dressing room since technical rehearsals had begun on Tuesday, but she had already transformed it. The walls were covered in posters advertising her various triumphs, or with sheet music featuring her face on the cover. Every flat surface was draped with material, as if one of Mrs Gardener's storage hampers had exploded, and the air smelt of roses and greasepaint.

'Yes, that's much tighter. I'll run it with Bill before the dress.'

Grace examined her as she reread the scene. Evie was normally so grand, you couldn't help looking at her, and for the first time Grace suspected this was something she could turn on and off. At this moment the switch was off, and she was an actress studying her lines.

'You'll be able to use it this afternoon?'

Evie shrugged. 'I don't see why not. Bill has a quick ear, and most of his lines are the same. The back and forth is like a dance, and he's quick at that, too.'

'You're amazing, Evie.'

'I am, but honestly, you should see what they put us through on Broadway. During out-of-town previews you're rehearsing one version of the show during the day, and performing a slightly different one at night.'

'I haven't shown it to Usher yet.'

'You better had, dear, though the thought of simply springing it on the old goat is appealing. The staging won't be altered. You really are very good, Grace.'

It was a sober, professional assessment.

'Thank you.'

Evie put down the paper and turned her attention to the mirror. 'Though that puts you in a bit of bind, doesn't it?'

'Does it?'

Evie ran her hand across her neck and shuddered. 'Of course it does. What are you going to do? I know there is a fashion for being one of these "new women" who spend their time in an office making their bosses look good. You've been doing that for Mangrave, and you could do it for Jack. But you are better than that. You have the vision, the creative talent. You need a helper of your own.' She reached for her powder puff and patted it under her chin. 'And, of course, writing is a lonely business. You'd miss all the fun of actually being here.'

Grace didn't reply; just looked at the notebook she held on her knees. Only a few months ago, the idea of writing anything that might actually be performed had seemed a ridiculous ambition. When anyone had even mentioned her writing she had grown hot with embarrassment. Being bright and efficient and saying 'good morning' to Frederick Poole every day had been exciting enough, but still safe. Now, here she was, with her own name next to Ruby's on the posters outside. She still wasn't sure if she was thrilled about it, or strangely upset.

Evie's eyes suddenly brightened; the switch had been flicked to 'on' again.

'Darling! I have it! Grace Hawkins – writer and director! That way you'll still be in the midst of the action – all the drama – but you'll be forced to retreat to your country pile for a couple of months every year with Ruby, to pen your next theatrical sensation. I am a genius.'

'Evie, I couldn't possibly . . .'

Evie held up her hand. 'Now, Grace, I'll have none of that. The world is full of shrinking violets who flutter their eyelashes and say "I couldn't possibly . . .", and then are vaguely surprised when people take them at their word. It's an awful habit we women have.' Evie pointed at her with the powder puff. 'And I know you can be as fierce as you want when you are working in the interests of the theatre. My agent has told me that. You just need to be a bit fiercer in your own interests. Promise you'll never say "I couldn't possibly . . ." ever, ever again.'

Grace laughed. 'I'll try. But I don't think I'm a country pile sort of girl, Evie.'

'Rubbish – you are one hit and a decent haircut away from being exactly that.'

'You know, Evie, I think I would like to direct. Perhaps not musical theatre, but maybe straight drama or comedy.'

'There you go. Tell Lillian that. You've had a masterclass, of sorts, from Usher.' She spun the paper round. 'Can we change the word order on this line? So I can really land on that "blessings"?'

Grace nodded. 'Yes, that's better.'

'Miss Evangelista?'

The two women looked up from the page to see Miss Fortescue at the door. She had a magical ability to know wherever anyone was in the theatre at any given moment.

'Yes?'

'Mr Barton is asking to speak to the company immediately in

the rehearsal room, before we break for lunch, then Lady Lassiter was hoping you might find her in her office.'

Evie stood up and Grace gathered together her notebook and the new pages.

'You look worried, Miss Fortescue. Is Lil all right?'

Miss Fortescue bit her lip. 'Yes . . . That is . . . Sir Edmund and his mother called on her a little while ago.'

'Those horrors would upset the constitution of an ox,' Evie said. 'Constance has probably made some poor waif accept her son as a husband and wants to give Lillian her marching orders from Lassiter Court. Now, Grace, you will go and speak to Lillian about directing, won't you? Don't wait to be asked.'

Grace made a note. 'I will.'

'Promise?'

'Oh, Evie! Yes, very well! I promise.'

'That's the spirit.' Evie checked her profile in the mirror one more time. 'I shall come and see Lillian as soon as Usher dismisses us, Miss Fortescue.'

Evie and Grace entered the rehearsal room in time to see Lance and Stella finish their new scene from the end of Act One. Most of the rest of the company were lounging around the edges of the room, watching in rapt silence.

Usher sat back in his chair, his hands behind his head, and smiled. Grace blinked to check she wasn't hallucinating.

Yes, that was definitely a smile.

'Well, that scene is considerably . . . warmer in tone.'

'I'll say,' Stella said, disengaging herself from Lance's embrace.

'Will you have time to learn the new lyric and lines for this evening's dress, Stella?'

'I shall, Usher. It'll be a pleasure to rehearse.'

A general ripple of laughter ran round the room. Stella ambled over to the side and pulled her cigarettes out of her bag. Two of the young men from the chorus pushed each other aside in the race to light it for her. Usher stood up.

'Not too bad, Grace. Who have you been studying with?'

Jack and Usher both looked, with some suspicion, at Lance.

'Lance has been a great help, but Stella took me in hand,' Grace said cheerfully, delighted the scene seemed to have gone over so well.

Now everyone looked at Stella. One of the male chorus members gave a nervous squeak. Stella only pouted her lips and blew out a cloud of smoke.

'Settle down, everyone,' Usher said. 'Well, the dress rehearsal is at five. It will, of course, be a complete disaster. Don't let that put you off. We have a good show. By the time the curtain goes up tomorrow evening, it will be an excellent one. Enjoy your afternoon. You are free until three. Gather on stage afterwards for notes.'

'You don't have any notes for us now?' Bill asked suspiciously.

'Not at the moment, Mr Barlow. I'll take my lunch at the Metropole, if anyone needs me.'

With that, Usher picked up his notes and left the room. Evie followed him.

'Well, I'll be damned,' Bill said. 'Whoever drugged his tea this morning, keep doing it.'

'Grace, that was very good,' Jack said softly. 'I mean, I always knew you could do it, but I didn't know you'd be able to do it this well.'

She smiled at him. Another moment of quiet, serious Jack; the intensity of his gaze. Something fluttered in her stomach.

'Grace?'

She turned away from Jack to Ruby. 'Yes, Ruby?'

'I must just check that lyric for the "Please Be Our King" number again. Can you come to my office for a moment?'

Grace would much rather stay right there and hear Jack expand on his theme of how talented she was. But she was always professional.

'Yes, of course. Jack, do you need anything from me right now?'

'Everything, always and forever,' he said, but in his brightest and most bustling tone.

The company began to fall into their usual groups – the little gangs who ate together or rehearsed together. Most fetched sandwiches out of their bags, but Bill and Lance decided on a chop for lunch. They asked Jack to join them, but he declined. He still had notes to go through. A comfortable quiet had descended on the room when Evie stalked in. She spotted Jack at once and slammed down her hands on the table in front of him, her face ugly with rage.

'Evie?'

'Don't you "Evie" me,' she hissed. 'You devil! She's selling! That's right – Lillian is selling. The theatre and the production company, all to Joe Allerdyce. Heaven knows what will happen to us, and it's all your fault!'

'What in God's name are you taking about?'

Jack stared at Evie in complete bafflement, but for once in her life Evangelista D'Angelo seemed to have run out of words. She stared at Jack with an expression of disgust, then stalked back out of the room.

Jack followed her, then turned towards Lillian's offices. He wondered if Lillian had been offended by that drubbing he had given her about doing the work of a producer, but she had been absolutely magnificent five minutes afterwards, and in the days between then and now she had been clear and decisive about any decisions which came up. Perhaps Joe had been right and Lillian had just 'put on a show' in the last couple of weeks while secretly hating it, and so had now decided to throw it all in. *But why do it on the day of the dress rehearsal?* Jack thought. *We open tomorrow! The show is superb. Even if Lillian has decided to give up the theatre again, how can she do it today? The theatre and producing company to be sold at once to Joe Allerdyce, and in total? The man can close down the musical just for the hell of it. And why is it* my *fault?*

Jack could feel the blood beating in his ears as he reached the outer office and walked past Miss Fortescue, who rarely got to announce anyone, then he shoved open the inner door.

'What on earth are you doing?' he said, all thoughts of due deference and politeness driven out of him. 'How dare you do this to us all?'

Lillian was standing at the window with her back to him, and when she turned, he saw her face was white.

'Jack! Evie told you? For goodness' sake! I can't discuss it now . . . The theatre will be sold and that is that.'

'But can't sell us down the river now. This is insanity!'

'I don't have a choice!' Lillian exclaimed. 'Perhaps you should have thought of that before you stole a hundred pounds from the Veterans' Fund!'

Jack felt himself rocked back on his heels; it was like the pressure wave from an explosion – the sudden sense of the air being torn out of his lungs and his body strangely weightless.

'*What?*'

'There's no use denying it! My God, Jack! How could you? David Tompkins and Sir Jonathan Foss both contributed fifty-pound notes. They remember it quite distinctly and have signed letters to that effect. Constance kindly left copies of them for me. Neither of those notes arrived at the bank – I've seen the cashier's receipts.'

'I'm sorry to hear any money has been stolen from the fund,' Jack said, 'but why would you think *I* took it?'

'Anderson Hargreaves, the accountant, found one of the notes during a search of your belongings downstairs.'

'Nonsense! I would never,' Jack said slowly, 'never in a million years – not even if I was starving in the street – steal from anyone, and damn you, Lady Lassiter, for thinking that I would.'

'I know you were hard-up when you arrived here. Mrs Gardener told me you had hardly anything but the clothes you stood up in, and Flo had to feed you until your first wages came through, but to take money from the fund! Money that would be going to your old comrades like Danny! I suppose the other note went on your making yourself so comfortable. Fresh flowers every other day, they tell me.'

'Dash it, that's just not true. I had twenty pounds of my own when I arrived here. Yes, I didn't have any evening wear, but I had a decent suit and half a dozen shirts. I had no call for much else, working behind a shop counter in Paris. Mrs Gardener is romanticising if she says anything else. She found me decent clothes for the gala, and I thank her for it. Flo gave me two tins of biscuits, but I bought my own dinner every night from the restaurant behind the theatre. And as for the flowers – they were ones which wouldn't fit into Stella's dressing room.'

'I . . . But the fifty-pound note?'

'I've no idea how it got there, but it is nothing – *nothing* – to do with me.'

Lillian covered her eyes with her hands. 'Edmund says he saw you acting suspiciously near the donations box, Jack. That's why

Hargreaves agreed to search your things with him. You had much better just admit it.'

'Edmund!' Jack spoke the man's name in a sort of disgusted gasp. 'Lillian, for God's sake, tell me you don't believe a word that man says.'

'Why shouldn't I? I don't like him very much, but he is a war hero and Barney's grandson.'

'Lillian, he's . . .'

Jack stopped himself. Whatever he thought of Edmund was between him and the men they had both served with. He turned away from Lillian, desperate for a moment just to think. When he did, he discovered he had questions, not answers. He turned back towards her slowly.

'Why am I talking to you and not clearing this up with a member of the local constabulary?' he asked, his voice icy calm.

Lillian paused. 'Constance suggested that she and Edmund would be willing, if I agreed to the sale, to say no more about the theft. To avoid scandal.'

'That doesn't make sense.' Jack shook his head. 'You didn't hire me. What's the worst thing anyone could say? That Grace gave a veteran a chance and he turned out to be a bad lot? You'd get sympathy, not scandal. And besides, I didn't do it.'

'Then how did the note end up in your book?'

'It didn't! Not by my hand, at any rate. Let them accuse me. I'll see Edmund in court.'

She spoke in a rush. 'No, Jack, you can't risk it! A theft like that – it's six months' hard labour at least.'

'I don't care,' he said simply. 'All you're doing is robbing me of the chance to clear my name, and meanwhile betraying the trust of everyone in this theatre – Stella, Evie, Lance, Grace . . . And after everything Grace has done for The Empire, you're just going to announce to her she'll be working for Allerdyce, if she's lucky, and you're off?'

Lillian shook her head. 'It can't be helped.'

Jack was baffled. 'Lady Lassiter, have you gone quite mad?' he said. 'Oh, Lord, is this for my mother's sake? For a woman you knew over twenty years ago? I've no idea what you think you owe her, but I can tell you this as sure as I stand here – she'd tell me to stand up for myself and tell them all to go to Hell.'

'It's n-not up to you,' she stammered. 'I have made my decision.'

'It *is* up to me! Do this and I'll tell everyone. I'll tell them what I was accused of, and that I'm innocent.'

She put out her hand. 'No, no, you can't, Jack! Six months' hard labour and the scandal – you'll never work again. Edmund said he would testify he saw you hanging around near the collection box.'

'And Stella will say that's nonsense. I left the party with her. We had a glass of champagne at the Metropole and listened to the music, and it was a wonderful end to a marvellous evening.'

She laughed. 'The word of an actress won't be taken over the word of a baronet, Jack.'

'Would you believe her, though?'

'Yes – yes, I would, but in a court of law—'

'It's my choice to risk that.' He took a step towards her desk. 'I've told you, I'm innocent. I've told you what my mother would say, but you still insist you'll sell The Empire to protect me? We're practically strangers, Lady Lassiter, so what in God's name is going on?'

He reached the desk and saw something under the blotting pad: a familiar brand of cheap stationery, handwriting that was desperately familiar. Without thinking, he plucked it free.

'What . . . What's this?'

'No, Jack!'

Lillian stepped forward, but he held up his hand.

'This letter is from my mother,' he said very slowly. 'So you were in contact . . . Why did Mam never mention . . .'

He read on.

'But this is all about me. This is . . . This is from years ago – my school report, and me getting into trouble for playing in the hay barn. Favourite foods, the books I borrowed . . . There are pages of it. Why on earth would she think you'd be interested in all this?'

He looked at her, and as he did, in that long moment of silence, a thousand tiny moments from his life prickled into his consciousness: the people who said he didn't resemble Bessie or Fred; the moments he felt as if his parents looked at him like he was some wild changeling. The time – he couldn't have been more than six – when a neighbour had complained about morning sickness, and his mam had replied she wouldn't know about that, then got embarrassed and said something about charcoal biscuits. His height. His fancies. His impetuous nature. The scrapbook, and that message which had taken so long to reach him.

He spoke it out loud.

'"When Jack gets home, tell him to go and see Lady Lassiter." Lillian, what . . . what are we to each other?'

'Jack . . .' She lifted her hands, a sort of appeal or prayer. 'Jack, I am your mother.'

Jack felt a rushing in his ears. It was as if everything he knew – everything he had seen or heard or thought – had simply been an image in a mirror, and someone had just struck a hammer blow through it.

'I thought you were dead,' Lillian said, speaking quickly. 'Bessie wrote and told me you were missing, presumed killed. Then never wrote again. I didn't know it was because she and Fred had died themselves. She promised to write every year, as long as I didn't try and find you, and she did. Photographs, too, sometimes – though the last one was taken before the war. She promised to tell you about me when you were twenty-five, but she didn't live to . . . I thought you'd died without ever knowing . . . without knowing that . . .'

'That I'm your son.'

'Yes.'

Jack couldn't move.

'I have dreamt of seeing you every day, Jack, always wondering where you were, if I might walk past you in the street some time. I saw you at the gala, but I thought I was just seeing ghosts again – you were dead, after all. Then when I was in New York, I saw your name in the newspaper. We came home at once. I can't tell you what it was like, watching from the upstairs as you got out of the car at Lassiter Court. I thought I would die of happiness, or excitement, or shame. It was the best moment of my life. Then seeing you every day since, being so proud.'

'So Evie knows?'

'She always did. When I met her in Paris, I was still recovering, but she is the only person who does. I never told Barney. It was the only secret I ever kept from him.'

She approached warily, inching towards him round the desk.

'Who is . . . my father?'

'I don't know.' She saw an expression of surprise on his face and she hurried on. 'No, Jack, please, it's not like that. I was young and stupid and had just had my heart broken. Your father . . . Well, he was just a man. He managed to get me alone, and thought . . . thought he was entitled.'

'Is that why you gave me up? Because he—'

'No! Oh, Jack, please – never think that. You were innocent! I gave you up because I was poor and afraid. Bessie and Fred had always wanted a child and I knew you'd be safe with them – and loved. Oh, it broke my heart, but I knew they'd look after you.'

He couldn't look at her, couldn't stop looking at her. He needed to get away and think for a second. He thought of his mam and dad, the wrenching pain of losing them, and now, this impossible thing.

'I need to . . . I . . .'

He started towards the door, but she grabbed hold of his arm.

'Jack, the theft—'

He shook her off. 'I stole nothing. You trusted Mam and Dad – Bessie and Fred – to raise me, so you should know they raised me a great deal better than that. I need to think, Lillian.'

He walked out stiffly through the outer office and into the corridor, but she followed him.

'Jack, please! Don't go!'

Then he turned back towards her. She looked so fragile in the doorway, so heartbroken. Whatever his own feelings, he couldn't help feeling a stab of pity for her. He opened his arms. She collapsed against his chest and he held her, his head on his shoulder.

'Don't worry. I'll be back. I'm stage managing the dress rehearsal this evening, after all.'

She gave a small gulping sob, and he gently released himself from her embrace. Then he turned and walked away. Neither of them noticed Grace watching, pale and open-mouthed, at the other end of the corridor.

ACT III

CHAPTER TWENTY-FIVE

Ivor French, actor-manager of the French Company Players, could have picked a better moment. As soon as he had decided a visit to The Empire and its people would be wise, Ivor had left on the first train to Highbridge, and it was only when he arrived that he realised he had done so a couple of hours before the dress rehearsal of a major new production. He consoled himself that the only thing worse than turning up before the dress would be to turn up just before the first night.

At least this time he could afford to stay in a decent hotel. Ivor had enjoyed – no, more than enjoyed – he had revelled in the most successful summer of his entire career. *Macbeth!!* had been playing to packed houses around the provinces. He had been fêted in Edinburgh, celebrated in Newcastle, and brought the house down in Birmingham. It was possible it had all gone to his head a little. Certainly, when he approached the stage door of The Empire, he was a great deal better dressed than previously.

However, even after his recent triumphs, and while blossoming in his new prosperity like a freshly repotted houseplant, Ivor French was not without worries. A London producer, a man who regularly staged musical entertainments in the best theatres of the West End, had been present on one of their triumphant nights in Glasgow and taken Ivor and his wife, Sylvia, for a splendid supper afterwards. Ivor had never seen so much cutlery and clean linen, and had to restrain himself from stealing a fork as a souvenir. So far, so pleasant. The producer had thought the show stupendous. He wanted Ivor and his company in London, but he wanted something new. The same wit, the same comedy, the same mix of music, mirth and Shakespeare, but not *Macbeth*. The London audiences would want an Ivor French production all of their own. How about *Much Ado About Nothing*?

Ivor agreed – and then was forced to admit, to himself at least, he had no idea what had made *Macbeth!!* a success. He put together a few songs, cast himself as Benedict and his wife as Beatrice, then in a panic decided to return to the magical place where his fortunes had been transformed and beg Grace, Jack and Ruby for help.

Ollie stood up in his basket and barked at him. This was accompanied by a tail wag, however, which was encouraging.

'Good afternoon, Ollie. Is Mr Treadwell here? Jack, dear boy, it is I!'

A figure of about the right height was standing with his back to Ivor, but when he turned round, Ivor saw a man whose face was half-covered in a mask.

'Sir!' Ivor exclaimed. 'What a marvellous aspect you have! I am Ivor French, actor-manager of the French Company Players. And I very much hope to have a word with my good friend Jack Treadwell, or Miss Grace Hawkins.' He put out his hand.

The other man shook it. 'I'm Danny Moon.'

'Ah! Son of Charlie Moon, once manager of this establishment?'

Danny nodded. 'I never had the pleasure of putting on a production here under your father. He and my agent never could agree terms, but I have heard only good things about him.'

Before Danny could reply, the internal doors opened and Evie appeared in a black skirt and vivid scarlet blouse, dotted with ornamental buttons and black embroidery. She also wore sunglasses, which Ivor had seen only in magazines before, and found fascinating.

'Miss D'Angelo!' Ivor breathed, and swept a low bow. 'What an honour this is.'

Evie offered him a hand. 'Charmed, I'm sure. Danny, if Lillian needs me, I shall be at the Metropole, resting.'

'Y-yes, miss.'

Danny made a note in his book. While Ivor was still bowing over Evie's fingertips, the doors opened again. This time it was Jack who came through them, but not with his usual tumbling enthusiasm. His shoulders were hunched and his eyes down.

Evie whipped her hand away from Ivor and held it to her chest. 'You!'

Jack glared at her. He seemed angry. Ivor found this fascinating, too – through all the slings and arrows and sound and fury of the restaging of *Macbeth!!* he had seen Jack look disappointed, confused, mildly horrified and desperate, but never angry.

'Dash it, Evie, I'm not a thief! From the Veterans' Fund? I can't believe you thought it possible, even for a second.' He caught sight of the others. 'Oh, hello, Ivor.'

Ivor opened his mouth, ready to launch into one of the little speeches he'd prepared, but Jack just held up his hand.

'I can't stop now, Ivor.'

And with that, he was gone. Ivor had never seen him that close to discourteous, either. It was an afternoon of revelations. He swivelled his eyes back to Evie. She removed her sunglasses, and a slight blush coloured her cheeks.

'How could I not believe it? A fifty-pound note found among Jack's possessions, two fifty-pound notes missing from the donations box at the gala! While Jack was dressing out of lost property, and Edmund told Lillian . . .' Miss Evangelista D'Angelo had momentarily lost her poise. 'Though, of course, it seemed out of character. Oh, it's all hellish! Poor, poor Lillian.' Late for an actress of her experience, she remembered her audience. 'Good gracious, I oughtn't to have said a word. Don't say anything, will you, Danny, and . . . Mr French, isn't it? Lillian wouldn't want it talked about.'

Danny nodded.

'I am the soul of discretion, Miss D'Angelo,' Ivor said in his lowest and most sonorous tones. 'And a request from an angel, such as you, has the weight of a command from the Lord God Himself, to me.'

She smiled at him. 'You are sweet.'

She put on her sunglasses again, lifted her chin and made a creditable exit.

Ivor stared hard at the door through which she had left, then swivelled towards the young man behind the desk.

'Mr Moon, do you know the character of that young man, Jack Treadwell?'

'Yes, Mr French. We s-served together in the . . .' He trailed off.

'Did you, Danny? Did you indeed? Jack and I, too, in a manner of speaking, have served together. In the trenches of the theatre, under the barrage of time, dodging the rifle bullets of critical disdain, and then on to the sunny uplands of a magnificent victory. I would trust that young man with my life and stake my soul on his integrity.'

There was a slight pause as Danny caught up. 'Me too, sir.'

'Indeed.' Ivor leant on the counter and flung the longer end of his scarf round his neck. 'It seems to me that some skulduggery is afoot. Would you agree, young man?'

Danny nodded.

'The Fates have sent me here, Danny. I see that now. I came to ask for help, but instead I shall offer it.'

Ollie barked and wagged his tail, which Ivor acknowledged with a graceful nod of his head.

'Are you a detective, Mr French?' Danny asked hopefully.

'No' – Ivor raised his eyebrows and nodded to himself – 'but I have played the renowned sleuth Sherlock Holmes twice, and I immersed myself thoroughly in the role each time.'

The young man's face glowed with enthusiasm in the most gratifying manner. 'And I know about . . . about the note!'

Ivor removed his jacket and scarf and came round the counter to hang them on the coat rack.

'The Fates again, you see? We shall be discreet, we shall be thorough and thoughtful. Reputations are obviously at stake, and no doubt there are darker doings behind this of which we know nothing.'

'I know about Edmund, too. He's a c-c—'

'A cad?' Ivor supplied, his face now twisted into an expression of deep sagacity. 'Undoubtedly. I, too, have encountered the young baronet. I was a guest at his club in this very town during my run, and heard him speak disrespectfully to the waiting staff. | I had him down as a blackguard from that moment onwards. Now, let us put our heads together and clear the name of our noble friend. Coffee first!'

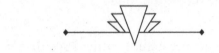

CHAPTER TWENTY-SIX

It had been clear from the moment Evie stepped off the train in Highbridge and posed for the photographer of the *Highbridge Illustrated News* that she and Stella would be competing for the best dressing room. Grace had rather cleverly pre-empted the problem, designating the two best available dressing room one and dressing room A. Evie's was a couple of square feet larger, but Stella's was three feet nearer the stage. Bill and Lance had decided to take the principal chorus room to share. It was almost as close to the stage, and it had enough space in it for them and an ancient leather sofa which they took turns sleeping on when not needed on stage during the technical rehearsals. The arrangement suited Bill well. His demons seemed in awe of Lance and shut up when he was around, or at least quietened down considerably.

Changed into street clothes, Bill opened the door and leant against it, waiting for Lance to finish combing his hair so they could go and eat their lunch.

'You're pretty enough already, sweetheart,' he said.

Lance glanced at him over his shoulder. 'You might get away with your rough good looks, Bill, but my public like me to look as if I've just stepped off the film set.'

Bill grunted. 'You looking forward to getting back to the flicks when all this is done?'

'I will be in a couple of weeks, when we're into the run. Naturally, when I'm back on set, being yelled at to look more in love and angry and tender at the same time, I'll miss this. I might even miss you.'

Bill grinned and looked out into the hall. Grace was walking towards them, very fast, her face drawn and eyes red.

'Grace, love!' he said. 'What's happened? You're not nervous about the dress, are you? You've written a great show. You and Ruby should be proud. If we muck it up, it's on us.'

She shook her head. 'I'm just . . . I just want to be alone and there's nowhere in this theatre to have a minute to yourself! Even my place outside the rehearsal corridor, on the flat roof – I thought no one knew about that, but the chorus has taken it over. There's always someone singing or sunbathing out there. Or tap-dancing. They've taken a bench out there! Lord knows how they managed to get it through the window.'

Bill put a hand on her shoulder. 'Hang on, pet. Lance! Grace needs a hiding place for a minute – she can have our room, can't she?'

Lance joined them in the corridor, shrugging on his elegant wool coat. 'All yours, Grace, with our compliments. At least until three. Say, are you all right?'

Her resolve broke amid all this masculine sympathy and she dissolved into tears.

Grace was shepherded in by the two men and guided to the

sofa. A very clean handkerchief and a rather dusty glass of water were placed in her hands.

'I . . . I'm probably just overtired.'

The men murmured their agreement.

'It's none of my business, not really. I don't know why I'm upset. It's a shock. I think Jack and Lillian . . . She's so much older than him, but then she's very beautiful. And he looks at Stella, and I'm just not that type.'

'Honey,' Lance said, crouching in front of her. 'Even *I* look at Stella—'

'But I saw the way Lillian held him! Oh, maybe I'd better come to America with you after all, Lance. Get away from this place.'

'I don't quite know what you're talking about, pet,' Bill said, 'but you need an hour of peace and quiet. Cry, sleep, it's up to you, but curl up there.'

He turned round to pick up a cloak hanging off the back of the door. It was spangled with magical symbols – no doubt the lost or abandoned prop of a passing magician. Now it was their blanket, and though neither of them would admit it, their good luck charm.

Grace couldn't think of anything else to do, so she kicked off her shoes and curled up on the sofa. Bill spread the cloak out over her, and Lance tucked it in.

'You'd be very welcome to come to America with me, Grace. I'd love it if you did. But we'd better get the dress and the first night out of the way. When did you last have a full night's sleep?'

'Oh, I can't remember. Even when I'm asleep I just dream of Evie counting her lines.' She pulled the cloak round her, looking very young. 'I'm such a fool. I really thought he . . . Lord, he probably just thinks I'm like his little sister or something. Helpful, sensible Grace. And I let myself get all worked up.'

'Look, you have a snooze and a weep,' Lance said. 'Within these walls you don't need to be practical, brilliant Grace for an hour or two.'

This kindness seemed to undo her entirely, and she hid her face under the spangled collar of the cloak. Lance patted her shoulder.

'Come on, Bill. Let's give the girl some room.'

Bill held the door while Lance walked past him.

'Light on or off, Grace?'

'Off,' came a small snuffling reply.

He flicked the brass switch, closed the door, then stood in the corridor with Lance.

'Lillian and Jack?' he said softly. 'I don't see it. And the way that lad looks at Grace . . . I don't for a second think he sees her as a little sister.'

Lance shrugged. 'Theatre makes some strange bedfellows, Bill. We all know that. But I'd agree with you. I've already picked out an engagement present for them.'

'But you invited her to America?'

'She's a super writer, and I didn't get this far by ignoring talent. I have every intention of being on top of her "to call" list, wherever she ends up.'

They took two steps along the corridor, then Bill stopped. 'Lance, are you happy to go and eat alone? I think I've got something to do.'

He nodded. 'If you won't have lunch with me, I'll go and have steak with Usher at the Metropole.'

'Have a fine afternoon. I shall see you at three.'

Lance raised a hand in farewell, and Bill doubled back, crossing the stage where Little Sam and his crew were still hammering and painting, and headed upstairs towards the rehearsal studio and Lillian's office.

*

Edmund returned to the offices of Lassiter Enterprises in a good mood after his visit to The Empire. Not just good, but exultant. Lillian had been a blight on his life since the day she returned from Paris on his grandfather's arm. Siegfried Rustman, an anglicised Hun at his prep school, had found a postcard of Lillian dressed like a tart in a production of *The Queen of Paris*; it was from one of her 'fallen from grace' scenes, where she exposed an indecent amount of flesh. Siegfried had made a great show of slavering over it, and when Edmund had lashed out in humiliation and frustration, tearing the card from his hand, Siegfried had beaten him for it.

Edmund dated his strange unpopularity at school from that incident, but he had kept the card, hating the slut but strangely fascinated by the picture. When Lillian showed up at speech day at the end of that term with the rest of his family, his humiliation had been complete. The boys clustered round her like puppies, but he had held himself aloof.

Their mutual hatred of Lillian had at least created a bond between him and his mother, even after she confiscated the postcard. Constance was the only female he didn't hold in contempt. The rest were all like Lillian, really. Even the ones moving around society, all proper and correct in their behaviour, were whores underneath their fine clothing. No better than the prostitutes in Paris, or the servant girls who swore they loved him, then wept when he showed them what love meant.

But today he had exacted some measure of revenge. Lillian had received them coolly in the office, and rejected out of hand their suggestion that the theatre be sold to Allerdyce. Then the dirty cow had had the temerity to ask why Edmund needed the money. She'd said she had heard rumours about his gaming debts, and had the gall to ask if he needed a loan. As if every penny she had, every stick of clothing she wore, hadn't been stolen from him!

He had enjoyed watching her go pale as his mother described the theft. Anderson Hargreaves was summoned in from the outer office to tell her about the fifty-pound note and where it had been found, then ushered out again. That was pleasing, too. Anderson had a way of looking at Edmund with baffled concern that was completely inappropriate for an employee. It was fun to see him being excluded from the rest of their conversation.

Then Edmund had revelled in Lillian's confused protestations that Jack Treadwell could have done such a thing. That glorious moment when Constance had pulled one of the purloined letters from her handbag and slid it across the desk towards Lillian! Her overpainted face had all but collapsed in shock. It was good that Constance had had her moment, too, telling Lillian that she knew she had inflicted her criminal bastard child on Highbridge before her poor deceived husband was even cold in his grave.

And when Edmund had said he would testify against Jack – that he had seen her scandalous whelp fiddling with the contributions box after the gala – he had felt a satisfaction which made him shudder under his immaculately tailored coat.

Naturally, he knew that Jack had escorted Stella from the reception without going near the contributions box, a little while before the fatal notes had been jammed into it. He had watched them go, wondering how the doorman managed to leave with the star while he waited for his mother. Perhaps if it came to court, Stella would testify on Jack's behalf. It did not matter. Who would believe a bastard and a showgirl's word, when weighed against the solemn testimony of Major Sir Edmund Lassiter? And there were so many people coming and going round the lobby at the time, no one with any credit in the town would be able to contradict him.

'Sir Edmund?'

'What?' Edmund barked, annoyed at being pulled out of his delicious reverie.

'The manager of the North End cutlery factory is here and won't leave till he sees you. He says the testing of the new machinery isn't complete, the workers aren't trained properly on it yet, and he'll resign if you order them to start full production tomorrow.'

'Sack him then,' Edmund said simply. He was done trying to reason with these little men. 'Pay him till the end of the week and promote the foreman. The line will be at full capacity tomorrow. What better test could there be?'

The minion removed himself and Edmund felt a glow in his chest. He could feel how this victory over Lillian had put steel in his spine, pumped fresh blood through his veins.

He was, from this moment, he felt, a force to be reckoned with. Perhaps he would pop to the club for lunch.

CHAPTER TWENTY-SEVEN

Jack walked until he found himself in an unfamiliar part of town. His steps had taken him down the hill from the centre of the city, and when he thought to look about him, he found himself some way from the main river crossing and half a mile west of the great pool where the few canal boats still working loaded and unloaded. The feel of the city had faded into the semi-rural. The river was wide but shallow, and the clear waters rippled musically over the stones. A well-trodden path ran along the bank, shaded by sycamores and elms. He came to a halt and sat on the bank, took off his shoes and socks, rolled up his trousers and set his feet into the water, which carried a sharp chill from its birthing place high up in the dale. The feel of it reminded him of the becks and streams near Winchurch, the place he had always regarded as his ancestral home, land of his fathers. Or not.

He couldn't get his mind to hang on to the idea for long enough for him to think it through. He was Jack Treadwell, charming if occasionally wayward son of Bessie and Fred. Their changeling child. He knew the fairy tales from school, where a mother finds her own baby replaced with one of the strange infants of the fairy folk.

But Jack had not been a replacement. And he had been loved. Of that he was sure. His mam and dad weren't outwardly affectionate parents, not once he was out of short trousers. He had heard other parents – richer, more middle-class parents – call their children 'darling' or 'sweetheart'. They had called him 'Jack', or 'son'. When he went to war, Dad had shaken his hand. But he had said he was proud of Jack when he did. Mam had kissed him then, a rare thing, but she had never got out of the habit of ruffling his hair when he was eating his dinner at the kitchen table.

When they saw he liked to read, Mam had got him a card for the library in the next town, and slipped him the occasional shilling to buy story papers when he'd done his chores. Dad bought him aniseed balls whenever he passed the sweet shop in the village, even when Jack was on leave, and Mam . . . How many hours had she spent trying to keep him clean and decently dressed? She'd made her best fish pie when he came home from training, and Jack had heard her shushing Dad when he left the house in the morning, so as not to wake him.

The loss of them blossomed for a long moment as he watched the water swirl past him. The pain of being without them had become familiar, dulled, in the last few years since their death. But it was different now. He was the child of Lillian Lassiter. The shame of her, and symbol of her shame. A terrible secret she had been forced to get rid of. He looked at his hands. Did they look like Lillian's? Did he look like her? He never was any good at spotting likenesses. Did he look like his father? His hair was darker than Fred or Bessie's. Did he get his colouring from that man? Lillian was a platinum blonde. Maybe her hair was naturally this chestnut. Did the slight curl in it come from *him*? The mysterious man who had . . . Was that in his blood? Did it leave some mark – being created in a moment of violent cruelty? He hoped that, if so, the many kindnesses of his beloved Mam and Dad had been enough to wipe it out.

'Mind if I join you?'

He looked up to find Bill standing over him.

He didn't reply, but Bill took silence for consent and sat down on the bank alongside him.

'Not thinking of drowning yourself, are you, mate?'

Jack shook his head.

'She would have kept you if she could've done.'

'*You* know? How in God's name do you know? Lillian said she'd only ever told Evie.'

'Don't fly off the handle. I caught her at a vulnerable moment just now.' Bill took a knife from his pocket, bent down to cut a trio of reeds from the water's edge, then began to plait them. 'And I knew Lil before. A long time ago.'

'What?' Jack stared at him.

He paused in his plaiting to rub the side of his neck. 'The girl I left behind when I ran off from the the theatre – that was Lil.'

'You and Lillian? I had no idea, Bill.'

'She and I were joined at the hip for six months. I loved her, and she, daft girl, loved me. Then I met my demon voices' – he pressed a finger into his temple – 'and I left. Walked out without a word while she was on stage, telling myself she'd be better off without me. I was an idiot.'

'Did you come here, to The Empire, because of . . . because of her?' Jack asked, struggling to keep up.

Bill returned to plaiting the reeds. 'Yes and no. I thought if it all went bad, I'd be out of town before she got home. Then, when I did all right, thanks to you and Lance, I was expecting her to welcome me like an old friend. She didn't.'

'No?'

'Nope. Blamed me for what happened after that. I didn't know the baby she'd had was you until half an hour ago, but she told me a few weeks ago that she'd had a child, that it had split her life in two. And she was right to blame me. Told me she'd have given it all up – the marriage, the money, the title – for another day with you, and I believe her. So whatever you're thinking, don't think she didn't want you.'

Jack groaned and lay back across the grass, looking up at the pale blue sky. 'Then why give me up? Couldn't she have pretended to be a widow or something?'

Bill rubbed his hand over his eyes. 'She was a kid, Jack. And however bad things are now for girls who get in trouble, they were a damn sight worse twenty-odd years ago.' He twisted round to look at him. 'They were good people, weren't they, your mum and dad?'

Jack stared up at the sky. 'Yes, of course, but . . . They kept this from me my whole life. Telling everyone I was their son, while I'm really the child of Lillian and some monster. I don't know what I am now.'

'You're Jack Treadwell.'

'Blood matters, doesn't it?'

Bill stared down at his own hands. 'I can't say, Jack. You have taken to the theatre like one born to it, so there's that. But I've never heard a word said against you. Someone taught you right from wrong.'

Jack laughed harshly. 'Mam – Bessie – did. While never telling me the truth and writing those reports to Lillian every year.'

'I suppose Bessie was trying to do the right thing by you both. I don't claim to have direct experience, but all parents lie to their children, don't they? And to themselves. Have to, to keep sane. You should read those letters, you know.'

'Why?'

'I'm guessing you'll find a testament of love in them, Jack. You'll see how much Bessie loved you in what's written, and how much Lillian loves you in how they're falling apart from rereading.'

Jack didn't answer that for a long time. Bill let him think.

'She thinks I'm capable of stealing, though, Bill.'

'Maybe she did for a minute. Or maybe she thought you turning up alive and loved by everyone was too bloody good to be true. I mean, look at you! You arrived and set the whole city dancing to your tune. Jack the doorman to Mr Treadwell, spokesman and company manager, in a couple of months.'

'I couldn't have done any of that without Grace. She's the one who makes my nonsense ideas actually work.'

'Say that aloud more often, Jack. She saw you and Lillian outside Lillian's office earlier. Seems to have upset her a bit.'

'It upset her? Really?'

'It did.'

Jack said nothing, feeling too many different emotions to do more than frown into the cloud-studded sky for a minute. Then he sighed.

'She's too good for me and my clowning about, Bill. She's brilliant and beautiful and kind. I mean, I didn't think I was good enough for her yesterday – I still sleep on a camp bed in the stage door lobby! And now I find out I'm illegitimate and accused of theft, too. I'm absolutely not good enough for her now.'

'Enough of that,' Bill said gruffly. 'I've learnt my lesson. It's not up to fellows like us to make a woman's decision for her.'

'What am I going to do, Bill?' Jack sat up again and pulled his knees up to his chest.

'I've no idea. But Constance and Edmund know you are Lillian's son. They stole some of your mum's letters.'

Jack groaned and put his head on his knees. 'Of course! That's why they accused me of theft – to make her hand over her shares in The Empire. It makes some sort of sense now. Dash it, I'm normally a bit quicker than this.' He lifted his gaze and stared at the fast-flowing river. 'I'm not going to tell anyone I'm her son, but I won't have an accusation of theft, or even the *rumour* of an accusation, hanging over my head. Though if I fight it, Constance will tell the story of Lady Lassiter's illegitimate son working at the theatre all over the place. Lillian's reputation would be destroyed, and mine . . . tainted, I suppose. People will judge me. And everyone'll think I got the job here because of her.'

'When we all know for a fact that it's because Ollie approved of you, and Grace trusts that dog's opinion. It's a pickle, mate. I'm not saying otherwise. But you'd better get your socks and shoes on, because you've got a dress to run in a couple of hours, and I bet someone in the theatre needs you for something right now.'

Jack did as he was told. 'I did learn one useful thing in the trenches, among all the rest of it. Sometimes it's best not to look too far ahead. Just do what needs to be done right now.'

Bill put out his hand and pulled Jack to his feet. 'Sounds like a good idea for the moment.'

'I'd better find out why Ivor French is here, for a start.'

'That the older fellow? Face like a skull and a very thin moustache? When I came to look for you he and Danny were in the lobby with Mr Poole. Talking away, thick as thieves, though they went silent when they saw me.'

'I wonder what they could be up to?'

'Dress rehearsal first, working out the other stuff later,' Bill said firmly.

Then, with a flick of his wrist, he cast his plaited reed into the middle of the river. The current caught it and carried it away.

CHAPTER TWENTY-EIGHT

'I think it might be best,' Stella said as the cast and crew returned to the stage to hear notes after the dress rehearsal, 'to start drinking immediately.'

Lance took hold of her hand and spun her round, just as he did during the final number. Her long pleated skirt ballooned out, its silver and blue panels like waves reaching up to her waist. The back was cut very low.

'I'll buy you a drink, but you'll need to be fresh in the morning. You know Usher will want us to go through your change and the last number again, probably at ungodly o'clock.'

'I realise,' Usher said from the stalls, 'that every show has its challenges, and that most of you are not used to the sudden and sharp transition from the rehearsal room to the stage. It's a very different thing, miming opening a door or climbing a set of steps, to actually doing so on stage as you perform, but I have never seen a company which seemed so apparently terrified of a set.'

'Little Sam was holding up the flat backstage!' Evie protested.

'I was afraid if I went for it with that door slam, I'd break his arm.'

Usher ignored her. 'Chorus! The set is your home. Steps to the terrace, the grand staircase, the flights to the upper level of the club – the climbing frames up to the balcony. They are your playground. Stop acting like you think the entire place is about to fall down around your ears. Evie, Stella, Lance and Bill – step forward, please.'

The principals did as they were asked and Usher turned round and shaded his eyes, calling up to the gallery.

'Ruben, are you familiar with these four personages? You are? Good. Whenever any of them are on stage, I would like to be able to see them.'

The spotlight waggled in acknowledgement.

'Evie, that was one of the most bad-tempered performances I've ever seen an actress give. We are supposed to believe that you are magnetic, electric. This evening you were sour. Lance, I blame myself. I should not have let you have steak for lunch. You ended up dancing like a farmyard heifer. For the rest of the run, if anyone sees Mr Lancelot Drake take anything harder to digest than a little thin soup at lunchtime, dash it from his hands. His many fans will thank you for it. Stella, I'm sure whatever that young man was saying to you during the club scene was absolutely hysterical, but it is the one time when you are on stage and are *not* the centre of attention. The audience needs to focus on Lance and Evie downstage. Will you please not improvise a Charleston or whatever that was?

'Bill, I realise that winking at the audience is your stock-in-trade, but in this production you are an actor, not a song and dance man. It is your duty to bring the audience into the scene with you, not to remind them they are simply watching you jig about.

'Chorus – one more note for you. Your fear of the stage mechanics aside, you were mostly adequate.'

The chorus were shocked into a delighted silence.

'But I expect you all in at nine tomorrow morning, by which time Little Sam has assured me all the flats will be held upright by mechanical rather than human means, and we shall run through the opening number, the end of Act One, and "Please Be Our King" until you develop some degree of trust in the skills of the carpenters. And what must we remember about the opener of Act Two?'

'Hit the third beat,' the chorus shouted back at him.

'Stella: Mabel Mills and her band have agreed to come in again at three tomorrow. You will be there, too, and we shall work on your two numbers with them until you can convince me you've been singing with them every night for a whole year. You performed together like strangers this evening. You and Mabel are duetting. At the moment she is blowing you off the stage without visible effort.

'Mrs Gardener, the chorus looked as if they had been dressed out of the poor box in the club scenes. Glamour, please, for every single soul on the stage. Less than absolutely gorgeous is not acceptable. Ruby, you seem to have the theatre orchestra in hand. Grace, the book is closed. Jack, follow me. I have some other matters to discuss with you and our producer.'

Jack had been taking notes as Usher spoke, but he knew they were more confused than usual. He had returned to the theatre just after three o'clock, leaving Bill outside signing autographs for a cluster of dedicated fans near stage door; he'd gone in search of Grace, not sure what he would say, but eager to find her. Then he did: Lance was ushering her out of his dressing room, and Grace looked rather flushed and dishevelled. She had caught sight of Jack as the door closed, and he had got as far as saying her name.

She had looked past him – or through him – and said, 'Oh,

Jack. We must have a chat some time. I'm thinking about going to Hollywood with Lance when *Riviera Nights* closes. To write.'

Then she walked away.

Jack had thought he had felt every emotion possible that day already, but her appearance, her casual tone, meant that he could do nothing but gape at her. Bill had made it sound as if she'd been shocked or upset by seeing him hug Lillian. Bill had been wrong. And he'd almost made a total fool of himself, acting as if he had presumed there was something between him and Grace, when it appeared she had decided on a future with Lance. Why on earth wouldn't she? What on earth could Jack offer in comparison to him?

'Nine o'clock tomorrow morning, please,' Usher said again.

Jack shook himself into the present moment and followed him.

Lance leant towards Stella as Usher made his way out of the auditorium and whispered to her, 'Now we start drinking.'

Then Lance turned to the cast and crew and lifted his voice.

'The Royal Café, my dear children. I'm giving you all your opening night present a little early – a champagne supper for us all. We'll celebrate the praise lavishly heaped on our friends in the chorus, while the principals will soothe their egos with oysters and dancing. Party frocks on, please. Grace, Ruby, Tom – either come or be struck from my heart forever. Your call.'

Evie spoke over the general squeals of excitement.

'Lance, Bill and I must refuse. Our producer has invited us to a quiet supper upstairs, and you know I only get more bad-tempered after a poor night's sleep. You young folk have fun.'

Lance bowed and Stella dropped a deep curtsey.

'My Queen, I look forward to you rechiselling Usher's face into an ecstatic glow by the end of your first number.'

Evie smiled at him with genuine warmth, took Bill's arm and left the stage.

If Usher thought the atmosphere was unusually strained as he discussed a few last-minute alterations with his producer and company manager in Lillian's office, he did not mention it. Once he was sure they had understood his intentions, and he had listened to Lillian's sensible responses and comments, he wished them goodnight and left. Jack began to gather up his papers to leave, too.

'Jack, please don't go,' Lillian said. 'Have supper with Bill and Evie and me.'

He hesitated. 'You and Evie think I'm a thief.'

She put out a hand. 'No, don't say that! I was too shocked to think straight. You must forgive me, for making that mistake at least. Even if you can't forgive me for—'

'For giving me up?'

She nodded.

'Lillian, my world's just been turned upside down. Can you give me a little time to sort it out in my own head?'

'Of course, Jack. Only, please believe me when I say we did all love you – me, Bessie and Fred. It hurt terribly to read Bessie's letters, knowing you were growing up without me, but . . . Well, I was so grateful for the comfort of knowing how they cared for you.'

He leant back in the chair and looked up at the ceiling.

'Bill said something like that,' he said.

'It was probably very wise, then,' the man himself said, coming into Lillian's office with Evie on his arm. 'We're ready for supper, Lil. But Evie here has something to say to Jack first.'

Evie pouted, but Bill raised his eyebrows at her and she sighed.

'I'm very sorry I thought you were a thief, Jack. I asked Stella about the gala night during the dress. I didn't tell her about the accusation or anything, but . . . Well, anyway, she said Edmund was being a lech, and you rescued her and carried her straight off to the Metropole without even fetching your coat. So I'm awfully sorry.'

She put out her hand and looked at him from under her long eyelashes.

Jack got to his feet and took her hand. 'Ollie had requisitioned my coat at the time. Thank you, and apology accepted.'

'Will you stay for supper, Jack?' Lillian said nervously.

He smiled briefly and managed a nod.

Since the Mabel Mills Jazz Band had started playing at the Royal Café, the character of the establishment had shifted somewhat. There was still a dining room upstairs, reached by a commodious lift with a uniformed bellboy in situ, where the older denizens of Highbridge society could enjoy a civilised evening while a string quartet played foxtrots between potted ferns. However, the ballroom downstairs had been taken over by the bright young things of the area. Most of the ladies had their hair bobbed, though some still only pinned their hair to look that way; the men were clean-shaven, and everyone came to dance. The room shimmered in silks and satins, low backs, and witty headdresses making much use of peacock plumes and pearls. The vast majority of the crowd drank cocktails or champagne, and half of them smoked as avidly as Stella, pulling their cigarettes from jewelled evening bags, which looked too dainty to hold much more than a lipstick. They came in groups from country house parties, in pairs from the elegant town houses of the west end, the sons and daughters of industrial fortunes and modest competencies, the slender twigs issuing out at odd angles from old family trees – young people whose main purpose seemed to be to cram as much pleasure as they could into their short, sunny days. For most of them, this meant a certain amount of hunting, a lot of tennis, and as many nights at the Royal Café as their allowances would allow.

Mabel led the band, sometimes playing lead trumpet, sometimes conducting, taking them through a series of familiar favourites and throwing in a few new tunes every week to keep the crowd fresh and on their toes. It was, they kept telling each other, as good as anything London had to offer.

The arrival of Lancelot Drake and Stella Stanmore always increased the buzz in the room, and the management were happy to slightly reduce the space available for dancing in order to accommodate his large party this evening.

'I know you'll look after us,' Lance told the maître d'. 'Keep the champagne flowing, there's a good chap. Now, Grace,' he went on, taking her arm, 'I insist you sit next to me. Leave your worries at the door – we're going to be frightfully frivolous all evening.'

'Jack went straight up to Lillian's office after the dress,' Grace told him miserably. 'I suppose he'll be having supper with her, and Evie and Bill.'

Stella caught her other arm. 'And that's exactly the sort of thing we're not going to discuss tonight.'

In front of them, tables were being rolled into place, covered with white linen and flowers, glasses and silverware. It was like one of the transformations which Little Sam's crew enacted on the stage. Corks popped, a soft polite percussion of them; flutes were filled.

'They were odd this afternoon, though, weren't they, Lance?' Stella said. 'Evie was sour, and Bill was distracted.'

'They must know about Jack and Lillian, too. Evie probably thinks he's a fortune hunter. I feel like such a fool.'

Grace stared at her champagne as if she hated it. Lance wagged his finger at Stella, and she stuck her tongue out at him.

'Come along, Grace. Let's dance.' He stood up and put out his hand.

'Oh, Lance, I'm not sure I feel like—'

'I said, let's dance.'

Grace took his hand and stood up. Like half the chorus, she was dressed in borrowed finery, courtesy of Mrs Gardener. The wardrobe mistress herself was sitting at the top of one of their tables with Little Sam and one of the chorus boys, and obviously telling some of her more scandalous stories. At least raiding the costume department meant the dresses were designed to be danced in and looked at.

'Stella, honey,' Lance said as Grace dropped her napkin on the table, 'can I get you anything from the buffet?'

Grace looked in the direction he was nodding. A group of young men in evening dress were collected at the edge of the dance floor, looking at the theatrical crowd with a mixture of awe and excitement.

Stella twisted in her chair. 'Yes – send me the one in the middle.'

'At once.'

Grace found herself being swept round in a delicate arc. Dancing with Lance was a supernatural experience. Grace could dance, and liked to do so, but Lance was one of those partners who turned you into an exceptional dancer just by taking hold of your hand. Four long steps, a turn and an elegant dip, and they were in front of the male buffet. Lance focused on the young man in the middle.

'If you ask Miss Stanmore to dance,' he said, looking away from Grace momentarily, 'I think she might just say yes.'

The young man started and his eyes widened with delight, but

Lance didn't stay for an answer, simply sweeping Grace off into the centre of the crowd.

For the next four minutes Grace was distinctly less miserable. It was not that she stopped worrying about Lillian and Jack; it was simply that as she was whirled round the dance floor by Lance, she ceased to think at all. The walls were mirrored, the ceiling was hung with crystal chandeliers, and the music was fast and infectious and full of the fever of being alive. When the music stopped, the room filled with applause and cheers, and the feeling of dancing left Grace in a pleasant, champagne-bubble haze.

There was some movement around the stage, and to her surprise, Grace saw that Stella was being invited up to join the band. Mabel held up her trumpet and waited till the crowd had quietened.

'Ladies and gentlemen, we have a special treat for you this evening! As you know, some of my band and I will be featuring in the new musical opening at The Empire from tomorrow night. I am very pleased to present the star of that show, Miss Stella Stanmore, here with us this evening to give you a sneak preview of the title number. Music by Ruby Rowntree, words by Grace Hawkins, and the swing from your good friend Mabel and the band. So a royal welcome, please, to the one and only Stella Stanmore, here to give you the title number of the hottest show of this season or any other – *Riviera Nights*!'

'Good lord!' Grace said. 'Did anyone know they were going to do that?'

'Dear girl,' Lance said, as the band began and the theatrical tables emptied as the chorus poured onto the floor, whooping with excitement, 'there's nothing you can tell either of those fine ladies about publicity.'

Stella's ice-white evening gown seemed to give off an unearthly glow as she stepped forward. The intro snapped into silence, and as she delivered the first phrase of the song unaccompanied, starting right at the bottom of her range and reaching up to the strong beating heart of her contralto as she sang the words 'Riviera Nights', Stella raised her arms, holding the last note, then she brought them down sharply and the band kicked in, brassy and full of heat.

Stella flew like they'd given her wings. The chorus spun and stepped between the other dancers, joining in on the call-outs till the whole crowd got the idea. Grace was turning round in the middle of it all, in the arms of a film star, not thinking any further, for once in her life, than the next beat of her heart.

CHAPTER TWENTY-NINE

The conductor calling 'Highbridge' woke Wilbur just in time. He gathered the papers scattered around him and thrust them into his briefcase before climbing out onto the empty station platform. He had missed the fast train from Sheffield, and this one had rattled along so slowly it had lulled him into a doze. The walls were plastered with advertisements for the new musical at The Empire: *Riviera Nights*, opening tomorrow.

He had spent a day in London, then two more in Sheffield, and was beginning to feel guilty about the number of times that Edison had put his hand in his pocket and handed Wilbur fistfuls of ten-shilling notes for his expenses. Wilbur had kept a careful record in his notebook: lunch here; dinner there; a couple of quid to a doorman; buns and cakes for a typist.

It had been worth it, though. The buns and cakes had got him the address of a company Edmund had invested heavily in at the beginning of 1920. The company turned out to be one man, tinkering in a shed just outside Brixton, and his card-sharp cousin. The revolutionary synthetic dyes he claimed to have invented seemed to be nothing more than fantasy. Another of Edmund's investments for a new cheaper firing method for porcelain fancy goods had led Wilbur to an abandoned warehouse on the Old Kent Road. The neighbours told Wilbur there had been a fire there last year, injuring two workers, and the owners had disappeared in the same puff of smoke which had blown up the kilns. It seemed to Wilbur that Edmund's investment had gone the same way.

Closer to home, Wilbur had got rounds of drinks for workers from the North End factory. Buying this place had been one of those times Sir Barnabas had made a bold business move, innovating and diversifying at once, by bringing the processes of making cutlery and tableware under one roof. During the war it was converted to produce munitions, but the process of turning it back to peacetime work had been tortuous. Edmund had wanted to use stainless steel and new stamping machines, had not listened to his engineers, and employed whoever promised him the impossible.

Wilbur turned over the paragraphs in his head as he walked home, staring at the pavement.

Lack of oversight . . . gross mismanagement.

They would have to give Edmund a chance to respond, of course.

Then there was Mangrave – and Wilbur's trip to Sheffield. More meals and pints bought, this time for local reporters and their underworld contacts. They told him, quietly, that Mangrave had learnt how to launder money in their pubs and bars. Run their profits from illegal gambling through other businesses so it emerged clean and shiny. And Ray Kelly had heard about him, and come and fetched him.

'Kelly knows how to spot a man's weakness,' one old lag had

said, leaning against the bar. 'Bloody Mangrave wanted to be a gentleman and Ray Kelly set him up so he can do the same work but hobnob with all the silk-hatted shits in the gentleman's club, too. Good riddance to him. He had a temper on him.'

Wilbur had written it all down in his notebook.

The street was quiet. It was late in the evening, but even so, you'd usually see kids about while there was even a scrap of light in the sky. Wilbur felt his heart beginning to beat faster before he realised consciously that something was wrong. He looked up. The shadow of a man peeled itself away from the wall against which he'd been leaning and blocked the pavement.

Wilbur kept walking, touched his hat.

'Good evening,' he said calmly, and moved to step round him.

Another man appeared from the narrow ginnel on the other side of the road. The first man held up his hand.

Wilbur looked over his shoulder. Two more right behind him.

Christ, I didn't even notice the first one as I passed.

And now they had him trapped.

Can I run?

The first man laid one hand on Wilbur's shoulder and yanked the briefcase from him. The other three had come up close, silent as cats. All grey in the dark, in shirtsleeves, peaked caps shadowing their faces, the shimmer of violence coming off them like heat, like a bad smell.

The first man opened the briefcase. Pulled out a bundle of papers.

'What scholarship!' the man said, his voice rich with contempt. 'Were you a clever boy in school, Wilbur? Learnt your lessons and always a polite word for your teachers, I'll bet.'

'Those papers are nothing to do with you,' Wilbur said. 'Put them back and let me pass.'

'Scholarship's a wonderful thing, lads,' he said. 'So I'm told.'

'Can you even read?' Wilbur said, briefly more angry than afraid.

'Mr Kelly reads to us, sometimes. For our general improvement.'

He dropped the case on the ground, so the papers still in it scattered over the mud of the roadway. He pulled a matchbook from his pocket, lit one, and used it to set fire to the bundle he still held. He pushed the burning scroll of them close to Wilbur's face, half blinding him, his own face made devilish through the smoke. Wilbur watched his own neat handwriting being consumed.

'That,' the man said quietly, 'is what I think of your scholarship.'

He dropped the flaming spill onto the papers at his feet and the flames spread between them.

'You were warned, puppy. Should have kept your clever nose out of it.'

He stood back and lit a cigarette while the papers smouldered at his feet. Then nodded to the other three.

Wilbur tried to run, striking out with elbow and fist. The first blow he took showed him what an amateur he was. He cried out, and his cry echoed against closed doors and shutters. He twisted round, bringing his elbow up at the same time, and felt it connect.

Another of the men surrounding him grunted with pain as Wilbur's boot stamped on his instep.

'Stop playing and finish him,' the man with the cigarette said.

Wilbur heard a metallic click and saw the glint of a knife in the edge of the gaslight. He swung his whole weight sideways, twisted again. For a miraculous moment he was free. And he ran.

They were after him at once, inches behind. He was too frightened to think, too frightened to feel his own fear. He could only taste it, bitter in his mouth. Breathing was hard, each lungful painful, and they were within a finger's reach of him.

Where is everyone?

Wilbur sprinted down the ginnel, the familiar maze. Familiar to them, too, as at the back of Esk Lane one of them sprinted at him from his left and brought him down hard on the ground. He tasted blood in his mouth, his right knee screamed in agony.

Get up, Wilbur. Get up now, or never again.

He kicked back with his free foot, bounced into a crouch and ran forward, not knowing where – somewhere those men weren't, somewhere there were people.

Something zipped by his ear.

Dear Christ, they're shooting at me now.

Wilbur swung right on to another road, then left on to one leading out of the town, and found himself blinded by oncoming lights. He held up his arms over his face and turned sideways, as something slammed into his shoulder and he fell.

Agnes stamped hard on the brakes as the man pitched forward into the road in front of her. She was certain she hadn't hit him, but she could no longer see him through her windscreen.

Joe thrust open the door, and she could hear him above the thumping idling beat of the engine.

'Young man! Are you injured?'

Agnes got out of the car, too, to see Joe crouched in front of the grille, the young man, respectably dressed but scuffed and dirty, half-raised in his arms. Joe's white dress shirt was smeared with blood.

'Oh my God, Joe! I think he's been shot.'

Agnes peered into the darkness of the streets to the north: the Barrows, a patch of ground she had visited from time to time on charitable missions.

Are there movements in the shadows?

'Get him into the car. We must get him to the hospital.'

The man was still conscious. 'No hospitals, please. It's a scratch.'

'We need to get you out of here, at least.' Joe lifted the man to his feet. 'Agnes, can you still drive?'

'Of course I can. Do try and keep the blood off the leather.'

She held the door open as Joe manoeuvred the young man into the back seat. As she got back behind the wheel, she saw that Joe had found the source of the blood and was pressing his handkerchief against it.

'I've still got my notebook,' the injured man said faintly.

'Well done, young man.' Agnes put the car into gear. 'We'll take him to the farmhouse, Joe, and call the doctor from there.'

The doctor came quickly: a quiet, sensible man who had known Agnes for many years, but rarely needed to visit her. She showed him into the drawing room, and if he was surprised to see a stranger with a bullet wound on the settee, being tended to by theatre impresario Joe Allerdyce, he didn't show it. Wilbur was weak, bruised and in pain, but his greatest concern seemed to be the danger of getting blood on the faded upholstery.

The doctor carried out a careful inventory of Wilbur's wounds. The bullet had only grazed him, but it had still ploughed a furrow into the flesh of his shoulder. Not serious in itself, but close enough to his neck for them all to feel a shiver of mortality. The doctor gave Wilbur morphine, cleaned and stitched the wound, and tied a bandage neatly in place. For the knee, he could only recommend cool compresses. The cracked ribs and bruises would hurt like the devil for a couple of weeks, but heal on their own.

Wilbur was profuse in his thanks to his rescuers and to the doctor. The latter accepted a brandy, which he tossed off in a single gulp, then he left without asking any questions about how

Wilbur had come by his injuries. Wilbur thanked Joe and Agnes again, and started to make enquiries about how to get home.

'And where is that?' Joe asked, proffering him more of Agnes's best brandy.

'The Barrows,' Wilbur replied, then, seeing the sceptical looks on their faces, 'Yes, I know it's where I was attacked. I could go to my mum and dad, but I don't think walking will be easy tomorrow and I want to be as near to the newspaper offices as I can. I have to go and see Mr Potter first thing and tell him—'

'You can tell him before then,' Agnes said, 'and enter into negotiations with him about how to get home, too. He's on his way here now.'

'Is he?'

'Yes, I called him at the same time I called the doctor. He was still at the offices, seeing the morning edition to bed.'

'How did you know who I was?' Wilbur asked, feeling comfortably woolly thanks to the morphine.

'The woman is a witch,' Joe answered cheerfully. 'It's why her horses do so well.'

'That reminds me, I have something in the kitchen which should help with your knee. Joe, ring the bell for me, would you?' Joe did so. 'No witchcraft in knowing who you are, however, Mr Bowman. You mentioned your notebook, and there was a little picture of you in the *Illustrated News* with that article you did about my great-nephew, Edmund.'

'Of course. My apologies, Miss de Montfort, I should've recognised you.'

She smiled. 'I have undergone something of a transformation recently. Who attacked you?'

'It was a mugging,' he said, avoiding her eye.

'Forgive me, but I doubt that. If that had been the case, you would have laid less emphasis on your notebook and seeing your editor.'

Wilbur nodded slowly, but said nothing else.

Agnes's housekeeper arrived to gather up the dirty linens, cast a blizzard of worried looks at Wilbur, and tell them she had a ham available if they were hungry. Agnes ordered hot water, a chafing-dish and the crock of Preparation Four. This caused some nervous looks between Joe and Wilbur, but did not seem to trouble the housekeeper.

'Straight away, madam. And Mr Allerdyce,' she added, 'one of your people came here with a message this afternoon. Bicycled up from town and wouldn't even take a glass of water for his trouble, dusty and sweaty as he looked, on the off chance you'd drop by here.'

They waited.

'Did he leave a message, dear?' Agnes said at last.

'Oh . . . Yes!'

She fished an envelope out of the pocket of her apron and handed it to Joe, before carrying off the stained travelling rug and a further order for sandwiches and beer.

Joe unfolded the note.

'What is it, Joe?'

'I'll be damned! Jesus bloody Christ. The office had a call from Edmund Lassiter this afternoon. Lillian's agreed to sell: The Empire is mine.'

CHAPTER THIRTY

The stairs weren't easy for Danny. Most of the flights were short, with relatively low risers, but there were plenty of them. Ollie remained at his heels throughout his climb, a reassuring and comforting presence, and Ivor French hummed something jaunty, giving no sign of impatience. The ache in Danny's ruined muscles threatened to turn into something sharper and less manageable, but he remained, in the wholeness of his conviction, almost immune to the pain. When they stopped finally outside the door to Lillian's flat, though, it ran through him in needling waves.

Ollie barked, and Lillian herself opened the door in response.

'Danny! What are you doing here?'

'W-we want to speak to you. This is Ivor French.'

'Come in, please.' Lillian offered her hand to Ivor. 'I heard you were in the theatre. A great pleasure to meet you, Mr French.'

Danny limped in and looked around him. Jack, Evie and Bill

were all present. The atmosphere had that slightly strained feel of an important discussion being interrupted.

Then Jack and Lillian swept into action. Ivor was introduced to Evie and Bill while Lillian fetched drinks. Even so, Danny felt that the conversation they were interrupting had not been a pleasant one. He lowered himself into one of the higher chairs near the dining table, which was easier on his leg, and scratched Ollie's ears to thank him for the company.

Lillian handed him a heavy cut glass tumbler with a good inch of drink in it. He took it gratefully, and felt the grumbling in his muscles grow muted as he drank.

'What's up, Danny, Ivor?' Jack said.

'We . . . we wanted to speak to you in private, Jack,' Danny said. 'You and Lady Lassiter. About what you and Miss D'Angelo were discussing.'

'I'm sorry, Lil,' Evie said. 'Jack and I had words about the theft at stage door.'

'Bill knows about the accusation made against Jack, Danny,' Lillian said gently. 'And I am sure we can trust Mr French to be discreet.'

'Not just discreet,' Ivor declared, finding his voice at the bottom of his own whisky glass, 'I aim to be Jack's champion.'

The others exchanged curious looks.

'Danny and I have had some very fruitful discussions this afternoon, haven't we?'

Danny nodded.

'But I realise my role is to assist. In this production I am Watson, not Sherlock. Danny, my dear friend, the floor is yours.'

Danny breathed in and out to try and steady himself. 'Th-they say you took two fifty-pound notes?'

'Yes,' Jack said.

Danny tried to say something more, but his tongue and lips had grown reluctant. He pulled a pad of paper from his top pocket, wrote on it, and showed the page to Jack.

'Yes, that's right. They say I took them from the donations box on the night of the gala. A couple of swells put them in, but they weren't paid in to the bank the following morning. Yes, it's the donation box Mr Poole keeps in his office.'

Found where? Book? Danny wrote.

'Yes, Mr Hargreaves found one there – he's the accountant for Lassiter Enterprises. They think I spent one, saved the other.'

Danny wrote again, and when Jack read the page he raised his eyebrows.

'What is it, Jack?' Evie asked from the settee.

'Danny says he was watching the search through the window, and Edmund was fiddling with the books before Hargreaves looked through them.'

'The bastard,' Bill said. 'But good for you for keeping an eye on them, Danny.'

Who has note now?

Jack repeated the question and Lillian answered this time.

'Anderson Hargreaves. He took it for safekeeping when it was discovered among Jack's things.'

Ollie sensed Danny's excitement and barked, shaking his tail.

Ivor and I want to go and see him in the morning.

'Danny?' Jack said. 'What are you thinking?'

Danny breathed in hard and set down his pen. 'T-trust me, Captain.' He tapped Ivor on the arm.

Ivor cleared his throat. 'We have an idea, but we are basing it on what Danny saw through the window in the briefest of moments, and would rather . . . We would like to confirm our suspicions before we share them. But it is possible . . .' He looked sideways at

Danny for permission and confirmation. 'Just possible it may go some way to exonerating you, Jack.'

'Then I'd be most profoundly grateful to you both,' Jack said.

'We all would! Edmund claims he saw Jack acting suspiciously near the collection box on the night of the gala, too,' Bill added.

'He's a liar and a coward.' Danny spoke the words more steadily than usual.

Jack didn't reply, just put his hand on Danny's shoulder and let it rest there.

Lillian stood up and walked towards the telephone. 'I'll ring Hargreaves at home and ask him to see you before he goes into the office.'

'I'm sorry to put you to this trouble,' Wilbur said.

He tried to sit up and winced.

Agnes put down a cloth and the heated chafing-dish on top of it to save her carpet. The strange green Preparation Four had the consistency of thick mud.

'Let's take a look at that knee. I think we can do better than "cool compresses". Doctors are an overrated bunch.'

Wilbur delicately pulled up the blanket, which was preserving his modesty, to the middle of his thigh, and Agnes nodded.

'Swollen as a balloon. Right, stay still. This will feel hot, then cold, but it will help.'

'Miss de Montfort – I really—'

'Oh, hush, man! I use this on the horses all the time.'

Joe chuckled. 'I'd let her do what she likes, son. Don't want her fetching her shotgun to put you out of your misery.'

Agnes applied the dark green paste from her dish around Wilbur's knee. He flinched, then blinked in surprise.

'That really does feel good.'

'A recipe of my own. Used it on Bonny Lass in 1920.' Agnes began to bind the knee with clean crêpe bandages. 'Thought we were going to have to shoot her, but she won the Epsom Derby a year later.'

'I'm not sure I'll be able to do that,' Wilbur said.

Agnes snorted with laughter, then sat back on her heels for a second to admire her work. Satisfied, she wiped her hands and Joe helped her to her feet.

'I'll send you home with a pot of it, Mr Bowman. Needs thinning with linseed oil, and heating. And you'll need to change it every day. Leave it too long and you start smelling like overcooked cabbage.'

The bell at the front door clanged and Joe went to answer it, returning moments later with Edison Potter on his heels.

'What in God's name?' Edison began. 'Someone shot at you, Wilbur? What were you playing at? Good evening, Agnes.'

'Edison.'

Agnes raised her glass to him, then took a seat to enjoy the show.

'They were Ray Kelly's men. They mentioned him by name. I spoke to Mangrave's wife a few days ago, though he had warned me off asking any other questions about him. She said they'd been in Sheffield, so I went and asked around. I suppose that got back to Mangrave, and so to Kelly.' Wilbur looked suddenly shocked. 'Sorry, boss, I must have turned daft. I shouldn't be saying anything in front of Miss de Montfort and Mr Allerdyce.'

Edison dropped himself onto another of the armchairs and ran a hand through his thinning hair. 'I asked the question, lad. Agnes, can I have a drink?'

'Of course, Edison.'

Joe made another trip to the brandy decanter and Agnes lifted up her own glass for a refill.

'Miss de Montfort sold her shares in Lassiter Enterprises when Sir Barnabas became ill two years ago,' Wilbur continued.

'You're remarkably well informed, Wilbur.'

'It's a matter of public record, Miss de Montfort.'

'I suppose so, and I think as we are now on intimate terms, you may call me by my Christian name. But what has Mangrave got to do with Ray Kelly? I know of him, of course – his people are a blight on horse racing in this county.'

Wilbur looked at Edison, but didn't reply.

'Reporters!' Joe snorted. 'Always asking you for the ins and outs of your own life, but will never answer a straight question themselves.'

He pulled the note from his pocket and handed it to Edison.

Edison read it. 'Lady Lassiter is selling you The Empire?'

'So it would seem,' Joe muttered into his glass. 'But I don't like it.'

'That's what you wanted, isn't it?' Edison asked him.

'Well, yes. I thought Lillian would get bored in the end, but let's be clear, I reckoned it would take a mite longer than this for the novelty to wear off. From what I hear, she's at the theatre every damn day and the new show's coming together nicely. Why would she suddenly decide to hand everything over to me now? And here is this young man, bleeding on the sofa and linking the names Mangrave and Kelly. I don't know what links it all together, but I bloody well don't like it.'

'I always thought you were something of a "fair means or foul" sort of businessman, Joe,' Edison said, pulling a cigar out of his pocket.

'I have my limits, Edison, I have my limits. And no smoking in the house.'

Edison put the cigar back in his pocket hurriedly.

'This connection you've suggested between Mangrave and Kelly,' Joe said at last. 'Am I right in thinking you believe Mangrave's moving money through the theatre?'

The two gentlemen of the press said nothing, but their silence spoke volumes.

Agnes set down her glass. 'I don't like it either, Joe. Not one bit.'

Edison finished his brandy and stood up. 'Wilbur, you're staying in my guest room tonight. I shan't take no for an answer. Now gather yourself. I'll take you there myself, and then I intend to convey my thoughts to Ray Kelly about harm coming to my reporters going about their business.'

Joe held up the blanket so Wilbur could put his trousers back on without offending Agnes's delicate gaze, but her thoughts were obviously elsewhere.

'Joe, what were you planning to offer for the theatre?'

'Eighty-five thousand,' he said promptly.

'But you won't make the deal just yet, will you?'

'No, Agnes. I'll send Constance the figure in the morning, but I want to speak to Lillian myself. We'll be there tomorrow evening, for the opening night. If she can look me in the eye then and tell me she wants to sell . . . well, I'll see. Why?'

'I think I might call on Lillian myself tomorrow.'

Wilbur indicated that the blanket was no longer necessary.

'Don't be late for tea tomorrow,' Joe reminded Agnes as he folded the blanket neatly over his arm. 'I'm looking forward to introducing you to my sons.'

Late evening turned to full inky night.

Grace lay in her bed, buffeted by images of Jack and Lillian, the sound of a theatre full of expectant theatregoers, the blast of Mabel Mills's trumpet.

Jack put together his camp bed in the dead silence of the theatre and stared at the ceiling, wondering if he dared trust his fate to Ivor and Danny, and trying to imagine what The Empire would be like without Grace. It felt terribly bleak. He thought of Lillian and Bessie, and only fell asleep when Ollie abandoned his basket and settled beside him in a position that was awkward for them both, but somehow better.

The chorus danced through their dreams; Ruby's and Tom's were full of fluttering manuscript paper, and Usher Barton sat up into the small hours, studying his book and questioning every artistic decision he had ever made.

Constance and Edmund Lassiter slept very well indeed.

CHAPTER THIRTY-ONE

The following morning, Edison Potter was woken by a persistent rapping on the back door.

'What is it?' his wife asked sleepily.

He told her to stay where she was and made his way downstairs. The door to the guest room was still closed. The morphine Wilbur had been given would have put him into the deepest of sleeps. The light was creeping through the windows, but the shadows were still thick and damp, so it was too early for the daily help to have arrived. Edison pushed open the door to the kitchen. A stranger was boiling a kettle on the range, and another man was sitting in one of the rocking chairs next to the old fireplace.

Ray Kelly.

Edison stood on the threshold.

'So you knock, then let yourselves in, Mr Kelly?'

Kelly looked up at him. 'A tricky bit of etiquette, we concede,' he said, and the whites of his eyes seemed to glint. 'We've no wish to take the household by surprise, no wish to dawdle around on the street waiting for you to find your slippers, Mr Potter. I promise Sharps will be careful with your crockery, and he knows to warm the pot.'

Edison lowered his bulk into the rocking chair opposite Kelly's without comment.

'Your message was conveyed to us last night. My associate who took your telephone call informed us you made use of colourful language.'

Edison didn't answer at once, only watched Ray Kelly for a long cool moment before replying. 'That offend your delicate sensibilities, Kelly? I'm happy to repeat the language now – and the message. If you think breaking into my house and making tea is going to intimidate me, you're wrong. Your men tried to murder my reporter last night. If you think I'm going to let that lie just because you've shown you can walk into my kitchen, you have another think coming.'

Kelly looked offended, holding up his hand. Sharps poured tea and passed them both cups. He was using the kitchenware, the mixed blue and white the staff used day to day, not the upstairs china. Edison sipped. Strong and sweet, it was welcome in the chill of the morning. Sharps sat on a stool by the table, pulled out his knife and began cleaning his nails.

'You are labouring, Mr Potter, under a misapprehension,' Kelly said, 'in thinking we're the moving force behind this attack on Mr Bowman. The Barrows reside in a dangerous part of town. The young man's smart attire might mark him as a target for violence from some of the unhappy youth. We live, we should not need to tell you so, in uncertain times. Might you not, as an arbiter of truth in your position as an editor, consider these other explanations, rather than leap to any conclusion?'

Edison snorted. 'Nonsense.'

'The young man is sleeping upstairs, is he not?'

'What's that to you?'

'Nothing at all. We wish him pleasant dreams. Why is my suggestion nonsense, Mr Potter?'

'The street was cleared in preparation. Doors and shutters closed. No jeering, no attempt at robbery. And Wilbur's had nothing but courtesy from his neighbours and returned the same to them. Those were your men. They named you. They were acting in your name. And I know why. You are protecting that wife-beating bastard, Mangrave, who's been cleaning your money for you through The Empire.'

A fluttering upset crossed Kelly's strange features, an expression of almost saintly suffering and restraint.

'We understand how you may have come to this conclusion, Mr Potter. We see that now, but we have certain rules. This attack would be in contravention of those rules.'

Edison felt curiosity stir within him. He was certain that if Ray Kelly had ordered the attack, he would say so. But if he hadn't ordered it, it seemed some of his men had acted without his authority.

'Your rules are your business, Kelly. But I know you're a crook, pure and simple. Claim you have a code, if you like, but you are no gentleman thief. You're a stain on this city. If you think I'm going to fall into line, ignore what you do as long as you only kill the weak and your fellow criminals—'

Sharps stood up fast enough to knock the stool backwards, and the knife in his hand glimmered.

'Sit down, Sharps!' Kelly barked, then continued more quietly, 'We'll give the man licence to say what he likes in his own kitchen.'

Sharps picked up the stool again and sat as ordered, but kept his eyes fixed on Edison and the knife loose in his hand.

'We came to make enquiries and offer our assistance. If the young man has lost anything of value, or has medical expenses to be paid—'

'If he takes a farthing from you, for any reason, I'll sack him. I know where your money comes from. No decent man should touch a penny of it.'

Kelly snarled. 'Be quiet! Take care you don't push us too far. We are a part of this city – part of what keeps it moving and breathing, just as you are. We will keep our own house in order, and you, you pious prick, will get up every day and know you can still suck down your cigars and enjoy moving about in the sunlight because we are patient, and we are moderate, and we have bigger fish to fry than Wilbur Bowman and his scribbling.'

He got up quickly and the chair squeaked, then rocked. 'Come, Sharps, we are out of sorts. We swear if anyone crosses us before nightfall, there will be hell to pay and blood on your hands, Edison Potter.'

'Your sins are your own, Kelly,' Edison said, failing to bite back the retort.

Kelly didn't even look at him. Sharps jumped to his feet and held the back door open for his master.

Edison watched them go. The door slammed shut and he breathed out at last. His heart was thumping hard in his chest, and he knew the palms that held his over-sweet tea were sweating.

CHAPTER THIRTY-TWO

Anderson Hargreaves and his wife, Naomi, had their breakfast at the usual early hour and then waited. Unable to sit still, Anderson went to the bay window and squinted down the street. He owned, thanks to many years of diligent work for Lassiter Enterprises, a pleasant villa a stroll out of town, which was opposite a park. Naomi had taken their children there for their daily exercise when they were small, and now his daughter took her own baby there most mornings. He could see the gates from his window and noticed two odd figures sitting on a bench just inside them. The older one wore a scarf, thrown over his shoulder in a rather theatrical manner, and the younger one, somewhat obscured by his companion, seemed to be wearing some sort of uniform. His mind registered them as an oddity, but not the possibility these could be Lady Lassiter's emissaries, waiting till a decent hour to announce themselves. His thoughts were too clouded by his concerns at work as he peered down the street for more plausible candidates.

He was often plagued by such worries these days. He saw strange fluctuations in the Lassiter accounts – payments made and strange spasms of cash received – and he found Edmund's airy dismissals of his concerns unnerving.

Sir Edmund's, I should say now.

Then he realised he recognised the man in the uniform. It was the stage doorman from The Empire – the one he and Edmund had asked to wait outside while they searched the area.

The carriage clock on the shelf struck eight, and at almost the same moment the odd couple got up from the bench and began to walk towards his house.

'Anderson, what are you peering out of the window for?' Naomi asked with a laugh, looking up from her copy of the *Highbridge Gazette*.

'I think you had better make more tea, my love,' he said. 'We are about to have visitors.'

On cue, they heard the brass door knocker. Anderson opened the door, and his wife got up from the table to gaze with frank curiosity around his shoulder. The doorway was filled by an older gentleman with a scarf, a thin moustache and dramatically swept-back hair. Behind him stood the doorman from the theatre.

'Mr Hargreaves?' the older man asked.

Anderson admitted as much.

'My name is Ivor French. And we have a great deal to discuss.'

There wasn't much in the way of discussion at first. Mr and Mrs Hargreaves provided tea, and luckily there was still some of the fruit cake from her midweek bake. When everyone was settled, they were treated to a monologue from Ivor French, which began with what an honourable and talented man Jack Treadwell was, but veered often and extensively into a history of Ivor's own theatrical career, which entailed a lot of quotations from *King Lear*.

Anderson's teacup was cold and empty when he finally managed to interject.

'How may I help you, Mr French?'

'Ah, yes! Yesterday morning, you searched the stage door area which our good friend, such is his devotion to the arts, has made his home over the last months.'

Naomi made a move to stand, but Ivor held up his hand.

'Pray, do stay, dear lady! There is nothing here that you should not know. A simple misunderstanding that my friend Danny Moon and I are eager and willing to clear up.'

Naomi needed no further encouragement to remain. This was by far the most interesting visit she had had in five years. She freshened the teapot in preparation.

Anderson cleared his throat. 'Yes, Mr French. I did search that area, at the request of and in the company of my employer, Sir Edmund Lassiter.'

He kept his voice very neutral, but Naomi couldn't help but glance at him as she refilled their cups. Anderson was the soul of discretion, but she had the impression her husband missed Sir Barnabas very much.

'And you discovered a fifty-pound note?' Ivor enquired over the rim of his fresh cup of tea.

Anderson nodded.

'Marvellous. You have it still in your possession?'

'I do,' Anderson replied. 'My understanding is that it is evidence of a particularly despicable theft. I understand from something Sir Edmund said later in the day that the matter is to be resolved quietly, without any prosecution of Mr Treadwell.' His face flushed. 'Though I tell you frankly, Mr French, I think a man who would steal from a fund for veterans should be drummed out of town forthwith – and the money will be returned to the fund.'

'I'm afraid that particular note doesn't belong to the Veterans' Fund. We'd like it returned, please.' Ivor sipped from Naomi Hargreaves' best china with extravagant care.

'I don't understand.'

'It's mine!' Danny said.

They were the first words the doorman had spoken, but he seemed to take great delight in saying them.

'Yours? Mr Moon, you are telling me that fifty-pound note is your property? Forgive me, but that is a large amount for any man to have lying around.'

'S-savings. I don't like banks.' Danny broke off a piece of cake and popped it in his mouth. 'Been saving since the war. I live at home.'

'You see,' Ivor said gently, 'when I called at the theatre yesterday afternoon, I found Danny in a state of distress, though, knowing that the dress rehearsal yesterday afternoon was consuming the attention of his friends, he did not wish to trouble them with news of this devastating loss.' Ivor clapped Danny on the back. 'Stout fellow.

'Not being caught up in the imminent production,' he continued, 'I was assisting him in searching the area when we heard in passing Mr Treadwell tell a friend he had been accused of stealing money – to wit, two fifty-pound notes – from the Veterans' Fund. One presumed spent, the other found among Mr Treadwell's books. The mystery of the loss of Danny's savings was immediately solved. You really must put the money into a bank, you know, Danny.'

'Y-yes, Ivor.'

'A quick word with Lady Lassiter after the stresses of the dress were over, and the mistake was clarified entirely. Thus the telephone call you received last evening, preparing you for our visit.'

Anderson opened and closed his mouth a couple of times.

'But, Mr French . . . You must understand, whatever this gentleman's claims, the coincidence is just too much! I have it on the word of the gentlemen involved that they each put a fifty-pound note into the donations box, and no fifty-pound notes were paid into the bank with the rest of the money collected that night. Sir Edmund recalled seeing this Treadwell, a recent employee, acting suspiciously near the box. Fifty-pound notes were stolen. A fifty-pound note was discovered.'

'*Aha!*' Ivor exclaimed, and Naomi slopped her tea into the saucer. 'My point exactly! *Our* point. It was Danny, my sagacious friend, who pointed out that a quick test could be made.'

'A test?'

'A test which is also the proof, Mr Hargreaves! The proof that this is some unfortunate error. You have just told me you have the note in your possession – well, Danny and I have the donations box. Mr Hargreaves, fetch the note! Danny, produce the box!'

Anderson felt that this was all getting out of hand. 'I'm really not sure . . .'

'Indulge us,' Ivor said, in a low purr which could have carried from the back of the stage to the gallery, and helped himself to more cake.

'Yes, do indulge them, Anderson,' Naomi agreed.

In the face of such persuasion, Anderson could do nothing else.

Anderson went to fetch the cash box from his study. He had been uncomfortable during the search, and even more so when showing Lady Lassiter the note and offering his word as to where it had been found. It had all seemed unnecessary, and the glee on Edmund's face had been distasteful. He could not understand why

Edmund and his mother had wanted him there, then shuffled him out of the room again once he had told Lady Lassiter where the note had been discovered.

He had left feeling rather used, and resenting it.

He returned with the note in a large envelope.

'Before we go any further, may I ask, Mr Moon, exactly where you were keeping this money?'

'A big green book,' Danny said promptly.

Anderson nodded.

In his absence, the large rosewood donations box had been placed on the table and the tea things moved to make room for it. And everyone was standing up.

'Is that note you now hold the very one you took from the book yesterday morning?' Ivor asked, with all the dramatic import of a conjuror asking a mark to identify his card.

'It is.'

'And you were there on the night of the gala, Mr Hargreaves. This is the donations box, is it not?'

'The very same,' Naomi interjected. 'Such lovely wood. I noticed it as I put in a five-shilling note.'

'You are a truly kind lady.' Ivor bowed to her. 'Could you, Mr Hargreaves, put that note, the one discovered in the book, the very one which is alleged stolen, into the box, just as one of those very generous gentlemen did on the night of the gala?'

Anderson frowned at them and took the note out of the envelope, then proffered it towards the slit in the top of the donations box. It had been folded once, so as to fit conveniently into a man's wallet. And he saw the problem.

'This cannot be the note,' he said. 'Look, Naomi! It has been folded only once, but one would have to fold it again to get it through the slit in the top of the box.'

To his surprise, he felt an enormous swell of relief. He beamed at his strange visitors.

'Yes, yes! My sincere apologies, Mr Moon!' He handed the note to Danny with genuine enthusiasm. 'I do think, as Mr French says, you'd be much better off putting this in a bank. But it cannot be one of the notes Foss and Tompkins contributed. That much is obvious.'

'Marvellous work, Mr French!' Naomi said, clasping her hands together but managing to stop just short of applause. Then her husband's face darkened.

'But it remains a fact, Mr French, that one hundred pounds is missing from the fund, and Mr Treadwell was seen near the donations box.'

Ivor smiled. 'Many people were! Foss and Tompkins were. Mrs Hargreaves has just told us she was, too. But I have proof absolute that whoever took those notes, it was not Mr Treadwell!'

'Oh, but how?' Naomi said delightedly.

'The c-case of the missing umbrella!' Danny said, grinning.

'Indeed.' Ivor nodded at his audience. 'During our discussions with Mr Frederick Poole yesterday – the best front of house manager in the country, in my humble opinion – Danny and I ascertained a number of key points.'

Even Anderson found himself agog at this point.

'*One!* The donations box was not left unguarded as a matter of course. No, no, no! The Empire is not so casual about your five-shilling note, Mrs Hargreaves. For the duration of the party, and as the guests were leaving, a young lad named Marcus was stationed nearby to keep an eye on it. But . . . *two* !'

Naomi jumped.

'At one point, Marcus was sent upstairs by Mr Poole to fetch an umbrella from lost property, so one lady in particular would have her feathered headdress protected from a sudden spring shower. For a few crucial minutes, as Mr Poole dealt with the departing dignitaries, no one was watching the box.'

'Lady Foss was wearing feathers!' Mrs Hargreaves said, and was rewarded with a nod.

'And, dash it, Sir Jonathan said in his letter he thought to put the note in the box while waiting for an umbrella to be fetched,' Anderson added. 'But how does this prove Jack Treadwell innocent?'

'I have already said Mr Poole is the best front of house manager in the country,' Ivor said quietly, then built to his crescendo. 'So why was there not an umbrella waiting in the lobby against such an eventuality as a spring shower? Why? *Because*,' he thundered, 'as Mr Poole can testify, Jack Treadwell, with Mr Poole's agreement, had already taken it to protect Miss Stella Stanmore on the short walk to the Metropole! That is why Marcus had to leave his post!'

Naomi did applaud this time, enthusiastically. 'So Mr Treadwell left before the notes were even in the donations box! That's magnificent, Mr French!'

'It does seem unarguable,' Anderson agreed with a smile. 'I suppose some miscreant off the street must have seen their chance and dashed in at just that moment.'

'Very unfortunate,' Ivor agreed. 'I'm sure Lady Lassiter will be delighted to make good the loss to the fund. And Mr Poole has resolved to keep two umbrellas to hand in future.'

'So Edmund must have been mistaken?' Naomi said, with a glance at her husband. 'I'm very glad Mr Treadwell's innocence has been proven, though.'

'Jack . . . he saved my life.' Danny put the fifty-pound note into his pocket and spoke slowly. 'Not just mine, either. We were g-going over the top. Trying to get across no-man's-land. Companies got mixed halfway. Major Lassiter panicked. Tried to take cover, make the rest of us go on without him. To save himself. Then he got stuck, couldn't make it back. German artillery were finding their range. Jack rushed back for him, pulled him out of the shell hole and ordered us all forward, gave us the commands that Major Lassiter should've been giving. Edmund Lassiter almost got us all killed. Jack saved us.'

Naomi looked at her husband, expecting him to be shocked, or to say something to defend his employer. His complete lack of surprise and his silence were instructive.

The donations box was packed away, compliments and thanks for tea civilly offered and received, and the Hargreaves ushered their guests out into the morning. Naomi closed the door behind them and turned to her husband.

'So how did Sir Edmund know a hundred pounds had been stolen, Anderson?' she asked quietly.

He didn't answer her directly; he only gave one of those shakes of the head which could mean everything or nothing, then picked up his coat.

CHAPTER THIRTY-THREE

The theatre hummed with nervous excitement even before the company arrived, as if the bones and bricks of the place could feel it coming.

Bill gave up trying to stay at his digs, and arrived at eight in the morning to find Ollie guarding the door and most of the company already present. The chorus were either having final fittings with Mrs Gardener or practising their steps in the halls. Frederick Poole was polishing the brass fittings of the box office, Little Sam was making his crew rehearse the most complicated set changes again and again, and even some of the musicians had turned up early and were playing in the pit under Tom's cheerful guidance.

At 9.30, Jack found Bill and Evie running through their lines in Evie's dressing room.

'They got it!' he told them, a grin splitting his face from ear to ear. 'Ivor and Danny! Edmund can say what he likes – they proved that note wasn't one of the ones missing from the box. And that I couldn't've taken either of them!'

'And what about the other thing?' Evie said, lowering her voice. 'What if Constance threatens to tell everyone that you're Lillian's son?'

'That's up to her, Evie,' Jack replied. 'But I don't think Lillian's minded to hand over her shares in the theatre to Edmund now, no matter what they do.'

He disappeared again, almost with his old energy. The hum of excitement in the building ticked up a notch.

Grace had lost the fizzy oblivion of the night before, but she was so taut with anticipation, she couldn't think straight either. She didn't want to leave The Empire, or go to Hollywood. She wanted to write plays here instead, but could she bear to stay if Jack and Lillian were together? She wandered the theatre, through the corridors, through the promenades and bars where flowers were being arranged, glasses polished, linens smoothed, not because she had anything to do, but because the thought of staying still was impossible. After half an hour of wandering, she opened the doors to the dress circle and went through. Below her, on the stage, the chorus were now treating Sam's set like a playground, as instructed. Doors were slammed, steps jumped off, chairs and props in general brandished. Then Grace noticed a figure sitting at the front of the circle. For a second she thought it was Jack, then Jack crossed the stage below her, calling out to the chorus to remember to leave the props table as they found it.

'Hello?'

The man turned towards her. He looked relatively young, but had an old-fashioned collar and Victorian sideburns. He smiled at her in a friendly manner, then disappeared. Grace sat down very suddenly, remembering the story of the theatre ghost who only turned up for hits.

'Oh. Good Lord. I hope you're right, whoever you are.'

'Grace! Anyone seen Grace?'

She went down to the front of the circle and waved. 'Ruby? I'm here.'

'We need to double-check the intro line for the cabaret number!'

'I'm coming!'

Grace headed towards the nearest door, her heart suddenly light in her chest.

Constance's reasons for taking the papers to Lillian herself were purely practical. It was efficient for her to get the document gifting the shares in The Empire to Edmund signed today. She would then be in a position to have the papers drawn up for the sale to Joe Allerdyce as quickly as possible. There would be the usual inevitable delays which occur when dealing with the transfer of a large piece of property, but that was no reason not to hurry along at this stage. That she would get to see Lillian's humiliation with her own eyes was a bonus, and one she felt she deserved after all these years of playing second fiddle to her showgirl stepmother-in-law.

News of an accident at the North End factory, in which a worker had been injured, had cast a shadow over her morning, but then Joe Allerdyce's telegram had returned a spring in her step. Eighty-five thousand pounds! She had to admit, he had kept his word, offering a fair price for the whole humiliating package. Constance wished him well.

The front of house manager offered to show her up to Lillian's offices, but she reminded him tartly she had visited before. Her confidence in her memory was misplaced. The backstage corridors all looked alike, and after ten minutes' searching she found herself in danger of exiting the building again through the stage door. That new doorman was there, and a strange tall gentleman with a long scarf. They regarded her coldly, and their dog growled at her. Eventually the doorman gave her directions and she returned to her search, finally arriving in Lillian's outer office a little late and a little out of breath.

No matter. The secretary went in to announce her, and Constance had a chance to smooth her hair and glance in the mirror. This was one of her good days. She definitely had the March nose, even if it made her small eyes look smaller; still, it was nevertheless proof of her own superior breeding.

Finally she was ushered in. Lillian stood up from behind the desk to greet her, and they took their seats opposite each other. Lillian did not offer her tea or coffee, which irritated Constance, because she had been looking forward to turning it down.

She set the brown envelope containing the necessary documents on the desk, her handbag on her lap, and started pulling off her gloves.

'You've brought them yourself,' Lillian said coldly.

'Yes. And I've received a telegram from Joe Allerdyce. He is quite delighted to hear that the sale will go ahead and has made a very reasonable offer.'

Lillian took the envelope, opened it, and read the documents it contained. Then she set them down again. 'No.'

'What do you mean, "no", Lillian?' Constance gave a little laugh. 'I know you can be a little flighty, but I'm sure you can't have forgotten our discussion yesterday.'

'You mean when you threatened the son whom I had thought was dead with prison, in an attempt to defraud me of my share in this theatre? That conversation?'

'You thought he was dead?'

'Yes. I thought he had been killed in 1917. In fact, he had only been taken prisoner. I have had the chance to see him again through the narrowest stroke of luck, and because the friend who raised him was a very honourable woman.'

Constance didn't like that emphasis on 'honourable' or the word 'defraud'.

'I am ridding the Lassiter family name of the stain of this theatrical adventurism, preventing scandal and protecting the jobs of our workers.'

'So you think there is something noble in your attempt to blackmail and defraud? What a supple ethical thinker you are, Constance.'

Another word Constance didn't like – 'attempt'. And Lillian really looked far too comfortable. Constance had expected there might be some hysterical resistance, some further protests that Jack could not have done such a thing, tears, even . . . but this? Lillian sitting back in her chair and looking at Constance down her nose? Constance had not expected this. She shoved Lillian's pen towards her in a spasm of petulance.

'Just sign the papers, Lillian.'

'No. I will not. I have had visitors myself this morning. And I telephoned Joe Allerdyce a little while ago and explained to him that you were mistaken. I intend to hold on to my shares in The Empire.'

She picked up the papers and tore them in two with a sudden violence that made Constance start.

'You know what I found interesting, Constance? Joe sounded relieved. Like he suspected there was something sordid in the whole deal, and was glad not to have to sully his hands doing business with you and Edmund. How does that feel, I wonder, to know that good old Joe Allerdyce, king of the cheap ale and dirty songs, would rather not befoul himself by associating with you?'

The woman is mad, Constance thought.

'How dare you speak to me like that! You are nothing but a common little slut, and your son is a thief. Your only choice is to sign those papers.'

Lillian stood up. 'Jack Treadwell is no thief. We can prove he left before Foss and Tompkins had their spasm of generosity, and the note found in his book was never put in the donations box. God, Edmund really is a fool, isn't he? I can't believe he didn't notice it had only been folded once, so would not have fitted through the slit. The money has already been returned to Danny Moon by Mr Hargreaves, with his sincere apologies.'

'But it didn't belong to Danny Moon!' Constance said before she could stop herself.

Lillian raised an eyebrow. 'Didn't it? He says the money is his. The only way Edmund could deny it was Danny's would be if he admitted he put the note there himself. Did Edmund withdraw a fifty-pound note from the bank yesterday? Did you?'

Constance went red, but didn't say anything.

Lillian put her hands on the table and leant over towards Constance, the light from the window behind her making her resemble an angry angel.

'You actually made me think he could be guilty for a second, Constance. My God! You question my morals, but you make me look like a saint. You should have known that once I looked into Jack's eyes, I'd know he'd never take money from the Veterans' Fund! You should have known that a man like him, raised by decent people, not a creature like you, would have friends who would defend him. I should have known that, too. Perhaps a little of the stain of the Lassiters rubbed off on me. Of that I am heartily ashamed, and I hope my son will in time forgive me.'

'I'll tell everyone you had a child before your marriage – I'll tell everyone you gave your son away!'

*

'Publish and be damned. I'll happily give tearful interviews about my terrible choice to the *Highbridge Illustrated News*, if necessary. It will be dreary in the extreme, but this is 1922. We don't live in a Dickens novel, and I very much doubt people will care very much or for very long. Do your worst, but if you ever say anything to question the honour of my son, or the honour of the very fine people who brought him up, you should know there are a lot of men in this town who would be willing to discuss Edmund's behaviour in the war, should they be asked to do so.'

Constance opened and closed her lips, her mouth dry and tasting of ashes. 'But Lassiter Enterprises, Lillian . . . I see you have no family feeling for Edmund, but what of Tom? He is Sir Barnabas's grandson, too. What of your husband's legacy? What of all the workers? Edmund has made some foolish decisions . . . but we have to save the company.'

Lillian hesitated. She had been a worker in a Lassiter factory once. So had Bessie Treadwell. She knew enough about the lives of the workers to realise the sudden collapse of Lassiter Enterprises would destroy hundreds of families in the city.

'How much did Joe offer you?'

'Eighty-five thousand.'

Lillian thought of the other visitor she had greeted that morning. 'I can't afford to buy Edmund's shares, but I know who might.'

Usher Barton dismissed the chorus and told them to rest and ready themselves for opening night. Then he climbed the shallow staircases to the rehearsal corridor and Lillian's office. To his surprise he saw Ivor, Danny, Jack, Bill, Evie and Miss Fortescue clustered tightly together, their ears pressed to the door of the inner office.

'What on earth are you doing?' he asked, and was roundly shushed.

At one point, Ivor and Danny looked particularly gleeful and their fellow eavesdroppers whispered congratulations of some sort. At another, all eyes turned to Jack.

It was like watching the audience of a pantomime without being able to see or hear the action. The phone on Miss Fortescue's desk rang. She gave it an agonised glance, but didn't move, so Usher lifted the receiver with a sigh.

'This is Usher Barton. Yes, Miss Fortescue is . . . otherwise engaged at the moment, and I happened to be passing. Can I be of service? I shall put you through to the box office with my compliments, Sir Jonathan. I am sure Mr Poole will have reserved tickets for you.'

The group around the door broke up with sudden speed. Bill and Evie sprinted into the corridor and began practising dance steps. Ivor dragged Jack towards a far corner of the office and began talking to him about his early theatrical triumphs. Danny simply stood very straight next to the coat rack, as if that might make him somehow inconspicuous. It did not.

Almost at once, the door opened and Constance emerged. Her cheeks were very red and she had a sort of sniffy look about her. She glanced round quickly, though no one other than Usher was looking at her, then scuttled out.

The door opened again and Lillian put her head round it.

'Miss Fortescue, if you would be so kind . . .' She stopped, seeing all the people gathered, not very casually, around the outer office.

They burst into applause – all but Usher, who had missed the performance. Lillian paused, then smiled and made them all a careful bow, before offering her own applause to Danny and Ivor.

In the weeks that followed, Usher thought of that woman, bitter and humiliated, leaving along the corridor. He wondered if she had heard that applause, and what difference it might have made.

CHAPTER THIRTY-FOUR

Agnes joined Joe and his sons for afternoon tea in the Metropole. She noted, in the same way she noticed horseflesh, that they were both handsome young men, steady in their bearing, and she was rather gratified by the way they leapt to their feet at her approach and the warmth of their welcome.

'It's a great pleasure to meet you, Miss de Montfort!' the elder one, Arthur, said. 'We've been wondering why Dad isn't in the office at all hours the way he used to be. I thought he'd been kidnapped when he was three hours late calling and asking me about the weekly takings.'

'And I almost sent for the doctor when I wrote asking what he thought about my choice of pantomime and he started his reply, "Whatever you think best, son!"' the younger one, Francis, added.

Joe chuckled, and Agnes was pleased to see he seemed to enjoy this mild teasing from his sons.

'Of course,' Francis continued, 'he followed that up with

three pages of notes about the staging and who my principal boy should be.'

'I hope you don't think I'm damaging your father's business at all?' Agnes said as they took their seats again.

The two men laughed.

'Lord, no,' Arthur replied. 'I'm delighted to think he won't work himself into a heart attack. I understand you don't like the new house?'

'I loathe it. But then I'd have said the same about the songs from musical revues three months ago, so I concede that opinions may change.'

'"How elastic our stiff prejudices grow when love once comes to bend them."' Francis raised his teacup, then caught a look from his brother which made him stammer. 'W-we just did a stage version of *Moby Dick*, that's a line from it . . . I didn't mean to be offensive, Miss de Montfort.'

She pushed the silver stand towards him. 'Do have a cake. The miniature sponges here are very fine.'

Joe did not seem embarrassed, but to cover his sons' confusion at any rate, he changed the conversation. 'Lady Lassiter rang me this morning, Agnes. She's decided, it seems, not to sell her shares to Edmund after all.'

'Are you disappointed, Dad?' Arthur asked, a look of genuine concern on his face.

Joe shook his head. 'I'll reckon I'll survive. Though, let me tell you, I'd like to see Mangrave off the scene.'

Agnes helped herself to a cake of her own. 'I think he'll find his employment at the theatre ending suddenly and very soon, as it happens, Joe.'

'Do you, now?'

'Yes. That was why I was a little late for this delicious tea.

As you know, I came into a large sum of money very recently, selling my north paddock. I decided to reinvest it. I bought Edmund's stake in The Empire an hour ago. Lillian and I thought we'd fire Mangrave together this evening. Our first joint managerial action.'

'Hang on a second,' Joe said. 'Let me get this straight. You've bought his stake in The Empire?'

Her mouth being full of cake, Agnes could only nod in reply, looking at Joe with an expression which approximated wide-eyed innocence.

'You, Agnes de Montfort, who'd barely been seen a play until a few months ago, now own forty-nine per cent of the largest theatre in Highbridge?'

Another nod.

'And you have bought it with the money I paid you for that land?'

She swallowed. 'Yes, I did. You don't mind, do you, Joe?'

Joe Allerdyce's sons looked at their father, and for a moment his face was completely immobile. Then he let out a great bark of laughter, just as he had when Agnes had mistaken him for a footman. It was so loud that it startled a waiter on the other side of the dining room into nearly dropping an egg sandwich into the lap of Lady Foss. And then Joe kept laughing, till tears ran down his cheeks. Agnes put a comforting hand on his shoulder and offered him a glass of water, but that only seemed to make him laugh more.

Opening night. It was actually, finally, terrifyingly, time. Grace stood in the shadows of the wings stage right, her heart in her mouth as the house lights went down and the audience settled. The performance space was in darkness. Lance, standing beside her, straightened his cuffs.

'Break a leg, Lance,' she managed to say in a slightly strangled voice.

He winked at her, then strode out onto the stage. A single spotlight speared the darkness and he lifted his arms.

'Ladies and gentlemen, welcome to the Hotel Riviera!'

The lights flooded the stage, illuminating the set. It was a magical sort of cutaway, showing the hotel ballroom and the beautiful summer's day outside. The orchestra struck up and the first number was all of a sudden underway. Half the chorus were playing the staff at the hotel, the men in tight trousers and waistcoats, the women in black and white maids' uniforms. Usher had given them all props – table linens and dusters, vases of flowers. It was actually happening. Grace tried to remember to breathe.

Now the character actors and the rest of the chorus came on as the guests. Ruben and Clifford had bathed the whole scene in a bluish light which made it look as if every beam was reflected off an azure sea. A pearl spotlight found Stella appearing at the top of the grand staircase, singing her verse. Lance's face as he looked at her was a picture of longing.

'I think they're going to like it.'

Grace jumped and found Evie standing behind her.

'You might try and enjoy it, too, Grace! We're almost four minutes in and no one's fallen over yet.'

Evie was wearing her widow's weeds and dark glasses, with her suitcase in her hand, ready for her big entrance at the end of this song. She didn't seem nervous at all.

'Is something wrong, darling?' she asked.

Grace couldn't help herself. 'I know about Lillian and Jack, Evie. I feel such a fool, but it's got me terribly upset. I thought . . . I know it's silly, but I thought perhaps he might be starting to . . . like me. But that's all over now I know about him and Lillian!'

On stage, the welcome number closed to whoops and applause. The stagehands took over, flying scenery in and out and narrowing the stage to the reception area.

'You're not going to let *that* put you off, Grace? Are you so conventionally minded? Oh, wait there.'

Evie swept on and the audience cheered her arrival. Grace watched, open-mouthed, as Evie struck the bell on the front desk and Lance emerged through the reception door. Grace knew that theatre people could be a little bohemian about matters of the heart, but she didn't understand how Evie could act like it didn't matter at all. She felt suddenly very small and wished she hadn't said anything.

'I'm Katherine De Freuendes Saxon Fitzwilliam Grange,' Evie announced in an American drawl. 'Are you the proprietor?'

She managed to make even saying her name sound vaguely indecent. The audience applauded her again. They seemed to have got into the habit.

On the other side of the stage, Jack was gripping the book so hard he was afraid it was going to snap in his hands. Stella had paused next to him to watch Evie's entrance.

'Blimey, they love her, don't they?' she said with wry affection.

'They certainly seem to. Go and change, Stella.'

'I've got plenty of time, darling. Wow, nothing sour about this performance. If they keep applauding her every word like this, I'll have time for a cocktail in my dressing room, too.'

Jack looked at her and she held up her hand.

'I'm joking, sweetie! Just joking! It's going swimmingly. Why do you look so glum?'

Jack sighed. 'Stella, I think Grace is in love with Lance.'

She gave him a long look. 'How do you figure *that*?'

'I saw her coming out of his dressing room before the dress rehearsal. And she says she's going to Hollywood to write with him. Why *wouldn't* she be in love with him, anyway? He's so much better-looking than I am. And brilliant. And talented. And I'm just . . .'

'So you *do* have feelings for Grace! I knew it!'

'Please just go and change, Stella!'

He reached out and took hold of the arm of a passing dancer, moving him out of the way of a descending sandbag.

Evie exited the stage, kicking her heels as she did, to further applause. Milly was waiting for her; they had three minutes to get her into evening dress. On stage, the set turned into the Hotel Riviera nightclub, and Mabel Mills was revealed with her jazz band, to more tremendous applause. Bill began the tap sequence, leading the chorus back and forth across the stage and snapping his heels. Grace watched him. If he had any nerves this evening, she could see no evidence of them.

'I know people can have old-fashioned attitudes,' Evie said, as if their conversation had never been interrupted. 'But even if it comes out about Lillian and Jack, would your family really mind so much?'

Grace stared at her. 'Evie, *I'd* mind!'

Evie put her arms forward and Milly smoothed on her silk evening gloves. 'But why?'

Grace was suddenly close to tears. 'Evie, I don't want to get involved with a man who is sleeping with another woman! I suppose I might be terribly old-fashioned, but I . . . It would break my heart!'

Evie went still. Then Milly tapped her arm and she leant on Milly's shoulder as she stepped out of one pair of shoes and into another. 'Oh . . . Good gracious. Grace, dear, it's not what you think. You must talk to Jack.'

'But I saw them together . . .'

'Am I secure, Milly?'

'Yes, Miss D'Angelo.'

'Thank you. We managed that marvellously. Grace, my dearest, I can't explain, but honestly, it's not like that at all!'

Then Evie swept back out on stage again.

Jack had started counting his breaths. Everything was working and the audience seemed to be lapping it up, but every time he stopped counting, he thought of Grace, and that offhand way she'd talked about going to Hollywood with Lance, and his heart was squeezed.

Then Lance himself came off after the nightclub sequence, where he and Bill had been dancing alternately with Stella and Evie. He caught his breath, while on stage Stella interrogated Evie about her previous husbands. The audience were laughing in all the right places. Lance pulled off his bow tie and handed it to Jack, ready to go back on for the clearing-up scene with Bill.

'Grace isn't in love with me, you idiot,' he said conversationally. 'She's in love with you.'

'I . . . What?'

'Stella told me what you said earlier. Look, Grace told me she didn't want to write for Hollywood when I first asked her. She wants to do plays here, if this show goes well. If she said anything else to you, it's because she thinks you and Lillian are . . . you know, having an affair.'

'An *affair*? But— Wait, so you and she—'

'Just talk to Grace, Jack.'

And with that, Lance slouched back on to the stage, every inch the star-crossed lover.

*

Frederick Poole stepped quietly into the royal box, where Lady Lassiter was hosting Agnes, Joe Allerdyce and his sons, along with Ivor and Danny.

'I've been informed, Lady Lassiter, that Mr Mangrave has just come in to his office.'

'Thank you, Mr Poole. Will you ask him to stay there so I may have a word with him at the interval?'

Poole removed himself with a nod, and Joe leant over to Lillian.

'This is torture. Whatever you paid Usher Barton, it was worth every bloody penny.'

Lillian smiled. 'Lance managed to get him for quite a reasonable rate,' she whispered. 'There will be champagne and refreshments in the royal retiring room during the interval, Joe. Usher will be there. If you're feeling brave, you can try hiring him for something while I'm out of the way.'

'And where will you be, Lillian?'

'Agnes and I will be sacking Mangrave, as planned. Why wait until after the show?'

Joe smiled. 'Your champagne'll taste all the sweeter for knowing that.' Then he returned his attention to the stage.

FINALE

CHAPTER THIRTY-FIVE

Edmund and his mother watched the performance from the centre of the dress circle, and remained in their seats during the interval. As soon as the old duffers, the lords and the well-heeled of Highbridge had shuffled off to the bar, Constance put her hand on Edmund's arm.

'Edmund, this is a setback, of course. But we must put our best foot forward. We will give Mangrave that position, as we promised, then use the capital from the sale of the shares to deal with the most immediate problems at Lassiter Enterprises. The worker who was injured today must be compensated, naturally, and the manager you sacked persuaded not to go to the newspapers. The loss of a week at full production while they continue the testing is an annoyance, but the capital gives us some more time. The wages will be paid. I have a few names to suggest for the board to quiet these rumours about your impulsiveness.'

Constance was very dull sometimes. It was a great pity, Edmund thought. Like every other woman, his mother had disappointed

him in the end. So Lillian had called their bluff, and Hargreaves
had his doubts.

The idiot had just handed over fifty pounds to that damned
Danny Moon.

Edmund had told Hargreaves what he thought of that piece of
business. Then Hargreaves had resigned.

Good riddance.

Edmund was glad to see the back of the man. And these woolly
accusations of his poor business sense were nothing more than talk.

'I have a different approach, Mama,' he said. 'The shares, and
the money I get from their sale to Agnes, are part of my own
personal fortune. Nothing to do with Lassiter Enterprises.'

'Edmund!' his mother hissed. 'The reputation of the company
is being damaged. It is time to show your personal investment.
Leadership. A commitment to see the company through difficult
times.'

Edmund let her talk. He would say one thing for this show – it
was certainly giving him an appetite for a holiday. There was a
dancer on stage . . .

Josie – that's her name.

She'd been one of the professional dancers at the Royal Café
until this ridiculous musical came along. He'd tried to get her
alone a couple of times in the past, but she'd found some excuse
to stay in with other people, the little tease. Still, she'd be at the
party tonight. He'd be nice, flatter her about her dancing, and try
his luck again. Something to look forward to.

'Edmund, you're not listening to me!'

'No, Mama, I'm not. You know, perhaps I'll take Agnes's
money and start a little investment fund in London.'

'But, Edmund! You are the baronet. You cannot desert your
grandfather's company!'

'I'm not sure that running a bunch of factories is all it's cracked up to be,' he drawled. 'Perhaps Tom should run them. He might like textiles, and fancy wear and cutlery. Though I suppose you've been such a bitch to him, he might throw it all over to be assistant to Ruby Rowntree. God, what a ripping joke. He'd rather be subject to her than you.'

'Edmund, how can you be so cruel to me, after everything I've done for you?'

'Don't fuss so, Mama! Enjoy the show, then go back to your knitting circles and leave the business to me.'

Constance crumpled the programme in her hand.

Mangrave was sitting at his desk in the inner office when Lillian and Agnes came in. He was tapping a fountain pen on the blotter, his round flat face creased with irritation. He looked like a discarded napkin.

'Well, I've been waiting. What is it you want to say to me, Lady Lassiter?'

'I wanted to introduce you to my new partner at The Empire, Mr Mangrave. Miss de Montfort has bought Edmund's shares in the building and production management company.'

'And our first order of business, Mr Mangrave,' Agnes continued, 'is to fire you.'

His expression changed from irritation to boredom. 'I was aware I was unlikely to stay much longer at The Empire, no matter who owned it. Very well. I shall leave at the end of the week.'

'No,' Lillian said. 'You will leave now. At this moment.' *Did his watery grey eyes flicker towards the safe?* Lillian wasn't sure. 'Your keys, please, Mr Mangrave.'

He drew them out of his pocket and placed them on the blotter in front of him.

'And the combination for the safe,' she added.

Mangrave looked up from the blotter and smiled. 'I apologise, Lady Lassiter. I seem to have forgotten it.'

Agnes sighed. 'How tiresome. Don't worry, Lillian, the company can send a man in the morning to drill it. Goodbye, Mr Mangrave.'

Mangrave stood up slowly and tugged his waistcoat straight. 'There is nothing worse than a couple of old women trying to do the work of men. I find it faintly obscene.'

The bells indicating the interval was nearly over rang in the hallways.

Lillian smiled sweetly. 'We are naturally devastated to hear that, Mr Mangrave. It is true that gentlemen like you have a very different way of going about their business.'

'Yes,' Agnes chimed in. 'I thought the same thing, too, Lillian, when Joe and I found poor Mr Wilbur Bowman on the road last night. Thank goodness he escaped relatively unhurt, and with his notebook still in his pocket.'

Mangrave looked at her sharply.

'Yes, he is staying with his editor now,' Agnes went on. 'Edison Potter. Lovely man, though he has some strange acquaintances. Apparently Ray Kelly called on him this morning.'

'You know, Agnes . . .' Lillian folded her arms across her chest. 'I think Wilbur would be fascinated to see what's in the safe. Shall we invite him to see it opened?'

'Excellent plan, Lillian.'

Mangrave pursed his lips. 'Wilbur Bowman?'

'Yes,' Agnes said. 'Were you told he'd been chased into the river? You really cannot get the staff these days.'

'It is a struggle,' Lillian agreed.

A flush stole up Mangrave's face and he tensed his muscles.

Lillian refused to flinch, but she felt it – the sudden charge of violence in the air.

'Ladies?'

A young male voice called to them from the outer office.

'Arthur? We're in here,' Agnes replied, and Joe's tall, strong, capable sons came into the room.

'We don't want you to miss the opening of the second act,' Francis said.

'Thank you.' Lillian felt her shoulders relax a little as she picked up the keys from Mangrave's desk and tossed them in her hand. 'Our business is done and Mr Mangrave was just leaving.'

Mangrave looked at Joe's sons, then shouldered past them. When Agnes, Lillian and the two young men left the office, they locked the door behind them.

The second act was moving at the same blistering pace as the first, and the audience's enthusiasm seemed to build with every number. It was strange; now, at last, with an audience in the theatre, Grace could see the thinking behind some of Usher's decisions which had puzzled and frustrated her in rehearsals. It was as if he had been able to anticipate their reactions, and work them into the rhythms of the whole piece.

'Bill, darling, I'm going to blow the whole house up with this next number, so give me some room, won't you?' Stella said, smoking her cigarette carefully so as not to smear her lipstick.

'Of course, pet.'

He helped her up onto the rolling platform, where Mabel Mills and her band were ready and waiting. Then he turned to Grace.

'I think this is really going to be something!' He put his arm round her shoulder and squeezed. 'I hope you stay here, Grace.'

'I don't know what to do, Bill.'

'Talk to Jack. And you can write your own ticket with Lillian after tonight.'

'Do you really think so?'

'I know it.'

'Think we can make this even better than last night, Miss Mabel?' Stella was saying.

Mabel gave her a long, slow look up and down. 'I think you look like you mean business, honey.' She turned to the band. 'Gentlemen, let's leave it all out there.'

The stage crew steadied the platform, pushing it into place as the backdrop lifted, the lighting changed, and the beach was transformed back into the nightclub, festooned for a gala.

'You'll know it, too, Grace, when you and Ruby come out for your share of the ovations,' Bill said.

'What? Will I have to go on stage? And what ovations?'

'Come on, Grace, taste the air! This is a smash.'

Bill was right. Stella and Mabel's number got an ovation of its own. 'Please Be Our King' went like clockwork, with the audience catching the jokes and gasping at the choreography. Evie and Bill's duet, where he persuaded her to marry him and become a queen, was funny and moving in a way that surprised even Grace, and Lance and Stella's number sent shivers of longing around the house.

The second the final number ended, with the whole cast and Mabel on stage, the theatre exploded in wave after wave of applause. When Usher, Grace and Ruby were pulled out on stage by the principals, the cheers redoubled. For Grace, it was like dancing with Lance – a moment of pure sensation: the thunderous storm of delighted noise, the light on her face and the thudding of blood in her veins. Marcus appeared from the wings and handed them bouquets. Evie and Stella were already weighed down with flowers. Little Sam's crew lowered and raised the curtains a dozen times, until it became almost a joke.

'No more, Sam!' Usher called at last. 'Stop now, or Miss Mills will be late for her show at the Metropole.'

While the applause still sounded on the other side of the velvet, he turned to the company.

'Remarkable show, everyone. It has been an honour to work with you. Now, I understand Lillian is throwing you a party in the circle bar. Enjoy it.'

'No notes, Usher?' Stella asked.

'I only have one note – do *that* again. Do it every night, and you will make a lot of audiences happier than they have any right to be. My work here is done.'

The company applauded, and he bestowed on them one more of his strange and miraculous smiles.

CHAPTER THIRTY-SIX

The audience had left the theatre on a wave of collective happiness, leaving the company and the guests for the opening night party behind them. Lillian had been generous with the invitations, and the bars were still a crush and the atmosphere riotous. Jack moved through the party, receiving congratulations and offering them, trying to get nearer to Grace, but she kept moving away. There had been no chance to talk to her at the interval – twenty minutes of extreme activity as misplaced props were found, costumes repaired and the set rearranged. An hour or so into the festivities, Joe's contact rang in from the *Highbridge Gazette* with their notice. To no one's surprise, but to everyone's great delight, it was a rave.

When Lance took a seat at the grand piano in the bar, and Stella and Bill reprised their 'My Old Dutch' duet from the music hall revue, Jack noticed Grace disappearing through one of the side doors. He followed and found her at last, standing on the stage, waiting for him in front of the empty auditorium.

He approached with caution.

'Grace, please don't dash off again!'

She shook her head. 'I won't, Jack.'

'You've been avoiding me, though.'

She sighed and bit her lip. 'I have a little . . .' She squeezed her eyes shut. 'Everyone's saying I should talk to you, but I couldn't. Not with all those people around.'

'All those people congratulating you on your stunning success, you mean?' he said fondly.

'Yes. I suppose so. It's been smashing, but please, Jack, I have to . . . Look, are you and Lillian . . . well, having an affair? I saw you with her yesterday afternoon, but Evie was just so odd about it! Saying I shouldn't mind about your relationship, then she went sort of queer and started avoiding me, too, just telling me to talk to you! Bill did, too!'

'No! It's nothing like that. Honestly, Grace, I've never looked at anyone here in that way . . . apart from you. I swear I was still holding those feathered capes when I fell in love with you. But I was just a doorman, then I was your assistant and I was sure you'd never have a romantic notion about me.' He wanted to throw his arms around her, but she still looked upset and unsure. 'Then I saw you coming out of Lance's room looking dishevelled and you said you were off to Hollywood! I thought – well, why shouldn't you? He's a star, and I know you and he had been getting on so well . . .'

He tailed off finally.

'Oh, Jack, you goose! I was looking dishevelled because I'd been crying over you!'

'Really!' he said with a surge of delight. He took a step towards her, but she backed away.

'But, Jack, I *saw* you! That embrace . . . It meant something.'

He reached out and took her hand. 'It did. Lord, where do I start? Look, Grace, I . . . I found out yesterday afternoon that Lillian . . . is my mother.'

'What?'

'She . . . She had me when she was terribly young, so I was adopted and I never knew. Lillian thought I'd been killed in the war, but . . .'

Grace gasped and put her hand over her mouth. 'What your mam said! "Tell Jack to go and see Lady Lassiter!" Good Lord.'

'Yes! Lillian said Bessie had promised to tell me when I was twenty-five. Made that scrapbook so she could tell me all about Lillian when the time came, I suppose, but she never got the chance. Edmund and Constance found out, and they were trying to blackmail her into selling The Empire.'

'Jack!' Grace took his other hand and he felt her fingers close round his. It was better than all the ovations put together. 'It must have been a terrible shock. How do you feel?'

Her sympathy almost unmanned him. 'I've no idea. But, Grace, if it comes out . . . Do you mind that I'm . . . I know some people do care about these things. And Lillian's marvellous, but I'm afraid I have some bad blood.'

'No.' She gave her firm, sharp shake of the head. 'I don't mind in the slightest.'

'And what about Hollywood?'

'Bugger Hollywood. I like it here.'

She moved towards him. He stared for a long moment into her eyes, put his arm around her waist, and finally neither of them blushed or looked away. He lowered his face towards hers, then he felt her stiffen.

'Jack, did you hear that?'

Jack heard it now, too – Ollie's bark, high and alarmed.

They followed the bark, still holding hands.

They found Ollie stage right, in the corridor off the wings, in front of a door which led up to the royal box and management offices. His nose was down and his tail straight out.

'What is it, lad?' Jack said.

'Maybe he's seen the ghost.' Danny had come up the corridor behind them. 'What is it, Ollie?'

His work done, Ollie returned to Danny's side and had his ears scratched.

'Let's see,' Jack said. 'I quite fancy getting a look at the ghost. And he's good luck, isn't he?'

Grace put her hand on Jack's back, and he felt a wave of joy through his body which seemed to radiate from where her hand touched him.

'I saw the ghost earlier as a matter of fact,' she said. 'He seemed quite nice.'

'Did you really?' he said, smiling over his shoulder at her. 'I'd love to meet him some day.'

Then he pulled the door open. It was one of those threshold doors which studded each level of the theatre, dividing the plush and paint of the public areas from the bare plaster and ordered chaos of backstage. There was nothing to be seen, but Ollie started barking again.

'Smoke!' Danny exclaimed. 'I smell smoke.'

Jack smelled it, too, then saw it – a breath of grey along the ceiling of the corridor. He slammed the door shut on it.

'Danny! Ring the alarm! Grace, can you check the dressing rooms? Check all the fire doors are open? I'll head to the party – make sure they hear the alarm and clear out.'

Danny was shaking, but he moved as fast as he could back towards stage door, where the electrical alarm sat above the counter. It would make bells ring throughout the theatre, from the chop shop in the basement to the promenades and the auditorium itself, and summon the fire brigade at the same time. Jack knew it was time to move, avoiding panic, using all the doors. They'd be fine. He followed Grace, who had crossed into the middle of the stage again and was standing stock-still, staring upwards.

He followed her gaze. High above them, the painted canvas backdrops of sand and sea were roiled in flame.

How long have we been away? Two minutes at most.

He grabbed Grace's wrist and pulled her away from the terrible spectacle. Behind them, a wooden beam, wrapped in flaming painted cloth, plummeted to the stage and exploded in a shower of sparks.

She screamed, and he held her against him for a moment, then she pushed him away.

'Go, Jack,' she said. 'I'll drop the fire curtain – and be careful.'

'I want to see you leave.'

'There's no time. I swear, I'll see you outside in a minute. Just trust me.'

He had to. He went round the edge of the stage, scrambling across the edge of the orchestra pit, and ran through the stalls. The bells began to ring. He glanced over his shoulder, watching as the heavy asbestos fire curtain dropped hard and fast into place.

The theatre was on fire. Another truth his brain couldn't quite comprehend. The main stairs would most likely be blocked with people coming down from the party, now the alarms were ringing, and he needed to go up. He had to find a way. He climbed onto the backs of some stalls seats, got a hand up, and pulled himself into the dress circle, tumbling over the parapet in an untidy heap, then headed for the backstage stairs stage left and went up a level. Over the ringing of the bells he heard a piano.

He opened the door to Ruby's room. She was bent over the keys, Tom Lassiter at her side.

'The alarm!' Jack shouted at them.

'Is it a real one?' Ruby said, looking disappointed. 'We wanted to get away from the party. It's such a crush, and Tom's had a nice idea about the bass arrangement on the Act One closing.'

Tom took one look at Jack's face. 'It's real? How bad, Jack?'

'Bad. Get Ruby out of here.'

Ruby shoved her notebook into her carpet bag. 'Tom, check the rooms on the rehearsal corridor above,' she said. 'Miss Fortescue might still be working. I'll do this floor and below us.' Jack was about to speak. 'I promise I'll do it fast, Mr Treadwell.'

He nodded and ran to the end of the corridor, pushing the door open, and he was front of house in the upper circle. He could smell smoke here, too. The house lights were on, and he looked up. The dome of the auditorium was growing hazy with smoke.

'Is anyone here?' he called.

A head appeared over the parapet of the gallery above: Marcus.

'Auditorium is clear, Mr Treadwell! Mr Poole sent me to check.'

'Ta, thanks, Marcus. Stage left stairs are clear. Go now. I'll tell Mr Poole.'

The boy nodded and disappeared. Jack opened the door to the upper circle promenade. The bells were ringing and the partygoers were moving towards the main marble staircases in an unhurried fashion, carrying on their conversations, greeting friends. The chorus and crew were signing programmes as they made their way across the promenade; others were finishing their champagne in a leisurely fashion. Jack opened his mouth, then he felt a hand grip his arm tightly and turned to find himself looking at Joe.

'Don't panic the crowd,' Joe said quietly. 'I've seen the smoke in the auditorium. This entire theatre can empty in minutes, but if you shout "fire" now and people panic, you'll bloody well kill someone.'

The impulse to shout – to scream at them to hurry – beat against Jack's heart and brain. Joe tightened his grip.

'Keep your mouth shut, lad.'

'Where are Lillian and Agnes?' he managed to say, his voice half-strangled in his throat.

'Below us at the dress circle bar, ushering them gently along. Poole's checking the side stairs. If they're clear . . .'

Before he could finish, the door at the far end of the bar opened. Poole came through it, shaking his head, and walked swiftly towards them.

'Too much smoke that side of the building. It's the main stairs only.'

Given how nervous Poole sometimes got, Jack was impressed by how calm he seemed now.

'Mr Poole, Marcus has finished his check of the auditorium. I sent him out down the rehearsal side stairs.'

Poole looked visibly relieved.

'Damn it,' Joe said. Then he raised his voice. 'Take your glasses, if you wish, my friends, but move along now! Lady Lassiter says this entire theatre can be cleared in five minutes, and we're just the party! Let's not make a liar out of her!' He clapped one man on the shoulder. 'Come along, George. Shuffle faster, otherwise you'll still be here when the fire brigade start dousing the place, and those lovely ostrich feathers in your wife's headdress will wilt!'

George laughed and took his wife's arm.

'Who's checking the dressing rooms?' Joe demanded.

'Ruby and Tom are checking the rehearsal rooms,' Jack replied. 'Grace and Danny are doing the dressing rooms.'

Every muscle in his body felt wired too tight, as if the tendons would start popping at any moment.

'Little Sam has the workshops,' Poole added. 'He went as soon as we heard the alarm. Mrs Briggs is checking the powder rooms.'

Far below them they heard a stifled shriek. Joe moved swiftly to the front of the promenade, where a wide half-moon window gave a view over the pavement and the town hall beyond. Below him a sea of faces were looking up, pointing, covering their mouths in shock.

'Jesus bloody Christ!'

'What is it, Mr Allerdyce?' Poole asked.

'The crowd outside've seen the smoke and the panic's is spreading back in. God damn it, they're blocking the entrance.'

'I can scamper down the back stairs,' Poole told him. 'To move the crowd back?'

'Do it.'

Joe turned to Jack as Poole dunked his handkerchief in the melted ice of a champagne bucket, held it over his face, and left them.

'We'll bring up the rear on the main stairs, Jack. Get Lillian and Agnes on the way. When d'you last do a fire drill? Your people seem to know their business.'

'During the music hall run.' Jack could smell smoke here now. 'The company assemble on the back road, Danny checks them off against the day book. But half the performers were here at the party, so it's bound to be awfully confusing.'

Joe reached the head of the stairs and ran his fingers over the dappled marble pillar for a second, his face heavy with regret, then returned to the business at hand.

'Right, move along now, everyone! Slow and steady!'

Jack looked down the staircase in front of them. Every step

seemed to take an infinity of time. There were Lillian and Agnes on the next landing, ushering people on with smiles fixed on their faces.

Someone in the lobby shouted, 'There are flames! I saw flames! Everyone, run!'

A tremor seemed to run through the crowd like it was a living thing, a spasm of terror.

'Just stay calm!' Jack heard his own voice before he even knew he was speaking. 'We'll all be out of here in a jiffy.'

'Listen to Mr Treadwell!' Joe bellowed. 'Nearly there, everyone!'

The crowd seemed to settle, just for an instant. Then came another voice from the lobby.

'There's fire coming out of the window!'

The crowd tumbled forward in panic. Just below Jack, a young man climbed onto the balustrade and jumped the remaining fifteen feet to the lobby. A woman screamed and the orderly walk downwards became urgent, dangerous. Jack grabbed the collar of the man in front of him, pulled him back.

'Are you mad? Stop shoving at those people in front of you!'

The man turned round and Jack saw a familiar expression. He had seen it in the trenches, under bombardment – a look of terror so complete you knew, looking into those eyes, that any rational thought had fled. He released the man as if holding him would infect him with the same fear.

'Jack!'

They had reached the next landing, where Lillian and Agnes stood just off the staircase. Agnes had her hand on Lillian's shoulder.

'Jack, how bad is it?' Lillian said.

He didn't know how to reply, just shook his head.

'Joe, your boys went to the Metropole to catch Mabel's late show,' Agnes told him. 'They left twenty minutes ago.'

He patted her arm.

'Come on, Lillian,' Agnes said, picking up a pair of napkins and dunking them in an ice bucket, as Poole had done.

'But . . . ?' Lillian looked confused.

'Joe and Jack are going to help anyone injured on the main stairs. We'll go down the back way.'

She thrust a damp napkin into Lillian's hand, then pulled her towards the doors at the other end of the bar. The electric lights flickered, and for a few seconds the world looked like a badly made moving picture, all jerky and confused.

Jack and Joe continued their painfully slow journey downwards. The stairway was opening up in front of them. A girl, her dress rucked up to her thigh, was lying on the half-landing, eyes closed. Jack crouched down beside her, noting her pulse felt weak, and as he lifted her, he could see a swelling on her forehead. Joe helped an old man to his feet, began to shepherd him down. A woman in evening dress was walking up the stairs towards them.

Joe used his free hand to stop her.

'What're you doing, madam?'

'My wrap,' she said, her eyes vague and unfocused. 'I left it. A present.'

Joe held her wrist. 'I sent my chauffeur down with it.'

'How kind,' the woman murmured, and allowed herself to be turned round.

The strangeness of humanity, Jack thought.

The young woman he was carrying stirred; her eyes half opened. She muttered something indistinct, then her eyes closed again.

Their way was hampered now by coats, discarded bags, the detritus of that last panicked rush. At the bottom of the stairs, Poole was crouching next to a young man.

'Silly fool jumped,' he said, looking up as they approached.

'Ankle's broken. Lady Lassiter and Miss de Montfort are outside.'

Joe freed himself from the man and woman he was guiding, shoving them gently towards the street exit. Marcus was already there. He took the woman's hand, pulling her out of the lobby and into the safety of the street like a tug pulls a tall ship out of port.

'This way, madam! Mr Treadwell! There's an ambulance outside. And Danny has the day book. Bill and Stella are helping him check it off.'

Jack deposited his fragile cargo on a stretcher, and saw Joe and Poole placing the jumper with the broken ankle onto another.

'Danny! Is anyone hurt?'

'N-no, I don't think so.'

He was going through the day book, occasionally looking up and marking off another name as he spotted them in the milling crowd. Ollie barked and sat down as if he'd just issued an order.

Lance put his hand on Jack's shoulder.

'We're all right. Ivor, Evie and I almost got trapped in the royal retiring room. Grace and Stella had to stop Bill trying to douse the flames himself. Had to drag him out by the collar.'

Bill hobbled up to them. 'Good to see you, Jack. This looks bad.'

'You hurt, Bill?'

'Bit of a twist on the knee. Feels worse than it is.'

Grace burst through the crowd and straight into Jack's arms. She smelt of smoke, but she was there and alive and whole. He refused to wait any longer; he gently pushed the hair away from her forehead and kissed her. She kissed him back, and the world stopped. He felt the slow boom of his heart, and for a second the world was perfect and consisted of just him and her.

'I'm missing one!' Danny shouted. 'Has anyone seen Josie?'

The moment was gone.

Jack released Grace, but kept a firm grip of her hand.

'She went off with Edmund Lassiter!' one of the chorus boys said, his voice rising with panic. 'He was giving her champagne. They said they were going ghost hunting!'

'Where? When?' Jack said. 'Bill, can you see Sir Edmund?'

Bill stared into the crowd, shook his head.

'I'll look,' Grace said.

Jack was forced to let her hand slip out of his, and she started pushing through the baffled onlookers.

'I don't know!' the boy said. 'It was ages ago, not long after the party started. Stella was still carrying her flowers.'

Lance swore loudly.

Grace ran back to join them. 'No sign of Sir Edmund. His mother thought he'd gone to his club, but they've sent a message back saying there is no sign of him. She's hysterical.'

'Where would he go? Where haven't we checked?'

'Lillian's flat,' Jack said.

They looked up. The dome of The Empire was already wreathed in smoke, and fire showed, ghastly, in the windows on the right of the building.

'There are no fire alarms up there,' Danny said.

CHAPTER THIRTY-SEVEN

'Everyone, stay here. I'll go and look for them,' Jack said, taking off his jacket and rolling up his sleeves.

Grace grabbed hold of his arm. 'The fire brigade will be here any second!'

He looked at her. 'Tell them to get a ladder up when they arrive. South corner.'

Grace nodded and slowly released him.

'I'm coming with you, Treadwell,' Lance muttered. 'You weren't the only man to put on a uniform, you know.'

'Take this,' Danny said, handing Jack a heavy torch.

'Here you go,' Poole said, arriving just in time to thrust another torch at Lance.

They went before any of the others could stop them, back into the theatre and up the main stairs. For the first two storeys, the theatre was eerily quiet. The electric lights had gone out and the beams of their torches showed nothing but heavy, slightly smudged shadows. The fire was a presence, though, close by on

the other side of a door, above or below them. They could sense it like a man walking through the forest at night senses the predator in the undergrowth.

They continued through the upper circle promenade – past the abandoned champagne glasses and finger sandwiches on little plates with The Empire painted on the rim – into the auditorium. The smoke around the dome was thick now, and Jack could see flames licking the edge of the fire curtain. The royal box was already alight, the velvet drapes aflame and fluttering into the pit.

Backstage now, to another staircase. The rehearsal corridor was full of smoke.

'Rope!'

Jack pushed open the door leading to the balcony from where some of the stagehands controlled the rise and fall of the scenery. He managed to get a hand on a coil near the door, then threw up his other hand to shield his face. The whole area of the stage was consumed by rippling orange flames, below and above him. They moved like water: surging waterfalls of fire. Lance grabbed his collar, pulled him back into the corridor and slammed the door just as the fire seemed to notice him, turn its gaze on him and pounce. Jack got to his feet again, and they ran in a low crouch to the end of the corridor and up the stairs. The door to Lillian's flat was locked.

'Josie?' Lance shouted, hammering at it with his fist. 'Josie, can you hear me?'

'Fuck off, Drake!' a voice drawled from inside. 'Get your own girl.'

Lance stepped back and Jack kicked the lock. It was designed for privacy, rather than protection – the pine splintered and the door swung open.

Jack looked around him. Josie was curled up on one of the

armchairs. Her party dress was torn, her hair was disarranged, and she held a broken bottle by its neck in her hand. She stared into the torch beam, her eyes and cheeks black with mascara.

'Christ! Josie, what happened?' Lance said, dashing towards her.

'Lance!' she exclaimed, dropping the bottle.

'Nothing. We're just waiting for the silly girl to calm down,' Edmund drawled. He was sitting in the centre of the room, a single candle lit on the dining table beside him, a full glass in his hands. His face looked bruised. 'What happened to the lights?'

Jack crossed to him in three steps, lifted him by his collar and punched him once, hard, on the jaw. He fell backwards, loose with drink, and ending up sprawled on the floor. He looked surprised.

'Defending a chorus girl's honour again are we, Treadwell? How wonderful.'

Lance had taken off his dinner jacket and was persuading Josie to put her arms through the sleeves.

'The building's on fire, you little shit,' Lance said in an almost conversational tone. 'We're getting Josie out of here. You can stay and burn for all I care.'

'What?' Edmund scrambled to his feet and smelt the air. 'Oh, dear God! How do we get out?'

'Josie, can you walk?' Lance asked, half-lifting her to her feet.

'Yes,' she said. 'I'm a bit dizzy.'

'Dizzy?'

'He hit me,' she said simply. 'He said Lady Lassiter had a Degas painting up here, and I wanted to see it. Then as soon as he got me in here he locked the door and tried to . . . I fought him and he hit me. I hit him back, though. Then I got the bottle and told him if he came near, I'd cut him. He wouldn't let me leave.'

Lance smoothed the hair off her face. 'Good for you, darling.

I've every intention of killing him but we need to get out of here first.'

Smoke was drifting in from the corridor. Jack turned away from Edmund with disgust, slammed the door and ran over to the huge rose window at the east end of the room.

'Lance! We've got to go over this bit of roof. Get to the corner tower and wait for the ladder.'

'Give me the rope. I'll tie it this end and you smash the window.'

Jack grabbed a candlestick from the top of the grand piano and used it to smash out the lozenge-shaped bottom pane. It was big enough for them to climb through.

'Josie, get a blanket. Something thick to save us from the glass.'

She nodded and headed a little unsteadily for the bedroom.

'What are you doing?' Edmund got to his feet. 'We can't go out of the window!'

'No choice,' Jack said shortly.

He took the blanket that Josie handed him and laid it over the glass still embedded in the wooden frame.

Lance had tied a bowline round the leg of the grand piano, jerked on it hard to test that the knot held, then paid it out till he was standing by the window with Jack and Josie. He peered out.

'Can you get to the corner tower, Lance? Tie up the other end there?'

The roof looked suddenly steep and narrow.

'You know my film stunts are normally done with camera tricks, don't you, Jack?'

'I'm a true believer. Josie, what's wrong?'

Josie had sat down rather suddenly on the floor.

'My head. I . . . '

He put his hand briefly on her shoulder and shot a look of loathing at Edmund.

'She slipped!'

'Lance, go!'

Lance went. Jack watched him as he let himself down carefully from the window onto the steeply sloping apron of slated tiles, and started to walk, catlike, across them towards the corner tower. Jack could hear bells ringing in the distance, orders being shouted below. Lance was twenty feet from the tower . . . ten.

'Jack?' Josie had her hands on the polished wooden floor. 'Why is the floor hot?'

A sudden cracking groan – an explosion of splintering timbers outside the window. Jack turned in time to see Lance leap forward as the tiles under his feet were split apart, and a great gout of flame burst through the hole and into the night. Jack covered his eyes, momentarily blinded by the hungry flames.

'Lance!'

The spurt of flame dropped back into the darkness, and Jack saw him, clear of the great hole in the roof, looping the rope around a statue of Tragedy, then around his waist. The rope hung across the new, terrible hole in the roof. Jack looked at Josie, who looked woozy and weak. He didn't think she'd be able to get herself across that gap alone.

'Edmund, you go next. You'll have to go hand over hand across that bloody gap. Then help hold the rope and Josie and I will come together.'

Edmund didn't need to be told twice. He threw himself out of the window, walked along the remaining part of the roof, then went hand over hand across the gap, his legs dangling below him. The statue of Tragedy tilted under his weight. Lance braced himself against the tiles. Even at this distance, and through the smoke, Jack could see his muscles were straining as he took Edmund's weight.

At last, Edmund hauled himself up onto the other side of

the chasm. He grabbed the remaining end of the rope, tied it around his waist, and stepped back towards the tower to take his share of the strain.

'They're putting up a rescue ladder!' Lance shouted. 'Just get over here.'

'Josie? It's time.' Jack put out his hand. 'I'm going to carry you over the gap. But I'll need my hands, so you're just going to have to cling on to me. Arms round my neck and wrap your legs tight around my waist.'

'I'm sorry . . . I feel so . . .'

'Just use all your strength to hang on to me, all right? Pretend I'm just giving you a piggyback in the park.'

'Okey-dokey – oh!' She pointed.

Smoke was beginning to rise through the floor around Lillian's Turkish carpets.

They didn't have long. Jack climbed out of the window, then turned to help her out.

'Promise me you're going to hang on. Promise me, Josie!'

'I promise.'

Jack put his right hand on the rope, held her hand with the other, and they inched towards the chasm along the slates. Then he crouched down and she climbed on his back, arms tight around his neck. Her limbs were light and strong.

He put both hands on the rope.

'Are you ready to take the weight, Lance?'

'Ready!' Lance yelled.

'Just hurry up, won't you?' shouted Edmund.

Jack said a brief prayer for Lance at one end and the piano at the other, sat on the edge of the hole and closed his hands around the rope.

'Shut your eyes, Josie. Tight.'

Then he pushed off. The rope sank under their weight and Jack was floating free. He released his right hand, gripped the rope ahead with it; same with his left. He could feel Josie's breath on his neck.

This is fine, he told himself. *Just like climbing the rope at school. Easier. Just hand over hand.*

'Hurry up!' He heard Edmund's voice above him. 'The statue's going! Let them go, Lance! Drop the rope! We'll be dragged in, too!'

Jack swung forward faster.

'Edmund, no!' Lance screamed.

The rope slackened, they dropped, and Jack looked down.

It was hell. Darkness resolved into smoke eighty feet below them, and all around the edge of this sudden dark void was flame – running in currents along the timbers with an urgent hunger. It had gorged itself on the fittings and furnishings – the fine velvet seats and carpeted tea rooms and bars – and now, in a frenzy, it was gnawing on the bones of the building.

In the weightless second, Jack saw everything: that the fire was alive; that he and Josie would die at once; that perhaps he should have left Edmund shivering in that shell hole in France. He'd have lived a longer life, but if he'd done that, it would have been a small, guilty life. This was better. He had come home. He had kissed Grace. He had been happy. He knew all of this, with perfect clarity, in the moment between the rope slackening and it miraculously tightening again.

He moved fast, hand over hand, his lungs on fire and his muscles screaming. Josie got a hand on the rope, too, as they reached the remains of the roof at the far side of the chasm. She pulled herself off him and onto the tiles, then Jack hauled himself up. Lance was on the very brink. Jack looked sideways, and saw the statue of Tragedy had fallen. Lance had almost followed them into the abyss.

'Josie!' Lance shouted. 'There's a sort of ledge round the tower. Get there and hang on!'

She struggled into a crouch, then her eyes widened. 'Lance! The rope!'

The roof timbers of the flat itself gave way, and another burst of flame shot into the night air as the blaze sucked in the fresh oxygen. Lance worked at the tightened knot around his waist, then the rope went taut as, back in the flat, Lillian's grand piano fell into the flaming void below. Burning debris flew up into the air around them, smashing down, left and right.

Lance was pulled back, twisted in the air. Jack grabbed him, seizing hold of his friend's forearm as the rope whipped from around his waist, then flew free. They fell forward, Jack still holding on to Lance. Lance's weight was pulling him down, dragging him across the tiles, and again he was looking down into the void. Josie threw herself forward, grabbing his ankle, bracing herself against the fallen statue. His slide into the deep stopped, but he was half-hanging into the abyss.

'Lance! I can't hold you long!' Jack looked down into the man's ridiculously handsome face. 'Give me your other hand!'

Lance closed his eyes, and for a horrible second Jack thought he was going to let go. Then he swung up his left hand, took a grip on Jack's outstretched arm. There was nowhere to get a hold, no purchase. Lance was a dead weight, dangling free over the fire and darkness, and Jack's arms felt as if they were being torn from their sockets. Josie was using all her strength to keep Jack from slipping across the tiles to his death.

Lance looked up, framed by smoke and the flickering of fire far below.

'Now what, Treadwell?'

'Just hang on!'

'They're coming, Jack!' Josie shouted. 'The firemen are coming!'

It might have been ten seconds . . . thirty . . . No more than a minute of complete and perfect agony, then Jack felt strong arms around his waist, heard Josie's sob of relief. Other hands were reaching for Lance now – fresh strength in blue serge uniforms. They hauled Lance out of the hole together.

Josie went down the ladder first, a fireman in front of her, then Jack, then Lance and their other rescuers. Their friends were there to meet them at the bottom. Stella kissed Lance, then took immediate charge of Josie. Bill put a blanket round Lance's shoulders. Jack winced when Grace hugged him, and put out his hand to Lillian. She took it and squeezed his fingers, but had no words to speak.

'Where's Edmund?' Jack asked.

Then he noticed the figure being loaded onto a stretcher and into another ambulance. Constance was clambering into the vehicle after it.

'What happened?'

'Oh, Jack, it was terrible!' Grace shuddered. 'Almost as soon as the ladder went up against the tower, he started coming down. Then there was that terrible explosion and something burning hit him. He didn't fall, but it knocked him out. He seemed to be hanging there, his clothes on fire, for ages before the firemen managed to get him down. Then they went straight up for you.'

Jack kept his arm tight around her. 'The poor devil. Though he almost got us killed up there.'

He told Grace simply and without drama what had happened.

'I hope he—'

'Don't, Grace. We made it, that's what matters.'

Her face was small and tight with rage, but she didn't say anything. He kissed the top of her hair.

'Lillian, what's your butler doing here?'

Wiping the soot from his streaming eyes, Jack could make out Fenton Hewitt and his footmen moving around the crowd with Ivor and Evie. They were offering blankets and hip flasks. Lillian had gone white listening to Jack's account of what had happened on the roof, but she took her lead from Grace and shook herself.

'Someone telephoned Lassiter Court and they came at once,' she replied. 'Hewitt? I'll take something for Mr Treadwell, his voice sounds terrible.'

Jack did feel that his throat as well as his eyes were burning.

The captain of the firefighters approached.

'I'm very sorry, Lady Lassiter,' he said. 'We have the hoses on it now, and we can stop the fire spreading to other buildings, but I don't think the structure can be saved.'

Lillian had tears in her eyes, and her voice caught as she answered him.

'I quite understand. Please do thank your men for their heroic actions saving our friends. I am so very grateful.'

The captain nodded and withdrew as Hewitt handed Jack a stirrup cup. The mixture was, he could tell, extremely alcoholic, but oddly fruity. It warmed parts of him he didn't know were cold.

He couldn't look at the flaming ruins of the theatre any more, so he looked at the crowd. Joe and Agnes were there with two tall young men. The chorus girls had blankets or men's dinner jackets over their shoulders, while one of the boys from the chorus was hugging Mrs Gardener. The others were helping Ivor distribute drinks. Ruby and Tom were sitting on Ruby's carpet bag, watching the slow, sorry collapse. Tom must have seen what happened to his brother, yet for some reason he had decided to remain here.

Jack turned to Danny. 'If you can get any information about Edmund from the hospital, can you see it reaches Tom?'

'I will. And I d-don't know if you want it, Jack, but I saved this for you.'

Danny had saved Jack's book – his copy of *Riviera Nights* with all the staging and cues, props and costume lists.

'Thank you.'

Jack suddenly found the smoke was getting in his eyes again.

Gradually the bustle was stilling, and all faces were turned in miserable silence towards the theatre. Only the reporter, Wilbur Bowman, was still moving, leaning on a cane as he went from person to person, taking their testimony.

'Lady Lassiter,' Hewitt said. 'The car is here – we can take you home whenever you wish.'

She patted his arm distractedly. 'Thank you, Hewitt, but no. I'll stay till the end.'

CHAPTER THIRTY-EIGHT

By the time dawn broke, the fire was out. Some of the frontage still stood, and the two towers, but the rest of the theatre was black, dripping rubble, and the stench of smoke was heavy in the air. The fire crews were beginning to roll up their hoses.

Most of the guests had left, but none of the company could tear themselves away. Only Josie had been persuaded to go. Usher had insisted on booking her a room at the Metropole, so she could rest peacefully under the care of their inhouse doctor, and had carried her off with sincere fatherly concern.

'A sad beginning to your career in the theatre, Agnes,' Joe said. 'I'm very sorry. She was a beautiful theatre.'

She examined him for any sign of mockery, and saw none. 'She was, wasn't she? And it *is* a sad beginning, though the building was fully insured. I did check that before I bought Edmund's shares.'

'You could probably still cancel that deal.'

Agnes shook her head. 'No. I shan't be doing that.'

Joe took out a cigar and lit it. Agnes didn't move away. She was coming to appreciate the scent of his tobacco.

'I didn't think you would,' Joe said. 'Mr Bowman is hovering.'

Agnes nodded to Wilbur and he hobbled over to them.

'Wilbur! This is dedication to duty. You were shot at and are back out reporting the next day?'

Wilbur opened his notebook. 'The presses never sleep, Miss de Montfort – I mean, Agnes – and our theatre critic went to bed as soon as he'd submitted the notice of *Riviera Nights*, so I took the chance to cover this. I understand you purchased Sir Edmund's stake only yesterday. This is a sad beginning to your career in the theatre, isn't it?'

Joe smiled into his cigar smoke.

'Let's call it a dramatic opening,' Agnes replied. 'But let me introduce you to Lillian, Lady Lassiter. If anyone gives you a comment, it should be her.'

They joined the group round Jack, Grace and Lillian, but before Wilbur could ask anything, Arthur Allerdyce and his brother, Francis, approached them.

'Dad, can I have a word? Francis and I have been talking. That was a fantastic show. We can't let it just disappear after one night. We were thinking we could restage it at the Palladium in Manchester. The revue I've got on there is starting to wind down.'

A breath of something like hope passed like a breeze among his listeners. Joe sucked on his cigar. 'Sets will need rebuilding, and all the costumes remaking. Then we'll only have the principals till Christmas.'

'It'll make a great story, Mr Allerdyce,' Jack said hopefully.

He felt Grace grip his hand more tightly.

Joe sniffed. 'It will.' He was quiet for a long time, then nodded. 'But it'd be best to make it a Highbridge story. The goodwill's local. Arthur, find out where Aaron Cooper is and get him here. He's got a bloody fine revue that can transfer to the Palladium. We'll stage *Riviera Nights* here in Highbridge, at the Palace of Varieties. That way we can use all the backstage crew from The Empire who already know the show. Lillian, Agnes and I can go through the details. I'm more than happy to split the costs and profits fairly. Not that there'll be much profit after a rebuild, but it's a good show. It ought to be seen.'

'That would be smashing, Mr Allerdyce,' Grace said.

'Call me Joe, kid. But I have a condition!' Joe added, lifting his cigar. 'I'll do this . . . but only if you marry me, Agnes.'

Agnes frowned at him. Everyone else gasped.

'Now, let's be clear, you can keep the farmhouse. You can carry on living there, if you like. You're an independant kind of woman and I respect that. But I want something out of this deal for myself, and I want that something to be you.'

This time, it only took Agnes ten seconds to decide. She laughed, put a hand on Joe's lapel and reached up to kiss his cheek.

'Very well.'

Wilbur was writing furiously. 'Can I put all this in the paper, too?'

'Fine by me, lad.'

'If you wish to, Wilbur, write away,' Agnes added.

Lillian took a deep breath. 'Thank you, Joe. From the bottom of my heart. And my congratulations to you both. Jack, could you speak to everyone?' He smiled at her and she sighed. 'You're going to tell me to do the job myself, aren't you, dear?'

'I am, Lillian.'

She nodded, and beckoned to the fire chief.

'Sir, may I borrow the back of your fire engine for a moment?'

'Certainly, Lady Lassiter,' he said.

Lillian removed the man's dinner jacket she had been wearing over her evening dress and handed it to Grace.

'Would you make sure that gets back to Ivor, Grace? And I do hope you'll find time to help him with his new production. He's been rather a hero, you know.'

Grace took the jacket. 'I will, Lillian.'

Lillian took the fire chief's hand, stepped elegantly onto the back of the tender, and stared back at the ruins of The Empire over her shoulder.

Such a palace!

She remembered how proud Barney had been of it . . . of her.

Dear Barney. What would he have told me to do? Grieve if I need to, then get on and rebuild something even better.

The company gathered around her. She looked at their faces: her lost son, her new partner, her old friend, and her former lover. Her heroes, her friends, her employees, her rivals, and her writers, dancers, stars and musicians. Her company.

'My friends,' she said in a loud voice, 'we have suffered a terrible loss tonight, and perhaps the loss is all the more bitter because it comes on the heels of our great triumph. At least everyone who attended the first performance of *Riviera Nights* at The Empire can say they had a genuinely unique experience.'

There was a ripple of rueful laughter.

'But as I stand here now, in front of the ruins of a place that I have loved, I realise we have a great deal to be thankful for. Sir Edmund Lassiter has been gravely injured, and our thoughts are with those who care for him.' Her eye lighted on Tom, but he looked away. 'Josie is resting, and the two audience members who were hurt will, I am told, make complete recoveries.'

Someone applauded and it washed wearily around the crowd. They were grateful, but looking at the ruins, it was hard not to regret all that lost splendour, all that work.

'Although the building has been destroyed,' Lillian carried on, raising her voice a little, 'we have had the chance to see something remarkable. I am not talking about the show, magnificent as it was from beginning to end. And thanks to Joe Allerdyce, *Riviera Nights* will be reopening soon. No, I am talking about the bravery and heroic behaviour of our company tonight – of Danny Moon and Ollie who first raised the alarm, of Mr Poole and Marcus who guided so many to safety with exemplary calm, of Ruby and Tom, Grace and Little Sam – all of you who risked your own safety to ensure the safety of others. This ruin behind you is a mirage. You all saved The Empire tonight, because you saved the company, and one another. And, of course, Lancelot Drake and Jack Treadwell, who rushed back into the flames to rescue Josie, and it turns out she, the remarkable girl, saved them right back. Jack and Lance, we knew already from your service that you were both heroes, but it was proved again tonight. No wonder Lance is so good at playing the hero on the stage – it seems he's not acting at all!'

'Please don't ask for your money back,' Lance called out.

He and Stella were sharing a blanket over their shoulders. They managed to make even that look glamorous. This time the laughter was warmer.

'I think you'll need it if you continue to treat the whole company to champagne suppers at the Metropole,' Lillian replied.

Evie cupped her hands to her mouth. 'He's invited the entire fire brigade to join us next time, Lil!'

Lillian joined in that laugh, then waited for them to settle. 'A very good idea. *Riviera Nights* will play on, and I promise not one of you will lose a day of pay or a moment in the spotlight. So, my friends, remember we have lost nothing but bricks and mortar.

The Empire will be rebuilt, bigger and better than ever, and we have also made something tonight. We have made a family, and one I am very, very proud to be part of.'

The cheers and applause were sincere and sustained this time. As Lillian watched, the crowd began to turn to one another in earnest conversation. She could feel the fresh hope and energy radiating off them: Jack and Grace, already talking earnestly about something; Tom and Ruby, with their heads together; Wilbur, writing as fast as his pencil would move. She looked down and saw Bill smiling up at her. He offered his hand, and she took it to step down from her fire engine stage, conscious that her performance had been creditable.

'Nice speech, Lil.'

'Thank you, Bill.'

He waited while the magical Fenton Hewitt handed Lillian a fur wrap to replace Ivor's dinner jacket. She threaded her arm through Bill's and looked around the crowd.

'What is it, Lil?'

'I was just thinking about Mangrave. We certainly won't have a chance to examine the books now. I wonder if he really did leave at the interval?'

'You think he . . . ?'

Lillian shook her head. 'I don't need to think about that now. I just need to be glad everyone is safe.'

He squeezed her arm. 'Chap from the Metropole turned up just before you gave your speech. They're offering breakfast to the company with their compliments.'

'Then let's continue all these conversations over hot coffee.' She turned. 'Jack?'

'Yes, Lillian?'

'We're having breakfast at the Metropole. Gather the company.'

CURTAIN CALLS

SIX MONTHS LATER

T he party at Lassiter Court was in full swing. The occasion was the engagement of Grace Hawkins and Jack Treadwell, and even if some of the more censorious members of Highbridge society had decided not to attend, Lillian had discovered she still had more than enough friends to fill even her house.

The story of Jack's birth – or at least part of it – had been published in a sensitive article in the *Highbridge Illustrated News* written by Wilbur Bowman. It had caused a scandal in the city, but coming as it did in the wake of the fire and Sir Edmund's injuries, not as much as it might have done. Most people's reactions were coloured by sympathy rather than judgement. None of Lillian's people had left her, and in fact Anderson Hargreaves had applied for the position of financial manager at the theatre. She and Agnes had appointed him at once.

Lillian spotted the reporter himself across the crowd of friends and family at the Court; he had his notebook in hand. She plucked a glass of champagne from the tray of a passing waiter and carried it across to him.

'Mr Bowman! Put your notebook away. You are an invited guest, and I'm sure Edison will allow you to stop work long enough to have a drink. My congratulations on your promotion.'

Wilbur tucked the notebook away with a smile and they both glanced towards Edison, who was chatting away in an animated fashion with Agnes and Joe on the other side of the room.

'Thank you, Lady Lassiter! I can't help myself, I'm afraid, making notes. I hope you're well.'

'Very,' Lillian said firmly. 'One or two of the ladies of the town still make a point of crossing the road when they see me coming, but not enough to disrupt the city's traffic, and none of them are people I liked talking to a great deal anyway.'

'I hear Mr French's new production is doing very well in London,' Wilbur said.

'Yes, he sends us all of his cuttings. Piles of them. I think helping him was rather a solace for Jack and Grace in those first weeks after The Empire burnt down. Though their greatest solace was almost certainly each other.'

She sought out the engaged couple in the crowd. They were standing side by side, very close together, talking to the Moons – Alma, Charlie and Danny – and Grace's parents.

'Ruby wrote Ivor some excellent tunes,' Lillian continued, 'and Tom helped arrange them.'

'Is it true that you've given Tom Lassiter rooms here at the Court, Lady Lassiter?'

She eyed him carefully over the top of her champagne glass. 'Are you asking as a reporter or as a guest?'

'A guest,' he replied with a smile.

'Yes. It's unofficial, but the poor boy finds the atmosphere in the town house difficult, so we make him welcome here whenever he wishes to come. Edmund is in Switzerland now, they hope the climate will help with his recovery.'

'Constance seems to have steadied the ship at Lassiter Enterprises in his absence,' Wilbur said with a sigh.

Given that Edmund's injuries meant he couldn't respond to any questions, Wilbur's stories about the company had been put to one side. His remarkable accounts of the fire, however, and of the heroism of Lance and Jack – and Josie – had been syndicated across the country.

'Constance impressed the new board with her clear vision for the future, I'm told,' Wilbur went on. 'She made good the gaps his poor investment caused with the money from the sale of his Empire shares. She has his proxy and *says* she communicates with him regularly, though he'll not be able to resume his duties for many months yet. And, in my opinion, she's much better at the job than he was.'

Lillian nodded. 'Mr Bowman, have you had any luck discovering what became of Alexander Mangrave? Has he been seen at all since the fire?'

He looked at her sideways. 'No, but that is a serious subject for such a lovely day, Lady Lassiter.'

'Nevertheless, I'd like to know.'

He considered for a moment. 'Mrs Mangrave has returned to her brother in Newcastle, and according to his last letter to me, her health and spirits are gradually improving. I wish I could write and give them a clear answer on what happened to Mangrave, though – put her mind at rest.'

'But you have your suspicions?'

He nodded. 'I do. He overreached himself – gave Ray Kelly's men orders to stop me asking questions – and Kelly has a harsh way of dealing with people who displease him. I think Mangrave was summoned to account for his actions and never came back down the dale.' He paused. 'But it looks like Constance's connections with Ray Kelly's gang are far from over. She's just has appointed a lawyer named MacDonald as manager for the Lassiter Fancy Goods works. He's one of Ray Kelly's men.'

Lillian sipped her champagne. 'I exchanged my shares in Lassiter Enterprises for full and free title to this house, so I'm glad to say I shall have nothing more to do with the factories. Constance must choose her own way, but I can honour Barney's legacy with the new theatre, at any rate.'

Wilbur got out his notebook again. 'Any news on the reopening?'

'You will have to wait for my speech to find out, Mr Bowman.'

She nodded her farewell and went to join Bill and Evie, who were gathering round the piano with Tom.

Jack and Grace had been so busy receiving the congratulations of their friends, they had hardly had a moment to speak to each other, but as people began to drift towards the piano, Jack put a hand round Grace's waist and hugged her to his side. He still couldn't believe he had persuaded her to marry him at last.

He'd proposed the day after the fire, but she'd shaken her head and told him that she wanted to be asked out to dinner at least once first – and that perhaps before he proposed, he should work out where he was going to live, and even meet her family. He had accepted these conditions cheerfully, and considered it was kind of her not to mention he only had the clothes he stood up in. Even his good coat had gone in the fire. Finding somewhere to live had been straightforward enough, though. Danny had appointed himself Jack's assistant. The first thing he did was arrange for Jack to take lodgings in his own home, under the benevolent eye of

Alma and Charlie, and a conveniently short walk from Grace's family house. Ollie went with him, and it was an arrangement which pleased them all.

'This is perfect,' Jack said to her. 'I only wish Lance and Stella were here. I suppose Hollywood and the West End couldn't wait any longer for them.'

'They'll be back, dear,' Grace replied. 'I'm just so glad all of Highbridge got to see them in *Riviera Nights* before they went.'

'Me, too.'

He leant towards her. The upset of discovering the true story of his birth had begun to recede at last, and he had Grace to thank for that. She had been patient and caring, encouraging him to talk, and he had found it helped. He had told her about the war, Edmund's behaviour in no-man's-land, the loss of Bessie and Fred, and his wandering years in France. He had discovered slowly that he could accept Lillian was his mother, and be proud of her, without loving his mam and dad any less. He was grateful to them. Mam had sent him to The Empire, after all, and if she hadn't done that, he would never have found Grace.

A glass was chinked and they turned back towards the piano.

'Ah, time for Lillian's announcement!' Jack said.

Grace stood up on her tiptoes to kiss him on his cheek, and the world felt more champagne-soaked and shining than ever. He was so terribly proud of her. Grace's new play, a neat little comedy she had been commissioned to write by Joe Allerdyce, would be put on at the Playhouse. She would also direct. Rehearsals were due to start as soon as she and Jack got back from their honeymoon at the end of May. Lillian had insisted on paying for that as a wedding gift, and they were, naturally, going to spend it on the Riviera.

'Ladies and gentlemen,' Lillian began as the crowd quietened. 'As you know, we are gathered here to celebrate the engagement of two of the best young people it is my privilege to know – Grace Hawkins and Jack Treadwell!'

The crowd cheered, and Frederick Poole applauded so hard Jack feared he would do himself an injury.

'No one here doubts for a second, I think, that they make a remarkable team,' Lillian added once the applause subsided.

'I know that to my cost,' Joe called from the back of the room. 'Those two cost me a bloody fortune!'

Jack and Grace smiled amid the general laughter.

'I am so, so pleased that they are a part of my family, and our family at The Empire,' Lillian went on, to a general chinking of glasses and 'hear, hears'.

'And I have another announcement to make. The rebuilding of The Empire is well underway, Agnes and I have appointed Jack as our theatre manager, and we shall have the privilege of staging as our opening production Grace and Ruby's new musical. Have you got a title yet, Grace?'

'Not a clue,' Grace replied confidently, raising her glass. 'But I'll find one!'

The crowd laughed, and there was a fresh and enthusiastic round of applause.

'So I would like to propose a toast,' Lillian said. 'To new beginnings, new adventures, and, most of all . . . to Grace and Jack.'

'To Grace and Jack!' the guests chorused back.

The music began. Amid loud cheers, Jack led Grace into the space the guests had cleared for them.

The sound of music and laughter poured out of Lassiter Court well into the night. The deer in the park cropped the grass, unconcerned, and lay down to sleep, lulled by the sense of hope and happiness that seemed to flow out of the lighted windows and reach even the city and the dales, the factories and farms, the houses and shops. The people for miles around dreamt of love and glamour, and smiled in their sleep.

The glow did not reach Constance Lassiter, writing letters in her cold and empty town house, however, or Ray Kelly, reading in his cottage. They went about their work steadily, and untouched by its warmth. Kelly contemplated expansion – a new chapter in his business dealings. In these dark hours of the night, Constance thought only of revenge.

But at Lassiter Court, the music played on. Lillian looked round at her guests, happier than she had been for many years. Then Bill dragged her into the centre of the room, and Jack, Grace, Evie and the others discovered to their delight that Lady Lassiter had not forgotten how to dance.

ACKNOWLEDGEMENTS

Despite spending my whole life performing and creating and writing songs, I never thought I would realise the dream of writing a book. But here I am, writing the acknowledgements for my debut novel. Wow! I don't know about you, but I always love reading the acknowledgements in books and seeing how many people it takes to make a book possible. Turns out it's quite a lot!

Bringing *The Empire* to life has been a team effort and I have adored working with every single person who has helped me on my journey to becoming a published author. Bloody hell, that feels good to type! I hope I've remembered everyone, but if you've been involved in the making of this book, or my career up until now, please know I am incredibly grateful, it has been a joy from start to finish – if a bit of a whirlwind.

Firstly, I want to thank you – yes, you – for picking up this book, whether as a print book, ebook or audiobook. Without your support, I wouldn't be writing this, so a huge thank you. When you perform, it is always with one thing in mind: the audience. I've now learnt that writing is much the same.

Of course, a massive thank you to my Cathy. This book is dedicated to you as a small thank you for all that you do and for being the inspiration for all of the strong, kind and determined women in this book.

Thanks to my agents, Gordon Wise, Alastair Lindsey-Renton, Helen Clarkson and Sarah Spear at Curtis Brown for making this dream a reality and translating all the publishing terms.

My publishers, Bonnier Books UK, made sure that the whole process has been the most fun. I first met Kate Parkin and Sarah Bauer over Zoom, and during that call, as I told them my ideas and they joined in enthusiastically, I knew we'd get on. Since then, we've had many brainstorming sessions – sometimes fuelled by cheese – and they've all been the most enormous fun. Thank you to Sarah, my editor, for always supporting my idea (and for stopping me when I got "too creative" with some of the plot ideas!) and for steering the ship and the deadlines. Thank you to Katie Lumsden, Salma Begum and Katie Meegan for working with Sarah to create the book; to Vicky Joss, Ellie Pilcher and Stephen Dumughn for all your inventive marketing; to Clare Kelly and Francesca Russell for helping me publicise the book far and wide; to Stuart Finglass, Mark Williams, Andrea Tome, Elise Burns, Vincent Kelleher, Sophie Hamilton, Kate Griffiths, Phoenix Curland, Stacey Hamilton, Amanda Percival, Ellie Pilcher, Kim Evans, Ruth Logan, Stella Giatrakou, Nick Ash, Ilaria Tarasconi and Amy Smith for selling *The Empire* around the world. Thanks to Jenny Richards and Michael Crampton for the most beautiful cover and to Alex May, Ella Holden and Eloise Angeline for making it into an actual book. A huge thanks to Ciara Lloyd for being my biggest cheerleader at Bonnier and to Alex Riddle and

James Asare for always making me feel so welcome. Thanks to my copy editor, Steve O'Gorman, and my proofreader Jane Donovan. Phew! It really does take a village.

Thanks also to the team at Livenation for looking after me – Sarah D and Phil B. They keep me on track, and I appreciate it more than they know. And to the wonderful Andrew for always knowing where I should be and what I'm meant to be doing, even when I don't – which is most of the time.

Finally, but probably most importantly, thank you to the theatres up and down the country – those I've worked or performed in, those that I've sat in the audience of, those that have inspired me and the hundreds of thousands of people who visit them every year. Thank you to everyone who performs and works in them. It's been a tough time of late for many of us – performers and audiences alike – but I think it's reminded everyone just how important the arts are. This novel may be fiction, but I was only able to write it because I've been lucky enough to spend so much time in so many incredible theatres – and *The Empire* is a love letter to each and every one.

Thank you.

Love, M xx

READERS' LETTERS

Hello my lovelies!

Thank you, thank you, thank you from the bottom of my heart for picking up *The Empire*. I can only hope that you enjoyed reading it half as much as I enjoyed writing it!

I've come to realise over the past few months that writing a book is a lot like staging a show. First, you're struck by an idea, then you workshop it or – as in my case – bounce increasingly bonkers ideas off my ever wise and patient editors. Then bit by tiny bit, word by word, note by note, it starts to come together . . . it becomes magic . . .

The Empire really is a love letter to the years that I've had the privilege of spending on stage, to the theatres that have been my home, to the amazing casts and crew who have come to be my family, but most of all to you, the audience, the reader, without whom none of this would have been possible.

As a thank you, I would love to ensure you're the first

to hear about my writing, upcoming bookish events, cover reveals or even a few cheeky giveaways. That's why I set up my readers' club, Behind the Curtain. You can sign up here: **https://bit.ly/BehindTheCurtainBall** to become part of the Behind the Curtain readers' club. It only takes a few moments to sign up; there are no catches or costs.

Bonnier Books UK will keep your data private and confidential, and it will never be passed on to a third party. We won't spam you with loads of emails, just get in touch now and then with news about my books, and you can unsubscribe any time you want.

And if you would like to get involved in a wider conversation about my books, please do review *The Empire* on Amazon, on GoodReads, on any other online store, on your own blog and social media accounts, or talk about it with friends, family or reading groups! You can also use the hashtag **#FromStageToPage** to join in the conversation. Sharing your thoughts helps other readers, and I'd love to hear what you think.

Thank you again for reading *The Empire*, and for all your gorgeous support so far. It really does mean the world to me.

Much love,